WRITING BETWEEN THE LINES

An Anthology on War and Its Social Consequences

WRITING BETWEEN THE LINES

Edited with an introduction by

Kevin Bowen & **Bruce Weigl**

Foreword by DENISE LEVERTOV

University of Massachusetts Press   Amherst

Copyright © 1997 by
The William Joiner Center for the Study of
War and Social Consequences
All rights reserved
Printed in the United States of America
LC 96-9591
ISBN 1-55849-053-1 (cloth); 054-x (pbk.)
Designed by Richard Hendel
Set in Janson and Franklin Gothic types by Keystone Typesetting, Inc.
Printed and bound by Braun-Brumfield, Inc.
Library of Congress Cataloging-in-Publication Data
Writing between the lines : an anthology on war and its social
consequences / edited with an introduction by Kevin Bowen and Bruce
Weigl ; foreword by Denise Levertov.
p. cm.
ISBN 1-55849-053-1 (alk. paper). — ISBN 1-55849-054-x (pbk. : alk paper)
1. War — Literary collections. 2. Vietnamese conflict, 1961–1975 —
Literary collections. 3. War and society. I. Bowen, Kevin, 1947–
II. Weigl, Bruce. 1949–
PN6071.W35W75   1997
808.8'0358 — dc20   96-9591
                                                           CIP

Permissions to reprint selections in this book have been granted gratis by
the authors, owners, and copyright holders. Their names and the sources of
the selections are listed on the final pages of this book.

This book is published with the support and cooperation of the University
of Massachusetts Boston and the William Joiner Center for the Study of
War and Social Consequences at the University of Massachusetts Boston.

British Library Cataloguing in Publication Data are available.

For the Children

Contents

Aftermath

Going Back

Foreword

Strangely, my own most vivid memory of Vietnam, from my one brief visit to Hanoi and the North in November 1973, is of a pristine dewy morning in the country, and not of all the evidences of war and the personal tragedies I also witnessed. I had slipped out of the village guest house where we had spent the night; my companions were not yet up. During this trip I was seldom alone except for the few hours of diary-writing and exhausted sleep at the end of each busy day, and I treasured this moment of solitude in a beautiful scene which had the added charm of not having been visible when we'd arrived the previous evening. The chalet-like guest house stood among trees — palms and others — close to a small clear pond. On the far side of the pond I could see a small boy silently leading a water-buffalo along the narrow path. Everything was still, and quiet, and green. A light mist was rising off the water. The tops of tall palms just barely stirred, as if dreaming, then held still again. I had the sharpest sense of *being here*, being in the very midst of Vietnam, this country that for almost a decade, by then, had been so prominent an entity in my mind and in that of everyone I knew, and yet had remained, until this journey, essentially an abstraction. My companions and I had made the trip to see it for ourselves; but no moment until now had given me so palpable an encounter with Vietnam's most essential reality as these few minutes of immersion in the beginnings of a day in the green, green countryside unmarked by any sign of war. The children in the Bach My Hospital, missing feet, legs, hands, their heads bandaged; the bomb craters that encircled the hospital; the stricken faces of mourners — unforgettable and excruciating sights such as these reinforced our horror of war and provided specific knowledge of its immediate consequences. But that morning I experienced intensely the beauty and patient endurance of the land, qualities that are reflected in its peasant people, who have suffered so many invasions through the centuries. This was the ground that sustained them, the steady pulse underneath the tumult of wars.

Reading through the varied contents of this anthology I kept thinking about the audience who will also be reading it. For some, it will link itself to their own memories, gained as G.I.'s or relief workers; some readers may be Vietnamese themselves, now living in the United States, and a few, no doubt, will read it in Vietnam. Others will have memories of the war years here in the States, whether they supported or opposed the war — memories of waiting for people to come home, either from the armed forces or from imprisonment as draft resisters, or from Canada or Sweden. Memories of demonstrations, of hopes for social change. Of their mental images of a country they had never seen, a place whose name became the name of an era.

But I thought, too, of those too young to remember all that, many of them born after the war was over. And perhaps it's to them especially that such an anthology may speak — may begin to make real what the era was at its core: not Woodstock. Not Woodstock but mortal wounds inflicted on and by real people in a real country. And not a war movie, even the better of which show the war as experienced by U.S. forces, people far from home, not as lived by the Vietnamese, military or civilian, inside their own country.

A contribution like Linda Van Devanter's account of her return after the war, visiting the North which she'd never seen and the area in the South where she had been an army nurse, reveals something of the way in which the Vietnamese remained unknown, essentially *unimagined*, to the invaders:

> I saw art and history and music, and I began to get a sense of these people as I'd never understood them before. There had been no time during the war to go to history museums, and I had never known how many eons these people had faced war. America had been only the last in a long line of countries that had tried to conquer this nation throughout its existence of thousands of years. . . . War destroys so many things, and one of the first casualties is the ability to think of the enemy as human beings with a history and a future.

A sense of that long past and of hope for the future infuses the work of many Vietnamese contributions, even though all are also full of deep, persistent sadness. An unknown soldier wrote in 1967 that "Vietnam is a country of great seas / And long rivers," and a stanza of his poem "Hope" reads,

> The burning and killing will pass.
> The enemy will be driven from our country.
> Although our legs are weary,
> Our voices hoarse,
> We sing the songs of rebuilding.

It's a tone of sober, not euphoric, hope.

Those American readers who remember only their own wartime experiences need to be reminded of the character and actuality of the peasant people against whom they fought (often unwillingly, with pain and disgust at their own enforced actions, and, for so many, with lasting trauma) or with whom they tried to stand in solidarity as participants in the antiwar movement, yet whom they never really knew. And the young, to whom it is all history, a jumble of rumor, they above all need to be awakened to what it was really like: what war itself is really like. If they understood more, would they so easily break out in that rash of yellow ribbons which greets each military adventure, such as Grenada, Panama, the Gulf War? There are so many factors involved—above all, economic factors—in the repeated acceptance of war; and education about it can't, by itself, change that. But certainly an anthology such as this can contribute to more understanding. It is a reminder, and we need reminders. "We can't afford to heal," writes George Evans. "If we do, we'll forget, and if we forget, it will start again." Marilyn McMahon—an army nurse who will never bear a child because she has seen too many of her fellow nurses, exposed, like herself, to dioxin, give birth to physically or mentally damaged babies or suffer one miscarriage after another—writes in the same vein:

> Wounds heal from the bottom up
>   and from outside in.
> Each must be kept open,
>   must be probed
>   and exposed to light.
> Must be inspected
>   and known.

The *psychological* impact of war is bound to be different for the invaders and the invaded; far more devastating, in the long run, for the former, as the countless war-related suicides and drug-addicted veterans in the United States demonstrate. The *physical* effects—the deaths, bereavements, mutilations, and ongoing ill health—are shared; that's another thing an anthology like this makes one remember, even by simply placing writings from both countries side by side. Indeed, though the point is not specifically made, it may cause a reader to reflect on how the technological sophistication of U.S. weapons (such as the devilish plastic fleshettes, indetectable by X-rays, of which Lady Borton reminds us) and the poverty of Vietnamese medical resources combined to make the amount of sheer physical suffering greater on the Vietnamese side; and to recall that any consideration of Vietnamese casualties has to include a vast number of civilians. We may never know how many American soldiers were damaged by Agent Orange—but we have even less recognition of the numbers of women, children, and the elderly injured by this and other poisons. And for the Vietnamese, the postwar shortages of food, medicine, and other necessities, resulting from punitive trade embargoes, as well as the presence of unexploded mines and the devastation of land, roads, and buildings, caused wartime suffering to be prolonged far beyond the cessation of fighting.

As the editors point out in their introduction, the collection is by no means comprehensive but is drawn exclusively from the work of those writers, U.S. and Vietnamese, who have been associated with the Joiner Center in the first eight years of its Writer's Workshop. It is, then, a sampler. We need to see more of such pairings, such accounts of parallel experience — which are never simply mirror images, because one side was in its native land and knew what the war was about, while the other was thousands of miles from home and had only confused ideas of whom and why they were fighting.

Especially, I think, we need to see published in America much more writing from Vietnam. A book like this one is a beginning, not a summing up. Testimony, evocation: vivid writing, in prose or poetry, breaks through the abstractions, takes us into concrete reality. We need to find ourselves, not once but many times over, *in that place*, not in the era but in the land at the still center of the era's maelstrom, as I for a moment found myself, that green dawn by the pond, in the unchanging Vietnam over which so many wars have swept. Only so will we arrive, belatedly, at some better comprehension of what *that* war was.

Introduction: Completing the Circle

The bus lurched over the last bumps on the road leading out of Danang to the highway south to Nha Trang. It was January 1988 during our third trip back to Viet Nam. The conversation turned to writing. A fresh paperback copy of Larry Heinemann's novel *Paco's Story*, winner of the National Book Award for 1986, was being passed around our small group of mostly university professors and students, including a delegation from the Joiner Center of UMass/Boston. We talked about the great weight of writing that had come from the war and the fact that, twenty years after the U.S. war in Viet Nam had ended, American veterans were still writing novels, nonfiction, poetry, and plays and were winning some of our most prestigious national literary awards. We talked about the country we were traveling through, its roads still pockmarked by the war, abandoned tanks and military vehicles still straddling the highways, and we wondered who the great Vietnamese writers of the war were and what were their stories?

On that bone-rattling trip down Highway One through Quang Nam Province in 1988, the idea for the William Joiner Center Writer's Workshop first took form. We were intrigued by the question of what would happen if we brought together a group of veterans who had written about the war and created a space for them to teach, a workshop to draw other veterans and writers struggling with similar issues and themes. A month after we had returned from Viet Nam, during a conference in February 1988, that marked the twentieth anniversary of the Tet Offensive, Center codirectors David Hunt and Kevin Bowen met with Bruce Weigl, Bill Ehrhart, and John Balaban to try out the idea. After some initial hesitation, everyone agreed that the workshop was worth pursuing. Planning began immediately, and in the summer of 1988, the Joiner Center Summer Writer's Workshop convened at the University of Massachusetts Boston with T. Michael Sullivan, the Center's veterans resource project coordinator, guiding the first group through workshops offered by a teaching faculty of Weigl, Ehrhart, Larry Rottmann, Lamont Steptoe, and John Balaban.

Two things have distinguished the Joiner gathering for writers from other workshops: its remarkable faculty comprising primarily Vietnam veteran writers, and the participation of visiting writers from Viet Nam. During that first summer, Le Luu, an award-winning novelist and veteran of the North Vietnamese Army, and Nguy Ngu, a short story writer and veteran of the Army of the Republic of Vietnam, traveled to Boston to join the American veteran writers. Their presence generated enormous energy. In 1989, Le Luu returned with Nguyen Quang Sang, an award-winning short story writer and filmmaker and the director of the Ho Chi Minh City Writers' Association and Nguyen Khai, a highly respected short story writer from Ha Noi.

Inspired by the workshop model, writers convened in Ha Noi the following year for the first International Conference of U.S. and Vietnamese Veteran Writers, cosponsored by the Vietnamese Writers Association and the William Joiner Center. A delegation of American veteran writers, including Jointer Center codirectors Kevin Bowen and David Hunt, as well as Phil Caputo, Bill Ehrhart, Larry Heinemann, Bruce Weigl, Yusef Komunyakaa, Larry Rottmann, and George Wilson met with their Vietnamese counterparts for three remarkable days. These meetings were followed by similar gatherings in Hai Phong, Hue, Da Nang, and Ho Chi Minh City.

Many more exchanges followed. Distinguished Vietnamese writers such as Huu Thinh, Le Minh Khue, Nguyen Quang Thieu, Pham Tien Duat, Tran Dang Khoa, To Nhuan Vy, Nguyen Duy, Van Le, Cao Tien Le, and Chu Lai have visited the workshop in recent summers. Their visits have resulted in major collaborations between "American" and Vietnamese writers.

Literary anthologies are inherently problematic for their editors, their reviewers, and to a certain extent, their readers. The most common criticism of anthologies of all types is that they are, for a variety of reasons, exclusive, that the editors have left out significant work. This anthology shares that difficulty but is distinguished from most literary anthologies because what inspired and enabled this collection, and what determined which writers would be represented in its pages, was the belief of the editors that every writer who had participated in the Joiner Center Workshop since its inception be represented.

If our editorial decisions were difficult, this was because the list of contributors included so many important and accomplished writers, whose collective body of work could easily fill a hundred anthologies. Choices had to be made, but we gladly accepted this challenge. As we immersed ourselves in our task, we discovered important commonalities among writers, encountering people who had come to their art after having borne witness to war, political brutality, social injustice, ideological isolation, or some combination of these forces. What sets this group of writers apart, however, is their emergence not as victims but as survivors who, through the very act of their art, exemplify what is enduring, resilient, and moral within the human spirit. That they witnessed and sometimes endured coercion in different forms and then went on to write of that coercion with eloquence and clarity is profound proof of the power of the forces of good.

In the introduction to her monumental anthology *Against Forgetting: Twentieth-Century Poetry of Witness*, Carolyn Forché (herself a Joiner Workshop teacher and a contributor here) writes that "the poetry of witness is itself born in dialectical opposition to the extremity that has made such witness necessary." Assembling the poetry, fiction, and nonfiction for this anthology, we were struck with how well that characterization suited the work gathered here, and how well it describes the depths of commitment these writers have made to their art and to telling the truth of their experiences.

This anthology, therefore, has grown (and has been assembled) as the workshop has grown: from a first rather tentative gathering of Vietnam veteran writers and their students, struggling to find their individual voices as well as a common diction, to what is now one of the most vital and exciting writing workshops offered anywhere. More than forty poets, fiction writers, and nonfiction writers from Viet Nam, the United States, Puerto Rico, Nicaragua, and Guatemala have participated as faculty or as visiting writers. Notably, they have worked not as antagonists of their various traditions but as contributors to and refiners of those traditions. This anthology then, is an homage to them, and to their students, and it is a celebration of what the workshop has come to stand for: the power of the word in the face of that which threatens the word.

To reflect the variety of experiences, perspectives, and literary styles represented here, we have divided the book into five sections. "In Country," the first section, includes poetry and prose that chronicle firsthand experiences *during* the American war in Viet Nam. This particular grouping is distinguished from most other Vietnam War–related anthologies because both American and Vietnamese sides appear here, providing for the first time in English a fuller and more honest literary accounting of that long war than we have had. Section two, "Aftermath," gathers work by Vietnamese and American writers who confront the horror and waste, the social and political upheaval left in the wake of war. Construing the recent wars in Central America as part of the same fabric as the war in Viet Nam,

"Across Borders," section three, includes a remarkable variety of poetry and prose that focuses on these wars and that tries to break down geographical, moral, political, and artistic borders, to promote the notion of world citizenship. The fourth section, "Going Back," includes the work of combatants and noncombatants who participated in the American war in Viet Nam and who subsequently returned to that country in peace. The anthology concludes with "Mountains and Rivers," a collection of poetry and prose of Vietnamese writers, beginning with their oral tradition, extending to the present time, and distinguished by its fierce prizing of life that manages to maintain some form of normalcy and hope in the face of war. Concluding this collection with the work of our Vietnamese colleagues and some of their literary ancestors seems appropriate. The circle that was broken by war, begins to reform.

Acknowledgments

As has been the case with Thanh Nguyen and Bruce Weigl's *Poems from Captured Documents* (University of Massachusetts Press, 1994), and Linda Ditmar and Gene Michaud's *From Hanoi to Hollywood* (Rutgers University Press, 1990), proceeds from this volume will go to support the Joiner Outpatient Pediatric Clinic at Hue Central Hospital. We thank all the writers and publishers involved for waiving their reprint fees. From its beginnings, the Writer's Workshop has been firmly embedded in the center's efforts at reconciliation and assistance to Viet Nam. On that drive down Highway One in the winter of 1988, we visited hospitals, clinics, and rehabilitation centers. We met old and young men and women who had fought for the North and South. During those days, the U.S. embargo still in effect, Viet Nam was an extremely poor country, still suffering from the consequences of the war and the embargo. We rarely saw cars or motorcycles. Electricity was irregular at best. Hospitals had few medicines, and the clinic pharmacies were bare. Men, women, and children were still being maimed and killed by ordnance strewn across the country. Yet everywhere we went we were deeply touched by the openness and dignity of the people. With the help of John McAuliff and the Indochina Reconciliation Project, we arranged a return visit to Ha Noi at the end of the trip to meet with officials at what was then the Ministry of Labor, War Invalids, and Social Welfare, and we began a series of programs that would send medicines and medical equipment to rehabilitation centers in Ha Noi, Dong Ha, Hoi An, Hoc Mon, Tay Ninh, My Tho and to hospitals in Ha Noi, Hue, Ho Chi Minh City, and Tay Ninh. Other visits have followed, including those of several medical delegations of Vietnam veterans led by Ralph Timperi, who set up training programs and established the Joiner Outpatient Pediatric Clinic at Hue Central Hospital.

The list of other friends of the Center, staff members, and workshop students who have also made significant contributions to the workshop during the past nine years and therefore, to this anthology, is long. David Hunt, the Joiner Center's codirector until 1994, needs to be particularly acknowledged here, as well as T. Michael Sullivan, who since its inception has guided the workshop through hectic times. Leslie Bowen, Frank Boback, Julia Perez, Jaime Rodriguez, Paul White, Anne Marie Madden, David Monahan, Keith Snyder, Art Galasso, Alex Walker, and Maura Branley have all put in long hours on workshop activities over the years. Among others, we are grateful to the many who have opened their homes to visiting writers, including Joan and John McIntyre, Cheri Rankin and Chris Myers, Ralph Timperi and Jennifer Corchran, and David Hunt. Special thanks to the families on Melville Avenue, to Leslie Bowen, Lillian Shirley and Tom Davidson (and their children Katherine and Sean), and to Jim Austen and Cathy Overholt for sharing their beautiful backyards, their gardens and trees each summer. Special thanks to Norm Oppegard and Joan McIntyre for their tireless devotion to this manuscript as well as their hard work throughout the year, to Vu Tu Nam and Chinh Huu of the Vietnamese Writers Association for assisting us in bringing Vietnamese writers to the United States, to our translators during the workshop, Thanh Nguyen, Hien Tran, Ngo Vinh Hai, Ngo Vinh Long, Ha Huy Thong, Le Thi Hoai Phuong, Thuy Hunt, and, especially, to Nguyen Ba Chung for his invaluable assistance. A special thanks is owed to the Lannan Foundation, whose assistance at a critical time kept the workshop from going under and whose continued support has allowed us to keep tuition reasonable over the years. Thanks also to the Ford Foundation, whose generous support has funded visiting writers from Vietnam over the past five years, to the Overbrook Foundation and the Public Concern Foundation for similar support, to the William Joiner Foundation, and to Bob Glassman for his many generous contributions.

Finally, we would like to remember two friends: Leo Cawley, a Marine Corps Vietnam veteran, writer and activist who died in 1992; and Paul White, a U.S. Navy veteran, former Joiner Center staff member and critical figure in the early days of the workshop, who died in November 1994. We will not forget.

IN COUNTRY

Him on the Bicycle

There was no light; there was no light at all. — Roethke

In a liftship near Hue,
the door gunner is in a trance.
He's that driver who falls
asleep at the wheel
between Pittsburgh and Cleveland
staring at the Ho Chi Minh Trail.

Flares fall,
where the river leaps
I go stiff,
I have to think, tropical.

The door gunner sees movement,
the pilot makes small circles:
four men running, carrying rifles,
one man on a bicycle.

He pulls me out of the ship,
there's firing far away.
I'm on the back of the bike
holding his hips.
It's hard pumping for two,
I hop off and push the bike.

I'm brushing past trees,
the man on the bike stops pumping,
lifts his feet,
we don't waste a stroke.
His hat flies off,
I catch it behind my back,
put it on, I want to live forever!

Like a blaze
streaming down the trail.

How to Tell a True War Story

This is TRUE.

I had a buddy in Vietnam. His name was Bob Kiley, but everybody called him Rat.

A friend of his gets killed, so about a week later Rat sits down and writes a letter to the guy's sister. Rat tells her what a great brother she had, how together the guy was, a number one pal and comrade. A real soldier's soldier, Rat says. Then he tells a few stories to make the point, how her brother would always volunteer for stuff nobody else would volunteer for in a million years, dangerous stuff, like doing recon or going out on these really badass night patrols. Stainless steel balls, Rat tells her. The guy was a little crazy, for sure, but crazy in a good way, a real daredevil, because he liked the challenge of it, he liked testing himself, just man against gook. A great, great guy, Rat says.

Anyway, it's a terrific letter, very personal and touching. Rat almost bawls writing it. He gets all teary telling about the good times they had together, how her brother made the war seem almost fun, always raising hell and lighting up villes and bringing smoke to bear every which way. A great sense of humor, too. Like the time at this river when he went fishing with a whole damn crate of hand grenades. Probably the funniest thing in world history, Rat says, all that gore, about twenty zillion dead gook fish. Her brother, he had the right attitude. He knew how to have a good time. On Halloween, this real hot spooky night, the dude paints up his body all different colors and puts on this weird mask and hikes over to a ville and goes trick-or-treating almost stark naked, just boots and balls and an M-16. A tremendous human being, Rat says. Pretty nutso sometimes, but you could trust him with your life.

And then the letter gets very sad and serious. Rat pours his heart out. He says he loved the guy. He says the guy was his best friend in the world. They were like soul mates, he says, like twins or something, they had a whole lot in common. He tells the guy's sister he'll look her up when the war's over.

So what happens?

Rat mails the letter. He waits two months. The dumb cooze never writes back.

A true war story is never moral. It does not instruct, nor encourage virtue, nor suggest models of proper human behavior, nor restrain men from doing the things men have always done. If a story seems moral, do not believe it. If at the end of a war story you feel uplifted, or if you feel that some small bit of rectitude has been salvaged from the larger waste, then you have been made the victim of a very old and terrible lie. There is no rectitude whatsoever. There is no virtue. As a first rule of thumb, therefore, you can tell a true war story by its absolute and uncompromising allegiance to obscenity and evil. Listen to Rat Kiley. Cooze, he says. He does not say bitch. He certainly does not say woman, or girl. He says cooze. Then he spits and stares. He's nineteen years old — it's too much for him — so he looks at you with those big sad gentle killer eyes and says cooze, because his friend is dead, and because it's so incredibly sad and true: she never wrote back.

You can tell a true war story if it embarrasses you. If you don't care for obscenity, you don't care for the truth; if you don't care for the truth, watch how you vote. Send guys to war, they come home talking dirty.

Listen to Rat: "Jesus Christ, man, I write this beautiful fuckin' letter, I slave over it, and what happens? The dumb cooze never writes back."

The dead guy's name was Curt Lemon. What happened was we crossed a muddy river and marched west into the mountains, and on the third day we took a break along a trail junction in deep jungle. Right away, Lemon and Rat Kiley started goofing. They didn't understand about the spookiness. They were kids; they just didn't know. A nature hike, they thought, not even a war, so they went off into the shade of some giant trees — quadruple canopy, no sunlight at all — and they were giggling and calling each other yellow mother and playing a silly game they'd invented. The game involved smoke grenades, which were harmless unless you did stupid things, and what they did was pull out the pin and stand a few feet apart and play catch under the shade of those huge trees. Whoever chickened out was a yellow mother. And if nobody chickened out, the grenade would make a light popping sound and they'd be covered with smoke and they'd laugh and dance around and then do it again.

It's all exactly true.

It happened, to me, nearly twenty years ago, and I still remember that trail junction and those giant trees and a soft dripping sound somewhere beyond the trees. I remember the smell of moss. Up in the canopy there were tiny white blossoms, but no sunlight at all, and I remember the shadows spreading out under the trees where Curt Lemon and Rat Kiley were playing catch with smoke grenades. Mitchell Sanders sat flipping his yo-yo. Norman Bowker and Kiowa and Dave Jensen were dozing, or half-dozing, and all around us were those ragged green mountains.

Except for the laughter things were quiet.

At one point, I remember, Mitchell Sanders turned and looked at me, not quite nodding, as if to warn me about something, as if he already knew, then after a while he rolled up his yo-yo and moved away.

It's hard to tell you what happened next.

They were just goofing. There was a noise, I suppose, which must've been the detonator, so I glanced behind me and watched Lemon step from the shade into bright sunlight. His face was suddenly brown and shining. A handsome kid, really. Sharp gray eyes, lean and narrow waisted, and when he died it was almost beautiful, the way the sunlight came around him and lifted him up and sucked him high into a tree full of moss and vines and white blossoms.

In any war story, but especially a true one, it's difficult to separate what happened from what seemed to happen. What seems to happen becomes its own happening and has to be told that way. The angles of vision are skewed. When a booby trap explodes, you close your eyes and duck and float outside yourself. When a guy dies, like Curt Lemon, you look away and then look back for a moment and then look away again. The pictures get jumbled; you tend to miss a lot. And then afterward, when you go to tell about it, there is always that surreal seemingness, which makes the story seem untrue, but which in fact represents the hard and exact truth as it *seemed*.

In many cases a true war story cannot be believed. If you believe it, be skeptical. It's a question of credibility. Often the crazy stuff is true and the normal stuff isn't, because the normal stuff is necessary to make you believe the truly incredible craziness.

In other cases you can't even tell a true war story. Sometimes it's just beyond telling.

I heard this one, for example, from Mitchell Sanders. It was near dusk and we were sitting at my foxhole along a wide muddy river north of Quang Ngai. I remember how peaceful the twilight was. A deep pinkish red spilled out on the river, which moved without sound, and in the morning we would cross the river and march west into the mountains. The occasion was right for a good story.

"God's truth," Mitchell Sanders said. "A six-man patrol goes up into the mountains on a basic listening-post operation. The idea's to spend a week up there, just lie low and listen for enemy movement. They've got a radio along, so if they hear anything suspicious — anything — they're supposed to call in artillery or gunships, whatever it takes. Otherwise they keep strict field discipline. Absolute silence. They just listen."

Sanders glanced at me to make sure I had the scenario. He was playing with his yo-yo, dancing it with short, tight little strokes of the wrist.

His face was blank in the dusk.

"We're talking regulation, by-the-book LP. These six guys, they don't say boo for a solid week. They don't got tongues. All ears."

"Right," I said.

"Understand me?"

"Invisible."

Sanders nodded.

"Affirm," he said. "Invisible. So what happens is, these guys get themselves deep in the bush, all camouflaged up, and they lie down and wait and that's all they do, nothing else, they lie there for seven straight days and just listen. And man, I'll tell you — it's spooky. This is mountains. You don't know spooky till you been there. Jungle, sort of, except it's way up in the clouds and there's always this fog — like rain, except it's not raining — everything's all wet and swirly and tangled up and you can't see jack, you can't find your own pecker to piss with. Like you don't even have a body. Serious spooky. You just go with the vapors — the fog sort of takes you in . . . and the sounds, man. The sounds carry forever. You hear stuff nobody should ever hear."

Sanders was quiet for a second, just working the yo-yo, then he smiled at me.

"So after a couple days the guys start hearing this real soft, kind of wacked-out music. Weird echoes and stuff. Like a radio or something, but it's not a radio, it's this strange gook music that comes right out of the rocks. Faraway, sort of, but right up close, too. They try to ignore it. But it's a listening post, right? So they listen. And every night they keep hearing that crazyass gook concert. All kinds of chimes and xylophones. I mean, this is wilderness — no way, it can't be real — but there it is, like the mountains are tuned in to Radio fucking Hanoi. Naturally they get nervous. One guy sticks Juicy Fruit in his ears. Another guy almost flips. Thing is, though, they can't report music. They can't get on the horn and call back to base and say, 'Hey, listen, we need some firepower, we got to blow away this weirdo gook rock band.' They can't do that. It wouldn't go down. So they lie there in the fog and keep their mouths shut. And what makes it extra bad, see, is the poor dudes can't horse around like normal. Can't joke it away. Can't even talk to each other except maybe in whispers, all hush-hush, and that just revs up the willies. All they do is listen."

Again there was some silence as Mitchell Sanders looked out on the river. The dark was coming on hard now, and off to the west I could see the mountains rising in silhouette, all the mysteries and unknowns.

"This next part," Sanders said quietly, "you won't believe."

"Probably not," I said.

"You won't. And you know why?" He gave me a long, tired smile. "Because it happened. Because every word is absolutely dead-on true."

Sanders made a sound in his throat, like a sigh, as if to say he didn't care if I believed him or not. But he did care. He wanted me to feel the truth, to believe by the raw force of feeling. He seemed sad, in a way.

"These six guys," he said, "they're pretty fried out by now, and one night they start hearing voices. Like at a cocktail party. That's what it sounds like, this big swank gook cocktail party somewhere out there in the fog. Music and chitchat and stuff. It's crazy, I know, but they hear the champagne corks. They hear the actual martini glasses. Real hoity-toity, all very civilized, except this isn't civilization. This is Nam.

"Anyway, the guys try to be cool. They just lie there and groove, but after a while they start hearing — you won't believe this — they hear chamber music. They hear violins and cellos. They hear this terrific mama-san soprano. Then after a while they hear gook opera and a glee club and the Haiphong Boys' Choir and a barbershop quartet and all kinds of weird chanting and Buddha-Buddha stuff. And the whole time, in the background, there's still that cocktail party going on. All these different voices. Not human voices, though. Because it's the mountains. Follow me? The rock — it's talking. And the fog, too, and the grass and the goddamn mongooses. Everything talks. The trees talk politics, the monkeys talk religion. The whole country. Vietnam. The place talks. It talks. Understand? Nam — it truly talks.

"The guys can't cope. They lose it. They get on the radio and report enemy movement — a whole army, they say — and they order up the firepower. They get arty and gunships. They call in air strikes. And I'll tell you, they fuckin' crash that cocktail party. All night long, they just smoke those mountains. They make jungle juice. They blow away trees and glee clubs and whatever else there is to blow away. Scorch time. They walk napalm up and down the ridges. They bring in the Cobras and F-4's, they use Willie Peter and HE and incendiaries. It's all fire. They make those mountains burn.

"Around dawn things finally get quiet. Like you never even heard quiet before. One of those real thick, real misty days — just clouds and fog, they're off in this special zone — and the mountains are absolutely dead-flat silent. Like Brigadoon — pure vapor, you know? Everything's all sucked up inside the fog. Not a single sound, except they still hear it.

"So they pack up and start humping. They head down the mountain, back to base camp, and when they get there they don't say diddly. They don't talk. Not a word, like they're deaf and dumb. Later on this fat bird colonel comes up and asks what the hell happened out there. What'd they hear? Why all the ordnance? The man's ragged out, he gets down tight on their case. I mean, they spent six trillion dollars on firepower, and this fatass colonel wants answers, he wants to know what the fuckin' story is.

"But the guys don't say zip. They just look at him for a while, sort of funny like, sort of amazed, and the whole war is right there in that stare. It says everything you can't ever say. It says, man, you got wax in your ears. It says, poor bastard, you'll never know — wrong frequency — you don't even want to hear this. Then they salute the fucker and walk away, because certain stories you don't ever tell."

You can tell a true war story by the way it never seems to end. Not then, not ever. Not when Mitchell Sanders stood up and moved off into the dark.

It all happened.

Even now, at this instant, I remember that yo-yo. In a way, I suppose, you had to be there, you had to hear it, but I could tell how desperately Sanders wanted me to believe him, his frustration at not quite getting the details right, not quite pinning down the final and definitive truth.

And I remember sitting at my foxhole that night, watching the shadows of Quang Ngai, thinking about the coming day and how we would cross the river and march west into the mountains, all the ways I might die, all the things I did not understand.

Late in the night Mitchell Sanders touched my shoulder. "Just came to me," he whispered. "The moral, I mean. Nobody listens. Nobody hears nothin'. Like that fatass colonel. The politicians, all the civilian types. Your girlfriend. My girlfriend. Everybody's sweet little virgin girlfriend. What they need is to go out on LP. The vapors, man. Trees and rocks — you got to *listen* to your enemy."

And then again, in the morning, Sanders came up to me. The platoon was preparing to move out, checking weapons, going through all the little rituals that preceded a day's march. Already the lead squad had crossed the river and was filing off toward the west.

"I got a confession to make," Sanders said. "Last night, man, I had to make up a few things."

"I know that."

"The glee club. There wasn't any glee club."

"Right."

"No opera."

"Forget it, I understand."

"Yeah, but listen, it's still true. Those six guys, they heard wicked sound out there. They heard sound you just plain won't believe."

Sanders pulled on his rucksack, closed his eyes for a moment, then almost smiled at me. I knew what was coming.

"All right," I said, "what's the moral?"

"Forget it."

"No, go ahead."

For a long while he was quiet, looking away, and the silence kept stretching out until it was almost embarrassing. Then he shrugged and gave me a stare that lasted all day.

"Hear that quiet, man?" he said. "That quiet — just listen. There's your moral."

In a true war story, if there's a moral at all, it's like the thread that makes the cloth. You can't tease it out. You can't extract the meaning without unraveling the deeper meaning. And in the end, really, there's nothing much to say about a true war story, except maybe "Oh."

True war stories do not generalize. They do not indulge in abstraction or analysis.

For example: War is hell. As a moral declaration the old truism seems perfectly true, and yet because it abstracts, because it generalizes, I can't believe it with my stomach. Nothing turns inside.

It comes down to gut instinct. A true war story, if truly told, makes the stomach believe.

This one does it for me. I've told it before — many times, many versions — but here's what actually happened.

We crossed that river and marched west into the mountains. On the third day, Curt Lemon stepped on a booby-trapped 105 round. He was playing catch with Rat Kiley, laughing, and then he was dead. The trees were thick; it took nearly an hour to cut an LZ for the dustoff.

Later, higher in the mountains, we came across a baby VC water buffalo. What it was doing there I don't know—no farms or paddies—but we chased it down and got a rope around it and led it along to a deserted village where we set up for the night. After supper Rat Kiley went over and stroked its nose.

He opened up a can of C rations, pork and beans, but the baby buffalo wasn't interested.

Rat shrugged.

He stepped back and shot it through the right front knee. The animal did not make a sound. It went down hard, then got up again, and Rat took careful aim and shot off an ear. He shot it in the hindquarters and in the little hump at its back. He shot it twice in the flanks. It wasn't to kill; it was to hurt. He put the rifle muzzle up against the mouth and shot the mouth away. Nobody said much. The whole platoon stood there watching, feeling all kinds of things, but there wasn't a great deal of pity for the baby water buffalo. Curt Lemon was dead. Rat Kiley had lost his best friend in the world. Later in the week he would write a long personal letter to the guy's sister, who would not write back, but for now it was a question of pain. He shot off the tail. He shot away chunks of meat below the ribs. All around us there was the smell of smoke and filth and deep greenery, and the evening was humid and very hot. Rat went to automatic. He shot randomly, almost casually, quick little spurts in the belly and butt. Then he reloaded, squatted down, and shot it in the left front knee. Again the animal fell hard and tried to get up, but this time it couldn't quite make it. It wobbled and went down sideways. Rat shot it in the nose. He bent forward and whispered something, as if talking to a pet, then he shot it in the throat. All the while the baby buffalo was silent, or almost silent, just a light bubbling sound where the nose had been. It lay very still. Nothing moved except the eyes, which were enormous, the pupils shiny black and dumb.

Rat Kiley was crying. He tried to say something, but then cradled his rifle and went off by himself.

The rest of us stood in a ragged circle around the baby buffalo. For a time no one spoke. We had witnessed something essential, something brand new and profound, a piece of the world so startling there was not yet a name for it.

Somebody kicked the baby buffalo.

It was still alive, though just barely, just in the eyes.

"Amazing," Dave Jensen said. "My whole life, I never seen anything like it."

"Never?"

"Not hardly. Not once."

Kiowa and Mitchell Sanders picked up the baby buffalo. They hauled it across the open square, hoisted it up, and dumped it in the village well.

Afterward we sat waiting for Rat to get himself together.

"Amazing," Dave Jensen kept saying. "A new wrinkle. I never seen it before."

Mitchell Sanders took out his yo-yo. "Well, that's Nam," he said. "Garden of Evil. Over here, man, every sin's real fresh and original."

How do you generalize?

War is hell, but that's not the half of it, because war is also mystery and terror and adventure and courage and discovery and holiness and pity and despair and longing and love. War is nasty; war is fun. War is thrilling; war is drudgery. War makes you a man; war makes you dead. The truths are contradictory. It can be argued, for instance, that war is grotesque. But in truth war is also beauty. For all its horror, you can't help but gape at the awful majesty of combat. You stare out at tracer rounds unwinding through the dark like brilliant red ribbons. You crouch in ambush as a cool, impassive moon rises over the nighttime paddies. You admire the fluid symmetries of troops on the move, the harmonies of sound and shape and proportion, the great sheets of metal-fire streaming down from a gunship, the illumination rounds, the white phosphorus, the purply orange glow of napalm, the rocket's red glare. It's not pretty, exactly. It's astonishing. It fills the eye. It commands you. You hate it, yes, but your eyes do not. Like a killer forest fire, like cancer under a microscope, any battle or bombing raid or artillery barrage has the aesthetic purity of absolute moral indifference—a powerful, implacable beauty—and a true war story will tell the truth about this, though the truth is ugly.

To generalize about war is like generalizing about peace. Almost everything is true. Almost nothing is true. At its core, perhaps, war is just another name for death, and yet any soldier will tell you, if he tells the truth, that proximity to death brings with it a corresponding proximity to life. After a firefight, there is always the immense pleasure of aliveness. The trees are alive. The grass, the soil—everything. All around you things are purely living, and you among them, and the aliveness makes you tremble. You feel an intense, out-of-the-skin awareness of your living self—your truest self, the human being you want to be and then become by the force of wanting it. In the midst of evil you want to be a good man. You want decency. You want justice and courtesy and human concord, things you never knew you wanted. There is a kind of largeness to it, a kind of godliness. Though it's odd, you're never more alive than when you're almost dead. You recognize what's valuable. Freshly, as if for the first time, you love what's best in yourself and in the world, all that might be lost. At the hour of dusk you sit at your foxhole and look out on a wide river turning pinkish red, and at the mountains beyond, and although in the morning you must cross the river and go into the mountains and do terrible things and maybe die, even so, you find yourself studying the fine colors on the river, you feel wonder and awe at the setting of the sun, and you are filled with a hard, aching love for how the world could be and always should be, but now is not.

Mitchell Sanders was right. For the common soldier, at least, war has the feel — the spiritual texture — of a great ghostly fog, thick and permanent. There is no clarity. Everything swirls. The old rules are no longer binding, the old truths no longer true. Right spills over into wrong. Order blends into chaos, love into hate, ugliness into beauty, law into anarchy, civility into savagery. The vapors suck you in. You can't tell where you are, or why you're there, and the only certainty is overwhelming ambiguity.

In war you lose your sense of the definite, hence your sense of truth itself, and therefore it's safe to say that in a true war story nothing is ever absolutely true.

Often in a true war story there is not even a point, or else the point doesn't hit you until twenty years later, in your sleep, and you wake up and shake your wife and start telling the story to her, except when you get to the end you've forgotten the point again. And then for a long time you lie there watching the story happen in your head. You listen to your wife's breathing. The war's over. You close your eyes. You smile and think, Christ, what's the point?

This one wakes me up.

In the mountains that day, I watched Lemon turn sideways. He laughed and said something to Rat Kiley. Then he took a peculiar half step, moving from shade into bright sunlight, and the booby-trapped 105 round blew him into a tree. The parts were just hanging there, so Dave Jensen and I were ordered to shinny up and peel him off. I remember the white bone of an arm. I remember pieces of skin and something wet and yellow that must've been the intestines. The gore was horrible, and stays with me. But what wakes me up twenty years later is Dave Jensen singing "Lemon Tree" as we threw down the parts.

———————

You can tell a true war story by the questions you ask. Somebody tells a story, let's say, and afterward you ask, "Is it true?" and if the answer matters, you've got your answer. For example, we've all heard this one. Four guys go down a trail. A grenade sails out. One guy jumps on it and takes the blast and saves his three buddies.

Is it true?

The answer matters.

You'd feel cheated if it never happened. Without the grounding reality, it's just a trite bit of puffery, pure Hollywood, untrue in the way all such stories are untrue. Yet even if it did happen—and maybe it did, anything's possible—even then you know it can't be true, because a true war story does not depend upon that kind of truth. Absolute occurrence is irrelevant. A thing may happen and be a total lie; another thing may not happen and be truer than the truth. For example: Four guys go down a trail. A grenade sails out. One guy jumps on it and takes the blast, but it's a killer grenade and everybody dies anyway. Before they die, though, one of the dead guys says, "The fuck you do that for?" and the jumper says, "Story of my life, man," and the other guy starts to smile but he's dead.

That's a true story that never happened.

———————

Twenty years later, I can still see the sunlight on Lemon's face. I can see him turning, looking back at Rat Kiley, then he laughed and took that curious half step from shade into sunlight, his face suddenly brown and shining, and when his foot touched down, in that instant, he must've thought it was the sunlight that was killing him. It was not the sunlight. It was a rigged 105 round. But if I could ever get the story right, how the sun seemed to gather around him and pick him up and lift him high into a tree, if I could somehow re-create the fatal whiteness of that light, the quick glare, the obvious cause and effect, then you would believe the last thing Curt Lemon believed, which for him must've been the final truth.

———————

Now and then, when I tell this story, someone will come up to me afterward and say she liked it. It's always a woman. Usually it's an older woman of kindly temperament and humane politics. She'll explain that as a rule she hates war stories; she can't understand why people want to wallow in all the blood and gore. But this one she liked. The poor baby buffalo, it made her sad. Sometimes, even, there are little tears. What I should do, she'll say, is put it all behind me. Find new stories to tell.

I won't say it but I'll think it.

I'll picture Rat Kiley's face, his grief, and I'll think, You *dumb cooze.*

Because she wasn't listening.

It *wasn't* a war story. It was a *love* story.

But you can't say that. All you can do is tell it one more time, patiently, adding and subtracting, making up a few things to get at the real truth. No Mitchell Sanders, you tell her. No Lemon, no Rat Kiley. No trail junction. No baby buffalo. No vines or moss or white blossoms. Beginning to end, you tell her, it's all made up. Every goddamn detail — the mountains and the river and especially that poor dumb baby buffalo. None of it happened. *None* of it. And even if it did happen, it didn't happen in the mountains, it happened in this little village on the Batangan Peninsula, and it was raining like crazy, and one night a guy named Stink Harris woke up screaming with a leech on his tongue. You can tell a true war story if you just keep on telling it.

And in the end, of course, a true war story is never about war. It's about sunlight. It's about the special way that dawn spreads out on a river when you know you must cross the river and march into the mountains and do things you are afraid to do. It's about love and memory. It's about sorrow. It's about sisters who never write back and people who never listen.

The Ivory Comb

Bathed in moonlight, the hut lay hidden in the heart of the Plain of Reeds, among a thinly grown mangrove belt washed by the rising water. A liaison post on a communication artery, it was small, but crowded with people. We had to wait for our turn to leave, so we alternated lying down and sitting cross-legged on a plank bed, feeling confined. To while away our time we told stories. I will never forget one elderly comrade, a gifted storyteller. His dirty jokes and his jokes about the resistance made us die laughing. To begin, he would always summon a smile and he looked funny. But that night there was something different about him. He insisted that it was his turn to talk, but when all agreed, he remained silent for a long time. He bent his head a little, sat very still, and looked out into the immensity of the water that surrounded us. We stopped joking in anticipation of something serious. Outside, a gusty wind blew, and the surf broke on the mangroves. The hut jolted and rocked like a boat. Some storks stirred uneasily, others flapped their wings, fluttering in the air. The waves and the wind seemed to remind the old storyteller of distant events. He strained as though he were listening to a distant voice. Turning away from us, he stared at the horizon and the bright stars. Quietly, he began his story.

"That day I traveled from Post M.G. to Post D.A.," he began. "As soon as we left the shore, everyone was eager to know who manned our boat. This was not merely out of curiosity; before our departure we had been told by the head of the liaison post that we had a long and dangerous journey ahead, and that we would have to travel by boat as well as on foot. By water, we could easily be spotted by choppers, and by land we could easily run into commandos. If choppers whirled overhead, we would have to remain calm and strictly abide by the steersman's orders. That meant we would place our fate in his hands. Naturally we wanted to know who he was. In the darkness, however, I saw that the steersman was a young slender girl, with a U.S.–made carbine slung on her shoulder, and a scarf around her neck.

" 'How many women are working at this post?' I asked.

" 'Only two, a cook and I,' she said.

"Hearing her voice, I guessed her to be eighteen, twenty at the most. I came to like her and wanted to ask her more questions, but seeing that she was busy, I gave up the idea. She stood straight and turned toward another boat nearby saying: 'I'll start first, all right?'

" 'Hear, hear, good journey!' the liaison men on the next boat said. Some men called her Sister Hai, as if she were the eldest; others, Sister Ut, believing her the youngest. Addressing her comrades as 'little brother,' her replies were clever. Then, politely, she told us to put all of our important things in our pockets or in separate parcels to avoid losing them in case we were strafed by helicopters or ambushed by commandos. Unlike the station master, she warned us against these possible mishaps in a rather mild and lovely tone. Then she bent forward and started the boat's motor. The boat left the thick mangrove belt slowly and then dashed ahead. There was a pleasant chill in the air. Following her instructions, the passengers busied themselves with their luggage. Nothing was more precious to me than my papers and my traveling money, which I always kept in my pocket. Suddenly I thought about the tiny ivory comb. I unpacked my bag, searched it out, put it with my papers in a pouch I slid into my breast pocket and carefully fastened this with a safety pin.

"The little comb was the only relic of a dear friend. Whenever I looked at it, I would feel loss, and some regret.

"During the first days following the restoration of peace in 1954, my friend and I revisited our native village. We had lived next door to each other, near an estuary of the Mekong River. We had joined the Resistance at the beginning of 1946 after the French had invaded our province. My friend stood sixth in his family and was accordingly called Sau. His only daughter was barely twelve months old. Every time his wife came to see him in the liberated zone, he would urge her to bring their daughter along the next time she came, something she dared not do because she had to go through the jungle. Even traveling alone the journey was difficult. Sau didn't blame her. For eight long years he only saw his daughter in a small photograph. Now, on the way home, he was stirred by the indescribable feelings of a father. The boat approached a landing place. Sau saw a little girl about eight, with bobbed hair, black trousers and a red-flowered vest, playing in the shade of a mango tree in the front yard of a house. Not waiting for the boat to reach the bank, he jumped out and shouted, 'Thu, my daughter!' I was close behind him. Sau expected her to bound toward him and fling her arms around his neck. He took a few more steps, bending forward and opening his arms, ready to catch her in a warm embrace. Startled by his call, the little girl stared at him with wide eyes; she looked lost and puzzled. Whenever my friend was seized with sudden emotion, a scar on his right cheek would turn red and was dreadful to look at. With such a face, and with his hands stretched out, he slowly advanced, mumbling in a trembling voice 'Come on, daughter! Come on!' The girl did not understand and blinked at him as though to ask who he was. Her face grew suddenly pale. She broke away in a run and cried, 'Mother, Mother!' Sau stood motionless. His eyes did not leave her. His face was distorted with pain and his arms dropped listlessly.

"As the trip had been rather long, we only had three days to spend at home, not enough time for Thu to get to know her father. That night she wouldn't let Sau sleep with her mother. She got out of her bed, and pulled Sau out of her mother's bed, protesting. Throughout most of the next day, he tried to comfort his daughter, but his efforts were futile. She wouldn't call him 'Daddy.' When her mother told her to call him in for dinner the girl said, 'You'd better call him yourself!' Her mother exploded in anger, snatched a stick and threatened to beat her, insisting that she obey.

" 'Come in for dinner!' Thu said in her father's direction.

"Sau sat still, playing deaf, waiting for the word 'Daddy.' His daughter remained in the kitchen; she raised her voice and said again: 'Dinner is ready.' Sau did not move. The girl turned toward her mother, angrily.

" 'I've done as I was told, but he still won't come.'

"Sau looked at his daughter, shaking his head slightly, and smiled. Maybe he was too hurt to cry.

"In preparation for the next meal, Sau's wife put a pot of rice on the fire and then went out to buy some food. She told Thu to ask for her father's help if she needed it. The pot was soon boiling. Sau's daughter opened the lid and stirred the rice with a big chop-stick. The pot was a bit too heavy for her to lift off the tripod to pour out the excess water. She looked up at Sau. He thought that she was going to give in and call to him for help. She looked around.

" 'The pot is boiling. Pour some water off for me, please,' she said out loud.

"Sau corrected her. 'You should say "Father, please help me pour out some water," ' he said.

"She ignored his words and said in a loud voice: 'The pot is boiling; the rice will be overcooked.'

"Sau stayed motionless. 'If you spoil the rice,' he warned her, 'your mother will surely beat you. Just say, "Daddy, help me." '

"Because the water in the pot was now boiling over, she was afraid and she looked down as if trying to decide what to do. Still, she held her ground. With a rag, she tried to lift the pot but couldn't. She looked up again. The pot boiled faster. Panicking, she was almost crying. She turned her eyes to the pot, then to Sau. She looked pitiful and funny. Finally she stretched out to reach a large spoon and used it to bail out the water, muttering something Sau could not hear.

"During the meal, Sau served her a piece of yellow fish egg. She set it aside in her bowl with her chop-sticks, then suddenly tossed it away, scattering rice all over. Angered by his behavior, Sau spanked her.

" 'Why are you so mule-headed?' he shouted.

"The next morning many relatives came to see Sau off. Thu was also there with her grandmother. Sau was busy receiving everybody and seemed not to pay attention to his daughter. His wife packed his belongings. Their daughter stood alone in a corner, leaning against the door, gazing at everybody around her father. She looked different, no longer obstinate, no longer frowning. Her long and upturned eyelashes that never seemed to flicker made her eyes look wider. She was obviously lost in thought.

"At the moment of departure, only after he had said goodbye to everyone else, did Sau look at his daughter. He noticed a flicker in the girl's eyes.

" 'Bye-bye,' Sau said softly.

"Sau thought she would keep standing in the corner, but unexpectedly she shouted, 'Dad . . . dy, Dad . . . dy.' This 'Daddy' broke out of her after being held back for many years. Stretching out her arms, Thu rushed toward her father and clung to his neck. Pressing herself tightly against his chest, she sobbed: 'Daddy, I won't let you go. Stay with me.'

"Sau hugged his daughter, who kissed his cheek, his hair, his neck, and the long scar on his face.

"The grandmother then told Sau what had happened the night before. Trying to understand why Thu refused to recognize her father, she asked the child why she wouldn't say 'Daddy.'

" 'No, he is not Daddy,' Thu said, turning over in bed.

" 'Your Daddy has been away from home for a long time,' the grandmother said, 'maybe that's why you don't recognize him?'

" 'This man does not look like the daddy I see in the photograph,' Thu said.

" 'Still,' her grandmother said, 'he is your father. Maybe he looks older after such a long time?'

" 'Not older,' Thu said, 'Daddy doesn't have a scar on his cheek.'

"Now the grandmother understood everything. She explained to Thu that her father had been away, fighting against the French and had been wounded. The next morning, Thu asked her grandmother to take her home.

"Sau's daughter kept pressing herself tightly against her father's chest.

Sau could not contain his emotion, but he didn't want her to see him cry. He carried her with one arm and wiped his tears with the other. He kissed her hair and said, 'Let Daddy go. I'll be back again soon.'

" 'No,' the girl screamed, and tightened her grasp around his shoulders, clinging to him with her arms and her legs. It was time to leave. People tried to comfort the girl.

"Sau's wife told her daughter, 'Thu, my love, let Father go. He'll come back and live with us when our country is reunited.'

"Then the grandmother touched Thu's hair and said: 'My good girl, let Daddy go. Tell him to buy a comb for you.'

" 'Buy a comb for me and bring it home, Daddy,' Thu said. Then she let go of him and dropped to her feet.

"Some time later, Sau and I went to East Nam Bo. The years 1954 to 1959 were dark ones. The U.S.–Diem regime hunted down former Resistance members, so we had to live in the jungle.

"We would spend the night in our hammocks with a plastic sheet as a roof. Sau often told me that he felt terrible for having spanked his daughter that day. Once, he suddenly sat up and said: 'People here often hunt elephants. I should see if I can get a piece of ivory to make a comb for my daughter.'

"After that he slept with this hope. Not long afterward, running short of food, we thought that if we hunted with bows and arrows we could get food and still not disturb the jungle's silence. We didn't know how to hunt elephants, but by chance one came across our path. No one else showed much interest, so Sau decided to chase it. With a friend he hid himself in the bush where they waited for the elephant to come close then shot him in the eye.

"I was working under my plastic roof when I heard someone shouting. I looked up and saw Sau rushing through the jungle. He raised a piece of ivory and his face brightened like a child's.

"We often saw him working on the piece of ivory to make a comb, with the skill and patience of a jeweler. I liked to watch him. He usually finished a couple of teeth a day. The finished comb was ten by one and one half centimeters. On the handle, Sau had painstakingly engraved the words: 'With my love and best thoughts for my daughter, Thu.'

"At the end of 1958, during the time we had no weapons, Sau was killed during a raid by American and puppet troops from a bullet fired from an American plane. Before he died, he put his hand in his pocket and took out the comb. Handing it to me, he stared hard into my eyes. Since that day, I often see him in my imagination, his eyes riveted on me.

" 'I will bring the comb to your daughter,' I said in a low voice, bending my head closer to him. Hearing this, Sau shut his eyes forever.

"I have to tell you that during those dark days, secrecy was observed by the living and by the dead. We could not build Sau's tomb above the ground as was our custom because the enemy would desecrate it. Instead I carved a sign into the bark of a nearby tree as a reminder.

"Some time later I was at a relatively safe Resistance base, and a relative visited me. I wanted to send the ivory comb to Thu, but my relative said that Thu and her mother had left for Saigon or for the Plain of Reeds. The Americans and their puppets had organized propaganda courses indicting the communists in their village; they conducted terrorist raids, burned down people's houses, and herded the villagers into concentration camps. Eventually the place became completely desolate.

"I held the comb in my hand. The sight of it gave me much pain.

"The boat's motor went on humming. I was eager to have a close look at the face of the liaison girl on whom my safety depended. The night was not dark and the stars were covered only here and there with some hazy clouds. In the faint light I could only distinguish the girl's profile, her rather round face and her unusual eyes. I thought I had met her somewhere before.

"Suddenly someone shouted, 'A plane! A plane!' People screamed:

" 'Head to the bank!'

" 'Where's the plane?'

" 'I see its light behind us.'

" 'Turn to the bank! Turn to the bank! It's a jet coming.'

" 'The liaison girl slowed the boat and looked at the sky. 'No, it isn't a plane,' she said. 'It's the light of a star.' Her calm voice brought order back to the boat.

"Later, the passengers were quiet, enjoying the trip when the liaison agent stopped the motor and shouted, 'Planes.'

"She steered the boat toward a bamboo bush. Another boat behind us also took shelter there. We could hear the drone of American helicopters.

"The boat rocked and some passengers lost their balance; the liaison agent tried to soothe them, saying 'Keep quiet, uncles; the choppers are still far away. Jump onto the bank, spread out, and hide yourselves. Don't move if they drop flares on you.'

"As she spoke, everyone except me was already on the bank. I was about to jump when the girl said: 'Stay here, uncle, don't worry.'

"The choppers came up from the other end of the canal, their flares advancing toward us. They roared and drew nearer and nearer. The Americans typically used three helicopters: one lighting the way, and the other two doing the strafing.

"The girl repeated her advice to me: 'Camouflage yourself carefully with tree leaves and don't move.'

"This was the first time I had been caught by flares from helicopters. When they were directed toward me, I felt their intense light and the beating of the helicopter blades over my head. I was afraid that the boat was too visible. The camouflage was blown up as in a whirlwind, revealing the knapsacks underneath. I thought I was finished, and I tucked my head between my shoulders to make myself smaller. The girl tried to quiet me again.

" 'They can't see us as we see ourselves,' she said. 'They stage a show of strength, but they can't see anything. We only have to keep calm and not move.' Then she looked up at the field and called the passengers back to the boat. Some were soaked through, and they grumbled as they changed their clothes. The motor roared again.

"After midnight we landed on the bank and continued our trip on foot. We walked in a single line along the muddy, uneven, slippery ditches across a rice field. We carried our sandals in our hands and groped our way step by step. At a point near the riverbank, the liaison girl ordered us to stop, and sent two scouts ahead to reconnoiter the area.

"Within half an hour the scouts encountered enemy commandos. The enemy hadn't hidden in the gardens along the riverside as they usually did, but lay in ambush in the open field. Shots were fired from all directions and bullets flew close overhead.

" 'Brother Tu, guide the group away, I'll stay here,' the liaison girl ordered. I felt a strange urge to tell her to come with us, but she had already faded away. Bullets continued to fly, whistling, then dropping in the distance. We lay as close to the ditch as we could, being careful not to raise our heads. I heard a carbine shot to our left which instantly drew all the firing to that direction. I realized the liaison girl had purposely drawn the enemy's attention to her.

"Run away, Tu,' came the order. Our group rushed forward. I was not used to the firing, but I was not afraid, thinking only of the fate of the liaison girl. We ran helter-skelter across the field into the bush ahead, and from there to the river, which we crossed safely.

"Fleeing the commandos as quickly as possible, we arrived at the appointed place earlier than had been arranged but we did not have to wait long for our new guide from the D.A. post. We gathered in a pineapple field so damaged by toxic chemicals sprayed by the enemy that the plants did not bear fruit.

"We were all very tired. The guides allowed us one night's rest. Some of us did not even bother hanging our hammocks and we lay down on the ground, using our bags as pillows, and soon began to snore. I could only doze, fitfully. I dreamed I was on my way home to my native province; many of the villages looked strangely different; people had been forced to dismantle their houses and go live in concentration camps, which they later destroyed. The gardens, too, had completely changed.

"I pictured Sau, handing me the comb which I still kept. From time to time I woke and thought of those who had stayed behind to check on the enemy's pursuit, especially of the liaison girl. I wondered what had happened to her and to the others. I fell asleep from exhaustion.

"I heard the faint sound of footsteps, then voices, and laughter. I woke and saw that it was dawn. A stripe of clouds hung in the sky. People were talking excitedly. The liaison girl was there, soaked through, her clothes caked with mud, but she had joined us in time.

"I saw her more clearly this time. Although she had just fought against the commandos and had escaped from a dangerous place, she looked as though nothing serious had happened to her. She was sunburned, her eyes shined, and she looked to be no more than twenty. She stepped toward me. I wanted to express my admiration and gratitude. I greeted her with a smile and said, 'I was worried about you. Are you the youngest in your family?'

" 'I'm the first,' she said.

" 'Why do they call you Sister Ut then? Is it because you're not mar . . .?

" 'No,' she said without giving me time to finish. 'I'm the first and the last born. I'm the only child of the family.'

" 'What's the name of your village? I think I've met you somewhere before.'

" 'I come from Culao Gieng.'

"I shuddered hearing the name of my own native village. Looking into her eyes, I said 'Culao Gieng of Cho Moi district, Long Chau Sa province?'

" 'Yes' she said.

" 'What's your name?' I asked.

" 'Thu.'

" 'Thu?' I asked, surprised. 'Is your father's name Sau and your mother's name Binh?'

"She was so astonished, she couldn't say a word and stood looking at me from head to toe. The D.A. post guides urged us to get ready to leave but I paid no attention. 'Your father's name is Sau, isn't it, my niece?' I said.

" 'Yes . . . but how do you know?'

" 'I'm Uncle Ba. Do you remember the day your father left home and promised to buy a comb for you?'

"She nodded slightly: 'Yes, I do.'

"I took the ivory comb out of my pocket. 'Your father sent you this. He made it himself.'

"She took the comb; I thought it seemed to remind her of the day her father left her. She was happy and I didn't want to trouble her happiness. I thought I should lie: 'Your father is well, he couldn't return home and he asked me to bring this to you.'

" 'You're wrong,' she said, 'this comb is not from my father.'

"I was disappointed and anxious so I asked her again, 'is your father Sau and your mother Binh?'

" 'Yes, they are.'

"She was about to cry, but she stopped.

" 'If you're not wrong, then you're lying because you don't want to hurt me,' she said. 'I know my father is dead.'

"Tears rolled down her cheeks. 'I can take the pain' she said. 'Don't be afraid to tell me the truth. I learned two years ago that my father had died; that's why I asked my mother to let me work as a liaison.'

"She wanted to say more, but the words died in her throat. She bowed her head and looked at the ground: her hair trembled. I kept silent. My comrades shouted, urging me to leave. I knew I couldn't stay any longer. I asked for her address and inquired briefly about her mother and her family's health.

"The joy of meeting Thu lasted only a few moments. I glanced at her and instinctively said: 'Good-bye, my daughter!' She murmured something I couldn't hear. From a distance I turned around and saw her following us. She stopped by a ditch. Small rice plants stirred by the wind looked like waves dashing towards her. Behind her, defoliated coconut trees looked like giant fish skeletons hanging in the air. New leaves sprouted which, when seen from a distance, offered the spectacle of a forest of swords raised skyward."

1966

From *Ugly Deadly Music*

I stood stiffly with my feet well apart, parade-rest fashion, at the break in the barbed-wire fence between the officers' country tents and the battalion motor pool. My feet and legs itched with sweat. My shirt clung to my back. My shaving cuts burned. I watched, astonished, as the battalion Reconnaissance Platoon, thirty-some men and ten boxy squat-looking armored personnel carriers — tracks, we called them — cranked in from two months in the field, trailing a rank stink and stirring a cloud of dust that left a tingle in the air. One man slowly dismounted from each track and led it up the sloped path from the perimeter road, ground-guiding it, walking with a stumbling hangdog gait. Each man wore a sleeveless flak jacket hung with grenades, and baggy jungle trousers, the ones with large thigh pockets and drawstrings at the cuffs. The tracks followed behind, like stupid, obedient draft horses, creaking and clacking along, and scraping over rocks hidden in the dust. There were sharp squeaks and irritating scratching noises, slow slack grindings, and the throttled rap of straight-pipe mufflers, all at once. And the talk, what there was, came shouted and snappy — easy obscenities and shit laughs. It was an ugly deadly music, the jerky bitter echoes of machines out of sync. A shudder went through me, as if someone were scratching his nails on a blackboard.

The men walking and the men mounted passed not fifteen feet in front of me. A moult, a smudge of dirt, and a sweat and grit and grease stink covered everything and everyone — the smell of a junkyard in a driving rainstorm. Each man looked over, looked down at me with the blandest, blankest sort of glance — almost painful to watch — neither welcome nor distance. This one or that one did signify with a slow nod of the head or an arch of the brows or a close-mouthed sigh, and I nodded or smiled back, but most glanced over dreamily and blinked a puff-eyed blink and glanced forward again.

The tracks, flat-decked affairs with sharply slanted fronts and armor-shielded machine guns (one fifty-caliber and two smaller M-60s), were painted o.d. — olive drab, a dark tallow shade of green, with large dun-colored numerals, faint and scratched but plain. The smooth straight sides and some of the curved gun shields bore thin bright gouges from Chicom claymore hits and deflected small arms. The confusion of scratches and scrapes was wonderful and brutal as fingernails dragged across the nap of velvet. Some of the tracks had nicknames: "Lucky Louie" and "Stone Pony" and "White Hunter" and "One Bad Cat" and "The Kiss-off" and "Scratch ⊬⊬ ⊬⊬ I ." Body count.

That summer the number would become fifteen and later twenty-six, and later still we would lose count and give up the counting, saying among ourselves, "Who fucken cares?"

The last track, the seven-seven, pulled into the motor pool, towing the very last, the seven-six. The seven-seven left the seven-six near the mechanics' quonset and pulled up and parked with the rest. A pathetic, odd moment of stillness settled over us as it finally shut down. Thick waves of engine heat rose through all the chicken-wire grillwork. The ground guides stood in front of the tracks, motionless and stoop-shouldered in ankle-deep ocher silt. The men still mounted, the drivers and gunners and TCs — track commanders — gazed at their hands or wiped dusted faces with dusted arms or stared down the broad slope at the rubber-tree woodline across from the perimeter wire, squinting darkened, puffy eyes.

With the tracks facing me on line I saw that all the machine guns — ten fifty-calibers and twenty M-60s — were still loaded and pointing down. It was the frankest kind of gesture. Down where the terror would be, pointing always at the closest trees, the likeliest part of a hedgerow, the nearest rice-paddy dikes, which everyone called berms. The driver of the downed track, wearing a football-helmet–looking thing, a CVC, roused himself. He pulled himself out of his hatch and stood on the seat, sloughing off his dark glasses and bulky flak jacket and CVC, leaving them where they fell. He wore a pistol holster clipped to his trouser belt and two leather cartridge belts buckled round his waist, studded with rounds. A thick dust, almost crusted, covered his short curly hair, the razor rash on his face and neck, and the sparse hair of his arms. A glistening sweat smeared the sides of his chest and back where his flak jacket had clung to his body in folds, and his eyes shone a glassy pink against his gritty black face. The sweat soaked through in patches and dripped in runnels from his chin and fingertips and belly. He worked his jaw and cheeks, hawking up phlegm, then spit a gob of white foamy spit to leeward at the woodline down the way. It disappeared into the dust. He heaved his chest, catching his breath, all the while working his hands open and closed until he reached his fists to his eyes, leaning his head back.

"Geeee-ahhh damn!" he bellowed. Everyone in the motor pool jerked their heads, then looked away or turned their backs completely, but still listened. The man swooped down, landing in a dry puff of dust, but caught himself from falling over with his fists. He turned quickly and drew a long-handled spade out of its strap among the other pioneer tools — shovels and tanker bars and other long-handled junk. He brought the spade back over his head and began beating on the front of the track with the blade end, like it was an ax.

"You goddamned half-stepping fuck-up track!" He said it low and slow and mean. "I'm gonna tear you apart with my bare fucken hands. I'm gonna pour mo-gas on your asshole and burn you down to fucken nickels, you short-time pissant mo-gas-guzzling motherfucker!" The blade end of the handle cracked and flew off on the upswing but he kept beating on the headlight mounts and the engine hood catch and so forth, shouting and cursing, the sweat flying from his forehead in an arc and his back rippling under the dirt. Then suddenly he stood mute, his arms hanging limp, his gaze fixed upon his boots and the dirt and the cracked and splintered tip of the spade handle. He let it slide from his fingers, then climbed the tread next to his hatch. He reached in for his shirt and steel pot and walked stiff-legged toward the mess hall and did not look back. I did not see him until later that night when he was drunk and incoherent, lying on his cot smoking dope and blowing large billowing smoke rings. The next morning he packed his duffel, sold his pistol and cartridge belts, said his goodbyes around, and went home.

The rest of the platoon, singly and by twos and threes, slowly went to work dismounting the guns for cleaning, and after a moment only one man was visible. He leaned against the sloped front of his track, stripped to the waist with a stub of cigar between his teeth. His trousers, soaked through around the belt, were covered with dirt and grease, stiff and puckered at the knees. He wore a faded web belt low on his hips; a knife on the right, a green plastic canteen on his left, and a forty-five-caliber automatic pistol in a black holster hung in front of his crotch. He told me later he wore the pistol for protection the way some people kept something thick in their breast pocket, "like a Bible or a fuck book, ya know?" He walked toward me with a slow ambling gait, smiled to himself as he passed, and went over to a fifty-five-gallon drum sunk in the ground, the Enlisted Men's Club piss tube. His hair shone with sweat, was matted and wild-looking. He had brown teeth and dark wrinkles around his mouth, gray watery eyes, and tiny inflamed scars across his stomach, like the deep and sweeping scratches of cats. His whole face seemed pulled together around the eyes, as though someone had squeezed it. He stood with his feet well apart, looking straight down at the stream of piss. There was a rich humus smell about him, not plain dirt or soft crumbling chunks, but powdery and damp, a thing that clings to everything it touches.

"Excuse me," I said. "Could you tell me where I can find the platoon leader?"

"Say? The El-tee?" His words came easy and weary and dry. "See that track on the end there?" He pumped his thumb over his shoulder without looking up. "He's aroun' back some fucken place. Ya can't miss him. He's the dude with the silver spoon in his mouth. You new, huh? M' name's Cross."

"I'm Philip Dosier. Well, I'll see you later."

"I don't doubt."

I walked around the side of the six-niner, making sure all my buttons were buttoned, pulling the slack out of my rifle sling, and adjusting my steel pot down over my eyes, garrison style, then walked around to the back. All the activity was there, all the way down the line. The ramp of each track was open, some swung all the way to the ground, some held level to the floors inside with water cans or wooden boxes. Everyone was stripped to the waist and bareheaded, going about his work with slow languid motions because of the heat; shaking out blankets and poncho liners in a cloud of dust and chaff and lint, or cleaning the stripped-down machine guns in cans of gasoline, or policing up brass cartridges by the armfuls and tossing the cartridges, cans, and all into fifty-five-gallon drums set out for junk. The gas truck, a deuce-and-a-half with two fuel tanks on the back marked "Mo-gas," had begun moving up the line, refueling. I thought gas-powered tracks were obsolete. I had never seen any before, except the two on display at the Patton Museum at Fort Knox.

Lieutenant Greer sat in the shade inside the back of his track on one of the low metal benches, folding a map. He was a husky, meaty-looking dude with short, shaggy, filthy hair and freckles and red wrinkle marks from his CVC across the forehead and under the ears. He wore back-in-the-world fatigues covered with dust; a brass armor insignia on one collar, his silver lieutenant's bar on the other, and a pair of amber-tinted driving goggles around his neck.

The first time I came down with heat exhaustion a couple months later, May or June it might have been, Lieutenant Greer called the dust-off chopper himself. He laid me out on the litter and held me up, leaning me against his thigh, and poured canteen after canteen of tepid water over my head. He held his canteen cup while I washed down half a handful of salt tablets, spilling mouthfuls of water down my chin and chest. I vomited twice, finally dry-heaving on my hands and knees while he soaked compresses on the back of my neck with more water. When the chopper came, the colonel's command chopper because the dust-offs were busy with Bravo and Charlie companies, the lieutenant walked me over to it and gave me a hand up, saying thanks to the colonel. I sat among the racks of the colonel's radios until he landed me at the battalion aid station, and late that afternoon the lieutenant came over to fetch me back to the platoon. Toward the end of summer when Greer went home we threw a party for him at the platoon tents, everybody getting ripped and red-eyed drinking quarts, drinking his health. He shook everybody's hand and wished us good luck and left, staggering out into the moonlight, and I never saw him again.

The inside of his track was very neat, much neater than any of the rest. There was a collapsed litter strapped close under the armor deck, three radios, ammunition cans neatly stacked on the floor under the TC hatch, waterproof duffel bags full of clothes along one wall, and boxes of fragmentation grenades and claymores, command-detonated antipersonnel mines about the size of the top of a shoe box and curved outward. The lieutenant's M–1 carbine and a sandbag filled with magazines hung on a hook behind his head.

I saluted and nervously introduced myself. After a moment of silly questions and silly answers and that same stupid lecture about bringing him my personal problems, the lieutenant called on the radio for Seven-zero, Staff Sergeant Surtees, the platoon sergeant.

Surtees was a heavyset Negro who wore the only shoulder-holster forty-five in the platoon and the only man, other than the lieutenant, wearing a shirt, the sleeves rolled in precise folds with all his insignia and rank patches: E-6 chevrons and 25th Division patch and name patch.

He smoked big cheap cigars which he rolled in his fingers as he talked to the platoon in formation, and would pause to spit tobacco for emphasis, but he could never get the hang of it and so always had spittle dribbled on his shirts. He loved to say, "E'ery swingin' dick," and here he would take pause to spit on his shirt, "in this platoon is chicken shit," and then would bug his eyes, trying to flash fire. When he had an announcement for the whole platoon, that the mail was in or chow was ready or the water trailer had arrived he would call us on the radio and say, "Rom-e-o, Romeo. This is Seven–ze-ro!" and then say whatever it was he wanted to say.

In the fall when his 1049 came, his transfer to division, it took him fifteen minutes to gather his gear and sign out of the company. Word came down to the tents that Surtees was shipping out and a bunch of old-timers went down to see him go. When he slid into the jeep for the ride up to the airport, Quinn, a dude who transferred into the platoon that summer, walked up beside him, dropped a small package in his lap, and said, "It's a special belt, see? Ya take yer dick an' strap it to yer leg, get it stretched out good an' long, say 'bout fifteen or twenty feet. Then some night when yer good and fucked up on that NCO Club booze, just real down home fucked up and horny, why just whip it out, rub it up, an' shove it up yer fat nigger ass." Then everybody laughed, even the driver, who hardly knew him.

Sergeant Surtees stood in front of the lieutenant at mock attention and gave me the "Teamwork, fight like hell, and sleep on your own time" speech that he would give every new replacement. "Falling asleep on guard duty is a court-martial offense; incorrect radio procedure will not be tolerated, the FCC monitors all frequencies; and you will at all times address me as Platoon Sergeant Surtees. Is that clear, Pfc?"

"Yes, Platoon Sergeant Surtees," I replied. I didn't know any different. I was still garrison. I had just come from Fort Knox, the armored cavalry, where I called everybody sir or sergeant.

Then he said, "Well, Lieutenant, wheredaya wanna put'im?"

Greer stood above us on the ramp brushing dust from his shirt, looked down the line of tracks, and said, "Put him on the seven-three. They're first in line, I guess. Got a note here from the sergeant major that three more'll be here this afternoon, so you make sure you're at battalion to pick them up. Otherwise, they're liable to get lost in one of the line companies. That's all, Sergeant. Glad to have you with us, Pfc."

Surtees walked me down to the seven-three, talking the whole way. "Putting the poop" to me, as he said. There were two men inside. One sat spraddle-legged over an ammunition can filled with gasoline on the driver's-side bench with his trousers rolled to his knees, scrubbing caked carbon from an M-60 bolt with a toothbrush. The other swept the metal floor with a short-handled Viet broom and stacked ammunition cans under the TC hatch, bent over at the waist because of the headroom.

The inside of the track was painted a light foam green. Everything was covered with road crud, mud-splattered and filthy. It was crowded and awkward and smelled sharply of gasoline, but there seemed to be room enough.

"Trobridge," Surtees said, "this man is on your track. Replaces Murphy." Then he turned and walked away.

The man bent over backed out and stood up, wiped his hand on his trousers, put it out to me, and said, "I'm Sergeant Trobridge, the TC. This here is Pfc. Atevo, my number-one gun." Atevo dropped the bolt into the can and shook hands firmly, nodding. The backs of his hands were red and raw from the gasoline. "And the dude that drives this thing is around here someplace. Cross? Hey, Cross!"

"Yeah," came a voice.

"Come around back and meet the new man. What did you say your name was?"

"Dosier. Philip Dosier."

"Yeah, Dozer. Name's Dozer, Cross!"

"Already met 'im. He'll do."

With that Atevo reached into the gas can for the bolt and motioned with the toothbrush for me to sit down. Trobridge slumped down next to me to take a break.

Atevo was about my size. He had a light, bushy mustache with tips that twisted around the sides of his mouth nearly to his chin, large and dark boyish eyes, and a dusty olive tan. Beside him a twelve-gauge pump-action shotgun leaned against the gas-tank armor. The gun was covered with dirt and a powdery rust that a person could rub off with his fingers. He wore a bowie knife on his belt in a black leather scabbard — riveted, not stitched.

The knife itself, easily the biggest blade I had ever seen, was gunmetal black with a dark wood handle. A gift from his uncle, he told me once, hand-forged and blade-heavy. "So it will always hit," he said. But he never threw it by the blade, always the handle. "All you will have time for is the draw and throw," he told me. He had a clear, keen eye and a good arm, and again and again I saw him throw it into a dirt-filled sandbag to the curved hilt. "But you must throw a knife only if you know it will strike its mark," he would say as he yanked it loose with a flick of his wrist. "For to throw it is to disarm yourself, and to disarm yourself is to be naked." He carried a whetstone in a small cedar box. He would spit on the stone, move the knife forward and draw it back and move it forward, keeping time with his breath. Sharpening both edges. Sometimes he would strop it on the leather toe of his boot for hours, especially after we had smoked some smokes, then test the cutting edge against the calluses on the heel of his hand.

Trobridge was on the chunky side with a flabby face and thick wetted lips. He always sweated more than anybody and wore thick black-rimmed GI glasses that slipped to the end of his nose, so he was always pushing at them, and for some reason he never tanned. He had a smallish waist and wide fleshy hips, and since he wore his trousers high on his waist, the fatigues did not bag the way they did on the rest of us.

He was one of those fat, sloppy, cushy dudes who would walk into his basic training company mess hall for the first time, and there would stand one of those barrel-chested, bad-ass-looking NCO's. He'd have his bad-looking Yogi Bear hat set at an angle down over his eyes and his arms folded across his chest, real badlike, and a pair of light-blue-tinted PX aviators. He'd spy Trobridge up one side and down the other, and say in a deep, gruff baritone, the humor and irony just dripping out of his mouth, coming in gushes, "Hey, *Fat*boy? How much you weigh, *Fat*-ass?" And Trobridge would stand there in his brand-new rumpled and shiny olive-drab fatigues, not knowing whether to shit or piss or go blind, and he'd answer, "T-t-two hundred and seventy pounds, sir," in a high-pitched voice. "Don't call me sir, *Fat*boy!" "Yes, Sergeant." "We gonna run about a hunnurd poun's offa yer ass, *Fat*boy. You gonna sweat an grunt a hunnurd poun's off'r die in the a–tempt." Then Bad–ass would turn on his heel and lay his eye on the cook behind the serving line. "Dursey, no potatoes fer Fatboy," he'd say, then he'd whirl around, coming down nose to nose with Trobridge. "An' Ah catch you with potatoes on yer breath, Fatboy, an' yer gonna wish you was never borned. You got that, Fatboy?" "Yes, Sergeant!" "Okay, *Fat*boy," he'd yell, and snap his arm straight, pointing to the serving line. "Eat it!" And every morning when the company would fall out for the mile run Bad–ass would scream in Trobridge's face, "You drop out, Fatboy, and you git this size-ten boot straight up your ass. You drop out and you'll be in the front leaning rest poundin' out eight-count push-ups until every hair on yer ass is white as ash. Now double-time! An' let me hear you grunt, Fatboy! Grunt!" Trobridge was just the perfect sort of no-talent loser the army sops up the way a desert soaks up a two-day rain. Not a week later it looks as though nothing happened at all. He gets room and board and a new pair of boots now and again, and the army baby-sits him for twenty or thirty years, telling him when to go to bed and when to eat, what to think and how to say it, and his desolate and destitute imagination never knows the difference.

Cross came around the back with a double armful of chilled beer, so the four of us sat in the shade inside awhile, drinking and talking. Where are you from? How come you wound up here? What's happening back-in-the-world? Were you drafted?

Besides the machine-gun ammunition stacked under the TC hatch where the fifty was, there were wooden boxes of frags and claymores and M-16 magazines, a captured AK-47 wrapped in clear plastic hanging from the radio, neatly folded ponchos atop a pile of neatly folded blankets and poncho liners, and two cloth hammocks tied front to rear just under the armor deck. A pair of Ho Chi Minh sandals and a red bandanna held at the neck with a twenty-four-carat gold ring hung from the rubber eyepiece of the infrared scope. There were duffels and waterproofs, spare barrels for the machine guns, wooden boxes, cardboard boxes, cooking gear, canteen cups, everything. I sat facing the gas tank, decorated with tits and thighs cut from magazines and covered with acetate and green cloth tape. The four-color paper was beginning to fade into yellows and washed-out pale greens. And behind me was the envy of the whole platoon, a genuine Igloo water cooler strapped to the top of the battery box. Cross had swiped it from the PA & E dudes, Pacific Architects and Engineers, across the road from the motor pool. They were the civilians who operated the camp's water purification gismo, among other things, and had it made. We could see them from the motor pool, taking a nap in their pickups or breaking for lunch or knocking off for the day or sitting on the veranda of their office, listening to the machinery hum and catching flies.

On the ground behind the ramp two bags, a beat-up waterproof and a duffel sealed with a padlock, leaned against each other with an M-16 and a steel pot on top.

Atevo kept scrubbing gun parts and we kept talking. He laughed down at the gas can when Cross spit tatters of cigar into the dust, saying something about "that fucked-up nigger, Surtees." Atevo let the parts dry in the sun, wiped them down with an oil-soaked shaving brush, and slapped the two M-60 machine guns back together. Then he turned his attention to his shotgun next to him. He broke it down quickly, cleaned it, passing a rag through the barrel, oiled it, and reassembled it, reloading all the shells. When he finished he stood up, put on his shirt not bothering with the buttons, grabbed his steel pot, and jumped off the back.

"Hey, Dosier, Cross, you want to go eat?" he asked.

I nodded and got up. Cross slouched lower on the bench and shook his head no.

"Atevo, why don't you take Murphy's gear up to the Orderly Room on your way?" Cross sat with his legs outstretched, pointing to the bags.

"Okay." I took the duffel and the steel pot, which was covered with a cloth camouflage cover, faded and stretched tight to the helmet like everyone else's. Atevo walked ahead with the waterproof and rifle. We stood in the shade of the supply room tent along with the rest while the first sergeant and the supply sergeant filled out forms. There were a dozen or more sets being turned in. It took longer than I expected because there were questions and answers and stories.

"It was raining and I couldn't see, but . . ." said one.

"That was two months ago, seems like, back in January somewhere. The afternoon we got those six gooks in the open, for Christ's sake," said another.

"These are the two that got it at the same time. They were sucking a smoke and the round hit right between 'em."

One guy had had his leg taken off by an RPG, whatever that was, and another guy had written from the States to say he and some other guy were doing fine and bragging about the Fort Ord Hospital pussy. When it came our turn Atevo said, "Sergeant Sean Murphy. KIA, eighteen February. Issue gear is in the duffel. Personal gear is in the waterproof," while the first sergeant wrote it down. I tossed the duffel with the issue gear on the pile behind the counter. Atevo set the waterproof in the back of the supply room deuce-and-a-half, then we went to eat.

As we walked along the ditch that split the company street I asked Atevo, "What's KIA?"

"Killed in action. Dead." He said it with a quick turn of his head.

I wanted to ask about Murphy — his story — but I looked at the side of Atevo's dusty, fuzzy face, the droop of his mustache, the way he hefted the shotgun easy over his shoulder, and thought it better to keep my peace.

Fragile as a Sun Ray

I was never able to understand why, even in the lightest moments, my mother remained depressed. Our family has not done badly. My parents have opened a private practice and have quite a few patients. I have followed their path into medical school and I often return to give them a hand. My younger brother has won numerous awards in competitions for exceptional mathematics students. Both he and I love our father and mother.

What did she have to be sad about?

My mother is just over forty and very beautiful — yet there is a deep sadness in her eyes. She immerses herself completely in mundane, everyday activities. Sometimes she loses her temper. Sometimes she cries. She argues with the neighbors. She is no different from anyone else. I have never been able to understand why she is so melancholy — but I did try to find out. And one day I discovered the reason, by accident, and I learned not to assume anyone was ordinary. Never can the heart rest easy.

Late one afternoon, the military ambulance turned onto a small trail so that the members of the medical unit could rest and wait for darkness before trying to cross the mountain pass. They were on their way to the South. The senior doctor and the two male nurses hung up their hammocks and immediately went to sleep. But my mother, new to the war, felt like lingering. She wandered down to the creek. It was shallow — if she tried to cross she would barely get her ankles wet. On the other side a strange sight caught her attention and made her heart beat quickly. About ten men in camouflaged fatigues were sitting on the clean pebbles next to the stream, each eating from his mess kit.

"These are prisoners from the battle of Route Nine," the soldier next to her explained.

She sat on a boulder on her side of the creek, took out her kerchief and washed it slowly. This was the first time she had seen people from the other side, but strangely enough the only emotion she felt was curiosity. Most of the enemy prisoners were busy eating and there was nothing extraordinary about their faces. Except one. He was quite young, in his twenties, and looked slender but strong; his face seemed delicate and balanced. He held

(35)

his mess kit in his hands but didn't eat, only stared off into space. She'd never seen a face like his in real life, but at home she would lie under the mosquito netting in the morning and listen to the noises from outside and daydream until her mother called her. In those half-dreaming, half-waking moments, a face would come to her, its form vague; she couldn't see any of its features in detail, nor could she even, in fact, describe it in general. But in her dreams she knew that face would come into her life.

Her heart pounded and her hands and feet suddenly turned icy cold. Rinsing the kerchief she looked across the narrow creek. The enemy soldier stopped staring into space and glanced down at his mess kit. Then he suddenly discovered her. Their eyes met. With a flash, a frightening thunder exploded in her wandering soul.

Startled, as if by guilt, she shot to her feet. On the other side of the stream, the enemy soldier reflected her startled motion. His movement stopped his guard's conversation and, with the point of a gun pressed to his temple, the prisoner sat down. But his eyes remained locked to hers, his look still burned into her. She walked back to the ambulance in a daze. She took out her hammock and hung it between two trees and lay down. Her heart revolted; she felt suffocated by fear. She could not be allowed to think these thoughts — he was clearly the enemy.

As the afternoon wore on, she stayed in her hammock. The senior doctor had risen and awakened the others; she heard him tell them to eat and clean up — they were going to depart as soon as it got dark. She floated in an indescribable melancholy. Bits and pieces of conversation between the doctor and someone she didn't know drifted into her sadness.

"You're a physician, comrade?" she heard the stranger ask.

"Yes, I am."

"Maybe you can give us a hand — we have a prisoner, an officer with an infected wound. We have to leave on a mission tonight — unless we can do something . . ."

"A prisoner?"

"Just captured."

"I'll come over and have a look."

She sat up erect in the hammock and stared intensely at the senior doctor. He looked at her. "Ah, yes, come with me. Bring the medical kit along."

It was him. His eyes were clear and innocent, his face peaceful; it was a face that existed outside the war. Her fear of herself increased: how could she dare look into this face, this enemy officer's face? But she was unable to take her eyes away. The late afternoon sun shone through the leafy foliage. The sounds of gunfire were silenced, but the war seemed to intensify in the cold face of the patient's guard. She followed the motions of the senior doctor's hands intently as he examined the thigh wound. He frowned when he spotted the infection. She washed the wound with cotton and antiseptic: she could hear the patient clenching his teeth, but he didn't cry out. When the doctor stopped, turned aside, and let the guard light his cigarette, she spoke softly to the prisoner:

"Try to hang on."

"Yes, doctor. Do you know where I'm being taken?"

"No, I'm sorry. I wish I did."

"I'm a doctor also."

"Really? How did you end up here?"

"How does anyone? The war knocks on every door. I tried to avoid it, but . . ."

"I know."

"Can you do anything to help me, doctor?"

"No one can do anything. Perhaps when the fighting is over . . ."

The senior doctor and the guard turned around.

"Finished?"

"Yes. I've given him the injection," she said, trying to avoid the prisoner's burning look. It wasn't a look of fear, or of pain, or of pleading. It was a look of surprise at the discovery that there could be someone who belonged to you, understood you, could possibly share a life with you. And that there was no chasm, no division between people . . .

The senior doctor looked at the wounded man worriedly. "Can you walk?"

As if he'd been pushed up from behind by some powerful force, the prisoner stood, his face pale with pain. Yet when he answered, his voice was firm:

"Yes, I'll try."

She realized at that instant that her presence had given him the resolve to continue. War couldn't dissolve the thread of love connecting two hearts. But what would happen to him, with his wounded leg, with his determination? She picked up the medical kit and followed the older doctor across the creek. The prisoners were preparing to leave. The guards raised their steely voices. Stealthily he raised his hand in her direction. Sadly, hopelessly, pleadingly gesturing toward the future . . .

Now twenty years have passed and many different fences have been torn down. And yet her hope has never been fulfilled. How wonderful it would be if they could meet again, even if only for a moment.

My mother is still melancholy, even as she keeps herself busy with the daily tasks of her life. Everyone possesses a secret, a sadness, a memory. I know that she survives today because of such a secret, such a sadness, such a desire.

Translated by Ho Nguyen and Wayne Karlin

Armed Forces Recruitment Day, Albuquerque High School, 1962

After the Navy,
the Air Force, and
the Army,
Sgt. Castillo,
the Marine Corps
recruiter,
got a standing ovation
when he walked up
to the microphone
and said proudly
that unlike
the rest, all
he could promise
was a pack,
a rifle, and
a damned hard time.
Except for that,
he was the
biggest
of liars.

First Day, Headquarters Co., 101st Airborne, Phan Rang, Viet Nam

The wounded back from the hospital
readying their rucksacks to return to the line.
Line doggies coming out of the bush.
Their lost year done.
Worn rosaries around their necks.
Christ nailed to a tree.
A man prayed out there.
So many trees out there.
So many nails.

First Encounter

You have stopped for a break, stand up
to put your gear on and hear shots,
see the flash of the muzzles.
You have been followed.
The whiteness of the branches
that have been cut along the way
tells you you're on a new trail,
but the sergeant is a stateside GI:
barracks inspections, rules and regs.
You are probably surrounded.
There are five others beside you.
You are twenty-three.
You look around you:
the sky, the trees.
You're far from home.
You know now that your life
is no longer yours.

Hearing the Argument of the Little Prisoners

The enemy opened the cell doors a few minutes each day.
The small prisoners — three and five years old — crawled out into the sun.
On the perimeter a calf chewed on grass.
The small prisoners told each other it was an elephant.

Hearing this, the guards broke into laughter,
Then tears fell down their cheeks.

Cu Chi, 1972

Translated by Nguyen Ba Chung with Bruce Weigl

Disasters of War

"Goddamnit, sir, he had a grenade!"

The marine's eyes were bloodshot. He'd probably been up all night, guarding this worthless bridge, the captain thought.

"Gook's walkin' at me with a freakin' grenade, what'm I supposed to do?"

The whole village seemed to be there. All were staring at him and the two marine sentries with silent, unreadable expressions, except for an old man whom the captain took for the village elder. He wore a long white goatee and was gesturing and talking nonstop. The captain couldn't understand a word. Nearby, a woman, whom the captain took to be the boy's mother, sat in the dust beside the corpse (it wasn't even that, the captain thought, it was just a mess). She sat looking off into space. Someone had covered what was left of the body with a couple of reed mats, but the captain could see enough of it to feel a little queasy. He could not understand how the woman could sit so near it without getting sick or hysterical. She just stared at nothing and chewed her betel nut. A man in a dark shirt and cork sun helmet, holding a pair of sticks, walked along the riverbank, looking at the ground and into the bushes.

"So help me God," the red-eyed marine was saying, "I didn't throw no grenade at him. I shot him. He musta had the pin pulled, because the thing went off in his hand. Boom."

The old man kept talking, standing on tiptoe so he could shout into the captain's ear.

"Did you see anything?" the captain asked the second marine.

"No, sir. I was makin' a head call. But I heard the shot. First the shot, then the grenade." He grabbed the first marine's rifle, which was propped against the sandbagged bunker where the two had sat up all night, guarding the bridge. "Here, sir, take a look at the barrel."

The captain jacked the bolt back and held the muzzle to his eye. He could see the powder grains inside the barrel. That did not prove anything; the marine could have thrown the grenade, then fired his rifle, and persuaded his buddy to back up his story.

"Son, this is a friendly ville. They're solid here. Hasn't been an incident here since nobody can remember when. Solid friendlies. Why would that kid be coming at you with a grenade?"

"How the freakin' hell do I know, sir? Why would I kill a kid for no good reason?"

Up all night, thought the captain. Waiting, listening, looking into the darkness, scared, and fed up, that's why.

"Please sir, you can't run me up. I didn't do nothin'."

The man by the riverbank picked up something long and thin and pink with the sticks, carried it delicately up to the village, then placed it under the reed mats. The captain was sure he was going to be sick. The woman looked off into space and spat a stream of betel nut. The elder talked and talked. The captain held a hand in front of his face to stop him from talking.

"I . . . don't understand," he said. "Do you speak any English? English? Eeeeeng-leeesh?"

The old man looked a little baffled and pulled at his goatee.

"Pas de l'Anglais," he said. "Mais, je parle français. Parlez-vous francais?"

"Eeeeng-leesh," said the captain.

The old man started talking again, this time in French. The captain could not understand a thing, but he heard the old man repeating one word over and over. Pishee or pashay or peshee, something like that.

"Skipper, I don't know what this old dude's tellin' you, but the kid had a grenade. I didn't do nothin'. You gotta believe me."

"Anybody in your company speak French?" he asked.

"Yes, sir," the second marine said after thinking a moment. "Doucette. He's a French Canadian, I think."

"Get him here chopchop."

The elder kept pointing at the river and saying pishee pashay peshee while the man with the sticks picked up every shred of the boy he could find and brought each one back, placing it under the mats. The woman's eyes stayed on the point in space. How could she be so impassive? Was she in shock? Maybe these people just don't have normal human feelings, the captain thought. Finally, the marine returned with Doucette, who began speaking to the village elder in French. The captain heard that word again. Pishee pashay peshee.

Doucette turned to the captain.

"Sir, the old guy, he says the kid was goin' to go fishin'. Just goin' down to the river to fish, then he gets shot."

The red-eyed marine raised his hand as if he were going to swat the old man.

"He wasn't fishin'! He had a freakin' grenade!"

The captain understood now and told Doucette to ask the elder if the boy was going to fish with a hand grenade. Doucette translated the question. The old man answered, "Oui, oui, oui." The captain understood that, but nothing else of what the old man said.

"What he's saying, Skipper," explained Doucette, "is that the kid's family lost their sampan and their nets a few days ago. So the kid got a grenade from somebody and was goin' to toss it in the river and pick up the dead fish, but then he got shot."

The marine with the bloodshot eyes seemed to be trying to smile.

"Told you, Skipper. What was I supposed to do?"

The captain did not say anything.

"How'm I supposed to know the kid's goin' fishin'? You go fishin with a fishin' rod, not a freakin' grenade. I see a gook comin' toward me with a grenade, I grease him. What would you have done, sir?"

Still, the captain said nothing. The man with the sticks brought the last piece of the boy and tucked it under the mats. He said something to the woman, who suddenly started howling, throwing her hands up and down and howling. Why had she waited so long? What had the man said to her? the captain wondered. Damned people made no sense. He turned to the marine.

"OK, carry on," he said.

The marine blew out his cheeks in relief.

"Told you I didn't do nothin'."

The Sound of Night

Viet was about to veer the truck to the left when he found the road ahead blocked by rocks and fallen trees.

"Plowing through will only wreck the radiator," Viet murmured to himself. He released the brakes and allowed the truck to roll backward to hide under the forest canopy. Layers of the rain forest formed indistinct waves against the horizon.

"If I don't reach my destination point I'll have to crouch in some crevice all day until my backside gets sore," Viet worried. "I'll really get it if I don't get this supply truck to the unit up front. Hmph! . . . Some lead driver I am!" Although he had known that it was going to be pitch dark tonight, he had nevertheless volunteered to take the truck to the destination point before sunrise.

"Who is laughing out there?" called Viet. Usually young female trail guides would converge on him as soon as they heard his voice and would begin to chatter on endlessly. But Viet was irritable tonight because he knew that their laughter was to be followed by a description of the problems on the trail ahead. Unfailingly the women hoped to use their laughter to erase the signs of irritation on the faces of the male truck drivers. But this only worked with less experienced and less hot-tempered drivers. With a veteran like Viet, such laughter had little effect.

Viet slammed the truck door and reached down to adjust the screws of the shock absorbers. He heard faint footsteps approaching, breaking the stillness of the night.

"Why didn't you use your under-carriage lights?" a female voice inquired.

Viet knew that it was because of him, or, to be more precise, because of his truck that the girl had come. But he maintained his self-important air as he spoke deliberately through his nose:

"Under-carriage lights! With this many inclines . . . that would be like signaling the enemy."

"Open the door for me," the girl called as she banged loudly on the truck.

"Can't you see the door handle? Are you blind or something?" Viet almost snapped before biting his tongue. Whatever happened, he had to maintain his composure in front of the girls. He should not lose his temper because of the destroyed road. The girls were not to blame.

Viet opened the truck door, sat back solemnly in his seat, and pressed the horn to fill the silence.

"Are you finished with the repairs yet?" the girl asked quietly. "Shall we go? I will lead you all the way tonight. Now, turn the truck to the right, OK?"

"Turn into a dead-end road in order to hide, huh?" Viet asked curtly.

"That's not it. At the end of the road I'll get off and lead you across the plateau by a short cut."

"The whole night through?"

"About ten kilometers," replied the girl. "It's quite rough. But there's no other way. The main road is full of antipersonnel bombs. Our troops are clearing them now. If we're lucky, the main road will be passable by tomorrow. Are you thirsty? Chew on these wild berries for now."

"So there is a way out," thought Viet. "I can still deliver the supplies in time."

Viet's irritation faded at the prospect of success and he could hear the rustle of the shoulder bag sliding toward him. Its strap gently pressed on his shirt and its flap sprung lightly open like the kick of a grasshopper.

"What kind of wild berries are these, Miss?"

"They're hard to describe. They are only as big as mung beans, but they grow in bunches. When they're ripe they're slightly sweet, with a hint of the fragrance of coffee. You see, in life nothing comes in a single taste. In a plum there is the sour taste of apricots and the fragrance of peaches. And in these *chut ngut* berries there is a slight tartness of plum."

"So she knows 'the things in life' already?" Viet thought. A dip in the road caused him to brake suddenly, almost slamming the girl's forehead against the windshield. But within a few seconds the girl's calm voice continued.

"We don't have these berries where I come from. But they grow all over around here. They're in season now. They're also medicinal."

Viet plucked a few berries and chewed on them, feeling a bittersweet taste on the tip of his tongue. He did not know whether it was the berries or the warm accent of the girl that perked him up, causing him to feel completely different from the way he did fifteen minutes ago. He wanted to listen to her and talk with her.

"In my experience," said Viet, "when you have not been to a place you feel that it is very far away. But once you've been there and get to know the trees, the vegetation, the fruits, and the people then you become as attached to that place as your own village."

"Yes, I feel that way too," the girl agreed. "I can never forget the villages in Ky Anh, Huong Khe."

In Country   (47)

"Can never forget," said Viet laughingly. "You're from a place where 'people enjoy three months of no work a year,' right?"

"Some jokers call us dirt farmers," giggled the girl.

At the end of the road, the girl struggled to open the truck door. Viet opened the door for her as he was saying:

"Your limbs are as slender as raw silk threads. It seems as if you just left your schoolwork at home only a few days ago. You'll have a tough job building roads and cutting through the mountains. I'll bet at night you're still weeping inside your blankets and calling out to Mama, right?"

"You get used to it, Brother," the girl replied, laughing.

Viet heard this laughter as coming from a person unused to hardship. It sounded quite nice and gentle and seemed to invite others to share in its freshness and joy.

The girl moved forward slowly, keeping a short distance in front of the truck. Her white blouse floated ahead in the pitch dark forest night. The truck followed her outline slowly. Now and then she stooped down to pick up something. Viet guessed that she was picking the *chum ngut* berries.

On a downward slope Viet braked to keep well behind the girl and to keep the truck from running out of control. Tree branches thumped on the truck body and thorny forest vines scratched noisily on the hood.

"Is something the matter?" the girl asked when she saw that the truck had stopped.

"Let's rest a minute," said Viet. "Aren't you tired? No other truck has passed by this route and there's a lot of thorny vines. My wrists are very tired."

Viet was not complaining but trying to prove that only he could have passed such an arduous route.

"You men have it so hard. We girls have hundreds of ways to counter the enemy. But then we are still encountering difficulties tonight. They have so many tricks. Please go easy on us and don't go around saying that the female guide on the Truong Son trails . . . By the way, can you tie my shoelaces for me? They kept getting untied. Maybe I should wear boots next time." Then the girls voice trailed off like a faint breeze: "But perhaps there will be no other times."

"What?" asked Viet. "Are you going back to school? Or are you being transferred to another front?"

"My squad discovered this trail," the girl continued as if she did not hear the question. "I've been through here several times before, but it's so dark tonight."

"Been through here several time," Viet mimicked the girl's accent.

"I just don't know why I can't correct my speech," the girl laughed.

"Especially at meetings, I get so embarrassed when they laugh at the way I talk."

"What is your rank among your siblings?" asked Viet.

"I'm the youngest," the girl said.

"That figures," said Viet. "The youngest usually acts like a baby."

Kidding aside, Viet was feeling somewhat sorry for this schoolgirl who was not even able to tie her shoelaces tightly or to open the truck door. And yet she had already left her native village to serve in the most treacherous front lines.

Lately, as he earned more and more battle commendations, Viet's personality had undergone some changes. He became more verbose. At times it looked as if he was bragging about himself. But nobody seemed to mind. Instead they seemed to want to listen to him because they all loved him. The soldiers on the trails would raise their canteens above their heads and pounded them with their spoons to welcome Viet every time he trucked the salt in to save them from their apparent danger — trembling weak knees after a week without salt. Then the mothers would welcome Viet back, his hair completely matted with trail dust. Just washing his hair would turn a whole section of a slow stream dirt red. Viet had been wounded several times. One time he was hit straight on. The slowing bullet went through him and then ricocheted back. Viet had raised his hand to the wound and pulled out the bullet. He had felt dizzy and couldn't breathe. The air from his lung was hissing out of the open wound. He had no bandage, so he had forced the bullet back into the wound to stop the air leakage before staggering back to the first-aid station.

Viet usually treated people who were somewhat younger than him or who joined after him as if he were their teacher. And although he looked at other people, he saw his reflection everywhere as if he were standing in front of a mirror. He told the girl of the many times he had been able to take his truck through fire hoops and of the various tricks he used to fool the enemy. The girl listened to him intently, only occasionally punctuating his stories very gently with a phrase that was full of surprise: "God, what intensity . . . what skill!"

"Why don't you stay in the truck," said Viet. "I'll head the truck in the right direction myself. My nerves are very sensitive. Through the wheels I can tell where we are on the slope of the mountain."

"No, that won't do," the girl said very quickly as if she had suddenly awoken. "I'm used to leading the way."

She jumped from the truck and her white blouse indicated clearly the path the vehicle was to follow. At the top of an incline she stopped.

"What happened?" asked Viet.

"The wind uprooted a tree and it is blocking the way," answered the girl. "Please come down here and give me a hand."

"The trunk of the tree is only a few inches thick and yet this girl cannot pull it to the side," thought Viet.

Then he said to her jokingly: "I'm really tired of seeing a hefty girl like you not able to 'do' things. Girls from Thai Binh wade across rivers with baskets full of rice and not one grain ever gets wet. You're such a weakling. When we crossed the Tan De ferry I and three other men my size had to exert all our strength to lift a huge basket of rice and place it on the head of the smallest woman. And yet she walked briskly away, flapping her arms gracefully in the meantime."

The girl only smiled as she searched around the roots of the fallen tree.

"What are you looking for?" asked Viet.

"My hair clip. It got knocked off by a tree branch."

"It's pitch dark. Forget it."

"But the hair is in my eyes, and I'm having trouble seeing."

"Nobody can see you in a dark night like this, so you don't have to look good."

"I am not trying to look good . . . There are a lot of *chut ngut* vines here. Pleas pull one out for me."

Viet reached out for the shrub that he had just stepped on, yanked out the most flexible vine he could feel and handed it to the girl.

The girl shook her head to let her hair fall behind her back, brushing loose strands away from her forehead with her hands.

Translated by Ngo Vinh Long

From *Fire and Rain*

The next day they found themselves in the sandpile. If the road detail was tedious, the sandpile was noxious. The pile was not one main heap. It was three accumulations of dirt that had been dug out on the western end of the base. The earth at one time was to have been utilized for the construction of a bunker complex. The plans never congealed, the engineering units were reassigned elsewhere, and the excavated dirt was left standing in three hillocks. Sandbag emplacements still had to be built and, by a pact promoted between the Brig solons and the base commander, the Brig inmates were chosen to venture into the lot and fill the needed sandbags to cover the various positions. There was a surplus of cheap labor in the Brig and what better way to meet the increasing sandbag demand? The Brig was sandbags, there was no way getting around it. An inmate came to know sandbags intimately.

Taking a cue from the road works, the sandpile was a relatively flat area about the size of a small baseball diamond. It was barren except for a few holes that had been dug by the frequent testing of C4 chemical explosives. The three earthen heaps stood twelve feet high and were spaced about eight yards apart. To fill the required number of sandbags the detail was set into teams of two men working at the foot of the piles. One man would dig out the earth and shovel it into the sandbag held open by his partner, the partner would tie the bag and place it in a batch. Once all the sandbags were filled, the men loaded them up on a two-and-a-half-ton truck. The schedule called for one hundred and fifty bags to be completed daily. It was an eight hour process with one break for lunch at the nearby battalion mess hall. The group of men selected for the detail was assigned an escort of ten guards, all armed.

On the surface, the order for a hundred and fifty sandbags per day sounded reasonable. All the men had to do was bust heavy with the back. Identical procedure to the road party. But not quite, because the sandpile was bad news. First of all, the men were not dealing with sand but with hard dirt intermixed with rock particles that the Brig CO insisted had to be ground into sediment before they were poured in the bags. And the guards checked the sandbags after they were done, actually feeling the burlap surface, and if there were any rocks they tore open the bag and spilt the earth back on the ground. Another bag had to be filled again. If any rocks were felt once more, the same procedure, the bag was ripped open. It was a benighted, wasted effort which the prisoners resented.

Filling a sandbag was no easy task. The deal began with the prisoner digging into the base of the pile and pulling out a spadeful of earth. The principle of gravity came into play and the earth began to slide down as the prisoner advanced his shovel. In a short time he was wading in dirt. With combat boots it wasn't too bad, you couldn't feel the grinding in the leather; but as the day progressed and the sun became stronger, all the dirt seemed to fall on the men. There was no wind, and two hours after the men had begun they were caked all over. Dawson was reminded of the dusty rides on the convoys up north. Each man was covered in a coat that darkened his face in a poor imitation of a coal miner's grimy mark. They had removed their shirts and the veneer extended to their arms and shoulders. The dirt formed a glove over their hands, going up to the elbow; rings of dirt leafed around the neck and brown layers settled across their chest and stomach. And the black prisoners came out looking like copper-painted African warriors. The earth itched and teased the skin intolerably.

Dawson sneezed into his hand, and wiped the mucus on his trousers. After rubbing clean his fingers of any dust, he picked his nose. The fingers came out smeared with brown, no mucus, just dust. He spat to the side, disgusted. Placing the spade between his legs, he put his hands on the small of his back and pushed inward, straightening his upper body.

Chi-Chi was sitting in a pool of earth covering his legs halfway. A half-filled sandbag was spread between his thighs. He was holding the front portion of the bag open, waiting for the rest of the earth to be poured inside. "C'mon, man, fill up the mother," he said. "Ya still got 'bout fifty more t'go."

Dawson wiped his hands to dry up the sweat. "Cut me some slack, will ya? You another P or somethin'?"

"C'mon, fill 'er up. I don't dig holdin' up this bag."

"You ain't holding it up," Dawson said. "You just keeping it open."

"It's the same thing."

"You wanna switch jobs?"

No settlement with Chi-Chi. "Fuck no, I ain't gonna handle no E-tool. Think I'm crazy? That's hard work."

Dawson picked up the E-tool and frowned. "I know, that's why I'm doing it. I still don't know why I tossed you for it."

"Now, you know we chose the thing fair and square. We used the guard's coin to choose, remember."

Dawson dug the spade into the earth. "I'll be damned if I'll do it again."

He dug up a spadeful and poured it in the bag. "Pro'bly a double-headed coin."

"We chose fair and square," Chi-Chi reminded him.

"Yeah," Dawson grunted.

Miller passed by, cradling the rifle in his right arm. "Cut the crap, ladies." He went off in the direction of the next sandpile.

Chi-Chi scanned Miller's back. "That fucker is a bummer."

"A what?"

"Like a bad trip, dig?"

Dawson didn't know what Chi-Chi was talking about. "Oh, sure." He ladled another spadeful into the bag.

Chi-Chi wrinkled his brow in displeasure. "They's all bummers here, every single one of 'em."

"Who?"

"Everybody. All the fuckin' Ps."

"Just found that out?" Dawson asked with a sardonic tone.

"Naw, I din't just find that out, I've known it all along. If I had my way there be no fuckin' H&S Casual. You know what I'd do if I was in charge of this setup?"

"No, what would ya do?"

"I'd close this joint and send everybody home — guards, Ps, prisoners — everybody. I'd say, 'Fuckit, anybody wanna sky home can do it. If you wanna make your bird — git!' And then I'd extend that proclamation to all the troopies in the field, even Army." Chi-Chi grinned enthusiastically. "Wouldn't that be somethin'? Everybody' slidin' home and leavin' the Brig empty?"

"That's cool," Dawson said, "but if you take all the dudes outta the bush who gonna fight the war?"

"That's it, man. There'd be nobody to fight the war, so there'd be no need to fight one, dig?"

"Oh," Dawson said, not comprehending at all. "But what happens after everybody sky?"

"Nothing. That's it, nothing. We all go back home and fuck."

"Oh."

"Wouldn't you rather fuck than be here?" Chi-Chi asked.

"Yeah, I'd imagine."

"There." Chi-Chi nodded with conviction. "I should be a goddamn politician."

Dawson lifted a spadeful of earth. "Yeah, Chi-Chi, maybe you should be." He lowered the E-tool and rested. "What's your platform gonna be, a free fuck for everybody?"

"The bummer comin' back," Chi-Chi alerted him.

Dawson looked over his shoulder. Miller was coming their way. He stopped in front of the sandpile. "Man, you people are the most talkative dudes. I swear, can't you take a friendly warning?"

"We ain't doin' nothin', Miller," Chi-Chi said.

"That's right, you ain't doin' nothin'. And how 'bout standing up when I talk to ya, turd."

Chi-Chi sighed and got to his feet.

"That goes for you, too, turd," Miller told Dawson.

Dawson shrugged and slouched to something that resembled the pose of attention. He looked at the sky while Miller spoke.

Miller's voice was surprisingly mild. "Now, you people know you ain't suppose to gab while you're workin'."

Chi-Chi opened his mouth to protest.

"Stow it, Curly. I know you people was shootin' the shit," Miller grinned sociably. "That's a no-no. Ain't no no-no's allowed in this place. Admit it, you was gabbin'."

No answer.

About ten feet away, on the same sandpile, two black prisoners were also filling sandbags. They had ceased their work and were awaiting the outcome of this latest development.

"Sir, request permission to speak," Chi-Chi petitioned.

"Of course, prisoner, by all means, do speak." Miller sounded like a headmaster chastising some errant schoolboys.

"We wasn't talking," Chi-Chi said.

Miller showed his toothy grin. "Now, now, ladies, we know we're lying, don't we? Yes, we do." He picked up the E-tool that stood next to Dawson's foot, and looked at it admiringly. "Can't allow a no-no, ladies." And just as simple as you please, Miller went over to where they had piled the tent sandbags and commenced to rip each one apart with the digging end of the E-tool. He wielded the spade expertly, creating a foot-long gash on each bag that spurted sand like the stuffing out of a rag doll. In a minute every bag was ripped and sagging.

Dawson took a step forward but Chi-Chi gripped his arm and held him back.

Miller tossed the E-tool back on the ground. "Now I'm sure we won't talk no more. Will we, ladies?"

Dawson found Miller's grin obnoxious. "Miller, you mother — "

"There you go again, talkin' out of turn, without asking no permission, either." Miller took a leisurely step toward Dawson, but he wasn't grinning anymore. "Don't you heed no rules, turd?"

Dawson kept his eyes leveled on Miller. He looked past the blue of the irises and into the pit.

"Gault!" Miller called out.

Another guard came over. "What's up, Miller?"

"Cover me," Miller said. "I think we got a problem of discipline here."

"Aw, c'mon, Miller," the guard said.

"No, Gault, really. We got one of those disciplinary actions."

"Aw, Miller, they gotta get these bags done today."

"They will." Miller looked rigidly at Dawson. "Won't you, turd?"

Dawson stared back, regretting a little his boldness.

"What's your name?" Miller asked.

Negative.

"I asked ya your name, turd," Miller repeated.

The old sensation, as if Gunnery Sergeant Yeager were there. "Dawson," he replied, but it was a defiant retort, like an openhanded slap.

Miller's next request was cutting. "Dawson, you was talking, turd. I want an apology from you. I want you to say, 'Pfc Miller, I'm sorry I was talking, sir. I won't do it again.' Say it!"

Dawson tightened inside. Every nerve trembled, and his neck muscles were strained tight.

"I'm waitin', turd." Miller's voice was cold as the granite on a tomb. Dawson felt every eye in the sandpile on him. He wasn't concerned with his anger, only the agitation in his heart.

Miller raised the rifle to his hip. With his thumb he pushed forward the safety catch. "I'm waitin' for an apology, prisoner."

Dawson's mind was racing. He wouldn't shoot me here. He couldn't. Would he? He remembered Crooked-Nose. That fucker should be in the psycho ward. He felt his legs go weak.

Miller took a step back, giving himself more room with the rifle pointed at Dawson's stomach.

The guard in back of them grasped the sling of his rifle, looking at Miller with the profoundest consternation. Miller had gone to the point where he couldn't back out if the prisoner called his hand.

The prisoner did not call his hand.

"I apologize," Dawson said weakly.

Miller shook his head. "Uh-uh. You suppose to say, 'Sir, I'm sorry for talking. I apologize, sir.'"

Dawson forced it out. "Sir, I'm sorry for talking . . . I apologize, sir."

Miller nodded appreciatively. His Nordic face regained the luster it had suspended momentarily. "That's very good, Dawson. I accept your apology. Now pick up that E-tool and get to work."

With the greatest effort of his life Dawson limply took up the spade. He looked down, avoiding the other men, trying to forget what he would always remember.

Miller tired of the game. "Okay, you men," he told all of them and no one in particular, "let's git back to work."

Chi-Chi sat down on the earthen cushion and held up a new sandbag.

The black men ten feet from him were not as quick. One of them muttered, "Bitch."

Miller walked around the dirt pile until he was facing them. "You men on the same kick as Dawson over here?"

The two blacks continued filling sandbags, totally disregarding the new intrusion.

Miller began all over again. "You men talkin'?"

No reply. One of the men did look up for a second or so; he went back to his shoveling.

The same pattern. "I asked ya a question," Miller said. "Were you men talkin'?"

The prisoner with the E-tool dug it in the earth and very slowly raised his hand to scratch his sweaty chest. The other man was sitting down holding the sandbag. He tittered.

"What's so funny?" Miller demanded to know.

Chi-Chi and Dawson slowed their labor and watched the action.

The man who was sitting had a tacit response. He spat into the opened sandbag.

Miller's features became heavy. He attacked the only way he could. "You niggers think you're smart, huh?"

He noted killer glances coming his way, and it delighted him. The opposition of the two men encouraged Miller to push the issue a little further, a little deeper. An odious grin formed on his face. He looked at the sandbags the blacks had piled up. Substantially less than Dawson and his partner had produced, about seven bags maybe.

Seven or one, did it make a difference? Miller believed what mattered was the symbolic gesture. "Those bags look like they're full of rocks," he said, rubbing his chin. He looked over his shoulder. "Don't they look like they're full of rocks, Gault?"

The other guard scuffed his boot in the dirt. He did not answer.

Miller stood before the sandbags, surveying them like a surgeon deciding the correct angle of an incision. He extended his palm to the prisoner. "Lemme see your E-tool, turd. I wanna check it." He cast a sly grin at the other guard. "I wanna see if it's in workin' condition."

The prisoner observed how Miller stared at the sandbags. He wasn't about to let the MP scatter his efforts. Wasted energy? No, man, that don't get it. On GP alone, he couldn't let him do it.

"You want the E-tool, you come and get it," the prisoner said.

Miller unslung his rifle, aimed it at the inmate.

The prisoner held the E-tool menacingly, grasping the neck of the shovel and the bottom of the handle. His body was bent slightly forward at the hips in a blatant defensive position.

Miller held his rifle steady. "If you don't put down that E-tool, nigger, I'm gonna put a bullet hole right through your belly."

The prisoner saw Miller's hand grasping the stock of the rifle, the finger on the trigger. When rankled, even a prisoner was capable of unusual courage. "You kill me, dude, 'cause that's the only way you gonna get this E-tool," he declared.

Dawson lowered his shovel, anxiously awaiting the outcome. He could not believe the other man had actually challenged Miller's firepower. And when he saw Miller hesitate, that was incredible.

Miller's sweaty paws began to stain the fine varnished coating on the wooden handguard. His tongue protruded like a small dart from the corner of his mouth. In that fraction of a second he seemed like an aerialist uncertain of his balance. He looked at the other guard, who did not move from his square foot of ground; he gazed at the prisoner, thinking that once you pointed a rifle at a man he'd back down. What's with this nigger anyway? The prospect of killing the man appealed to him. The thought of being relieved of his sinecure as MP did not.

Dawson rubbed his hands on his thighs. He could picture the black man lying on the ground with a bullet hole in his stomach. The first time during that afternoon when he wouldn't feel the sting of the sun on his back.

Miller put down the rifle, forcing his voice to be crisp. "Gault, this prisoner is threatening us. We gonna have to remove the E-tool from him."

The other guard unslung his rifle. The bolt went forward as he cocked it.

The two guards approached the prisoner, rifles aimed dead at him. The black man picked up a spadeful of earth and hurled it at the guards. He did this two more times and then swung the shovel like a baseball bat, keeping the guards away from him.

Miller brushed the dirt from his shirt, and spat out some dust. "Why you motherfuckin' nigger."

Dawson saw the expression on Miller's face. The MP was going to shoot the prisoner. The knowledge leaped at him. Oh, God, he's gonna zap 'im.

"What's going on here?"

Everyone turned his head to see Master Sergeant Lidel standing behind them. He didn't look too pleased.

Miller lowered his rifle. "Top, this prisoner threatenin' me and Gault with an E-tool."

"He's doing what?"

Miller rushed his words. He was going to get the impudent nigger one way or another. "He says he gonna brain anybody who come near him, Top."

Lidel stared at the prisoner. "Put down that E-tool."

The prisoner tightened his hold on the shovel. "I will if they stay away from me. I don't wanna fuck with nobody but if they fuck with me I'll kill 'em."

No inmate ever menaced Lidel or one of his guards. He looked at the prisoner as if he were seeing a madman. "You gonna do what?" His eyes widened. He called for two more guards and they came running. "Take this prisoner back to the compound."

The four guards closed in on the prisoner. He swung the E-tool, barely missing them, driving them back. The guards approached him again. The cutting edge of the spade whipped the air. The men backed away.

"If you don't drop that E-tool we gonna hafta shoot you," Lidel warned. "You best put it down."

The prisoner pointed the shovel at Miller. "If he stay away from me I will."

"Miller, get outta here," Lidel ordered.

Miller gripped his rifle, then shifted his weight from one foot to the other. He looked down, he looked up, he looked sideways. He was riled.

"Go on, Miller, leave. Go to the next sandpile and stand guard."

Miller slung his rifle and walked away. The expression on his face was acidic.

Dawson exhaled.

Lidel extended his hand toward the prisoner. "C'mon, son, gimme that E-tool. It ain't gonna help you to get in trouble."

The prisoner opened and closed his grip on the handle of the shovel. He looked at his friend and, strangely enough, at Dawson. He was undecided.

Lidel's tone was low key. "C'mon, son, hand it over. I promise ya won't get the hole. We'll go back to the CO and get this straightened out."

The prisoner stood in his defensive position, his eyes set on Lidel.

"You're only making it worse. Hand over that E-tool and I swear no harm will come to you."

The prisoner gazed at the other men. But he was alone. The others dropped their eyes. The E-tool was moist and heavy, his hands very wet.

He lowered the spade. Lidel walked up to him and took the shovel, gently removing it from the prisoner's grasp. He placed a hand on the prisoner's naked shoulder as if he were going to guide him away from the sandpile — and just as sudden, with his free hand, he rammed a fist into the prisoner's lower stomach. The man doubled over, groaning for air. Lidel brought down his fist on the prisoner's neck.

The other black man lunged at Lidel. A guard tackled him, shoving a rifle butt into the prisoner's groin.

"Nobody ever threatens me with an E-tool," Lidel said. He called to the guards. "Pick him up."

Two guards lifted the black man by the arms, forcing him to stand upright. Lidel got in position in front of him, and struck him again in the same exact spot. The prisoner's legs warped and he went down. The guards forced him up.

Lidel stepped back, placing his hands on his waist. "Take him back to the compound." He glanced at the other man. "Take his friend, too."

The other man jumped to his feet, dazed, but still full of fight. Two MPs pounced on the prisoner and grappled him to the ground. Between the two of them they subdued the rebel and dragged him away along with his friend who stumbled weakly, held up by a guard on each side. The man coughed and sounded as if he had difficulty breathing.

"The rest of you men get back to work," Lidel ordered.

Dawson picked up the E-tool, gripping it fiercely. He gazed very evenly at Lidel. Chi-Chi tugged at his trousers. "C'mon, man."

Dawson watched the guards pushing the two prisoners into the back of a jeep. The realization was intolerable. He had backed down before Miller's threat. The black man hadn't. Dawson couldn't even get by on his pride anymore; his fear had neutralized him.

From *A Time Far Past*

The night after Sai's unit crossed the Bac and Silver Rivers, Sai had been forced to remain behind. Malaria attacks rolled through his body for three days. He was unable to eat, but still, when evening came, he had to roll up his hammock and walk, his body leaning hard into his walking stick. At times he lost consciousness. His eyes became wild, his skin black and blue, his jaw so stiff he couldn't even swallow the bowl of ginseng the nurse prepared for him. Finally, she gave Sai three consecutive shots. Then, with two soldiers from Sai's unit, she carried Sai to the medical station one day's walk away.

After six months in the hospital, Sai's health improved. Discharged, he was appointed a platoon leader of an engineering company in charge of *ngam ong Thao*, a part of the trail that went under the shallows of the Thao River, south of Xe Bang Hieng. Sai had always been a restless person, full of projects and longings. Now he was as silent as an old man. In spite of his dream of fighting the enemy and becoming a hero, he was content with this assignment. He was willing to accept any responsibility assigned to him; nearly a year had passed since he left the North for the front, and since then he had done nothing. Many of his companions-in-arms had been in difficulties and suffered hardships for him. If he could do anything to show his gratitude, to deserve his place among them, he would do it.

When Sai arrived at his new unit, he wanted to go straight to the trail, but the company commander decided that he had to take another week to rest. By having someone at that higher level of education in his company, someone who had been a teacher and had worked at the political department of the regiment, the company commander was sure that Sai would be very helpful to him. First of all, Sai would have to teach the new recruits from the ethnic minority tribes how to read and write, and then help the commander himself to write the company reports.

After these first days of rest at his unit, Sai was feeling much better, but he had a strong craving for some greens to eat. He didn't care what kind. It was a simple enough want, but as a new member of the unit, he was not allowed to cross into the steep mountains and defoliated jungles alone. To please Sai, the company commander decided to send Them, his contact man, to help Sai find greens, bamboo shoots, mushrooms, and sour fruits. The trip back and forth would take two days, but Sai and Them prepared by bringing enough shredded dried meat and other provisions for four days. Carrying their guns and rucksacks, the two left early in the morning. By afternoon, they had arrived at a forest of tall thinly growing trees, mostly ironwood and *bong tau*, trees round and straight with perfect white bark.

Them walked at a fast clip, talking quickly as he went, acting as if the jungle were his family orchard. He knew where to find the greens and mushrooms and where each spring led.

"Do you like honey?" Them asked as they walked. "We can come back here tomorrow, when we have used up our water and use a canteen to store honey."

Sai assumed Them had been to the area before, but he soon learned this was not the case. This was Them's first time in this part of the jungle, yet quick and daring, wherever he went, he noticed everything. In only a few hours, the two had filled a rucksack with bamboo shoots and a two-kilo bag of cat's ear. The trip would have been a great triumph if it hadn't been for the unexpected rainstorm. In fact, signs of the rain had been coming in on the forest since nine o'clock that morning. Them and Sai had walked in the day's stifling air, and both their inner and outer shirts were soaked.

At dusk, the jungle rustled and lit up in a sweet yellow. Devoting all their attention to searching for greens and bamboo shoots, the men scarcely passed a word and paid little attention to the sun or wind. When darkness came, they sat down to chew their dry provisions and drink their water. Climbing into their hammocks, they fell immediately asleep, without knowing in which direction the universe was moving.

The water level rose steadily all night. It was almost dawn when Sai felt cold at his back. He searched with his hand and found that his hammock was flooded with water. He turned around to wake Them. They flashed their lights and saw the area around them all white with water, only a few dozen meters away a swift current was sweeping everything downstream. The sound of running water had drowned out the sound of raindrops on their tents. The two soldiers jumped down from their hammocks into the water. They slung their guns and rucksacks over their shoulders, took down the tents to cover themselves and furled their mosquito-net hammocks. After a long struggle, they reached higher ground and built a fire, never bothering to take precautions to hide the smoke. In the midst of the deserted jungle on a rainy night they were not worried, and even had they worried, that night they would have reassured themselves that enemy planes couldn't smell smoke.

Before daybreak, a group of jets flew over their position and began bombing all around their fire. Volleys of bombs exploded fifteen meters from Sai and Them. Sai was temporarily blinded. He had been lying between the ribs of a huge tree. Perhaps that saved him, for all the shrapnel stuck in the tree. But Them, who was sitting a bit further outside the tree, was struck by the first series of explosions. After the attack, Sai raised himself up and saw that Them was not moving. He jumped over the fire quickly and held his friend. A bomb fragment had sliced off a piece of flesh as big as a hand from Them's left buttock. His left thigh had also been struck by three bomb fragments. Blood had made a pool under him. Sai wiped his hands off on his shirt and the mosquito net, then started to dress Them's wounds. He used both his own and Them's supply of bandages, but was only able to cover three wounds. He took a pack of water pipe tobacco, already soaked with water, from his shirt pocket and applied it to the last wound. He took off his T-shirt, tore it, and tied his friend's wound.

It was only after he had dressed Them's wounds and felt his chest to make sure he was still breathing that Sai realized what had happened. He wondered what to do next. He was standing in deep water; which way should he go? How could he bring Them home? Having lost so much blood, he might not survive the trip back to the hospital. Sai didn't dare to think about it. He took his shirt and a mosquito net to wipe one tent clean, then he spread the tent over the two mosquito nets in the hollow of the tree and carried Them over and placed him on it. He then wiped the other tent clean and stretched it above Them to protect him from the rain. Them was groaning softly; he mumbled, "Water, please give your little brother a sip of water!" How pitiful the word "little brother" sounded. Sai felt limp. He turned around to take the canteen full of water and carefully pour a small amount into the empty canteen. He hid the one with more water in a tree and took the canteen with only a cup of water and poured it into his friend's mouth. Them suddenly stretched his hands out to grasp the canteen. He held the canteen tightly to his mouth as if he were afraid Sai would snatch it away. In two gulps, he swallowed all the water. Them sucked, then licked all around the canteen's mouth. Sai felt his tears rising, but he couldn't let Them quench his thirst. Dipping the canteen over his friend's mouth, Sai muttered something as if he were pleading with Them. Them also knew the danger of drinking too much water in times like this. Them licked the canteen's mouth until his tongue and lips dried up, then he fainted into sleep, moaning softly.

Sai took his rifle and ran down the hillside through waves of thorn bushes. Layers of rotten leaves formed a soft bed under his feet. Every step seemed to make him shorter. Around him, the water still swirled swiftly by, striking the cliffs, splashing all over before running noisily down toward the mountain.

Sai ran until he was out of breath. He couldn't find the militia path. The later it got, the more he worried about Them's wounds, so the more he pressed on. Finally, Sai collapsed flat on a rock, pressed his face down on the hard cold stone, ready to pass out. A few minutes later, in desperation he decided to fire a few shots to draw aid. Perhaps there were units billeted nearby, or perhaps someone else was out looking for greens. Sai had barely enough strength left to lift his gun; he just rested it against the rock and clicked the bolt, pointed the gun slightly upward and fired two shots. The whole jungle stirred for a short moment. Sai again sank his head down to the gun's butt. He held the gun so he couldn't drop off to sleep as he wanted to, then he stood up and stretched his arm, still holding the gun. Looking down to the bottom of the mountain, he saw two men splashing across the stream. From their camouflage uniforms, he knew that they were two soldiers from the puppet army. The two must have slept on the same hill with Sai and Them last night. They must have been the ones who called the jets to bomb this morning. Sai stood up, leaned his gun against a branch of a tree, and fired two more rounds. The two men had reached the other side of the stream and were running along the side of the mountain to the left. Sai didn't see them, but he pointed his gun in their direction and fired five more shots. He knew he hadn't enough energy to pursue them, he fired hoping only to chase them off and give himself the opportunity to get away. Their path had shown him the way to the other side of the swirling stream. Crossing the stream where they had crossed and going in the direction where they had run was inviting death, but only by going along the stream could he hope to find the militia path. Calculating the odds of success, Sai ran back to wake Them. The thirst was still raging in Them. Sai took the canteen to pour out two more sips of water. Them licked the corners of his lips, but this time he didn't try to seize the canteen. Sai took the hammock from the backpack, tied its two ends together, and hung it across his shoulder. Them placed one hand on Sai's shoulder, the other on a walking stick. He put the wounded leg in the hammock-sling, immobilizing it. The set-up would slow them down, but there was no other way to get out of the jungle. The two men limped down the mountain, then started to grope their way across the stream.

Suddenly Them, puffing and panting, pushed Sai over and tumbled down on top of him, his mouth wide open. "Water, water . . . oh God . . . waaa . . . ter," he cried. Sai pushed Them up, then opened the canteen and poured more water into Them's mouth. Them held the canteen tightly. This time he was stronger than Sai. The water gurgled into his mouth, oozed out at the corners, and ran down to soak the collar of his shirt. Sai kept still for almost ten seconds before he snatched the canteen out of

Them's hands. He felt like the ground under his feet was dissolving; Them cursed and stared at Sai with vengeful eyes. Sai didn't dare look at the pain and misery that appeared in Them's face. He turned away and twisted the canteen tightly closed. He took off the bandage to squeeze out the water and redress Them's wounds. Sai was in panic when he saw that blood was still trickling from Them's thigh. Sai didn't know what kinds of herbs to look for to treat the wound, and there was nothing but his sweaty T-shirt to use as a dressing. Sai felt that all he could do, at this point, was find a way back to the unit as quickly as possible.

The sun was directly overhead. It was quiet except for the sound of the stream. Too quiet. At every step, Sai had a feeling that the two enemy soldiers were ready to jump out like tigers on them. Sai tried to concentrate only on finding a way out. He leaned forward. As he moved, he clung to whatever he could for support. He didn't care that he was scratched by thorns or that his head banged up against trees and rocks. He didn't care that hunger attacked and sweat drenched him like a shower. Sai half-carried his friend on his back and half-dragged him.

The jungle closed in on them. Them rested his head quietly on Sai's shoulder. Maybe he had dropped off to sleep. They came across a ledge of rock as wide as a house. Although it was only as high as his knee, Sai didn't have enough energy to climb over it. He lay down to wait for his strength to return. But strength from where? All the elements a living body needed had been used up. Sai fell into a deep sound sleep, oblivious to everything around him.

Eventually, the silence called back both the pain and the burning thirst that had forced Them to cry out. He called out again and again, but Sai didn't move. He had thought Sai was sleeping. He pushed himself up and away from Sai's back and crawled with his hands, dragging his wounded leg. He could see nothing in the dark night. He followed the sound of flowing water as if it were calling to him. His thirst had peaked. He would quench it, whatever the consequences; he would rather die tonight than drink for a hundred more years. Them kept crawling, sideway, dragging his wounded leg. The strength of the spring had brought Them to its edge. Leaning his hands against a piece of rock, he stuck his face to the stream and drank without stopping, without taking a breath. He kept drinking until his stomach was swollen, but the thirst was not quenched. He touched his face on the surface of the cool water, which splashed up as if playing with him. He leaned against the rock and stretched out his arms, so he could set his face against the water that was so generous and indifferent about bringing him the happiness and satisfaction he had never found in his life. The happiness was great enough to end pain and hope forever. It had been twenty years, two months and six days since the night Them had first been bathed in the warm water in the stoneware basin of the midwife. Now, all his ideals and capacity for love were going to end with this last touch of cool water.

Sai didn't know whether it was midnight or near dawn. He didn't know whether he was on the beach or in an airtight room. His back felt a little cold. He wanted to raise his hands but he could not. He had to make an effort just to open his eyes. Sai touched his back. Them was not there. He stretched his arm to feel around, and Them was not there either. Dripping with sweat, he jumped up. His legs almost collapsed beneath him. He flashed his light swiftly to every side. Everywhere the night seemed thick and dark, and it felt like the enemy was watching. Sai decided to call Them, but his tongue was tied, his throat stuck and dry, unable to utter a word, not even a soft, single word.

After a dizzying moment, Sai walked down to the spring, flashing his light, looking for his friend. He walked backward until the water came up to his knees; then he saw Them stretching his arms, lying face down at the edge of the spring. Out of joy, Sai rushed over to his friend. But when he touched Them, he shivered. Looking at Them, his face buried in the water, Sai knew what had led to this horrible end. He wanted to yell, but he didn't have the energy. He wanted to cry, but the tears wouldn't come. His anger at himself rushed over him. Ignoring his fear, Sai lifted Them, carried him on his shoulder and walked along the stream.

Numb, Sai wanted to believe his friend was still alive. He knew that with Them over his shoulder, he felt more confident.

Later, nobody could understand or explain how Sai could have carried his sacrificed companion, up and down hills, for fifteen hours. Finally, reaching the militia path, Sai fell flat down. He lay with Them on his side, so the two faced each other like two close friends talking. Sai held his friend's waist. Them's wounded leg lay wrapped over Sai's body. Even at a short distance, the two young soldiers looked sound asleep.

Translated by Ngo Vinh Hai

Song of the Hammock

(Bai ca canh vong)

The hammock chirps, the hammock sings.
My hand rocks to its cadence.
The three rooms of my straw hut
Fill with the hammock's song.

The hammock chirps, the hammock sings.
The summer noon spreads everywhere.
Settled on a single foot,
A bird nods drowsing on bamboo.

The hammock chirps, the hammock sings.
The custard-apple tree sleeps;
Its fruit looks through half-open eyes,
The sky burning blue.

The hammock chirps, the hammock sings.
The hammock softly sways.
There at the open window
A bird taps out a rhythm.

The hammock chirps, the hammock sings.
How many years rocked by my mother
To the same hammock's sound?
Far away the white egret flies.

The hammock chirps, the hammock sings.
Little Giang already sleeps,
Her hair moving to its sway,
Her lips sketched into a smile.

In her dreams
She runs by the edge of the river
Chasing a white stork,
A giant gold butterfly.

She sees our mother
Bending over in the rice field,
Sees the gunners on the watch
Guarding our blue sky.

Rockaby, my little sister,
My hand rocks in cadence.
Rockaby, my little sister.

The three rooms of my straw hut
Fill with the sound of the hammock.
The hammock chirps, the hammock sings.

Translated by Nguyen Khac Vien

Song of the Moonlight and the Dan Bo

(Tieng dan bau va dem trang)

The artists of the Song and Dance ensemble of the Liberation Army came to our village.

You play a tune on the dan bo
and clap out the rhythm with your hands.
You sit, you sing,
suddenly the light of the moon is immense,
the voices of night birds rise up,
the melody of stars wanders the sky,
From the dan bo
sounds
rise that speak of men, of earth,
sounds of love, of all times past,
of love today
waiting always in the string
which endlessly shapes the lovely tune,
the tenderness of Nam Bo's beauty,*
all the life of the people's ancient Quan Ho songs.†
The curve of the communal temple roof grows softer.
The factory on the other bank grows larger,
and all who listen recognize themselves in this music's warm human
       strains.
The young partisan who drives the tractor,
her big toe covered with mud,
the old people who have led so many generations to the parting shores,
and the children, so many of them . . .
all turned to poets
by the song of the dan bo.

The song of the dan bo,
vibrates and rises through the moonlight
over the two crops of rice.

*Nam Bo: the southernmost part of Vietnam.
†Song contests of alternating answering refrains common in the province of Bac Ninh.

The string seems to skim the finger
no longer,
but stretches into space,
sounds by itself the ancient strength of Vietnam.

And we children hold our breath. We listen.
Suddenly in the distance, bombs explode.
The shade of an areca palm spreads over the dan bo
passes

like a hand
erasing the harsh sounds that stir hearts
leaving only the song of the dan bo,
fresh as a stream at its source.

Written in 1972 when the author was seventeen

Translated by Nguyen Khac Vien

Driver of Lorries without Windscreens

No windscreen — not that the truck doesn't have one —
bombs thunder, bombs blast — the windshield shattered in splinters —
seated firmly in the cab,
we look at the earth and sky straight ahead.

The wind rushes in, whips our eyes which sting
and the road ahead runs straight to the heart
and the stars are suddenly wings of birds
like planets that fall bursting into the cab.

No windscreen so there's dust
the dust powders our hair white like old men.
Why wash it? — drag on a cigarette
look at each other — filthy faces — and burst out laughing.

No windscreen, clothes soaked.
Rain falls, streams in as in the open.
Why change — grip the wheel. 100 kilometers still —
the rain stops, the wind blows. Soon we're dry.

Trucks arrive from where the bombs fall,
returning in convoys.
When we pass friends along the trail
we shake hands through broken windscreens.

No windscreen. No headlights either.
No tarpaulin, floorboards falling to pieces,
the truck keeps rolling ahead — South:
if there's a heart in the truck, it's enough.

1965

Translated by Nguyen Khac Vien

Truong Son East, Truong Son West

You and I, let us hang our hammocks in the same mountain jungle.
You and I — at opposite ends of the long mountain chain —
the road to the front so beautiful in this season
The eastern mountains long so for the west.
One mountain, clouds of two colors.
There sun. Here rain. The sky too is different.
That's how it is with you and me, with South and North.
That's how it is with two slopes of one long single forest.

Western chain — I leave, my heart tight, my love
on the other slope under ceaseless rain, climbing shoulder of the trail,
      carrying baskets of rice,
swarming mosquitoes, thousands in the ancient jungle — pull down your
      sleeves.
Harvest over, where will you search for bamboo shoots now?

Your heart knotted, my love. And me, on the wintry slope:
streams dry, butterflies among the rocks.
You know, my head is high in unknown lands
but you think of the bombs that cut my path.

I climb into the truck and all the sky's rain pours down.
The windshield wiper brushes my nostalgia away.
You walk down the mountain and the sun sets in splendor.
Tree branches keep our sorrows apart.
The trail that joins east to west carries no letters;
it carries bullets and rice.
On the eastern chain, a young girl in a green jacket, hard at work.
On the western chain, a soldier in a green jacket . . .

From your side to mine,
wave after wave, troops march to the front.
Like love that joins words without end,
the east meets with the west.

Translated by Nguyen Khac Vien

Tipping Point

Late blue light, the East
   China Sea, a half-mile out . . .
      masked, snorkeled, finned,

rising for air, longing for it,
   and in love with the green
      knife-edged hillsides, the thick

aromatic forests, and not ready
   for the line of B-52s coming in
      low on the horizon, three airplanes

at a time, bomb-empty after
   the all-day run to Vietnam.
      Long, shuddering wings, and predatory,

dorsal tail fins, underbelly
   in white camouflage, the rest
      jungle-green, saural, as if a gecko had

grown wings, a tail fin, and
   nightmare proportions. Chest deep,
      on the reef-edge, I think of the war smell

Which makes it back here:
   damp red clay, cordite, and fear-salts
      woven into the fabric of everything not

metal: tarps, webbed belts,
   and especially jungle "utes,"
      the utilities, the fatigue blouses

and trousers which were not
   supposed to rip, but breathe,
      and breathe they do — not so much

of death — but rather the long
    living with it, sleeping in it,
        not ever washing your body free of it.

A corporal asked me if he still stank.
    I told him no, and he said,
        "With all due respect, Lieutenant,

I don't believe you." A sea snake,
    habu, slips among the corals,
        and I hover while it slowly passes.

My blue surf mat wraps its rope
    around me, tugs inland
        at my hips while I drift over ranges

of thick, branching elkhorn,
    over lilac-pale anemones,
        over the crown-of-thorns starfish,

and urchins spinier than naval
    mines, over mottled slugs,
        half-buried clams, iridescent angelfish.

The commanding general said,
    "Every man has a tipping point,
        a place where his principles give way."

I told him I did not *belong*
    to any nation on earth, but
        a chill shift of wind, its hint of squall

beyond the mountain tells me
    no matter what I said or how,
        it will be a long swim back,
            complicities in tow.

Connections: Vermont Vietnam (I)

Hot summer day
On the River Road
swimmers of the Ompompanoosuc
dust in my eyes
       oh
       it is the hot wind of Laos
       the girl in Nhe An covers her face with a straw hat
       as we pass   she breathes   through cloth
       she stands between two piles of stone

       the dust of National Highway One blinds

me
summertime
I drive through Vermont
my fist on the horn, barefoot
    like Ching

Connections: Vermont Vietnam (II)

The generals came to the president
We are the laughing stock of the world
What world? he said
                    the world
                    the world

Vermont
       the green world
       the green mountain

Across the valley
someone is clearing a field
he is making a tan rectangle on Lyme Hill
the dark wood
the deposed farm
                    the mist is sipped up by the sun
                    the mist is eaten by the sun

What world? he said

What mountain? said the 20 ships of the Seventh Fleet
rolling on the warm waves lobbing shells all the summer day
into green distance

       on Trung Son Mountain Phan Su told a joke:
       The mountain is torn, the trees are broken
       How easy it is to gather wood
       to repair my house in the village which is broken by bombs

His shirt is plum colored, is brown like dark plums
the sails on the sampans that fish in the sea of the Seventh Fleet
                    are plum-colored

the holes in the mountain are red
the earth of that province is red   red
                              world

AFTERMATH

The Incense Smell on New Year's Eve

My family wakes at midnight, New Year's Eve.
Lamps blazing, my wife lights the joss-sticks.
Spirits of our ancestors
Whirl like dense smoke from the altar.

Like the silent wall, my children sit still,
Listen to my wife's inaudible call to the spirits.
I feel as if my throat is being choked,
Memories of past days and years come rushing back . . .

Days and years when we crossed the forest stirring dead leaves.
Bombs rained down before us, bombs fell behind us.
My battalion was three hundred men strong.
Only five were left when we reached Saigon.

But we shouldn't talk of the past.
Let's gather together dear friends, near and far.
Let's gather together friends of days past,
Friends with no place to go, no home.

Let's gather here where no one will be lost;
The scent of joss-sticks will lead the way.
Let's drink a cup of wine together;
Together let's celebrate spring.

The incense still burns in the urn.
My family stays up through the night.
Wind rustles leaves at the gate.
For a moment I hear my friends' footsteps coming home . . .

Translated by Nguyen Ba Chung and Bruce Weigl

Shell Shock

A few of the symptoms in the men suffering from shell shock, the popular term to describe an enormous mass of afflictions during the Great War of 1914–1918, were: tics, spasms, tremors, stammering, loss of voice, stupor, a state of fatigue, loss of muscular power, and delusions. Phobias, impairment of the skin sense, confusion, agitation, hallucination, diminished smell and taste, deafness, amnesia, forms of paralysis, and unbearable nightmares were common. Some of the stricken had been wounded, but not all of them. In March 1916 Robert Graves, a captain in the British trenches in France, knew that the war was breaking him. In his classic war memoir, *Good-Bye To All That*, he envisioned his wrecked self: "It would be a general nervous collapse, with tears and twitchings and dirtied trousers; I had seen cases like that." He was not yet twenty-one.

At first the War Office in London insisted that a man was wounded or a man was well. Physicians were hardly prepared to treat the thousands of cases of "war neuroses" and few were familiar with the work of Freud. It was thought that shell shock only became a problem after the beginning of the Battle of the Somme when British troops attacked German lines on a thirteen-mile front. In the catastrophe, 60,000 of their men were killed or wounded on the first day alone, July 1, 1916.

A pioneer in the use of psychotherapy to treat shell shock was the English psychiatrist and physiologist W.H.R. Rivers, who was highly respected for his anthropological research in India. When peace finally came, it was Dr. Rivers who wrote: "One of the most striking features of the war from which we have recently emerged — perhaps its most important feature from the medical point of view — has been the enormous scale on which it produced these disturbances of nervous and mental functions. . . ."

He deplored, as did so many others, the misleading nature of the expression "shell shock" which suggested that its sufferers had been solely damaged by proximity to bursting shells or by having been buried alive by these explosions. Dr. Rivers believed that the true origins of shell shock were a complex, defensive, emotional response to the trauma of war and used the writings of Freud, especially the theory of "forgetting," to treat officers under his care. Many others thought that the men who cracked were not stable, brave fellows to begin with, but Dr. Rivers wrote that "war calls into activity processes and tendencies which in its absence would have laid wholly dormant." In a country that valued a certain conduct based on concealing pain or helplessness, he challenged the widely held belief that, as he put it, "the forgetting of an unpleasant experience is . . . the most obvious and natural line of procedure." What he sought to teach was that the endless struggle to smother the threatening or loathsome memories of the war was injurious and debilitating to the soldier.

"We should lead the patient resolutely to face the situation provided by his painful experience," Dr. Rivers wrote. "We should point out to him that such experiences . . . can never be thrust wholly out of his life, though it may be possible to put it out of sight and cover it up so that it may seem to have been abolished. His experience should be talked over in all its bearings."

Not many British physicians spoke in that voice.

In the Craiglockhart War Hospital near Edinburgh where Dr. Rivers was in charge of one hundred officers who could no longer sleep at night, let alone command, one of his patients was the poet and writer Siegfried Sassoon. It was Sassoon, in his 1936 book, *Sherston's Progress*, who wrote of Dr. Rivers, using his real name in a fictionalized account of his life and the war that devoured him. A decorated officer who tried to denounce the war, Sassoon wrote this most haunting description of the hospital whose occupants were always under siege.

> One became conscious that the place was full of men whose slumbers were morbid and terrifying — men muttering uneasily or suddenly crying out in their sleep. Around me was that underworld of dreams haunted by submerged memories of warfare and its intolerable shocks and self-lacerating failures to achieve the impossible. By daylight each mind was a sort of aquarium for the psychopath to study. . . . Significant dreams could be noted down and Rivers could try to remove repressions. But by night each man was back in his doomed sector of a horror-stricken front line where the panic and stampede of some ghastly experience was re-enacted among the livid faces of the dead. No doctor could save him then, when he became the lonely victim of his dream disasters and delusions.

Because of his treatment with Dr. Rivers, whom he felt was a wonderful "dream friend," Sassoon decided that "going back to the War was my only chance of peace." It shamed him that he was not with his men at the front and so he went.

Others were far too frail and shattered to act on such a desperate decision. Their misery and panic are documented in *Instinct and the Unconscious*, a collection of lectures and papers based on the clinical experiences of Dr.

Rivers during the war. He wrote of one officer in the trenches searching for a missing friend. What the officer found was sections of a corpse. The head and limbs were no longer attached to the body so mangled was the dead man. In dreams, which persecuted the officer, his friend reappeared in this mutilated state or as a figure whose face had been eaten away by leprosy, always moving closer to him. Before coming to Dr. Rivers at Craiglockhart the officer had always been advised to keep all thoughts of the war from his mind as if it were merely a matter of willpower.

"The problem before me was to find some aspect of the painful experience which would allow the patient to dwell upon it in such a way as to relieve its horrible and terrifying character," Dr. Rivers wrote. He did this by making the patient eventually see that his friend had died instantly and thus been spared the prolonged and grim suffering of the severely wounded.

But Dr. Rivers sometimes failed when the experience the patient was struggling to forget was "so utterly horrible and disgusting, so wholly free from any redeeming features . . . that it was difficult or impossible to find any way to make its contemplation endurable." This described the case of a young officer whose earlier hospitalizations had been useless because, as Dr. Rivers put it, treatment was "isolation and repression." The patient was also told not to read the papers nor talk with anyone about the war. He wept when asked a question about the trenches during an interview with a medical board.

His story was short: the patient was flung down by the explosion of a shell so that his face struck the distended abdomen of a German corpse. The impact of the fall ruptured the belly of the dead man. Before the officer lost consciousness he realized that the foul-smelling substance which filled his mouth was human entrails. In his dreams it happened again and again.

Each month the war kept swallowing more men and new conscripts were urgently needed. The order came that all officers must be on duty or in the hospital, not recuperating at home. In August 1914 when volunteers enlisted in huge numbers, a man had to stand 5'8" tall to be accepted into the army. By early October the standard was lowered to 5'5" and then in November dropped again to 5'3". The British trenches, greatly inferior to those of the Germans, were sickening. In *The Great War and Modern Memory*, Paul Fussell wrote: "Their trenches were always wet and flooded — the stench of rotten flesh was over everything. . . . Dead horses and dead men — and parts of both — were sometimes not buried for months and often simply became an element of parapets and trench walks. You could smell the front line before you could see it."

The poet Wilfred Owen, before his confinement at Craiglockhart, wrote in a letter:

> After that we came to where the trenches had been blown flat out and had to go over the top. It was of course dark, too dark, and the ground was not mud, not sloppy mud, but an octopus of sucking clay, 3, 4 and 5 feet deep, relieved only by craters of water. Men have been known to drown in them. . . . Three-quarters dead, I mean each of us 3/4 dead, we reached the dug-out and relieved the wretches therein. The platoon had to move on to another dug-out which held twenty-five of them. Water filled it to a depth of 1 or 2 feet, leaving us 4 feet of air. . . . I nearly broke down and let myself drown in the water that was now slowly rising over my knees.

Men diagnosed as mental cases often feared they would go mad and lose their minds completely. Ignorance about their condition was widespread and many Britons thought men with shell shock had an irreversible condition or were malingerers, nothing more. "The sufferer is often haunted day and night by memories which torture him not merely by their horror but also by another aspect which is even worse: the ever increasing moral remorse which they induce," wrote Dr. C. Elliot Smith, Dean of the Faculty of Medicine in the University of Manchester. "A patient may be troubled not only by the terrible nature of the memory but by the recurring thought, 'If I had not done this or that,' it might never have happened."

It was assumed that this was more often the case with officers for their responsibilities were greater. Dr. T.A. Ross, a psychiatrist, pointed out that the training of a soldier in the 1914 war tended to make him regress to a childish attitude: "The soldier is above all things to learn to do what he is told at once without argument as a child is." Officers, however young, became the parent figure and it was incumbent on them not to give way to panic or confusion. Dr. Ross tried to make his patients see that they were not cowards, which many of them feared, although not always consciously, and to restore their self-respect. The patients would seem to improve but often fell back and forgot what had been discussed.

"Their illness as a whole was their sole respectable reason for being out of the war," Dr. Ross wrote in his book *War Neurosis*. "The illness itself was horrible but it was the lesser of two evils. When they had been nearly well for some days they began to think they were becoming eligible for the front. The depression caused by this would cause symptoms but they could believe in them only if my explanations were forgotten, i.e., repressed, and so it was easy to forget that one had not been a coward."

The war lasted four years and three months. After the Armistice in November 1918, interest in the multitude of mental disorders did not wane. In September 1920 a committee of the War Office convened for an inquiry into shell shock to record for future use its origins, manifestations, and treatment. The purpose, of course, was to discover ways to prevent it in the future. The committee, largely composed of high-ranking officers and medical men, held forty-one sittings and heard fifty-nine witnesses. There were no statistics on how many casualties from shell shock existed because the category was too vague.

There were the predictable opinions from men who clearly felt too much shell shock was detrimental to the honor of a regiment. A physician specializing in Nervous Diseases said that the effect of being blown up did not lead to the type of symptoms described as shell shock and complained that years of hospitalization often made a patient incurable.

He thought the best way to treat the sick men was to keep them under strict military discipline in rest hospitals behind the lines. The professional military tended to be suspicious of places like Craiglockhart War Hospital where they feared the officers were being cosseted and pampered.

A major said that if morale was kept up there would be no shell shock, as if ceaseless shelling, rats, vermin, and an abundance of corpses were incidental and the high rate of trench fever, trench foot, and trench mouth. It was his opinion, and shared by others, that good officers and medical officers could prevent shell shock if they did their jobs well.

One of the most eloquent witnesses, who had suffered a breakdown but recovered, was a squadron leader in the Medical Service. He said: "It is difficult to describe the clinical appearance of the men who broke down suddenly. The man looked obviously out of control: he gave way to involuntary movements, wringing his hands, his eyes became staring, and he got the look of a hunted animal — you cannot mistake it. When the crash does come he loses all shame and cringes."

Other witnesses suggested that soldiers suffered from a "hysterical" form of mental illness. (Until the war, hysteria was a diagnosis most often used for well-to-do women who were believed to be in need of rest and isolation.) But officers were vulnerable to "anxiety neurosis." These terms, now so old and meaningless, were still quite new to many in the medical and military.

Dr. Rivers reminded the committee that the things that men were trying to put out of their minds were "far too powerful" for the instrument of repression to be adequate. He was largely unheard. Others offered an eccentric hodge-podge of impressions on who could survive on the Western Front.

"You can never tell how a man is going to do in action until you have seen him there," a decorated major told the committee. "Some gay and sporting types which one imagines would do so well are useless; other foppish idiotic types do splendidly. Breeding and family tradition count much among officers. The typical Irishman does well, probably brilliantly up to a point but will not stick it like the typical Scot."

The barely concealed measure of contempt for the shell shock victim felt by so many professional officers was bluntly put by a colonel who was the consulting physician for gas cases in France. He volunteered his opinion that the man who broke down after prolonged exposure at the front was in a state of physical exhaustion — no witness disputed this — but classified the soldier as most likely to be "the tremulous, neurasthenic type." Only on the importance of poison gas as a factor in causing genuine symptoms was he more sympathetic: mustard gas could induce hysteria.

"In all serious forms of gas the respiratory organs are attacked, and there is nothing probably more liable to cause panic than the idea of being choked. It is rather akin to being buried alive — the dread of being slowly strangled," the colonel said.

Treatment for men considered to be suffering shell shock varied widely. There were electric shock treatments, baths, massage, hypnosis and hypnotic drugs, isolation, rest, and different methods of psychotherapy. Recovery was often quick but not for the more traumatized soldiers. Sometimes the physician used harsh methods to make men recover and was not interested in winning their trust, only in making them submit.

A twenty-four-year-old private, who was mute, was a survivor of the retreat at Mons, the battle of the Marne, and the two battles of Ypres, the names for the slaughter on the Western Front. He had also fought at Neuve Chapelle, Loos, and Armentieres. But his collapse came three months later when he was stationed in Greece. Dr. Lewis Yealland, who worked in a hospital for the paralyzed and epileptic in London, wrote in his book, *Hysterical Disorders of Warfare*, that here was an intractable case.

"Many attempts had been made to cure him," he wrote. "He had been strapped down in a chair for twenty minutes at a time, when strong electricity was applied to his neck and throat; lighted cigarette ends had been applied to the tip of his tongue and 'hot plates' had been placed at the back of his mouth."

The patient tried to escape the locked room but Dr. Yealland told him: "Such an idea as leaving me now is most ridiculous. . . ." After four hours of continuous treatment of electric shock, Dr. Yealland claimed to have restored speech and corrected the tremors which affected the patient's arms and legs.

Another private, buried by a collapsing trench with only his head sticking out, was hospitalized with his trunk rigidly bent forward and his head drawn back. The patient was so crooked his chest touched his thighs when he was seated. The unhappy man did not wish to answer the questions put forth by Dr. Yealland. The doctor said what the treatment would be and later wrote of the patient:

"He then began to ask me if the electricity was painful, but I instantly interrupted him, saying, 'I realize that you did not intend to ask me such a question and I shall overlook it. When I began to treat you I was aware of the fact that you understood the principles which are: *Attention*, first and foremost: *tongue*, last and least: *questions*, never.' "

What happened to the "cured" men, the untreated, or the untreatable and how they managed the rest of their lives is not known. The most unforgettable record of their suffering is not in the medical records but in the work of the poets of the Great War. It is these men who haunt us still and have been loved by generations of ordinary soldiers used up and hurt in the wars that were to follow.

Not many lived long enough to write about anything but their war. Honor them. No English poet of the Great War showed promise of great gifts than Isaac Rosenberg, a private in the First King's Own Royal Lancaster Regiment, killed in April 1918. The first lines of his poem, "August 1914," read:

> What in our lives is burnt
> In the fire of this?

Words for My Daughter

About eight of us were nailing up forts
in the mulberry grove behind Reds's house
when his mother started screeching and
all of us froze except Reds — fourteen, huge
as a hippo — who sprang out of the tree so fast
the branch nearly bobbed me off. So fast,
he hit the ground running, hammer in hand,
and seconds after he got in the house
we heard thumps like someone beating a tire
off a rim   his dad's howls   the screen door
banging open saw Reds barreling out
through the tall weeds toward the highway
the father stumbling after his fat son
who never looked back across the thick swale
of teazel and black-eyed susans until it was safe
to yell fuck you at the skinny drunk
stamping around barefoot and holding his ribs.

Another time, the Connelly kid came home to find
his alcoholic mother getting raped by the milkman.
Bobby broke a milkbottle and jabbed the guy
humping on his mom. I think it really happened
because none of us would loosely mention that
wraith of a woman who slippered around her house
and never talked to anyone, not even her kids.
Once a girl ran past my porch
with a dart in her back, her open mouth
pumping like a guppy's, her eyes wild.
Later that summer, or maybe the next,
the kids hung her brother from an oak.
Before they hoisted him, yowling and heavy
on the clothesline, they made him claw the creekbank
and eat worms. I don't know why his neck didn't snap.

Reds had another nickname you couldn't say
or he'd beat you up: "Honeybun."
His dad called him that when Reds was little.

So, these were my playmates. I love them still
for their justice and valor and desperate loves
twisted in shapes of hammer and shard.
I want you to know about their pain
and about the pain they could loose on others.
If you're reading this, I hope you will think,
Well, my Dad had it rough as a kid, so what?
If you're reading this, you can read the news
and you know that children suffer worse.

Worse for me is a cloud of memories
still drifting off the South China Sea,
like the 9-year-old boy, naked and lacerated,
thrashing in his pee on a steel operating table
and yelling "*Dau, Dau,*" while I, trying to translate
in the mayhem of Tet for surgeons who didn't know
who this boy was or what happened to him, kept asking
"Where? Where's the pain?" until a surgeon
said "Forget it. His ears are blown."

I remember your first Hallowe'en
when I held you on my chest and rocked you,
so small your toes didn't touch my lap
as I smelled your fragrant peony head
and cried because I was so happy and because
I heard, in no metaphorical way, the awful chorus
of Soeur Anicet's orphans writhing in their cribs.
Then the doorbell rang and a tiny Green Beret
was saying trick-or-treat and I thought *oh oh*
but remembered it was Hallowe'en and where I was.
I smiled at the evil midget, his map-light and night
paint, his toy knife for slitting throats, said,
"How ya doin', soldier?" and, still holding you asleep
in my arms, gave him a Mars Bar. To his father
waiting outside in fatigues I hissed, "You shit,"
and saw us, child, in a pose I know too well.

I want you to know the worst and be free from it.
I want you to know the worst and still find good.
Day by day, as you play nearby or laugh
with the ladies at Peoples Bank as we go around town
and I find myself beaming like a fool,
I suspect I am here less for your protection
than you are here for mine, as if you were sent
to call me back into our helpless tribe.

For the Missing in Action

Hazed with heat and harvest dust
the air swam with flying husks
as men whacked rice sheaves into bins
and all across the sunstruck fields
red flags hung from bamboo poles.
Beyond the last treeline on the horizon
beyond the coconut palms and eucalyptus
out in the moon zone puckered by bombs
the dead earth where no one ventures,
the boys found it, foolish boys
riding buffaloes in craterlands
where at night bombs thump and ghosts howl.
A green patch on the raw earth.
And now they've led the farmers here,
the kerchiefed women in baggy pants,
the men with sickles and flails, children
herding ducks with switches — all
staring from crater berm; silent:
In that dead place the weeds had formed a man
where someone died and fertilized the earth, with flesh
and blood, with tears, with longing for loved ones.
No scrap remained; not even a buckle
survived the monsoons, just a green creature,
a viney man, supine, with posies for eyes,
butterflies for buttons, a lily for a tongue.
Now when huddled asleep together
the farmers hear a rustly footfall
as the leaf-man rises and stumbles to them.

White Circle

Bomb smoke climbs to the sky in black circles,
white circles rise on the ground.
My friend and I go on in silence,
the silence expected after war.
Friend, there is no greater loss than death.
The white mourning headband takes the shape of a zero,
inside that white circle
a head burns with fire.

Translated by Nguyen Quang Thieu and Kevin Bowen

In the Labor Market at Giang Vo

I'm afraid to ask who you are,
selling your strength out on the street.
The rich need someone to put up their new houses.
They don't care who you are, where you come from.

I know who you are. You are the dark earth
torn from the river bend,
you are the jagged rock wrenched from the mountain,
one difference though — hunger eats at your gut.

These days every village must be a great city,
stacks of foods and goods shimmer and dance in the streets.
Not lack of work, but this new life gives birth to new lines of workers.
A new sky must mean new kinds of clouds.

Dusk crawls up the street. The crowd thins.
No one left but you. I recognize you now,
the look of quiet determination, the scar,
the last broken shard of the war.

1993

Translated by Nguyen Ba Chung and Kevin Bowen

Sitting with the Buddhist Monks in Hue, 1967

Cool spring air through the window,
birds waking rain in the white
limbs of the shaken birch,
I remember
I was led through an ancient
musky maze of alleyways
and rooms where people looked up
from their cooking
and their endless ledgers
as if I were a mean and clumsy spirit
lost among them.
Into darkness I was delivered,
only candlelight
to show the heads bowed
to the clasped hands
rocking in prayer.

I thought he was taking me to his whore.
They did not teach us
the words for prayer or for peace.
I'd watched his hands
gesture in the half-lit alleyway
and his hands told me to follow;
his eyes asked me for money.

I have tried to let the green war go,
but those monks looked at me
across their circle of knowing
and my body somehow
rose off the floor,
their voices
ringing in my skull
like gut wound in razor grass.

I was only a boy.
I didn't want to remember.
I only wanted the lily
to keep opening.

Waiting

I return to the village, to the place they call "Eighteen hamlets of Betel
      Gardens" — so many gardens, so many summers —
she waits, her face toward the night.
Twenty years longing for the sky to darken early;
twenty years, meals gone cold.

Tet should not come again and make my sister sad;
no one congratulate her for one more year of life.
She is no longer young, but out of love and respect, the villagers call her
      miss;
out of love, they don't show their children off in front of her.
Twenty years. When my sister climbs aboard boats loaded down with
      passengers,
she fears being drowned while still in her young and beautiful years.
Everyone knows of her faithfulness,
and he, he is still alive;
he shields the lamp at night, keeps it from going out.
Twenty years each night putting on her bright brocaded dress,
Still so full of life and yearning, though my brother, he is unaware.
My sister is not like the snake who sheds his old skin under every tree's
      shadow.
But without him, she lives like the odd relative at the festival.
In the midst of the family's laughter, she is lonely.
In the cold night, her one hand must warm the other.
She hears gun fire from the distant militia post.
At meals she still eats alone.
No matter where she sits, the scene falls out of balance.
She hides her youth beneath dimpled cheeks.
She misses him, longs for him,
sad as the flamboyant flower torn in two.
With those other youth who will never return
he's heard, and the plants and grass have heard,
that the leaves so love him, they volunteer to be his camouflage,
though they never can make him as cool as she does under her shade,
though they never can make him as warm as she under her hair.

As alive and bright as this day, as grass in the dry season,
her breath winds its way all through his life.
His bandanna should be a sail,
His bandanna of a time of tears.
One day it will wave in front of the veranda, a flag of happiness flying in
     the wind,
but tonight she is still sad,
the ring loose around her withered finger.
Dear sister,
with the burden of twenty years of waiting,
you count his footsteps heading home,
the night so black, the rooster's crow must be strong.
Is it possible he still carries the wooden walking-stick?
Is it possible I am only the river
that must turn bitterly before Binh Loi Bridge?
The whole company can't withdraw into the jungle at once.
Standing in the midst of so much suffering,
we can't look at the gathered stacks of guns
like extra bowls or chopsticks,
the excess so large, we who still live
don't dare to say they are the lucky ones.
During Tet Mau Than there were many plans.
She still believed them in the storybook endings of Kieu,
believed Mai flowers that bloom twice are lovers with second chances
believed the green autumn would arrive to answer moor hens' laments in
     June,
believed one day she would pick fruit for him
when the paddy rice blossomed . . .

The rice is blossoming.
He is returning.
The voice of the red-tailed treepie is a small piece of cloth covering the
     night.
He will recognize his own bright star.
Where are you this last night of waiting?
Night of the Thi,
dawn of the legendary Tam.

Translated by Ngo Vinh Hai, Nguyen Ba Chung, and Kevin Bowen

In Phan Thiet

Brother, nothing belongs to you,
not one blade of grass.
This hill covers much land,
but you don't even have a grave.

It was here you came upon the sea for the first time,
your tunnel leading out to it after days of climbing,
and it must have seemed immense after that hole
where sand turned you white at the slightest motion.

The stench of gunpowder and heat in that place
must have driven your heart wild with uncontrollable
beating, but then the wind rose, moist, warm, fresh,
and the sea rocked before you like a ship about to leave.

The stars always manage to shine, and by their light, you
and your comrades slipped through the hills cutting trails
towards the water. It was December, you were there, the sea moved
to embrace you, embrace you all, but it was a careless moment.

Bombs rained down where you stood
and you died with your face
a few feet from the water.

There you were, and I
had been looking,
searching everywhere,
dragging myself through
Tan Canh,
Sa Thuy,
Dac Pet,
Dac To.

The fevers you once had, I now had, soaked in the same
rain you were soaked in as it blanketed the forests.
But I never dreamed of the rain in Phan Thiet and a time
years later when I would sit in the back of a jeep full of soldiers
trying to hide my tears, searching for your bones.

The forest is still there, the battle ground still there.
A few steps, a few lousy steps
and you would have reached
Route 1.
But it was too far.

Did the vastness of the sea envelope you when it hit?

I still don't know the name of that hill
in Phan Thiet where you stand guard,
unaware the alert has ended,
unaware of news from home,
or of your brother's face.

Your home is not a cemetery.
You have remained on that hill,
burrowing into its green grass,
the blades of it our family's joss sticks,
and the hill our mother's inheritance,
leaving me to care for the rest.

The nights of Phan Thiet have grown darker.
The lights of the city light the way for a fisherman.
You do not sleep, and the fisherman does not sleep.
The sea tells both of you its stories night after night.

And day after day
Phan Thiet keeps my brother.

Translated by Nguyen Ba Chung, adapted by George Evans

Making the Children Behave

Do they think of me now
in those strange Asian villages
where nothing ever seemed
quite human
but myself
and my few grim friends
moving through them
hunched
in lines?

When they tell stories to their children
of the evil
that awaits misbehavior,
is it me they conjure?

A Walk in the Garden of Heaven

A Letter to Vietnam
for Huu Thinh, Le Minh Khue, and Nguyen Quang Thieu

1

They were talking when we entered the garden, two young people whispering with their hands, mist threads drifting from mountain tops on the raked gravel ocean. Islands afloat on the skin of infinity. The mind without its body.

"The moment I saw your face," he said, "was like walking into the Hall of A Thousand and One Bodhisattvas."

She had no idea what he meant, how it is to enter Sanjusangendo in Kyoto for even the fiftieth time and see row upon row of a thousand standing figures, carved, painted, and gold-leafed with a calm but stunned look of enlightenment, five hundred on each side of a larger, seated figure of their kind, miniature heads knotted to their scalps representing the fragments of a time when their heads exploded in dismay at the evil in this world, the way our heads exploded in the war, though we don't wear our histories where they can be seen.

Each statue has twenty pairs of arms to symbolize their actual 1,000 arms, these enlightened ones who choose to remain on earth and not end the cycle of death and rebirth some believe we go through until we get it right. They pause at the edge of nirvana to stay behind and help us all get through. It's easy to think they are foolish instead of holy.

But each hand holds twenty-five worlds it saves, and because each figure can multiply into thirty-three different figures, imagine the thirty-three

---

Garden of Heaven refers to Tenshin-en 天心園 , the Japanese rock garden at the Museum of Fine Arts, Boston. The three Vietnamese writers listed at the top of the first section, came to the United States for the first time in the summer of 1993 as guests of the William Joiner Center of Boston. I visited the garden with Mr. Huu Thinh and Ms. Lê Minh Khuê, both war veterans.

thousand worlds they hold, how much distress there really is, then multiply that by a thousand and one and think of what it's like to stand in an ancient wooden temple with all that sparkling compassion, even for those of us who believe in almost nothing.

It is said, and it's true, that if you search the thousand faces, you will find the face of someone lost from your life.

But the young girl in the garden was bored and looked over her lover's shoulder at a twist of flowers. Then so did he. The spell was broken.

We are older. There are so many wasted lives between us that only beauty makes sense. Yet we are like them. We are. They are the way it is between our countries. One talking, one looking away. Both talking, both looking away.

2

We entered the garden by chance. We were like the rocks there, plucked from some other place to be translated by circumstance into another tongue. And in the silent crashing of stone waterfalls, and rising of inanimate objects into music, we remembered there was a time we would have killed each other.

In the future we will think of it again. We might get drunk beneath a great moon and see one another's eyes in a pool of water, or remember in a glance across a Formica table in a kitchen filled with friends and noisy children, or while walking down the street. But it will not be the same.

It is called realizing you have lived, and it happens only once.

3

During Vietnam, which we say because the name signifies more than a place — it is an epoch, a paradigm, a memory, a mistake — during Vietnam, things were the same as they are now for those who are young and poor. We were standing around. There was no work, it was the beginning of our times as men, we were looking to prove ourselves, or looking for a way out. Some were patriots, and many were the sons of men who had gone to another war and come back admired. I don't remember any mercenaries. We were crossing thresholds, starting to lie to ourselves about things, and because we were there and ambitious or desperate, when they passed out weapons, we took them. We didn't understand the disordered nature of the universe, so disordered humans must try to arrange it, and if they get you young enough, you will help.

I'm grieved but not guilty. Sad but not ashamed.

That does not mean I lack compassion. It does not mean I sleep at night, or don't sweat at night. It does not mean it is easy to live.

In parts of my country, I'm considered insane.

4

Thinking of it in terms of your country, I could say I was the son of peasants. We earned or made everything we had. I learned to honor people for what they do, not for their positions. I've never been able to escape the rightness of that. To explain it in terms of my country, it means: if I didn't have enemies here, I would choose to live in exile.

5

We want the bones. We want all the bones. You will hear this. Good people will say it. They are all good people. They say it. They say: *We want the bones.* And they mean it, they mean what they say. They carry it into sleep, into their children, into the voting booth. *We want the bones. That's what we want. We don't want the ghosts. You keep the ghosts. We don't want them. Just the bones.*

Your ghosts are driving us out of our minds.

6

In my country we shift blame. After the war, those who went became pariahs. Not the ones who started it, not the ones who carried it. And because not everyone can overlook rejection or memory, more who went have died by their own hand than by your mines or bullets. There are more suicides among us now than names on our monument in the capital, our broken dash against the landscape, scar that would span the city if it listed the actual dead, black river that would surge across the country if it listed everyone ruined on every side.

I want this remembering to end, yet cannot let it. It's like drinking the ocean, but someone must remember, someone refuse to be tethered.

I visited your country at the wrong time, but if I had not I still would not understand the nature of things, would still think my country is paradise, which in many ways it is, but which it is not. It is built on graves, on bones, on promises broken and nightmares kept, on graves that howl deep in the earth, on skulls crushed with religious objects, on human skin used as rugs, on graves upon graves of graves. And we are always busy conquering ourselves.

Whatever it is holds us in a spell of wonder when we are children, abandoned me when the war began. I don't mean just me or just youth, I mean something about this country. But I don't mean just this country, I mean the world. I've spent my time searching for what it is, like a suicide who refuses to die, an optimist who is empty, a buoy on the sea.

7

In the dry garden where we walked, where stone represents water as well as itself, the Chinese characters of which mean the center or heart of heaven (天 for heaven, 心 for center or heart), there is a mountain represented, Mount Sumeru, the highest peak of every world, every world a Bodhisattva holds in its hands, every world in the universe, and every world we live in, but it also represents the center of infinity, and because infinity has only centers, we were standing everywhere at once, and exchanged what could not be stated except in language which could never be spoken.

But we must speak it. The question is, how many heads do we have and how many arms and how many worlds do we hold, and just how far will we go to end our war.

8

The order of the universe is that there may be none, not like glasses lined up, each dish upon its shelf. And what we think is wild is not.

I want to be reasonable, it is something that interests, even haunts me, but given certain knowledge, how to be is more hellish.

The room here is small, and at times the way wind kicks up over the fence lip reminds me of animal howling and that in turn of an even smaller room, a box of sorts within a building stilted off the ground beneath a tin washboard roof hammered by rain in your country.

Our rooms there were like boxes really, perimeters not unlike the skin, and came to mean everything for each one, for each had the need to live in containment where there was none, to confine ourselves, as one might a crazed dog until it calms.

Perhaps it is not the past I should concern myself with, but not to speak of it and face what is still happening is not possible.

The double bonds of living for something and dying for something are ribbons that trail from us, drag behind or flap from us, and if I could understand it now or ever this business would be done.

I want to be reasonable, it is something I crave and wish I knew how to pray for but cannot pray, not having the faith of it, having seen.

We have friends, then we do not have them because we reach some border across which words cannot manage, across which silence will not bridge, and in the manner of children we stand without explanation or understanding, and there is no necessity that we question it. We learn to ignore those events which remove things in the way that we know of as "Before their time." It's another weapon we aim at our heads.

9

When we stood in the garden and looked at the stone bridges connecting islands on the gravel ocean, I felt the war lift from us in flames, inch by inch flowing into stone like a river on fire.

We ended something walking together, and started something.

I've read the war is over for you, but have never believed it. Victory is no balm for loss. Any of us may celebrate a moment, but we live a long time, and finality is not what we need, compassion is what we need. Let the future think about the war being over, because then it will be.

We can't afford to heal. If we do, we'll forget, and if we forget, it will start again.

We've destroyed too much to be sentimental. We know that those above and those below the jungle canopy killed anything that got in the way, and we're all guilty of something. Wars are always lost. Even if you win.

10

I returned to San Francisco sorry about some things I was not able to explain. For example, the army of beggars in our streets, and how badly we treat the poor. The coldness of it, you see, is a symptom of killing nations at a distance, or even up against their breaths. It has also to do with how freedom can be like the end of a rope. It pollutes all notions of beauty, this living in the streets. My wife pointed out that Americans do help one another during floods, earthquakes, and conflagrations. "That's not compassion," I said, "it's convenience — only generosity when there is no disaster counts." I've become so wise, righteous anger makes me happy. We sat in silence after that. Actually, one was washing dishes and one was peeling potatoes, we could hear the rattle of a bottle gleaner digging through the recycle bin on our sidewalk, a jet was passing over, John Lee Hooker was singing on the radio, the neighbors were having a horrible fight, there was a crash in the intersection, one of our cats spit at the other, and the phone rang but we ignored it, so it wasn't really silent. Then she said, "We would all be wealthy if people were born honest." So. Not all understanding comes from the barrel of a gun.

11

Stretched flat in deep grass   resolute about the sickness of pursuits watching a moth on a beer can lip swing its curled tongue like an elephant trunk across the water dots.   The only thing I know about fame and success is that they are stumbling blocks when they commandeer my attention.   My real function is to think about things and listen, drunk and lazy, to the buzz in the grass, the millions of insects who do not care what I think.   I'm tired of the world of people — they're not to be trusted on the whole because they don't understand death.   It's not that they're unhappy, it's just that they don't understand death.   I'm not above or beneath them, I'm just sometimes not one of them.   I've seen too much to be fooled into thinking we know what we are doing.   Maybe I'm getting too arrogant for my own good, but even that sounds stupid in the face of death.   I understand the insects in the deep grass, even if I can't repeat what they say.

12

I've come out to the cliffs above the Pacific Ocean before sunset. I told you my childhood friends were all killed in the war, and you told me similar things. It wasn't difficult for me to also tell you I was never angry at your country. What was difficult, was to tell you how angry I am at my own.

Pelicans overhead. The rose-colored hood of a finch in the bushes. I sit on a railroad tie post on a high cliff at the edge of America.

Tourists drive up, take pictures, go home.

A cormorant. A sailboat. An Army gunship choppers over the beach.

Behind me, an Army base. In front of me, the sea.

I'm waiting for the sun to set, but it will not.

Manuel Is Quiet Sometimes

He was quiet again,
driving east on 113,
near the slaughterhouse
on the day after Christmas,
not mourning,
but almost bowed,
like it is after the funeral
of a distant relative,
thoughtful,
sorrow on the border at dusk.

Vietnam was a secret.
Some men there collected ears,
some gold teeth.
Manuel collected the moist silences
between bursts of mortar.
He would not tell
what creatures laughed in his sleep,
or what blood was still drying
from bright to dark
in moments of boredom
and waiting.
A few people knew
about the wound,
a jabbing in his leg
(though he refused
to limp);
I knew about the time
he went AWOL.

Driving east on 113,
he talked
about how he keeps
the car running
in winter. It's

a good car,
he said.

There was the brief illumination
of passing headlights,
and slaughterhouse smoke
halted in the sky.

Another night,
the night of the Chicano dance,
Manuel's head swung slow and lazy
with drinking.
He smiled repeatedly,
a polite amnesiac,
and drank other people's beer,
waiting for the dancers
to leave their tables
so he could steal the residue
in plastic cups.
It was almost 2 AM
when he toppled,
aimless as something beheaded,
collapsing so he huddled
a prisoner on the floor.

The shell of his body
swung elbows
when we pulled him up.
He saw me first,
seeing a stranger.
His eyes were the color
of etherized dreams,
eyes that could
castrate the enemy,
easy murder watching me
with no reflection.

This is what he said:
"I never lied
to you, man."

MARTÍN ESPADA

Memorial Day at the Viet Coffee House

Boston, Massachusetts

When the Memorial Day parade
rumbled past the Viet Coffee House,
the iron pachyderm tanks,
boys in green-brown camouflage
proud of crewcuts and memorized
steps to the march,
the clumsy bouquet of flags
and the migraine of the drum, drunken boom,
the objects in the Coffee House
did not stop their business:
the record player warped
a love song in French,
the cigarette smoke
kept whirling only to vanish
at the ceiling,
the pans sloppy with noodles
hissed on the stove.

Only the workers stopped moving,
as all their nightmares, fires
glowing in a darkened valley,
swept up together in a tidal blaze,
in the bombing mission
that swoops and roars
but never leaves this sky.

From Novel in Progress:

Over There Is the Horizon

While Nhi helped Vinh take off his water-soaked shirt, Vinh grumbled, "You've already pulled up a sizable catch, why do you want to set the net again, especially in such a filthy current? Do you want me to say here just to catch a few small fish?" Although critical of Nhi, Vinh's real discomfort came from finding himself alone with her. Whatever changes Nhi had undergone, she was still bold in her attitude toward him. Though she'd never made even the smallest hole in Vinh's defenses in all the years she'd known him, she never showed her displeasure or disappointment. She had always been direct, even regarding the most sensitive matters a woman would discuss. Even now, listening to Vinh grumble, she understood what was bothering him. She defended herself point by point: "If I go ashore I'll have to guard against the rats who eat the nets. On the boat there are fewer mosquitoes, and when the tide comes in I could make another run with the nets. Even if the current is dirty, it's better than no run at all. Would you leave me alone on this vast river with all the spirits of the deep?" Nhi laughed and jabbed a finger into Vinh's bare chest. "Get into the hold," she said, "and take off your clothes to dry or you'll catch cold!"

To give Vinh some privacy, she stepped to the bow and turned her eyes toward the mouth of the river. A few lamps flickered in the night mist like red eyes. "Throw out your clothes so I can hang them on the line to dry," Nhi said. She heard a sound behind her and reached around her back to grab the clothes and laughed when she saw his clothes consisted only of a pair of pants. She hung them up and said, "Wrap yourself with the wool blanket in the corner."

Vinh amazed himself. So far he had obeyed every one of Nhi's commands! Something else strange occurred to him: Why would old Nhat leave him all alone with Nhi on this pitch dark river? Nhi entered the hold, searching through a corner and pulled out a bottle of brandy that old Nhat had left behind. She poured Vinh a full cup and told him it would keep him warm. After only a few sips Vinh could feel the heat rise in him. Nhi poured another. Vinh was going to drink it all but Nhi stared at him so he stopped. Leaning against the hold, she peeled a grapefruit and ate it passionately. She stared at Vinh without saying a word. She took her time finishing the grapefruit piece by piece without offering a single bite to Vinh. The cutting morning chill and the brandy had made Vinh drowsy. Nhi appeared satisfied when Vinh lay down, pulling the wool blanket to his chin. There was enough space in the hold, but as if she were a thoughtful woman, Nhi pulled herself back slightly to give Vinh more room and put him at ease. She finished the grapefruit and brushed her hands clean. She pulled the storage bin open, looking for another blanket. Then with a long, satisfied sigh she lay down next to Vinh.

She was careful to show some consideration, and mumbled a word of apology before lying down in the opposite direction. Her thoughtfulness surprised Vinh. He would leave things alone and see what would happen next.

After about fifteen minutes, Nhi asked sweetly, "Are you leaving with Hai?" "What about you?" he said. "It's up to you," she said. He thought she might finally express her love but sensed a seriousness in her voice. "What do you mean it's up to me?" he asked. "Your husband has pleaded with you many times to join him in the United States." In the silence, one could hear Nhi's breathing. Then she asked calmly, "Can we talk seriously tonight?" "Of course my dear," he said, "I agree." Vinh had no idea why he had called her dear, a word he'd never used before with Nhi. It seemed to move her deeply. She was quiet. Vinh sat up immediately. He wanted to hear every word of Nhi's story.

"Why don't you lie down and rest, I have a long story to tell." She waited for Vinh to lie down before she continued. "My husband believed I was in love with you so he had to send you away." In the hazy darkness of the hold Vinh could imagine Nhi's bitter smile. "Tech was much more persistent than you. I was about eighteen then and I loved to dress up, loved to be wooed. Tech did everything to please me. The men around here were nothing but a bunch of ignorant jerks who wanted only to look at my legs and breasts. And you were lost in the clouds; Thu always in your heart. So I was taken in by Tech, but then he left for America without saying anything else about the wedding he had promised. That was the end for me. I promised myself I'd marry whoever proposed first, even if it was the beggar who cleaned the market. Hung asked first, so I accepted, but I had no real love for him. Do you understand?"

It was Nhi's turn to sit up. She gathered her hair that had broken loose from its knot; strands of it fluttered in the night wind against the silver mist outside as if the water's endless sound came from the hair as it moved in the wind. Nhi grabbed the cup of brandy only half-finished by Vinh. "Let me have a sip, it will cheer me up." She pushed Vinh's hand away, finished the drink and lay down, this time in the same direction as Vinh. Her voice was angry now. "And what's in the U.S. for me now? Happiness? Do I still need the fancy life and the coddling, or that jerk Tech to wait for me? He begged me to come to the States. And whom should I go with? Bao Thanh the con man?"

Sweat soaked Vinh's face. His hand clutched a wet towel. He gave it to Nhi to wash her face as if the gesture alone would soothe the passions that had risen inside him. He was surprised by the details of Nhi's story. Surprised too at the pain of the woman he had once looked down on.

Nhi wiped her face and threw herself to the floor, breathing unevenly. "Here I still have my parents. My old father would dive to the bottom of this river to be with me, even if lightning strikes. And here I still have . . . you. You believe that these are the things that hold me here, don't you?" Nhi pulled Vinh down, her two hands pulling him to her, her eyes staring as if mad. Vinh knew she had spoken of things that were deep in her heart. And in his own heart an uncommon respect for Nhi took root, and with that respect a sense of shame for how he had regarded her in the past. Even in her mistakes, Vinh thought, she is strong and honest.

Nhi made Vinh lie down while she sat up, turning her back toward him as if she were afraid he saw deep into her secrets.

Vinh could no longer tell if it was the liquor or the words that came from Nhi that choked him. His throat was dry, his eyes glazed over, and his mind heavy with swirling thoughts and emotions.

"You love Thu, don't you," she said. Nhi turned around, pulling the blanket to cover herself and Vinh, her face resting against Vinh's bare chest. "Tell me . . ." Nhi's voice trailed off, "You love Thu fiercely, don't you?" With those words Vinh could see an unfathomable sadness in Nhi's eyes. "Tomorrow I will wait for you at the Institute, even if you shake your head, even if you close your eyes, even if . . ."

Vinh felt his chest sting with Nhi's tears. He shuddered in a momentary dream: Thu was pressing her head against his chest, her sobs sounded far away. He held onto Nhi tightly. Nhi's voice brought him back and his arms dropped to his sides.

"My dear, can't you forget Thu for only a moment?" Nhi held Vinh tighter and tighter, her words a choked pleading. "One more hour," she said, "and it will be morning. Out of all your life can't you give me one hour?"

Vinh put his arms down to sit up but Nhi used her full weight to keep him down. He sighed; he could no longer be rough with her, especially on this night. He lay motionless in Nhi's arms and felt completely at peace, a strange and wonderous peace. It was as if he felt for the first time completely at home, and with Nhi whom he had thought of as so reckless. For the first time as a friend he said to Nhi, "Please don't force me to do the things my heart would rather not."

Nhi sat up quietly and pulled the blanket over Vinh's body. In the soft rush of early morning wind, Vinh could hear Nhi's breathing return to normal. But in the return of the quiet that seemed so precious, Nhi's voice was halting and did not sound like her own voice; her words like bullets sentenced to pierce Vinh's heart. "You're unworthy of Thu! Don't hold out hope that she'll be yours. You are worthy only of people like me, dear Vinh!"

Translated by Nguyen Quang Thieu

MARILYN McMAHON

Knowing

Recent research indicates Dioxin is the most potent toxin ever studied.
—*News report, September 1987*

I watched the helicopters
flying slowly north and south
along the DaNang River Valley,
trailing a gray mist
which scattered the sun
in murky rainbows.
I never wondered if I knew
all I ought to know
about what they were doing.

I knew that it was called
defoliation,
that the spray would destroy
the hiding places of snipers
and ambushing guerrillas.
I did not know to ask:
At what price?

Every evening,
the sunset choppers arrived
filled with soldiers burning
from jungle fevers:
malaria, dengue, dysentery.
We took them directly
to the cooling showers,
stripped their wet
dirt-encrusted uniforms
as we lowered their temperatures
and prepared them for bed.
I did not ask where they had been,
whether they or the uniforms I held
had been caught in the mist,

whether defoliation
had saved their lives.
I did not know to ask.

I knew part of the price
when nine other women
who had watched the helicopters
and seen the mist
talked of their children:
Jason's heart defects, and
Amy's and Rachel's and Timothy's.
Mary's eye problems.
The multiple operations
to make and repair digestive organs
for John and Kathleen and little John.
How lucky they felt
when one child was born healthy
whole.
How they grieved
about the miscarriages
one, two, three, even seven.
Their pain, their helplessness,
their rage when
Marianne died of leukemia at 2,
and Michelle died of cancer at 2 ½.
Their fear of what might yet happen.

I knew more
when I watched my parents
celebrate their fortieth
wedding anniversary,
four children, three grandchildren
sitting in the pews.
I knew what I would never know,
what the poisons and my fears
have removed forever from my knowing.
The conceiving, the carrying of a child,
the stretching of my womb, my breasts.
The pain of labor.
The bringing forth from my body a new life.

Aftermath (115)

I choose not to know
if my eggs are
misshapen and withered
as the trees along the river.
If snipers are hidden
in the coils of my DNA.

Wounds of War

1

He walks off the chopper
bleeding.
In his relief at being out of the fire zone
    he has forgotten that he hurts
    or that he was in terror.

2

The shell fragment is too large
it has invaded his heart
    his lungs, his liver, his spleen.
He will not survive the night.

3

In order that another,
    who has a better chance,
    might survive,
she must remove this patient from life
    support equipment.
Her professional smile calms the other patients,
    hides the anguished murderer inside.

4

Each wound receives the surgeon's scrutiny:
    this we will close, this we will drain,
    this entire area must be removed.
The eye surgeon, the chest surgeon,
    the orthopedist.

Each focuses on his own plot
    forgetting for a time
      their common ground.

5

Infection sets in.
The wound becomes a greenhouse
for exotic parasitic growths.

6

Wounds heal from the bottom up
    and from the outside in.
Each must be kept open,
    must be probed
    and exposed to light.
Must be inspected
    and known.

7

She sits at the side of the road
offering to sell stolen oranges
    to the jeep riders passing by.
She does not name herself wounded.
Two rockets blew away her home
and rice paddy.
    Her husband is dead.
    Her son has been drafted.
    Her baby will never cry again.

8

He wheels his custom chair
    through the crowded bookstore.

He focuses on narrow aisles and tall shelves
    avoiding images
    of jungle trails and buried mines
    of leaving in the mud
       his legs
       and his left hand.

9

In rage he shatters another window with his fist.
The glass shards never cut deeply enough
to cleanse the guilt.

10

She is afraid to trust again.
Her days are haunted
    by the texture of blood
    the odor of burns
    the face of senseless death;
friends known and loved
    vanished
    abandoned.
She sits alone in the darkened room
    scotch her only hope.

11

He stares at the gun he saved,
turning it over and over in his tired hands.
He is desperate to stop the sounds
    and the pictures.

12

*Wounds must be inspected
   and known.*

Must be kept open
and probed
and exposed to light.
Healing is from the bottom up
and from the outside in.

Beggars of the Past

Chapter One

The woman's name was Suong, Ba Suong. She had died before my eyes and I was the one who buried her. More than ten years later, the memory of the way Suong looked would still twist my insides with bitter regrets as well as sweet remembrances.

Yet Suong did not die, never died!

Oh God! Had I not come South like a bird fleeing the late cold weather, had I not accidentally run into her again, had she not survived, then perhaps my life would have . . .

It was a muggy summer night, presaging unending torrents of rain on the newly reforested land on the banks of the Hau River.

I had just arrived from the North to carry out an ironic and pitiful activity: To look for work, to find a place to stay for the remaining years of my life. Yes! I was about to turn fifty and yet I had had to leave my village in order to look for work, that's why it was so pitiful! But alas, there was no other choice! My aimless life reflected my exhausted mind. And I never intended to sit down and write these lines, for I trembled at my memories. Recount! How empty the word is! To recount is to relive. To relive those half-alive half-dead days is like dying twice! Recount! O, what a stinking job this is. And yet I have to retell, to record, as if I have been led along by some ghosts whose power I cannot resist.

I was forty-nine and unemployed. To be more precise, I had been fired. I was a reject, cast out onto the streets. I was 5′5″ but weighed less than 100 pounds. Haggard looking and showing signs of mental problems. My hair was gray in patches, my chest and belly were sunken, my eyes looked like those of a mud fish, my complexion sickly, my lips purplish, and many of my teeth had fallen out. I seldom smiled or talked and was afraid of light, noise, cities, and other crowded places. My shuffling footsteps and my half-crying, half-smiling lips revealed my broken will . . . In other words, I was just a pitiful scarecrow amidst a vast stormy field. And yet I had once been a strong man and not just a bag of skin and bones. Back then the forest on both sides of the Saigon River was full of mines and bombs. Had I not been hit in the head by fragment from a Claymore mine my body and my mind would still be whole. I had become a sick and depressed old man. But I digress. Wasn't I about to tell the story of a woman who had definitely died and yet suddenly was found alive still? So! When one grows old and decrepit, one tends toward self-pity and nostalgia.

Yes, my dear reader! I am still telling you the story of this woman. It was a muggy summer night . . . My mind is slipping. Why do people who reminisce usually begin with nighttime first? It could have been daytime, could have been morning or afternoon, and that would not have made any difference anyway . . . Perhaps it is usually with nighttime that one's memory reaches deeply. I am slipping. But had I not been troubled then I would not have stumbled into this most crowded, or perhaps second most-crowded, restaurant in the western half of the Mekong Delta. It would not have happened otherwise! As I stumbled into friends from my glorious past I realized that they were just as down and out as I was. They had mostly retreated into the countryside to rely on the support of their wives, to hide behind their wives' aprons, assuming that there were still women out there who would want to become their wives. Many of these friends were drunkards, lying around in their hammocks all day. Others worked in the fields and would gripe as soon as they opened their mouths. One guy was huffing amidst a group of dirty children and a rice bin that had nothing left in it except a handful of mildewed bran at the very bottom. Another friend was living all by himself. When asked where his wife and children were, he only lifted his bottle of rice wine and produced a twisted grin . . . Each of my former comrades-in-arms had fallen. I had missed them dearly until I saw them. But after visiting with them I was filled with sorrow for them and for myself. Most of the brave fighting men of my former brigade had been crushed by life into twisted and lonely lumps who could only be recognized by their leaden and glassy eyes. The past . . . Remembrance . . . Love . . . Everything had been buried in the dust of time. How sad! If I had known, I would not have searched out my old comrades. It only caused more pain and misery. Those forests of the past were now gone. The landscape had turned gray. And now hordes of strangers were pushing out the former inhabitants.

Among these people was our former messenger boy who was now a deputy district chairman in charge of finances. His name was Quan and he recognized me. But I didn't recognize him. Sixteen years had passed. He had been a small boy, around thirteen or fourteen. But now he was over thirty—a big man with a large chest, large belly, large behind, and a large smiling mouth. So how could I have recognized him? Such is life. Old men slow down, but the young move forward boldly. He asked me when and why I had come to the South. Why did I look so old, resembling the grandfather of our former squad leader, Mr. Hai Hung? Seeing me standing around uncomfortably, he hurried me into his car. He said that he wanted me to have a taste of the way girls in the western Mekong Delta take care of men. He said that northerners were naive and knew nothing about the finer things in life. I agreed to come along. It was quite unusual for old acquaintances to recognize each other, let alone invite each other out for a drink. I commented that he seemed to be doing well and that he behaved like an all-Indochina businessman. He said that it was an exhausting career, that he had to run around all the time like a dog on hot coals in order to drum up business . . . We chatted on as we nodded our heads. I was about to ask for news of old comrades when a blaring noise from the cassette player pounded into my ear drums and like the odor from an old secret tunnel the musty smell of the air-conditioner blasted into my brain. I was disgusted and tired. I did not want to talk anymore.

When evening fell we arrived at our destination. Eventually the car stopped in front of a huge restaurant deep in a plantation of water coconut that was crisscrossed by countless canals and waterways. How strange! As I stepped out of the car I was immediately flooded by the light of hundreds of electric bulbs and inundated with thousands of noises and sounds, suggesting both heaven and hell. I was at once overcome by a strange and nervous sensation. It was so extraordinarily strange that I had no idea what it was. So unexpected . . .

Yes! It was precisely at this plush restaurant filled with the peculiar atmosphere of the western Mekong Delta that I ran into the woman again.

Wait a minute! Before I ran into her again I met a beautiful young woman who was only half my age. She looked like a glamorous Hong Kong actress, both innocent and melancholy, like in the films of Quynh Dao. She was a bar girl. I suddenly found myself right in the middle of a huge sex bar, disheveled and reeking with the sour stench of sweat and dust.

What misery! Ever since I stepped out of the forest and stopped being a soldier I had not once been in a sex bar. I was both moved and surprised at the sight of a beautiful girl, delicious and fragrant as an ice-cream bar, hugging me and caressing me. With ethereal grace she opened and poured the beer, put food in my mouth, lighted my cigarettes, changed my chopsticks and spoons, murmured in my ears, smiled quietly, put things in my hands, leaned tenderly against my body, and oh my . . . The cold beer slid down my throat and into my chest, carrying with it the innocent but strangely melancholy gaze of a young girl whose eyes were painted with light green mascara. I drank. It had been a long time since I last drank. My entire body came alive . . . Hot and cold scented towels were placed interchangeably on my face, my forehead, my neck, and my chest. A dizzying mixture of sweet smells and sourness overwhelmed me. I sneered and then I laughed loudly. And I drank . . . The girl also drank. She drank as much as I did. Cans of Heineken beer kept popping like machine guns. Packs of 555 cigarettes were torn open. Specks of fire danced on smiling faces gleaming with fat and beer foam. We were all falling into a trance.

Translated by Ngo Vinh Long

From *Lost Armies*

Wheeler switched to boilermakers. After his fourth, John began eyeing him uneasily. The noise the college kids were making faded to a sea roar in his head. Their faces looked too young, too young. Smiles and eyes too luminous, mouths opening and closing without sense, no words coming out. A room full of ghosts. He could walk through them, into the past contained in this room, the past that had come back to cage him since the first deer had been found. Had they looked that young, acted that young, when they used to come here? Younger: Sid let them in, let them drink here when he and Dennis were still in high school. Nobody checked and Sid was afraid of Dennis. Wheeler had sat in this booth with Dennis, the night before the first pile of hacked deer had been left in the center of Concord Park. Twelve years before. Dennis had sent him a postcard then too, the same message on it.

He remembered the way he'd come back.

A smell of rotting felt from the pool table, a neon waterfall forever cooling a can of Old Bohemian, an obscenely shaped piece of driftwood over the mirror. The components of a time before the war, intact as in a museum. He let the memory of how it had been, the memory he'd come back here tonight to reclaim, unfold like a spring he'd been keeping tightly compressed in his guts.

He'd returned in the fall, on a late fall afternoon. The bar had been empty when he came inside. He'd looked around the room, searching for changes. Inside the glass trophy-filled case that once had occupied the space now held by a video game someone had clipped and taped up a headline from the *Reporter:* "Our Boys In Service."

When he'd looked closer he found himself in one of the newspaper articles stuck under it. The story about him was next to one about Dennis. The two of them were between a chicken-necked Ridge boy, who had just graduated from an air force jet mechanic's course, and Willy Looms, who had died. Wheeler looked at himself looking in the photographs under the glass. It was like seeing images in a series of mirrors — the man in his thirties he was now, looking at the face of a twenty-two-year-old looking at the face of an eighteen-year-old: two strangers who somehow, mysteriously, contained him. The face in the newspaper clipping was very young and looked thin under the white garrison cap — his slightly oversized boot camp dress blues were loose around the collar. The face of the boy staring at the photographs was young also, but his eyes were much older than they should have been. The boy stood looking at the photographs of himself and his friends and had thought that this was at last a homecoming, a finish.

Twelve years. He'd been two years at the University of Maryland by then, and though he'd come down to the country to visit his uncle Dan, he hadn't been in touch with Dennis at all. After Dennis had come to him at Phu Bai, had told him what he'd done, Wheeler allowed a distance to gather between them. Incountry he'd stopped writing to Dennis—he didn't know what to say—and after a while Dennis's letters and poems stopped coming also, as if after Trung Toan his poetry had dried up, as if he'd cut out his own tongue. There had been one final poem after their last frantic reunion in Okinawa, a sad attempt to reach each other through the bodies of whores, and Wheeler hadn't seen him since. Back in the States he'd kept track of Dennis only in the newspapers: a demonstration in New York, in Philadelphia, in Boston, finally Dennis's face staring at him in Turin-shroud vagueness from a grainy newspaper photo of the vets in their jungle clothes who'd seized the Statue of Liberty as a protest against the war's continuation. He wondered at Dennis's ability to tear open the sutures of his wounds, to endlessly relive the war on disbelieving American streets—while all he wanted to do was forget. Forgetting it meant placing all the distance he could between himself and Dennis, between himself and the abyss Dennis had shown him: he understood that his hands could do what Dennis's had. Yet when he'd gotten that first postcard—the second wouldn't come for twelve years—he'd driven back to the county as if Dennis had a wire hooked to his heart.

Twelve years ago. After he'd looked at the photos, he'd stood uncertainly in the darkness of the bar, and then Sid had come out of the toilet, wiping his hands on his hip pockets, peering at him through the gloom. "Wheeler, well, well. I should have known. Last week Slagel and now the sidekick. All the chickens have come home to roost." Wheeler watched Sid search his face for the war.

"When did you see Dennis?"

A frown crossed Sid's face. "You expectin' him here again?"

"He sent me a message to meet him."

Sid shrugged. Wheeler looked at him. Sid walked behind the bar and began to rearrange a pile of already neatly stacked glasses.

"Maybe I shouldn't say nothin'."

"Don't. Not about Dennis. Not to me."

Sid picked up one of the glasses and stared at it in the amber bar light, as if it were the most interesting glass in the world. "Hot shit," he said to it. "You both think you're hot shit. But all you did was lose a war."

"I'm sorry," Wheeler said.

The door opened and Dennis stepped inside. He was in a filthy khaki uniform, sleeves cut off raggedly above the elbows, collar rimmed with dirt and caked salt, faded areas where his ribbons and stripes had been. If a marine recruiting poster was the before, Dennis was the after, his appearance coaxed by parody: wrists bound with Montagnard bracelets, hair longer than Wheeler had ever seen it, framing his deeply tanned face, falling around his shoulders in dank, reddish-blond strands. He'd grown a drooping gunfighter's mustache: with his slitted arrogant eyes and the half-strut, half-bear shamble of his walk, he looked more than ever like a half-mad king robbed of his kingdom. When he drew closer, Wheeler saw that the flesh around his eyes was puffed and swollen from sleeplessness, fatigue.

Dennis grinned and ran his finger over Wheeler's face, testing to be sure he wasn't an illusion, then he put his arms around Wheeler and embraced him, his arms tightening. The jungle rankness of Dennis's shirt pushed into Wheeler's nostrils, and he felt himself suffocating, seized by an old panic, seized by the wild, seductive embrace of the war itself. He pulled away sharply. Dennis tilted his head to one side in puzzlement and stared at him. He immediately wanted to take it back, hug Dennis. But he didn't move, and looking at Dennis he ached for what he'd lost, what would never come again: for a boyhood of salt water and marshes, of unfettered distances, of fatherless freedom.

"How are you, man?" he asked lamely, gesturing at Dennis's clothing.

Dennis smiled, his stare still fastened to Wheeler. "Better than when I sent you that card."

"Jesus, Dennis. Cofferdam?"

"Cornball, but I figured it would get your attention. I felt like that too — come on in your green machine, extract me, I'm being overrun. They haven't been fiddle-fucking around with me."

"What did you think you'd get when you took the Statue — another Silver Star?"

"I deserved one for that, man. More than for the shit I did to get the first one."

Wheeler shrugged. "As long as you don't expect the government to feel the same way about it."

"Fuck 'em if they can't take a joke. The government plays its games and I play mine." Wheeler saw him glance at Sid, who was standing uncertainly behind the bar. "Come on, babe, let's sit."

They sat in a booth. "What's with you and him?" Wheeler asked.

"Sid's a mole." Dennis turned to the bar. "Scope him out—little pointy chin and little pointy cornholer nose and big pointy ears and his skin all gray and curdled like bad milk, like he crawled into a dark hole and rotted. See, what moles do is they crawl around in their tiny dark tunnels and listen to what people living up in the sunlight are doing. That's how moles and bartenders and pogues get all fat and sleek, that's why they're built the way they are—it's all part of nature's plan. Fuck with Mother Nature and what you get is an abortion like Sid." He bobbed his chin at him. "Look at him looking at me like he's going to cry. Don't you like what I'm saying, Sid?"

Sid came around the bar and stood, shifting his weight, his hands twitching helplessly, as if they were trying to get bigger to deal with Dennis. Wheeler felt like he should feel sorry for him. But he didn't. He didn't feel anything.

"You don't like what I'm saying, then don't listen," Dennis said. "Get out of here, mole. And if I find out anyone knows I was here tonight, I'll be back to visit you. You can bet your hairy little mole ass on that."

"You can't tell me to leave," Sid said uncertainly. "This is my place."

Dennis smiled at him. Sid stood still for a few moments, his face working. Then he stumbled into the toilet and closed the door behind him. Dennis got up and propped a chair under the handle.

"Jesus, Dennis," Wheeler said. Then he laughed. The action was pure Slagel. A new Dennis story.

"He's a fucking mole."

"Did you see the clippings he put up?"

Sid pounded on the men's room door.

Dennis went over to the bar. He drew two beers and brought them back with him. The pounding got weaker. "Yeah, I saw the clippings," he said. "The next best thing to being there. Never been in the deep shit, but he knows people who were, That's his ticket to life, man."

"And I bet you told him that too."

"Sure." Dennis was looking around the bar, tapping the table nervously, wired.

"He must really love you for it. Shit, you don't change, do you?"

Dennis turned back to him. "What the hell you going on about Sid, man? Yeah, I hurt his feelings, his mole soul. And the next time I came in here, waiting for you to come, man, and here the cops were, waiting for me."

"For what—aggravated insult?"

"They want me for jumping bail after I liberated the Statue of Liberty. The little scum bubble knew that—I told him—and he called them up."

Sid pounded again, subsided.

Wheeler said, "So fuck him."

"Yeah, the Marine Corps hymn. Hymn, hymn, fuck hymn."

"What happened?"

"What happened?" Dennis laughed. "They didn't get me." He laughed louder. "Yeah, I'm still out on bail, man. I'm so far out they'll never find me."

Wheeler laughed with him, unable to control it. Dennis the Menace. "You silly son of a bitch." He stared at the filthy clothes. "Where have you been hiding?"

Dennis looked at him. "You know where I've been, babe."

"Are you all right?"

"The charges are nothing, man. I'll beat them. Like you said, I should have gotten a medal for it."

"I didn't say that. Dennis, why did you send me the card?"

Dennis reached slowly across the tabletop and took hold of his shoulders, his arms telescoping out of Wheeler's nightmares; his wrists still circled with the Montagnard bracelets Wheeler had seen him wearing in Phu Bai, five on each wrist, one for each member of his team, one for each murder: bands, bonds that Dennis wanted to bind him with also, encompass him.

"What I am is alone, man. Alone. I want you with me, babe. The way we should have been together over there."

He stared, his eyes burning into Wheeler's head. They carried an invitation to step back into an intensity Wheeler couldn't, didn't want to deal with in the familiar, reasonable setting of the bar.

"Shit," he said. "You called me here to reenlist me."

Dennis looked at him strangely, as if seeing him for the first time. "I called you down here because I needed to see you, man. Because you came back and didn't call, didn't write, didn't do shit. Like I died over there, man. Like I was one of those dead you carried around in your green, vertical-enveloping motherfuck machine." He shook his head slowly. "Listen to me, babe. Consequences are coming down, don't you understand that?"

Wheeler felt a cold spot of sweat on his forehead, as if someone had pressed a finger on his skin and lifted it. Consequences were what you paid for carelessness in your movement through the world. For not noticing minuscule bulges or slight glints of metal or microscopic disturbances in the order of things. It was Dennis's word for booby traps and mines.

"Consequences," Wheeler said.

Dennis shook his head in disgust. "The operative word here is syndrome, babe. Syndrome. That's what they're trying to fuck me over with, put me away."

"Who?"

"All of them, man. The government, the VA, the Corps. Yeah, the USMC. Uncle Sam's Misguided Children. You Suck My Cock." He laughed strangely. "They don't like snuffies who sound off; they don't like brothers who find out they have other brothers and try to get them together. They're keeping me running, man, running. I know things, man. I was their big sneak and peeker."

"Have you spoken to anyone about how you feel?" Wheeler asked cautiously.

Dennis's face hardened. Instant suspicion, paranoia. Everything Dennis did was suddenly a symptom to Wheeler. It was a new way of looking at him that was almost a relief. His friend's sickness removed Dennis from himself, reduced him to a problem.

"What do you mean, how I feel?"

"I mean anyone who can help you."

"You can help me, man. I need a true brother. The only other one I ever had was a gook, and he's dead, he's butchered, man. And you act like I'm dead, like I got the disease of death."

Wheeler picked up his glass and stared into the gold of the beer, the play of amber light darkening the liquid like a curse of blood.

"I tried to call you," he said, lied. "But you were never in one place long enough to get hold of. And besides I didn't like the company you were keeping. How can I help you, Den? By doing what? I am your brother, nothing ever changes that, but don't ask me to be your buddy. You need money, a place to go, you want me to die for you, kill someone for you, I'll do it. But don't try to choose my path, man. What do you want me to do — with you? You want me to march with you and the other happy horse-shit vets, throw my medals away, take Smokey the Bear hostage? I don't like theater, Dennis; hell, I didn't even like the real thing. And I don't do parades, man."

"Hey, babe," Dennis said softly, touching Wheeler's hand. "Hey, man, speaking of parades, you heard that in places in Florida the alligators are returning to take back the land they were driven out of? See, there was this moratorium on shooting them, man, and they've multiplied, and now they're popping up everywhere. In this one condo development, see, the people there were woken up one night by the crash of falling garbage cans and they all rushed to their windows and looked out and saw all the pretty pastel colors from their streetlights bouncing off the scaly bodies and bulging eyes of a horde, man. This grunting, slithering parade of killers coming right up Main Street."

"Hey, Dennis, stop it."

"No, let me tell you about another parade, man, about a parade I was in last Veteran's Day, in Boston. I took this group of vets there and I asked if we could join in. The cops said no, but we said we were coming in anyway, so finally they said join, but at the end. At the end. You have to picture it, babe. Reservists in white ascots and chrome helmets, Boy Scouts and Girl Scouts and the Civil Air Patrol and drum majorettes and the sagging-gut Veterans of Wars Rumored to be Simpler, I mean the whole mythology, man, and then, limping along behind it, separated from it by a thin blue line of law and order, comes us — The Real Thing. The soldiers of the war. Stained jungle suits, missing arms and legs, wheelchairs, thousand-mile stares, stone jungle freakiness. Hi, folks. Here we are. And the cops all nervous lest we jump the Girl Scouts or something. And all the people on the sidewalks either booing us or cheering us and I couldn't figure which was worse, man, which was worse. And one woman, she has her hands over her kid's eyes and she's screaming at him not to look at us, that we weren't real, that we weren't real." Dennis smiled, his eyes gleaming in the red light.

"Enough," Wheeler said. "Enough."

"No, man, there's more," he said. "Much more. There's all the antiwar vet groupies there too, the nightmare suckers, all the corpse fuckers, yeah, they're cheering us on too, like the home team, and they don't see us either, no more than that mother. And then we go in front of the reviewing stand, near the Common, and there's some local bigwigs and a general in it, watching all this. So we had this troupe of mummers, black tights, white face, all that Marcel Marceau crap, break through the crowd there and pretend to be Vietnamese, and we surrounded them and slaughtered them, right in front of the reviewing stand, right in front of God almighty, mowed them down with our Mattel-it's-swell M-16s, ratta-tat-tat, ho hum, typical day in the Nam, everything but cutting out tongues, man, right? And suddenly there I was under the stand, screaming at the general to watch, pointing my finger at him like he's some dude 1,500 feet up in a helicopter, screaming at him to this time watch what we're doing, tell us not to do it, watch how we're blooding and bleeding on the ground, screaming at him that it wasn't mime, that it was mine, that it was Vietnam, not the *Nam*, screaming what I'd done up to him, man. And you're like a part of me and Willy the Gook would understand, I did it for him, man, did those people for him, but he's not here anymore and we need to do some-thing. Ask not what our country can do, right? Ask not what our own weak asses could do, and I'm trying to make up for the shit I did over there and what the fuck are you doing, man — you still think you're above it all, like my fucking audience and you can just come home and pretend like everybody else that you had nothing to do with it? You avoid me like I got a plague, man; Wheeler, listen to me, you did crimes too and you're the only one who knows what I did and I need you. I'm alone, man. Alone." The word burst out of his lips and hung on them like a howl, his mantra. "I'm alone. Alone."

Dennis leaned closer. His face looked unnaturally large and defined. Bulges and disturbances in the order of things. And Wheeler recoiled again, slightly, involuntarily.

Dennis looked at him and wagged his head in a pantomime of slow understanding. He smiled, the way he'd smiled when Wheeler had nothing to say about his poetry, a deliberate, terrible grimace. Wheeler couldn't meet his eyes. Dennis got up from the table, and left the bar.

After a few minutes, Wheeler had gone after him. The neon sign outside turned the Grand Pree's cinderblocks a sickly green and slapped a square of light on the black pavement of the parking lot, a spotlight that he'd stepped into. Where the audience would have been, there was only inky blackness. He called into it. There was no answer, no trace of Dennis. Moths and mosquitoes tumbled around the neon tubes, projecting frenzied shadows on the ground. The CLOSED sign glowed underneath: Dennis must have flipped it on to keep out any visitors, an old trick from when they were underage and Sid a friend. After a time, Wheeler stopped calling Dennis's name.

The next morning he'd gone out to Rector's Point, looking for him. He rented a boat at Smith's Pier and came around from the river side, landing at the mud flat that Dennis and he had always used during high school to start their forays into the marsh and forest.

He had tied the boat to a branch and splashed ashore, then stopped at the edge of the flat, looking for signs of passage. The marsh stretched on for miles to a fringing border of dark woods, a sun-pressed plain of gray-green marsh grass and tall cane reeds, its expanse broken by island clumps of loblolly pines, veined with a silver-glinting latticework of channels and ponds. He watched the blades of grass move sinuously over the plain in rhythmic waves, as if shudders were passing under them. It was absolutely silent. Here and there bright spots of marsh hibiscus burned like small white flames in the silence.

A shudder moved through him as though it had passed into him from the country. He was standing on their traditional take-off point into the jungles of their imagination, but he couldn't move. He couldn't go back into that jungle. It was a wall he couldn't breach.

He cupped his hands and called Dennis's name, over and over. But there was only silence, silence and then a sudden ink splatter of birds against the sky: a flock startled by something moving deep within the marsh.

Soon after, the mutilated deer had started to appear: reminders to Wheeler, evidence of crime.

KEVIN BOWEN

Playing Basketball with the Viet Cong

for Nguyen Quang Sang

You never thought it would come to this,
that afternoon in the war
when you leaned so hard into the controls
you became part of the landscape:
just you, the old man, old woman,
and their buffalo.
You never thought then
that this gray-haired man in sandals
smoking Gauloises on your back porch,
drinking your beer, his rough cough
punctuating tales of how he fooled
the French in '54,
would arrive at your back door
to call you out to shoot baskets, friend.
If at first he seems awkward,
before long he's got it down.
His left leg lifts from the ground,
his arms arch back then forward
from the waist to release the ball
arcing to the hoop, one, two, . . .
ten straight times. You stare at him
in his T-shirt, sandals, and shorts.
Yes, he smiles. It's a gift,
good for bringing gunships down
as he did in the Delta
and in other places where, he whispers,
there may be other scores to settle.

The Slope of Life

After the ban on playing prewar songs and disco music had been an-nounced, and some of the coffee shop owners on Tran Quang Khai Street had been arrested and taken to court for this offense, that part of the town became as deadly quiet as a cemetery. Once again, passers-by could hear quite clearly the crackling noise of dry tamarind pods tapping against one another in the slightest breeze. At such moments, as yellow leaves flew in the wind one would feel the memories of times past resurrected. The street sweeper would move her broom hesitantly across the surface of the street. And once in a while, the wind would change its direction, blowing dead leaves toward an empty coffee shop.

The owner of the shop, a woman as beautiful as Thuy Kieu,[1] gazed at the empty swimming pool now used as a dump for trash and dead leaves. The furniture inside the shop was hardly the kind that one would normally find in a real coffee shop; the two dark burgundy sofas with worn-out upholstery had probably been removed from some abandoned house, a china cabinet, made of teak and containing some dishes from Japan, re-placed the usual counter bar. Only a copy of *Echoes of the Days of Yore*, printed on rag paper, was needed to complete this collection of antiques. Near the front of the shop, off to one side and close to a cluster of La Nga bamboo, sat two customers. One, a man wearing dark glasses hardly spoke. Even when he did, his voice was so soft that from afar, one would have the impression that this other man with salt-and-pepper hair seated across from him was talking to a statue. This statuelike person was sitting with both of his legs on the seat, his arms hugging his knees, his face turned toward a bicycle that had been transformed into some sort of carrier and was now leaning against the trunks of the old bamboo hedge. In front of them, their two cups of coffee gradually ceased to steam.

When the shop owner shifted her gaze from the pool, the man with salt-and-pepper hair was still talking:

"No, I was wounded in Operation Lamson 719."

" . . . ?"

"Seven nineteen? Oh, that was the battle of Route 9!"

---

1. Thuy Kieu is the main character of Vietnam's most famous epic poem, *The Tale of Kieu* by Nguyen Du.

"Right, right! You folks called it the battle of Route 9, South Laos."

" . . ."

"I was still in Cong Hoa hospital on April 30. I had been readmitted because the amputation became infected again. I was not used to walking with a wooden leg, so I had tremendous pain. Anytime I put my left foot on the ground, it hurt so much that I couldn't keep from crying."

" . . ."

"Here it is! Oh, I forget that you can't see at all. Just below the knee. That's why I can still ride a bicycle."

" . . ."

"It was an antipersonnel mine, probably made in Communist China. You'd know it better than I do. I was told it was just this small!"

" . . ."

"Is it bigger? No wonder! I lost consciousness right after the explosion. I was really lucky that the helicopter could land and evacuate me to the hospital. When I came to, I asked to see my severed leg. And they showed it to me."

" . . ."

"Oh, nothing special! I felt a slight tingling up my spine. Mostly horrified. Or better yet, some empathy. Some strange feeling! Even though it had been a part of my body, it looked strange when severed. An imaginative writer of fiction would say that you'd hold it fast in your hand and burst into tears. The feeling was like my memory of my wedding day. Again, a writer would say all kinds of nice things about this, something like the bride and the groom would steal a glance at each other, or hold hands and walk on the shattered skins of firecrackers, or thrill at their vision of eternal happiness. All lies. I had to take care of every single trivial thing, only to be criticized by my aunts and uncles for minor details. I was dead tired. I think all of those complicated ceremonials were necessary for just one purpose: to warn the newlyweds that they must somehow hold on to each other. Anyone who has gone through a wedding day once would be so scared for the rest of his life he would never want to repeat it."

" . . ."

"Am I too cynical? Oh, perhaps I am. I am upset about losing money. When I came upon you, I was four hundred fifty *dong* poorer!"

" . . ."

"No. Thieves are swarming in Saigon nowadays, but even a thief still has a heart. No one would have the guts to deprive a disabled veteran of his meal. I have a friend who is also disabled, a blind man who earns his living by selling lottery tickets. Anyone could fool him. All you need is a crumbled, soiled piece of paper to pass as a fifty *dong* bill. Yet he never lost a cent! I lost my money because of an accident."

" . . ."

"Just before I met you. On the other side of Thi Nghe Bridge."

" . . . !"

"Oh, I have not yet told you how I earn my living. How stupid! I thought you could see my special bicycle! You would know if you could see. I carry goods for hire!"

" . . ."

"Yes, just like the carriers we used to see when we were going to school in Bong Son. But this one is modified to handle a much heavier load. Those carriers in the past were meant for tourists. Patrons, usually young female merchants, would normally sit on a bar between the driver and the handlebar. Her wares would be placed in the back, on an iron rack. Didn't we use to hear stories about those drivers! Some of them would take advantage of their position to embrace the girls, or would sneak a kiss on their hair or their white necks glistening with perspiration! They would even go so far as to compare them to a flower damp with morning dew! In that situation, you wouldn't mind even if you had to break your back pedaling uphill! Nowadays, there are 'drivers' who carry goods only. How boring!"

" . . ."

"Just guess!"

" . . ."

"No."

" . . ."

"Not at all. They're as bulky as they are fragile."

" . . . ?"

"I specialize in carrying big earthen vases. Those big ones people use to store rice or water. They are as bulky as they are fragile. I broke eight of them this morning."

" . . . ?"

"Eight. Yes, eight of them. Each costs fifty *dong*, eight makes four hundred. My fare is five a piece, from Bien Hoa to Saigon. The total . . ."

" . . ."

"How can I manage so many? Just a simple trick. When your stomach is flat, you figure it out. The trickiest part is to tie all eight of them to the carrier. A skillful driver can do it all. I had to hire someone to do the tying as I am new at this trade. I paid him ten *dong* for his skill. So it amounts to four hundred fifty *dong* in all."

" . . ."

"No, it wasn't a blow-out or a broken handle bar. I only regret that you can't see the carrier I parked at the bamboo hedge. No, you don't need a license to drive that carrier. The rear wheel was salvaged from an old motorcycle, its spokes taken from an old pedicab. The handle bar was cannibalized from a French-made Alcyon bike imported during colonial times. The pedals were made of steel tubes, seventeen centimeters in diameter, welded to the sprocket wheel. I use a hard wooden bar, one end cut into a U-shaped groove to support the frame when parked. And the pump is one people use to inflate automobile tires!"

The man in dark glasses raised his voice: "As handicapped as you are, why did you choose this trade?"

The skinny man with salt-and-pepper hair lowered his voice: "Show me an easy way then! I have a wife and four children to feed. Times have changed, and there is no easy way for an honest man to earn his living!"

"Oh, you're sarcastic again. Why not engage in a trade that doesn't need your legs?"

"Like what?"

"Sewing, weaving. Or even singing at bus stations, like many of your soldier friends are doing."

The man with salt-and-pepper hair smiled obliquely: "What song could I sing that would be moving enough for people to put money in my palms? Should I sing 'Forward March to Saigon,' or 'Ha Noi, My Hope and Love?' You know what would happen to me if I sang those songs that you hear at bus stations, don't you? Remember I was a detainee, released from reeducation camp."

"Oh, just a thought. There would be plenty of trades you could take up. You are still more fortunate than I am. You still have your sight. Sewing, weaving, sculpting, anything!"

The man with salt-and-pepper hair became pensive and quiet for a moment, then he went on, slowly:

"There are other ways, indeed! What I am going to tell you explains why I do what I do. You may or may not believe me. I don't want to engage in an easy trade, the ones normally reserved for women. I have chosen a difficult trade that requires the use of a pair of strong legs. I want to prove that I am not a good-for-nothing. Carrying goods on a bicycle requires strong legs, as you know, and you must be in good shape to be able to push the carrier up the slopes on both sides of the bridge. Even though skinny and one legged, I am capable of the work. The most difficult task in this trade is to be able to handle ten large earthen vases. I was able to handle eight."

"But you have failed! You broke all eight!"

"You're right! This is the first time that I broke my load, after six months in the trade. It was because of an automobile with a green license plate[2] that came to a screeching halt right in front of me while I was pedaling uphill with my wooden leg. I was so upset that I left the whole thing, bicycle and broken vases, scattered on the street and dragged myself to the curb. What happened was that the driver of the automobile suddenly stopped his car just as he noticed a woman signaling she wanted to buy gasoline from him. I am only a victim, not a perpetrator. I am still useful, not useless as they thought when they threw me out of the hospital on April thirtieth."

The man with dark glasses hesitated for a moment:

"We couldn't help it. We were so busy with numerous tasks at hand. There was no time for compassion. On the other hand, we could not leave our wounded in the hallways of the hospital."

The man with salt-and-pepper hair gave a quick reply:

"I already lost one leg. I wouldn't have taken up that much space."

"But you were lucky to have been airlifted to the rear by helicopter — that all you lost was one leg, from your knee down. I wish I were as lucky . . ."

The man with dark glasses felt a lump in his throat and couldn't continue. His friend became disinterested, said nothing but turned up his face. The two sat silent for a while. Moments later, the man with salt-and-pepper hair said timidly:

"You shouldn't have lost your sight!"

"Yes, if . . ."

"Was it too far away from the hospital! Or was it that you had a mediocre corpsman?"

"Both."

"Did your wife know?"

"I didn't want her to know. Moreover, . . ."

"Why?"

"I couldn't reach her even if I wanted to. It would take about a year, under normal circumstances. Please understand that communication was

2. Government vehicles are distinguished by green license plates.

not easy. On the other hand, information regarding a soldier's status had to be kept secret so as not to demoralize the rear."

Then, all of a sudden, the voice of the man with dark glasses became articulate, as if he were reciting a lesson:

"Compared to sacrifices of revolutionary soldiers who lost their lives in the war, my suffering is nothing!"

The bike rider looked at his friend with pity. He pushed the cup of coffee toward him: "Your cup is still full. Enjoy the coffee before it gets cold."

"Sure. Thanks," the blind man replied in embarrassment:

Then he slowly moved his hand on the table. Because the cup had been moved, he was about to spill it when his hand fumbled for the handle.

Seeing his friend find the cup handle, the bike rider changed the subject: "So your family has moved to the South!"

"That was our original plan. But . . ."

"But what?"

"Have you been back to Bong Son recently?"

"No."

"I wasn't at ease returning to our village after liberation. I wouldn't mind if I had become someone, but as you know, I am just a disabled person. It took me awhile to make up my mind. Knowing that I would no longer be able to see the coconut groves of my mother's land, I felt just as happy to hear the sounds of the water conveyors splashing in the Lai River, or to dip my feet in the cool water of the river of our youth. I have been wanting to be back in the village for so long. I could not afford the fare for the entire family, so I took my youngest one with me."

"Why didn't you bring your wife?"

"Oh, how much I would have loved to do that, but as I said, I couldn't afford it. My youngest one is only seven, so I can negotiate free fare for her on account of my status as a disabled person. It is good that my wife isn't here."

"My relatives had been displaced. I couldn't locate anyone. I was told they moved away first to Quy Nhon in 1972, then to other places I don't know. I was told that the coconut groves had been sheared off at their tops. I spent a night at the bus station, then left for Thanh Hoa the following morning. I didn't even have time to inquire of our schoolmates from Nguyen Hue High. Have you got any information about them?"

"Who do you want to know about?"

"Oh, that bunch of old classmates. Let me jog my memory for a moment. How about the one who sat at the end of the first table in grade seven. The boy who had a habit of blowing his nose all the time."

"That was Quang. After the Geneva agreement, he became a village chief."

"Woe, that's important! Did he incur a lot of blood debt?"

"I don't know. All I know is that after 1965, his entire family was massacred by a hand grenade tossed into his house while the family was having dinner."

The two friends remained silent for a while. The blind man continued the conversation, his voice soft again: "What about Luan? The one who took great pride in his Kaolo fountain pen, with a crystal nub."

"He became rich and owned several restaurants in Phu Cat. When American troops moved into the area, he wheeled and dealt in smuggled goods. He became rich practically overnight."

"Ah, a capitalist! And what about the bum who peed on little Ly when he jumped into the foxhole during an air raid?"

"That is Duc. We used to call him Duc Cong?"[3]

"Right. He became outraged any time we called him that. What became of him?"

"He joined the guerrillas in the early years. Back when we began to outlaw communists."

"With decree 10/59. How well did he make out?"

"I don't know. You should have better information about him than I do."

"What about yourself?"

"Nothing exciting. I moved to Nha Trang with my uncle after 1955. Went to high school and graduated with a diploma. Then I went on to college, but flunked math two times in a row. That's when I was drafted and was assigned to an artillery unit. I was wounded four times during my ten years of service. I lost a leg before I lost everything else. I was not so lucky as you."

The blind man turned up his face and asked: "What do you mean so 'lucky as you'? You must be kidding."

The rider stopped for a moment, then said: "Remember, when we were going to school in Bong Son, you had the reputation of being able to

3. Duc Cong: when the words are pronounced inversely as a pun on a person's name, the phrase translates as a pile of excrement.

commit everything to memory. I always thought, as long as someone has something to remember . . ."

The blind man remained motionless and quiet. The statuelike man was still squatting with his arms around his knees, his face showing signs of sadness. His friend spoke softly: "You don't feel well, do you? You want to leave?"

"Yes, I think we must. I have some errands to run."

The bike rider stirred his coffee with a spoon. The shop owner approached them and asked: "Would you like your tea now?"

The bike rider waved his hand: "There's no need for tea. Tell me how much I owe you?"

The blind man quickly dropped his feet: "It's my treat. How much is it?"

"Fourteen *dong*, please. Coffee is getting expensive nowadays."

"But not this expensive. I was told it would cost a *dong* a cup."

The shop owner politely explained: "Pure coffee is always expensive. Back when we were allowed to play music, it would fetch ten *dong* a cup."

The owner ran out of small change and had to give the man four cigarettes instead. Then the bicycle driver handed them all to his friend. The blind man, unaware of what was going on, groped for his aluminum cane. Realizing how forgetful he was, the bike rider earnest said: "Let me give you a ride, wherever you want to go."

"Oh, thanks so much. I wouldn't want to ride on your bike while your legs are like that. I can walk."

"Up to you, friend. See you later."

Then they parted. The blind man moved his aluminum cane to find his way out of the shop. The bicycle driver limped toward the bamboo cluster to retrieve his bike. Neither of them remembered to get the other's address.

Translated by Le Tho Giao

Do Len

When I was a boy I spent my days fishing at the Na Brook
or holding my grandmother's skirt in Binh Lam market
or catching sparrows on the great Buddha's ears
or stealing longans from the Tran Pagoda.

At night I played barefoot at the Cay Thi shrine
joined the crowds at the Song temple festival.
The white lilies smelled sweeter in the incense smoke,
the medium staggering in time with the old songs.

I didn't think of her hard life then. How my grandmother
scooped prawns and groped for crabs in the Quan field,
how she wobbled with those baskets of green beans on her shoulders
going to Ba Trai, Quan Chao, Dong Giao, cold freezing nights.

I lived between the banks of truth and untruth,
between my grandmother and angels, buddhas and gods.
I remember the year of famine and the *rong* roughly cooked.
Did I smell the fragrance of incense and white lilies then?

But soon the bombs began falling. My grandmother's house blew away
the Song temple blew away, the pagoda blew away,
the gods and Buddhas left together.
My grandmother sold eggs at the Len train stop.

I joined the army . . . traveling far from my village many years
the old river with one bank crumbling, one bank built up.
I found my love for my grandmother too late
a grassy mound all that was left.

Mother's Village, September 1983

Translated by Nguyen Ba Chung and Kevin Bowen

Moonlight

Our childhood, we had no time
to play by rivers and seas.
The war so soon upon us. In the jungle
the moon's halo, our only close friend.

Lives stripped bare under heaven,
we lived free as the wild grasses;
nothing to miss or forget,
only the moon's pure halo of relationship.

But from the time we came back to the city,
to movie houses, mirrors, and doors,
we began to believe that the moon's halo
had passed like a stranger across the road.

We thought the light bulb's filament too small
to fill those pitch black rooms;
hurried to throw the switch and saw
the full moon's halo shrink in the open window.

Tonight, I lift my face and look up
to see if anything shines,
shines as bright as the rice field,
as the ocean, as the river, the jungle.

Old round moon, so perfectly round,
look down on this indifferent one;
let your light, so calm and silent, absolutely silent,
be enough to awaken me.

Translated by Kevin Bowen

From *Chickenhawk: Back in the World*

Sundays were quiet. I read or worked on short stories. I wrote stories and thought of having them published someday. This Sunday I sat in a chair in the bedroom, reading. Suddenly my heart leapt and jerked. I sprang up, threw the book on the floor, and breathed out hard. I felt like I was dying.

"Patience," I hollered, "I must be having a heart attack." She rushed me to Beach Army Hospital, Jack in the back of the car. I took deep breaths with my face next to the air-conditioner vents.

I explained what had happened. The flight surgeon felt my pulse and smiled. Funny stuff?

"No," he said, "you've been hyperventilating."

"What's that?"

"You're accumulating more oxygen than you need because you're breathing wrong."

"Breathing wrong?" Been breathing for twenty-five years.

"Tension, maybe," the doctor said. "Next time you feel like this, try breathing in and out of a paper bag. That'll increase your carbon dioxide level and the feeling will go away."

Simple stuff. Drink myself to sleep at night and breathe out of a paper bag to make it through the day. Could be worse: just met a classmate, Wavey Sharp, best-looking guy in our class, but not anymore; his face was burned away in Vietnam.

Hughes trainers were falling out of the sky and no one knew why. Only helicopters with instructors were crashing; solo students weren't going down. No clues. The ships were found, what was left of them, pointing straight down. Veteran instructor pilots and their students suddenly dove to the ground and ended up as wet stuff in the wreckage. A guy in the flight unit who found one of these mangled messes cried about it.

An IP radioed while crashing. In the few seconds he had left on the planet he said that if you push the cyclic stick forward in autorotation, the Hughes's nose tucked down and the controls didn't work—

A few weeks later, a test pilot at the Hughes factory in Culver City, California, took a Hughes up very high and tried duplicating the condition. The dead guy was right. The Hughes tucked and stayed there, straining like a dowsing rod to reach the ground. The Hughes test pilot (wearing a parachute) tried using the opposite control—pushed the cyclic forward. Worked. The Hughes came out of the dive, taking fifteen hundred feet to recover. They sent the word back to us: don't let your students push the cyclic forward in autorotation and demonstrate the recovery to all Hughes instructors. Hoots in our Hiller flight room. Autorotations were done at five hundred feet, Pete. See it now: Peter Pilot pulls out of dive a thousand feet underground. Comical stuff.

My flight commander told me I had been selected to cross-train into the Hughes. I will fly a regular student load and learn Hughes in my off time. An honor, he said; he respected my flying skill.

Methods of Instruction again. Lineberry was gone. To Vietnam. A warrant officer pro-instructor took me out and tried to impress on me how nifty this little piece-of-shit helicopter was. Showed me the seven rubber belts that connected the engine to the transmission; claimed the system could operate even when only two belts were left. I nodded. We flew. Hughes buzzed a lot, but it was very maneuverable. I had trouble with the pedals. The tail rotor was too small and it was hard to move the tail around in strong wind. There was very little inertia in the lightweight main rotors, which made autorotations snappier, less forgiving of small errors than the Hiller. Pro-instructor climbed to three thousand feet and said, "You're supposed to see this." He cut the power and nudged the cyclic forward. Whap! Little shit dumped over on its nose. My goofy, friendly Hiller would never do that. (You can stop a Hiller on its tail during autorotation, slide backward, and then dump the nose down, accelerate, and get to where you're going—something you might have to do if you're already on top of the best spot to land—which you cannot do in a Hughes.) "Recovery is simple," pro-instructor said as we hurtled out of sky. "Just give the cyclic forward pressure, wait until the nose starts to come back up, and then resume normal control." He did that and the Hughes came out of ka-mikaze landing approach. Fun, but academic.

"Autorotations are always done from five hundred feet," I said.

Pro-instructor shrugged. "You won't be able to recover from five hundred feet, but this demonstration will make it hard to forget to keep your student from pushing the cyclic forward." Good point. Still haven't forgotten.

Two weeks later, when I finished the cross-training, my flight commander called me in again. They needed a substitute instructor in a Hughes flight—just one day. Just one day with that flight. But there was always a flight that needed a substitute. I now had a double load of work. I thought of the flight commander as an asshole.

I was having trouble at home. I drank more every night to get to sleep. I slept, but woke up exhausted. Argued with Patience—always cooked the same meals; sometimes forgot to cook at all; she wasn't sticking to our budget. Jack wanted to play.

Jack was learning to count. Sometimes I paid attention to his interests, but mostly not. He and I had a counting game. I held up my index finger and said, "One." Then I held up two fingers. "Two." And so on, until I popped up my thumb and said, "Five." He said he understood. We practiced: one, two, three, four, five. He said the right number when I added a finger. He understood. Quick-witted little guy. I held up my fist and raised my thumb. "Five," Jack said. Ah. Each finger was a number to Jack. We would have to work on this.

But I didn't. At least not very often. I didn't play with Jack enough, I didn't talk to Patience enough. I was drifting around in a fog of internalizations, talking to myself, fighting demons that kept coming back. Things just popped into my mind that I didn't want to see. I'm sitting alone in the living room at 2 A.M. I see twenty-one men trussed in a row, ropes at their ankles, hands bound under their backs—North Vietnamese prisoners. A sergeant, his face twisted with anger, stands at the first prisoner's feet. The North Vietnamese prisoner stares back, unblinking. The sergeant points a 45 at the man. He kicks the prisoner's feet suddenly. The shock of the impact jostles the prisoner inches across the ground. The sergeant fires the 45 into the prisoner's face. The prisoner's head bounces off the ground like a ball slapped from above, then flops back into the gore that was his brains. The sergeant turns to the next prisoner in the line.

"He tried to get away," says a voice at my side.

"He can't get away; he's tied!"

"He moved. He was trying to get away."

The next prisoner says a few hurried words in Vietnamese as the sergeant stands over him. When the sergeant kicks his feet, the prisoner closes his eyes. A bullet shakes his head.

"It's murder!" I hiss to the man at my side.

"They cut off Sergeant Rocci's cock and stuck it in his mouth. And the same with five of his men," the voice says. "After they spent the night slowly shoving knives into their guts. If you had been here to hear the screams—they screamed all night. This morning they were all dead, all gagged with their cocks. This isn't murder; it's justice."

Another head bounces off the ground. The shock wave hits my body.

"They sent us to pick up twenty-one prisoners," I plead.

"You'll get 'em. They'll just be dead, is all."

The sergeant moves down the line, stopping prisoners who try to escape. The line of men grows longer than it had been, and the sergeant grows distant. His face glows red and the heads bounce. And then he looks up at me. I jump out of the chair and get a drink.

I decided we should take a weekend trip to New Orleans with friends, Ray Welch and his wife. I felt excited about the trip, thought it would be the break I needed—it would distract me from my memories. Hadn't been away from the post except to go to my sister's wedding in Florida one weekend without Patience. My sister, Susan, asked me to wear my dress blues with medals. For Susan, I put on the bellhop uniform and medals. Drunk asked me, where was my flag? Loud. People all looked at the geek army guy—one of the guys losing the war. I walked away. Now, though, I'll be with Patience and my friend Ray; and we won't wear army stuff.

Missed the plane to New Orleans Friday night. Spent the night in a cheap Fort Worth hotel, laughing and drinking. Caught a plane the next morning, checked into a medium-priced (dumpy) hotel. The fun of the previous night wore thin. Wondered what I was doing in New Orleans. See the sights, Patience said. We got a cab, told the driver to take us to the sights.

Got out at an old park. Feeling bad. Held my breath because I didn't want Ray to see me breathe into a paper bag—too embarrassing. We walked to an ancient graveyard; I dropped back from the others, feeling faint. Squatted, head between knees, on the sidewalk. Patience comforted me. I stood up and walked inside the cemetery. Sank to my knees on the grass, inside cool walls, beside quiet vaults.

Made it to a sidewalk cafe as if it were a desperate mission. Sucked down whiskey, shaking. Four whiskies later, not shaking. Back to normal, telling stories. "Man," I said, "Don't know what that was all about, but I'm feeling fine now." I smiled. Ray and his wife looked relieved.

I needed to snap out of this feeling of depression. I took a Hiller out by myself one Saturday. I flew the riverbed alone, swooping from cliff tops to the valley floor and up to the other side. I felt okay in my helicopter.

I autorotated into the same place my student and I had the near-collision. Picked up to a high hover and floated slowly across a grassy ravine to a field, savoring the magic of levitation. No other helicopters were in sight. I put the toe of the left skid on top of a fence post and twirled around it. I practiced keeping the tail into the wind, hard to do smoothly. I turned around and saw a deer, a stag, bounding two hundred yards away, running to the tree line.

Dump nose and pursue. Intercept deer crossing the last clearing before the trees.

Deer veers away, leaping rocks, bushes, and ditches—eyes wide. Fly beside the running deer, alone, unaware of the helicopter strapped to me. Slide it front, facing the deer.

Deer turns. I block.

Deer stops for second, stares at the clamorous, hideous thing chasing it, stumbles backward, spins around to make an escape. No good. I'm there, too.

Deer sags, legs spread out. Chest heaves. Tongue hangs out from exhaustion. I back away, inviting it to run again.

C'mon, run! You asshole!

Deer stares, eyes glazed, immobile.

I have beaten this deer.

I'd been at Wolters for over a year. Coming into the main heliport with my last student of the day, I took the controls after the student came to a hover at the landing pad, because of the traffic. Hundreds of helicopters hovering to their parking spots made hundreds of rotor-wash storms, so the helicopters were tricky to control. The machine wanted to skitter off with every gust. My hands and feet moved the controls automatically, compensating. The Hiller hovered between spinning rotors, jittery, like a thoroughbred being led through a crowd.

Almost to the parking slot, I feel the helicopter tilt backward and immediately push the cyclic forward. Wrong. Not tilting back. I can see that, but it still feels like we're tilting back. I force myself to concentrate, ignore the feeling, fly reality. But the feeling is unshakable. Which is real? Bad time to experiment with relativity, so I tell the student "You got it" as I hover into the parking spot, student says, "I got it." Good student. Figures asshole IP is fucking with him again; probably wondering if IP will cut the power while he tries to park. Student sets the Hiller down like a pro.

Drive to the flight surgeon after leaving the student (he got an excellent grade), still dizzy. Flight surgeon impressed. No flying. They decided to watch me for a month to see if I got dizzy again. The flight commander put me in charge of our pickup truck. I drove it out to the stage fields and helped in the control towers, keeping track of the ships as they clicked in, made coffee. Gofer work. I felt horrible. No flying? That's why I joined the army. I went to the flight surgeon. Told him I felt great, sleeping like a fucking log. He believed me. I was back in the air two weeks after I was grounded.

Two months later it happened again. This time I was cruising straight and level, felt the ship rolling when it was not. My student landed, never knowing his IP was fucked up. This time I was grounded until they could find out what was wrong.

"What is wrong?" shrink asks.

"Dunno. Have a real hard time sleeping. Don't sleep."

"Do you have dreams?"

"Patience asks if I'm dreaming when I jump up at night. I dream, but I can't remember them — except one. But I'm never able to tell her this dream. I tell her I don't dream anything."

"What's it about?" shrink asks.

"I'm not sure where I am, but every morning a truck comes — "

"What truck?"

"A truck loaded with dead babies."

"You've seen this — in Vietnam?"

"No. I've seen lots of dead babies, but not loaded in trucks."

"Continue, please."

"The truck comes. I have to open the back door; I know what's out there, but I still go to the door. It's always the same. The driver backs the truck to the door and says, 'How many do you want?' He points to the pile of dead babies. I always gag at the sight. They all look dead, but then I see an eyelid blink in the pile, then another."

"That's it?"

Feeling bad; seeing it. "No. I always answer, 'Two hundred pounds, Jake.' I laugh when I say it. Jake picks up a pitchfork and stabs it into the pile and drops a couple of corpses on a big scale. 'Nearly ten pounds a head,' he says. Inside my head, I'm yelling for him to stop, that the babies aren't dead, but Jake just keeps loading the scale. Each time he stabs a kid, it squirms on the fork, but Jake doesn't notice."

Shrink watches me a while. "That's the end?"

"Yes."

"What do you think the dream means?"

"I was hoping you'd tell me."

"I'm more interested in what you think it means."

"I don't know."

The shrink sent me to Fort Sam Houston for loony tests. Fort Sam is a big medical post and the army's burn treatment center. In a hallway I saw many Vietnam veterans, kids with their faces burned off. New pink skin grafts were stretched over stunted noses. The public never saw this — bad for the war effort. I felt terrible; I was whole. Why was I here?

Diagnosis: combat neurosis. They prescribed Valium, so I could not fly. My new medical profile said: *Aviator may not be assigned to duty in combat area.* They were shipping pilots back to Vietnam every day. My new profile was known as the "million-dollar ticket" at Wolters, but I wanted to fly. Without flying, the army was a drag.

They found out I wrote stories. I told them, yes, I had many rejection slips to prove it. They assigned me to MOI as a platform instructor. I helped write the syllabus and gave lectures about being an IP. I worked with a captain, Robert Giraudo. Just the two of us ran the whole IP ground-school training sessions and had fun doing it. Giraudo eventually made major but turned in his resignation. He said the army was getting old. Giraudo was okay.

A year later, when they asked me if I was staying (I was getting near the end of my three-year obligation) I said no. The head of the MOI branch thought I was good in MOI and offered me a direct commission as a real officer, a regular army captain, if I stayed. No.

Out-process. Debrief. Gone. Leave in Volvo packed to brim. Go toward Fort Worth like a Saturday trip, but won't come back for twenty years. See helicopters flying over a butte; blink a lot.

An Old Story

We are sitting at a low table next to the wide open front door through which I can see a yard shaded by short, fruit-laden jackfruit trees and a sunflower-lined path littered with yellow blossoms. The wooden house that used to be a classroom has extra desks and benches and is too spacious for the woman and her daughter. Near the window by the front door stands a sewing machine. At one end of the room the customers' clothes make a colorful curtain, hiding the family bed. The whole arrangement reveals stability but it is sad and lonely.

The woman's appearance seems to confirm my impression. She is probably over thirty, pretty, without makeup, attractive but quite aloof, with a gaunt face, kind smile, and straight nose. Her deep eyes are full of passion but stare firmly. Coupled with a doubtful, narrow forehead, they reflect a constant attempt to judge her interlocutor. Her thick black hair is tied neatly at the back; her peasant's brown blouse is buttoned high and her fingers are dry and white. To lessen the intensity of her look, I assured her that I was not a reporter, but a man interested in the life story of a fellow countryman who came from a place I know well. When I repeat "I see," honestly for the third time, the woman's smile broadens, showing bluish lips and shiny even white teeth, and her judging stare fades.

She pours more tea into my cup, reassuring me that she does not smoke but will not be bothered by my cigarette. "I've lived among smokers. My father once burnt up two packets of Blue Bastos a day." She returns to her story that has two names I am now familiar with — Dien and Tu.

"Both were my older brothers' friends. In fact Dien was my first brother's age while Tu my eldest sister's. She didn't finish her elementary education, but the rest of us, together with Dien and Tu, went on to study at high school in town. Those who passed the junior high school entrance exam could attend state-owned class while those who failed went to private school."

"Nguyen Hoang School?" I say, to strengthen our intimacy.

"That's right. My second brother, Dien, and Tu studied at Nguyen Hoang; my first brother and I at Bo De."

"Bo De School on Tran Hung Dao street, on the way from town to the station?"

"Yes. You can still remember everything."

"Why, of course. I can even draw a map of the whole town."

"You must be my second brother's age?"

"We might have known each other. What's his name? What's he doing now?"

"He died then. I don't think you two met. He studied at Nguyen Hoang for two years, left for Hue, then south to Saigon and then back to Hue. After his first year in college he got a teaching job at a private school but joined the Liberation Front soon afterward and was killed."

"What about your first brother?"

"He was killed also. No sooner had he got his high school diploma than he joined the army and became a sergeant. He was able to come home several times but was killed even before he had a chance to marry."

"So both your brothers were killed?" Having seen literally hundreds of corpses, I felt my throat dry up with the question about the two unseen men.

"Both my brothers and my eldest sister," the woman calmly adds, continuing, "Like my second brother, she joined the Liberation Front, became a guerrilla, and was killed in my village."

"Three deaths for both sides." I try to keep my voice as calm as hers.

"I should have included my father," she goes on. "He fought against the French and sat with his radio and earphone listening to the Hanoi broadcast every evening. He was delighted when American planes were shot down in Hanoi. It's a little odd to include him though: he loved the Liberation Front, got killed by an American mine, but died beside a Saigon army officer." She pauses.

"Both Dien's and Tu's fathers fought the French. Tu's father was wounded and died several years after the Geneva Accords. He and my father were close friends. When Ngo Dinh Diem became president, they were arrested and beaten. This may be one of the reasons why my father liked Tu more than Dien. Dien's father was killed in the Resistance, his mother remarried a few years after 1954 and had another child. His step-father fought against the French too, but returned to work as a civil servant for the district government after 1954. He was ambushed and killed by guerrillas at the end of Diem's term. My father knew this had nothing to do with Dien, but he was somehow related and therefore couldn't be compared with Tu."

"And the other reasons?"

"Why my father liked Tu more than Dien? There are many: for example, Tu was motherless, gentle, and diligent. Tu was a good student and later became a lieutenant. Dien, meanwhile, lived with his mother and was the quiet and stubborn type who tried every means to dodge military service. If they failed to avoid service, they could only rise to the rank of sergeant."

"So why did you marry Dien?"

"Because I loved him," the woman responds instantly.

"Since you were a teenager?" I continued.

"When I was older, in fact; to be precise, after I failed the high school first certificate exam and became a home stitcher and then the village teacher. They seem to be my destined professions."

The woman sounded much more relaxed and confident now, apparently interested in talking about herself.

"At that time Tu had just finished his cadet training at Thu Duc. He was bolder than when he was in law school. He'd fallen in love with me, but was too shy to speak for himself; he felt so embarrassed that he avoided visiting me altogether. My second brother and I were very much alike in temperament, opposite to our father. My brother hated Tu. So did I. Well, not really 'hated' but I don't like the type of men who dare not voice their own likes and dislikes. He was born to be submissive and always tried to do his tasks as best as he could to please his bosses. The only risk he ever took was when he asked for my hand."

"Why was it a risk?"

"Don't you know? I had a bad political background — my parents fought the French, my brother and sister joined the Liberation Army? Tu's father himself was a Viet Minh follower during the French Resistance, and later jailed as a Vietcong spy. Our marriage would permanently stamp his name on the black list of the military security and cost him any future promotions. But he had at least managed to be an officer. Under Diem's term our situation could have been worse, especially as villagers. Those who were children of Resistance veterans could hardly obtain a junior high school education. As you can see, the obsession of one's so-called bad background and its impact on one's life are not only today's problems. Because of his background, my first brother had to attend a private school, which accounted for his death later. He continued his studies to some extent, but he couldn't tolerate the petty local officials who kept harassing my father, forcing him to attend 'communist denouncing classes' and then threw him into the district jail as a suspected dissident. My brother dropped out of school to volunteer for the army, insisted on becoming a parachutist because he wanted to get even. He came back home in that terrifying uniform, his eyes blood red, swearing, and uttering death threats. He confronted the local officials with a grenade and told them to leave our father alone. Then those bastards were too scared to speak and stopped molesting the old man. These things could only be done before the U.S. Army landed. Do you still remember that time? Swarms of GI's, convoys on the road, helicopters in the sky. The Tet Offensive, the campaign of 1972, the Road of Terror, refugee camps, New Life, and then Model hamlets . . . They were nothing like the former villages or hamlets that had been destroyed. Everybody left their hometown for somewhere else. Even the once cowardly militia had become parachutists. If my brother had survived, he'd have been unable to find any of his enemies at home. To tell the truth, I don't think he would have borne his grudge that long. The feeling of despair, you know; the roads littered with corpses. Only the military security maintained their black lists. That's why I thought Tu was such a daredevil. It was war that he disliked, not the high ranks, and he had kept an appropriately dutiful attitude to achieve a timely promotion. And as I said, his proposal to me, if accepted, would be devastating to his military career."

"You should have been moved?"

"I'm kind of a soft touch, so to speak, but I just couldn't stand his contradictions and his weakness."

"What about Dien?"

"There was no problem with him. Flunking the high school graduation exam, he didn't wait to take it again the following year like the others. He went home instead to work as an apprentice at his relative's rice grinding mill and soon became a foreman and mechanic. He was able to fix my sewing machine. Dien came to see me every day, mindless of my father's resentment. At that time my village became 'insecure.' Teenagers and students home for the summer, as well as the few militiamen who could only be seen in daytime, had to spend their nights in the town across the river opposite Dien's mill."

"Did Dien?"

"There was no other choice unless you joined the Liberation Army. Staying overnight at the village meant trouble with the local informers and undercover police. You would be arrested the next morning. Moreover, Dien was still trying to dodge military service."

"Didn't they know that?"

"Of course they did but they all were indebted to him in one way or another. He'd fixed their water pumps, scooters, and home appliances; he had money and was generous to all of them. So they knew they'd better keep on good terms with him."

"Was he as quiet as a fish?"

"Absolutely. Though he looked nice and mild, few could tell exactly how he felt. In fact I think he was a man of iron will. I loved and married him for such character. It wasn't a big deal for me then because he'd suddenly got drafted."

"By force?"

"Yes. It happened after the Tet Offensive. As you know the conscripts were chosen at random. The provincial police and military security would search the towns as if they were hunting beasts in the jungle. They crowded the roads, their trucks blocked all exits, and their speedboats lit up the river. Dien was caught, charged with being a communist suspect, and jailed at the provincial prison for several months before he was sent to a section of a draft center for evaders, and finally released as a private. Shortly afterward his papers were somehow mishandled and he was allowed to attend the school for noncommissioned officers and became a sergeant. That was when he was able to come home to see me again. My father was even more openly resentful of him, and I couldn't have been more annoyed!"

"What was wrong?" I must have sounded puzzled.

"On one side it was Dien. When he was working at the mill he could make much more money than all of the local officers, and their social status couldn't be compared, but Dien the sergeant was obviously inferior to them. On the other side it was my father, born at the end of the Nguyen dynasty, initially raised to become a mandarin, his Chinese was hardly good enough when he was forced to give it up. Because of his smattering of Chinese and Vietnamese he was saved from statute labor, but at the same time he was good-for-nothing: neither a peasant nor a landlord nor an official-to-be, a mass of contradictions. There were a dozen of his type in my village who'd supported the Resistance but didn't leave for the North in 1954 for fear of hardship, who often pledged loyalty to the Liberation and opposed the government, and resented the idea that any of their children would serve in the 'puppet' army for fear of losing face. They would gather together and whisper to one another over and over again that the Liberation Front would win the war in the long run. No wonder my father hated Dien. But the worse he treated Dien, the more I loved him. I told my father I would marry Dien by whatever means and must have sounded so determined that he was taken back."

"So you made up your mind just because of your father's attitude?"

"To some extent, yes. But I did love Dien and decided to be his wife at any cost."

"Didn't you care a bit about his inferiority to the other men?"

"Not at all, because, as you already know, more than anyone, I realized the foolishness of such hierarchies, like the high school graduate diploma for instance. Those who got it could become high-ranking officers; those who didn't, sergeants, like Dien. In my case, my diploma was useless. I turned out to be overqualified to be a village elementary teacher, let alone a home stitcher. And there were those who couldn't finish fifth grade but were promoted to captain or even colonel! It's an endless story. What's more, like my father, I believed in the prospects for peace after the U.S. withdrawal. As strong minded as he was, Dien could resume his study to get a B.A. or B.S. or even a law degree. Life always favors those who might be less intelligent but are strong and have luck on their side. And it would be fine if he chose to be a mechanic as he had been in the past, because he had been very good at that too. I had no doubts about his future. The other officers would be in trouble as soon as they left the army. Who would hire someone who was snobbish and bossy but good at nothing? That sounds like Tu, though he did go to college for a couple of years and was in fact better than most. This sense, coupled with my love for Dien, accounts for my resolute decision. At first my father was stunned, but soon he relented and began to haggle with me. As you can imagine, I sat patiently listening to him but turned a deaf ear to his argument."

"Did he give up in the end?"

"Yes, but in his own way, meaning he no longer considered me his daughter. He let me do everything without raising a finger; as a result, my wedding was too simple to deserve the title. But I didn't mind. I canceled all my work, left for our one-week honeymoon in Hue before we were separated — Dien sent back to his unit in Tay Nguyen while I went to live with his mother in a very insecure village. More often than not, the stillness of the nights was torn by bomb blasts from the local base, or gunshots from ambushes and confrontations between province commandoes and village guerrillas. Fire and death were no longer uncommon. I wrote Dien to tell him my plan to bring his mother south to Hue or Da Nang where it was safer, but my letter and a telegram announcing his injuries must have crossed in the mail. I put everything aside to rush to see him.

"He was actually wounded twice, rather seriously. As a result we could barely keep our heads above water with his salary, so I turned to teaching again. I was employed by a local Buddhist society to teach at a private school, and I worked as a stitcher at home. No sooner did he leave the hospital the second time than Dien got into trouble again. He broke a lieutenant's arm after the man bullied him with his handgun. I was forced to follow him from one military jail to another until he was transferred to a unit in Nha Trang. After we settled, I told him my plan to let his mother join us, but he rejected it. He didn't want to break her heart seeing his dog's life when hers had been miserable enough: married twice, both husbands killed shortly afterward, neither of her children with proper educations; Dien's half-brother was arrested once as a guerrilla suspect and Dien, who lived far away from home most of the time, could do nothing to help.

Sometimes I had the impression that he'd rather return to join the Liberation Army because 'at least they have a noble cause and something to die for.' But on the other hand, he didn't like to be called a quitter."

"What about you? What did you think?"

"I had no opinion except that I would follow Dien wherever he went. I had absolute trust in him and wasn't afraid of that prospect."

"You mean as a guerrilla couple, each with his or her own gun?"

"I guess so. In fact I couldn't think straight because I got so tied up with our daily hand-to-mouth existence in a city full of guns and soldiers. One day when he was on an operation, I received a telegram from my father telling me that my brother, Dien's mother, and his brother were all killed."

"Your second brother?"

"I read the piece of paper again and again but couldn't tell which one. My first brother was killed a long time ago; my second brother had joined the Liberation Army and gone north for further training. We don't say liberation soldiers are killed, but that they sacrifice their lives for their country. Once when I was still home, I heard about my sister's and her husband's deaths. When I managed to visit the spot, the villagers who buried them consoled me: 'They have heroically laid down their lives for our country.' My father should have used those words for my second brother, or maybe there were other implications. Too anxious to wait for Dien, I left the telegram on the table for him and caught the earliest bus home. Being a soldier, he could come back by military plane in no time at all since there were plenty of them at that time. As soon as I arrived home I realized my father hadn't meant to imply anything else but the three deaths. My village had become a battlefield for a whole week until nothing was left but a few charred remains, bomb craters, masses of steel, and, above all, the smell of decayed flesh. Bodies lay buried under the burning wood and ashes for weeks before the stink revealed them to their relatives or stray dogs. Thousands of soldiers, scores of heavy-armored tanks and jet planes had continually attacked the liberation troops there, among those dead was my second brother. The survivors who met my brother before his death told me he looked fat, healthy, and happy to see his countrymen again. Dien's mother and brother were killed by a napalm bomb and fortunately were found soon after the battle was over. Almost all the villagers had fled to another town or to the south; even if they had not wanted to evacuate, it wouldn't have been possible to stay. The battlefield was quiet but the battle wasn't yet over. Both sides were still ready to attack. The liberation troops increased their action around the area; the local region was shelled; and the local post was attacked in the middle of their afternoon roll-call. People were driven to another town and then to a large refugee camp in Da Nang, which used to be an American base before their with-drawal. Those who lived there could get rice-rationing booklets and re-ceive their rations of bread on a daily basis. My father had dragged himself there with the other villagers, so I stayed with him. He was half-dead at the loss of his three children. He knew nothing except burning one cigarette after another, repeating, 'Thieu's government can't stay long now that the U.S. troops have withdrawn. They don't have a noble cause like that of the Liberation Front whose course is clear and clean.' He said it in a low hoarse voice, partly because he had gotten so used to fear that he forgot it would have cost him nothing to speak a little bit louder, and partly because he was too tired to raise his voice. He even talked that way in front of Tu and his soldier friends. Tu was stationed near Da Nang and came to visit us every other day. They were getting along quite well with each other when I received another telegram informing me that Dien was wounded again. I rushed south to Nha Trang. He had learned about the other deaths only after being wounded, so he made me retell everything. I tried to sound as calm as possible. I can clearly see the scene in my mind as if it were yesterday. His complexion, originally dark, had become leaden gray due to loss of blood. His lips tightly clenched, his shining, calm eyes sank deep under his bushy eyebrows. The toughness I was so familiar with seemed strangely altered by his motionless figure on the bed and by his shifting look that moved from ceiling to window.

"I still remember that window, located between two patches of the dirty decrepit wall; it let me see a corner of the bright deep blue sky like the sky and stars over the Nha Trang sea in summer. The reason I remember is that I actually felt a little frightened then. Dien had been too quiet. Growing up with the war, I have witnessed all sorts of reactions to heart-breaking news, sometimes with sympathy and sometimes annoyance, espe-cially from those who were overly emotional. That sounds odd, par-ticularly coming from a woman, but perhaps I believe that people who cry too easily have a shallow heart. Consequently I rarely shed tears myself. I didn't cry then, but if Dien had shed a tear, I would have burst into tears, crying for him. He finally stirred. I was about to help him sit up but he shook his head and did it by himself. He stroked the hair back off his forehead, lit a cigarette, and smoked in silence. Meanwhile my eyes were glued to my hands on his pillow. His first words, 'So everything was over when you came back?' which was a phrase I had used more than once in my numbed and simplified story, sounded dull and dry. Then he said he would like to take a walk for some fresh air.

"All of a sudden he turned to the deads' obsequies, to my brother and how he died and whether he knew we were married. 'Your brother was my favorite,' he said as if to unburden himself. 'It's too bad we were parted early and now can never see each other again.' I burst out crying; my heart burning with love for my brother. When the news of his death was broken to me, I was just moderately moved, a normal feeling of a sister who had not seen her brother for a long time and now heard he was dead. I recalled the time we shared a room in town to go to school and the buses we took home every weekend, then the games, the books, the films, and the many other things we did together. Such memory brought tears to my eyes, but only when I heard Dien's words did I feel how terribly I missed him; it was as if my whole body were cut asunder, as if I could literally touch my own loss, painfully realizing that he was the brother closest and dearest to me, my cherished hope and pride. I seemed to become a little girl again but he wouldn't be there to come running toward me. He was dead. He was gone. There was no place on earth where I could find him again. I leaned my head against Dien's shoulder and cried as if to make up for the many times when I had clenched my teeth and swallowed my tears. Dien quietly stroked my hair."

"He didn't console you?"

"No, except for those few words."

"Only those few?"

"He might have said a little more about my brother and that was it. What I still can't understand is why I was so moved, as if he had touched me to the quick with his words."

"Dien was transferred to Division I?"

"That's right."

We have come to the turning point in the plot that leads to the next chapter, part of which I learned from the elementary school deputy head-master before I came to talk to this woman, who shared with me a common no-longer-existing town. But the turning point had eluded me then. With inspiration, and to revive the woman's memory and speed up the pace of the story, I told her what I knew and still remembered about the bloody military operations in 1971: February, Vietnamization of the war, Tchepone town, military bases, Lolo, Lizi, Sophia, Khe Sanh, Route 9, helicopters full of panicked people, and so on. She added more details: how operation forces had landed on the other side of the border and for the whole week, the Quang Tri–Thua Thien region seethed like boiling water.

"President Thieu solemnly declared the start of the operation on radio. The mass media in Hue and Saigon overwhelmed people with happy news of one side and frightening illustrations of the other on the front pages.

The operation was going full steam ahead. Day and night, the sky was crowded with helicopters and jets hovering and roaring. Along Route 1 endless convoys transporting ammunition to the front swerved off to Route 9. Following them were crowds of women from the nearby provinces who came to inquire about their husbands and had to go to the rear-base of Dien's regiment. During the last month the soldiers' wives had thronged there as if to a strange market fair; strange fair it was: no sellers, no buyers, everyone crying bitterly, waiting impatiently for any piece of news. A woman carrying her newborn baby had tried to stop an army truck to ask for her husband by throwing herself into the middle of the road. Their sounds of lamentations increased when news eventually came. Dien's battalion had left for the front with five hundred fully armed men. Seven of them now came back on the first run, literally in rags. They had run the risk of seizing a medivac helicopter to return to the base. The fire grew more violent. The water was about to boil over. Meanwhile, the Saigon radio station broadcast patriotic songs, news of victory, and praises of the operation: 'launching a direct attack on the very sanctuary of the enemy, cutting asunder the infiltration line of the Northern communists into the South, affirming the extraordinary growth of the Republic of Vietnam's Army, one of the strongest forces of the free world.' "

"Their propaganda drove me crazy. What made me more furious was what I saw on TV: President Thieu's visit to Khe Sanh to celebrate the victory and give decorations; the Marines wearing Vietcong sandals as spoils, dancing with the singers from the General Bureau of Political Warfare. In the meantime I was frantically asking for Dien's whereabouts. Then his unit sent me a telegram officially informing me he was 'missing in action' and asking me to come to receive the consolation money for the dead soldier's wife. Though well prepared, I felt it like a bolt from the blue. Something inside made me refuse to face reality. I wandered in the house like a ghost, waiting for his return. A week later I started to cry. It was the same as when I cried over the death of my second brother. When I saw soldiers come back in their coffins, I realized that it was all over. Like my two brothers, my sister, and the many other dead, Dien would never return to see me."

The woman paused, biting her lip. I silently had another smoke. "Life gradually became normal again," the woman returned to a calmer voice.

"That means I got used to Dien's eternal absence little by little and resumed my daily work except for the sewing. On one hand I had no interest in earning money; why on earth did I need it now that I was feeling deserted? I didn't go get the consolation money either. On the other hand, as a home stitcher, I had business from the soldiers. I made their uniforms and took it for granted that some would be wearing them when they were killed. On the very day after Dien's announced death, however, something awful struck my mind when I was sitting at the sewing machine. The heap of olive-colored khaki uniforms on the table looked like funeral clothes, just buried, then exhumed, and laid open in front of me. Without fear or disgust, I thought of Dien's body, shrunken and rotten in his dirty green uniform somewhere among the vast greenness of the jungles. Missing in action! When would his corpse be found? Would the metal ID card with his name, number, blood type as well as his plastic ID last so that his body could be identified? I didn't cry; I didn't want anyone to see me crying. I shut myself away from the outside world. The only person I did talk to was my father, who drank more and spoke less, and to my pupils, who all looked older than their ages. Such was the situation until the great battle in Quang Tri, later called the Summer of Fire. Division III was formed in Quang Tri; Tu was promoted to captain and transferred to this division to serve as deputy battalion commander. No sooner had it been formed than it was destroyed in a large battle and its generals and colonels ran pathetically to Hue and Da Nang. My father and I had to take shelter in a temporary refugee camp. This spacious place had unofficially become the rear-base of the defeated division. Soon after we came there, I decided to leave for Da Nang; then news of Tu's injury arrived. He had no one to turn to except us. When he saw me in the military hospital, Tu was so moved that tears filled his eyes. So was I.

"He told me about his escape from death and his visit to my house in town only to find that the whole neighborhood had been evacuated. My father joined me the following day and from then on I went to see Tu three times a week. After he left the hospital he came to my house to spend his sick leave. Then the Marines launched a counterattack in Quang Tri. Some homesick villagers managed to follow the Marines to return to their houses but rushed back to the camp, their plight worse than ever. I had gotten a teaching position at the camp and decided to stay there. Then came news of the truce, and the Four-Party Military Commission returned the POW's. I was, strangely enough, indifferent to this news. Since Dien's death I had no truck with the war. Then I was pregnant by Tu. I didn't try to hide it and turned a deaf ear to idle gossip. Who cares? Anyway, I loved my baby and anxiously waited for the moment it would come into life. I was almost thirty then."

"Ma . . . Ma . . ."

The woman and I look out into the yard. The little girl who led my way here was showing her house to the newsreporter. He sat next to me on the bus that took us to the opening ceremony of the local hydroelectric power station this morning. He was born and raised in the North, graduated from Teacher Training College but would prefer to become a reporter.

"Are you a teacher?" the reporter tries to start a conversation.

"Yes," the woman answers politely.

"He used to be a teacher," I add, to make up for my formerly simple introduction. But my "used to" has accidentally raised some doubt in the woman, and I have to say that he is a reporter. The invisible wall between them now has become insurmountable. I try to maintain the intimacy we've established anyway.

"You said you were expecting a child. So the little girl . . ."

"Actually she's not my daughter," she speaks so softly as if she didn't like the new "intruder" to hear her story.

"I found her in the street when Da Nang was liberated in 1975. She was about two years old then and was critically wounded. In fact, many passers-by thought she was already dead."

"Her parents . . ."

"They must have died in the crowd."

"How did you name her?"

"My poor girl! At first I gave her Dien's last name because I was still married to him officially. Our children, if any, would have been older than she was. When we returned to my hometown, however, I changed my mind and gave her my last name."

"Why did you do that?"

"I didn't want to hide her origin. I'll wait until she grows up to tell her the truth. You know my people: they'll do it if I don't. I also think it's the right thing to do."

"When did you learn about Dien's release?"

"The very day he came to the camp. His unit should have informed me but they didn't know my new address."

"Would you have gone to meet him if they had told you?" I emphasize the word "if" to avoid mentioning the fact that she was living with Tu then.

"Definitely," she instantly answers, but sits biting her lip for a while; her blank stare reveals her troubled mind.

"It was too late then. He was already in the camp."

"Didn't you go see him that day?"

"No, I didn't dare." She shakes her head and turns silent again. "I was afraid, not because I knew he would look down on me, which was a matter of course; I was afraid of his silence and indifference, as you already know."

"He went straight to the camp after being released?"

"Where else could he go? The Liberation Army had taken control of my village, half of the villagers were living in the camp."

"Didn't you go see him at all?"

"No, I was afraid and hesitated . . ."

"What about your father and Tu?"

"Like me, my father knew that Dien was released before he arrived at the camp but said nothing. Neither did Tu, especially when he couldn't do anything about it."

"When did you expect the child?"

"In four months."

"And when did Dien finally come to your house?"

"About ten days after his return . . ."

"Were you all taking a nap then?"

"No, we were having lunch on the front porch. I saw him walk, rather awkwardly, through the gate. He was wearing a uniform too big for his thin body, with both hands in his pockets. I was told before that he would sit drinking alone at a nearby shop so I avoided passing it altogether. I didn't even go outside. If I had gone to see him things would have been different, and I wouldn't have minded how he treated me. But I didn't, you know, I didn't. I was so overwhelmed with fear, shame, love, and sorrow that I couldn't stand facing him. Tears blinded my eyes when I left the table. I collapsed at the kitchen doorstep behind a water container."

The woman sobs. She buries her face in her hands and tries to swallow her tears. Her shoulders tremble. The reporter is left puzzled by what is happening. He nervously shifts his look back and forth from me to the woman. I already knew the end of the story.

I can visualize the refugee camp, one among hundreds of its kind at the time when the Thach Han River and other places were chosen for returning POW sites. That was where Dien had been released. The quiet man of iron will who never claimed to be a patriot wasn't killed in the Ha Lao Operation but was instead held as a prisoner of war. The local radio might have broadcast his message but the woman paid no attention to the radio. Her neighbors might have heard, but didn't tell her because she'd shut herself away from the world. They might have thought it just as well that she was happily living with Tu—apparently a better man than Dien, so why bother? Or perhaps Dien didn't leave a message, there were already so many of them; or maybe he was too proud to read a prepared message on the radio. Having given up hope of his survival, the woman didn't care about anything. Tu, meanwhile, was deeply in love with her and taking good care of her. She had heard about her husband's release only after she was pregnant by his friend. Dien would have firmly believed in his wife's loyalty until he returned home. What should a man of self-confidence do in that case? He remained silent and indifferent. If he had had power he would have tried to bend people's lives to his will. But he didn't, so he wouldn't let anyone alter his! The soldier's life and its misfortunes had dogged his heels. He didn't know whom he should be faithful to. He tried to stay faithful to himself, but what he perceived as his wife's betrayal had completely ruined him. After days of drinking by himself, and thinking it over, he'd decided what to do. The fatal day came. He tied a mine against his stomach under the new uniform, preparing himself for the coming battle. He kept his hands in his pockets to control the mine, walking straight to his wife's house. Silently, he watched her leave the dining table in tears, he looked straight into the faces of the two frightened men, then, with a look of complete indifference, exploded the mine. The blast, of course, was devastating. Thanks to the water container, the woman wasn't killed, but her baby didn't survive the wounds.

The sobs subdued, the woman looked tense again. She wipes her face and smiles shyly at me:

"I hope you weren't bothered. I feel relieved after crying, that's why I sometimes sob my heart out when I'm alone."

I look into the woman's eyes and try to convey my sympathy, but I am too embarrassed to be eloquent. Once again the woman speaks for me, this time in a pleasant but resolute way:

"I've shared my story with you because I know you understand, but let bygones be bygones. Sometimes I hear different versions of my own life but I don't care."

She pours more tea into our cups. I respect her will. The reporter will not learn anything more from me about her. He won't be able to make her an interesting character in his writing, though he will mention her in his article on the new power station built in the area. He will speak of her as a woman who had suffered a lot during the war but could settle down only a few years after the liberation and is now optimistic about her area's economy, thanks to electrification. She might read the article and agree with it. My story, on the contrary, is entirely fictitious and hence Dien, Tu, the storyteller, and the writer are all imaginary characters.

Translated by Nguyen Thi Kim Thu

Edited by Kevin Bowen, Bruce Weigl, and Edie Shillue

Returning the Missing

Boxes
smaller than bodies
returning the missing home
Dog tags
and wood
fragments of bone
All that's left
of Johnny
Jimmy
Jose
Leroy
Willie
or Jake
All that's left
of history
impassioned mystery
sundown of mistake

Parts

We saw
people
fragile as brown sticks
in black silk skin
living under
the shells of hats

We saw
rice paddies
We saw
water buffalo
We saw
snakes

I am
part snake
part water buffalo
part rice paddy

I am
part black silk skin
brown stick
living under
the shell of a hat

I am
the rainy season
I am
the dry season
I am
the red dust of the moon

Survivors

Some of us are drinking
Some of us are outlaws
Some of us are jailed
Some of us are lawmen
Some of us are high
Some of us are crazy
Some of us are gay
Some of us are bi
Some of us are transvestites

Some of us are alone
Some of us look like gods
Some of us look like devils
Some of us got money
Some of us don't
Some of us are Black
Some of us are Hispanic
Some of us are White
Some of us are Asian
Some of us are Red

Some of us are men
Some of us are women, too
Some of us got kids
Some of us don't
Some of us have killed
Some of us are still killing
Some of us need healing
Some of us give to others
Some of us take from others
Some of us still got our Mommas and Daddies
A lot of us don't anymore

Some of us are married
Some of us are divorced

Some of us have never been married
Some of us own our own cars or houses
Some of us have nothing
but apartments or rooms
Some of us sleep on vents
lay down in the biggest box we can find
Some of us have lost everything
owning nothing but what we can salvage
from the nearest dumpster
Some of us have turned to God
Some of us have left God
Some of us are cursing God
Some of us are painters, writers, poets,
actors, dreamers, musicians, dancers
Some of us are janitors, stock boys,
shoeshine boys, garbage men,
ditch diggers, mailmen, cooks,
window washers, bar tenders

Some of us see ghosts, hear voices,
wake up in the dark screaming
Some of us are lost in the maze of cities
like lab rats never finding the cheese
Some of us are blind
Some of us got no legs
or legs that refuse to work
Some of us live with old bullets
buried in the marrow of bone
Some of us are poisoned
dying little by little
Some of us got no hands, no feet,
no cock, no balls.
Some of us are shackled in padded rooms
Some of us have AIDS
Some of us are designing buildings,
making cars, managing money,
teaching school, opening stores,
buying a house, burying the dead,
aiding the physically challenged

Some of us are butchers, cops, salesmen,
con men, vendors, bankers, barbers,
hairdressers, gangsters, scientists,
lawyers, politicians, anarchists, hit men,
gardeners
Some of us are missing
disappeared in the mist of history
buried under tropic foliage
like lightning-felled trees
Some of us are ex-POW's
Some of us are fathers of Asian children

Some of us are prophets
ranting about the apocalypse
Some of us are fools
All of us are aging
Our footprints left forever
in the dusky purpleen-rose light
yellowing to amber night
We fall out of history like dominoes
tumbling into oblivion
like sideshow targets
in deer hunting season

The Examples

For my village's war widows

Time flows into the huge antique vase. Like locusts, the widows disappear one by one behind the grass. Red winds run back from the horizon and scratch at the ground. I stand on the village road, crying like a lost boy. I cannot turn over each grass blade around my country and search for them.

They have poles on their shoulders and move along ruts as if their backbones are deformed. They move in sleep through wild winds that rise up as the sun rolls its last circle into darkness. They move in sleep under prehistoric rains as dawn sits after the night fever. And I am a lunatic, standing to count them by one example.

My village widows — the examples — without shoes or sandals, they avoid roads that lead them to moonlight. Their breasts are tired and almost deaf, and could not hear love calling from the village men. And only the house mice eating rice in the casket can wake them. And they lie still, fearing their wooden coffin will be eaten hollow by termites.

Time flows silently into the huge ceramic vase. My village widows disappear behind grass, one by one, like locusts. I am a crying lunatic.

And when I have nobody to count, my village widows come back from the grass. They walk night lanes. Their hair spills moonlight. Their breasts reach for the sexual fire just kindled. After footsteps, after doors opening, I hear the strange song. The song penetrates the skulls of lunatics who cannot sleep, and who stand looking up at the moon.

And the lunatics open the doors and go out. They go with the song — farther and farther, to the place where there are no examples.

Translated by the author and Yusef Komunyakaa

Outside the Blue Nile

"Can you spare seven cents?"
       I drop two quarters into
               his paper cup,

& he runs after me, saying,
       "Man, I can't take this.
               I don't want to get rich."

I notice the 1st Cav. patch
       on his fatigue jacket. He smells like
               he slept in a field of mint.

He says that he's Benedict
       the Moor. Of course, I've
               never heard of the fellow.

Two days later, I spot him
       outside Cody's Bookstore
               & reach into my pocket,

fingering the pennies. He says,
       "I'm not begging today, brother.
               I'm just paying penance."

He goes back to scrubbing
       the sidewalk with a wirebrush.
               His black & white mutt

stands there, she guards him
       at night while he sleeps
               under a crown of stars.

I find what I'm looking for
       at the Berkeley Library.
               He was born in Sicily

on the estate of Chevalier de
        Lanza at San Fratello,
                the son of African slaves.

He sold the lumbering oxen
        he'd labored years to buy,
                gave the money to the poor,

& followed Father Lanza, pledging
        a Lenten vow. After the caves
                in the mountains near Palermo,

he went to live in a rocky cell
        on Mount Pellegrino where
                the Duke of Medina-Coeli

visited & built him a chapel.
        All the titles at his feet,
                Benedict the Moor

rejected. He couldn't
        read or write, but recited biblical
                passages for days.

Wearing just a few leaves,
        he predicted the death
                of Princess Bianca,

made the sign of the cross
        to give the blind sight. Here
                was a man who hid in a thicket

from a crowd's joy.
        The Duchess of Montalvo
                bowed often before him,

but she never saw his eyes.
        "Into thy hands, O Lord,
                I commend my spirit,"

were his last words. Three months
　　　later. I sit in The Blue Nile
　　　　　eating with my hands, folding

pieces of spicy chicken
　　　into spongy white bread
　　　　　thin as forgiveness,

knowing that one hand
　　　is sacred & the other is used
　　　　　to clean oneself with leaves

or clutch a dagger. No one
　　　touched Benedict the Moor's
　　　　　hands. Not even the Duchess.

They kissed the hem of his habit.
　　　In Palermo, the senate burned
　　　　　fourteen torches of white wax

in his honor. When I step out
　　　under Berkeley's cool stars,
　　　　　I see the face I thought

lost in the Oakland hills
　　　when eucalyptus created
　　　　　an inferno. I walk up

to him, fingering a nickel
　　　& two pennies. He says,
　　　　　"Can you spare three cents?"

Facing It

My black face fades,
hiding inside the black granite.
I said I wouldn't,
dammit: No tears.
I'm stone. I'm flesh.
My clouded reflection eyes me
like a bird of prey, the profile of night
slanted against morning. I turn
this way — the stone lets me go.
I turn that way — I'm inside
the Vietnam Veterans Memorial
again, depending on the light
to make a difference.
I go down the 58,022 names,
half-expecting to find
my own in letters like smoke.
I touch the name Andrew Johnson;
I see the booby trap's white flash.
Names shimmer on a woman's blouse
but when she walks away
the names stay on the wall.
Brushstrokes flash, a red bird's
wings cutting across my stare.
The sky. A plane in the sky.
A white vet's image floats
closer to me, then his pale eyes
look through mine. I'm a window.
He's lost his right arm
inside the stone. In the black mirror
a woman's trying to erase names:
No, she's brushing a boy's hair.

ACROSS BORDERS

It Was a Ragged Squadron

September 1978

No one wanted to cross that burnt field.
(Those silver ashes with a red spark or two from the final embers.)
You went out first and your body looked dark against the white.
Hidden in the brush, we others waited
                            until you made it to the other side,
then followed you.

I remember it in slow motion:
the sloping terrain, slippery and hot,
your hand around your weapon,
                            the stench of fire.
The sound the propellers made,
sporadic bursts of gunfire.

Your boots sank into the pliant earth
and you raised a whitish mist at every step.
(Time must have slowed down for us.)

Dionisio, all the comrades watched you,
our hearts beating uselessly
                    beneath the full moon.

Translated by Margaret Randall

Surreptitious Encounter with Joaquin Pasos

It's hard to talk to you as I deplete my energies,
It's not easy chatting, meeting you
in gas stations, in the waiting rooms of clinics and offices,
in traffic jams, Joaquinillo
      — may I call you that?

There's so much noise here: the impeccable linen of your
suits does not convince me
nor your rich boy's posturing.
                    I know
you are a sinner and Catholic, pure and immodest.
We are good for nothing, useless for anything
        but love and song.
But no one cares for love, no one needs a song.

What are we doing, Joaquin, where do we fit?
Your raucous laughter does not convince me either
and lizards make fun of us both.
Ah, how amusing, Joaquinillo, how amusing
is your broken spirit.

What inclement crossing waits for us?
All your ship's passengers are crazy
because a ship made of words
sails only on weightless seas of cologne.
I'd go to those countries of yours
   resplendent with metal trees against a nordic sun,
among good German boys made of cheese
I'd wander in your Luxembourg of tiny women
and we'd make mad love in one of the rooms
   of that hotel with the pink and gold dining room,
throw coins from our window at the Polish flutist
or gaze upon the orchestra of suicidal Gypsies.

Why do you weep for a dead fish?
Why does the body of a dead bird move you so?

I'd better go. There's so much noise here
and only busyness matters, although no one knows why
    or where we're going.
It's only fair for me to let you rest now, sheltered
    by your mortal and capital sins.
You've told me you're going to die of anguish
        at dawn one day.
You'll see, when you reach the shipwreck with your name,
        how many sighs of relief there are.
The family, relieved at last of the black or white sheep.

I'm growing deaf, can't find . . .
The parks and cemeteries are abandoned now,
a multitude of dead children look at us with sightless eyes.
Give me a sign, Joaquin, a sign for these distant latitudes.

Translated by Margaret Randall

Urgent Message to My Mother

All would be queens
and truly reign,
but none have been queen
in Arauco nor in Copan.
— Gabriela Mistral

We were educated for perfection,
so that nothing would fail and we would fulfill
our fairy princess destiny.

How hard we tried, eager to prove true
those years of hoarded hope!

But the bridal gowns grew old
and our hearts tired,
last survivors in struggle.
Into the reaches of ancient wardrobes
we've tossed the yellow veils, the wilted orange blossoms.
Never again will we be submissive
or perfect.

Forgive us, mother, for the impertinences
of presumptuous old hens
cackling the cuteness
of docile and innocuous daughters.

Forgive us for not having stayed
where tradition and good taste
directed us.

For daring to be ourselves
at the cost of all your dreams.

Translated by Margaret Randall

From *Testimony: Death of a Guatamalan Village*

Inside the Barracks

On entering the barracks, a wave of sadness and pain overtook the optimism I had silently nurtured along the way. That place of green tents and barbed-wire barricades over six feet high was even gloomier in appearance than I had anticipated; a place in which so many lives had been snuffed out had to seem no less mournful than one of the many clandestine burial sites lost among the mountains.

I felt the wings of death flutter above my head as I entered like a sleep-walker in that cursed place. I wanted to weep, but once again was stilled by the knowledge that the Almighty alone could dispose of my life.

The young officer led me by the rope to one of the inner patios, then left me in the hands of five soldiers while he retired inside to have a drink. After he'd eaten and drunk his fill, he asked to see the military commander.

"The lieutenant is dancing in the salon," the soldiers replied.

"Very well. Keep an eye on this one until I get back. Place him over there, by the pillar."

The patrol officer left me at the mercy of lower-rank soldiers who were uninformed about my background and how I got there.

One of the first to comment was a short dark sergeant whose eyes were inflamed from lack of sleep. He sneered at me and remarked aloud to the five soldiers who regarded me with a raw, vivid hatred:

"One more guerrilla they've brought us. We'll put this motherfucker away for good this very night." Before I could reply, he gave me a sharp blow in the gut that nearly broke something inside.

"Step back, faggot!" he snapped and shoved me until I was pinned against the corner pillar of that corridor. One of the soldiers brought a rope and they tied my arms down, then wound the end several times around the pillar, securing it with a large knot. They did the same with the rope I still had around my neck: they pushed my head back, banging it against the pillar, then strapped me down so that I was totally immobilized.

Once I was pinned to the pillar so that my chest jutted out, the sergeant approached once more. "All right, you shitface guerrilla. What kind of arms did you carry?"

I made no reply to his question.

Infuriated, he slapped my face and drew blood from my mouth.

"Speak up, son of a bitch, or we'll force you to talk in any case. What kind of arms did you use?"

He looked at me with so much hatred that the spittle frothed in the corner of his mouth. Despite his fury, I did not cringe, but answered him evenly:

"I don't know what you're referring to; all I can tell you is that I am a Christian and therefore respect the lives of my fellows. I believe in the Fifth Commandment. 'Thou shalt not kill.' "

"Speak up, motherfucker!" he shouted, hitting me again in the face.

I looked down and saw the blood dripping from my nose, staining my blue checked shirt. I maintained a hermetic silence.

"Look, I'll tell you what," he said. "Just give us the names of one or two of your companions, and we'll let you go."

"Senores, I've already told you the truth," I replied. "I am a schoolmaster dedicated to my work. My wish is to contribute to the betterment of my homeland."

"You don't fool any of us with your high-sounding jabber. You can rest assured that you won't get out of here alive." And they turned and went out into the street.

I breathed deeply to offset the effects of the beating and tried to keep my legs from collapsing with fatigue. It was now midnight, and my thoughts flew toward my wife and children, who would be alone in our home, worried sick over my absence. My clothes were stiff from the mud and water and stained with blood: they clung heavily to my body, causing my muscles to tense to repel the cold that bit at the marrow of my bones.

Through the open flap on one of the tents I could make out the soldiers who had been on patrol; they had changed their uniforms and were drinking hot coffee from plastic cups. I wanted something warm inside me to feel human again, but the blows by the hysterical soldiers drove even the desire for hot coffee from my mind. Never had my head weighed so heavily on my neck, as I recalled the missed opportunity for escape. I became angry with myself for falling so stupidly into death's clutches.

Weary from going over in my head what I could have done at the opportune moment, I let myself go blank and wondered how my life would end on that night of September 9. I spat out a thick glob of blood that slid down my nasal cavities, and then I remained inert, in suspension, listening to my labored breathing.

A little while later there was a change of guard in the barracks, and the soldiers who were relieved came down the corridor. They shouted from boredom and spouted profanities as they passed the pillar to which I was bound like a criminal.

The first ones to walk by stared at me with hatred and disdain and, without the least constraint, drove their fists into my chest while others struck me in the abdomen, causing me to cringe with pain.

"Too bad this chicken won't live out the night," they taunted me with hate-filled eyes, thirsting for my blood. After hitting me they retired casually to their bunks to undress, perhaps to sleep. I was horribly depressed. I was exposed to the elements and to any passing sadist with an impulse to lash out with a swift kick, a fist in the face, or a rifle butt in my belly. I felt like weeping, but I held back once more. I had to gather my strength so as not to buckle under. My bones felt cracked and pulverized from the chills that coursed up and down my body.

It was one in the morning, and I began to count ahead in my mind . . . two, three, four, five . . . sunrise. Still trusting in Divine Providence. I thought the new day might bring an improvement in my situation, unless, of course, they killed me that very night.

Time passed so slowly that 1:30 A.M. crept by, laden with my sighs and recollections of happier times. The dancing in the salon was coming to an end, for I heard the footsteps of the officers echoing in the corridor. They laughed boisterously joking and gossiping and swaggering like real he-men with beer and alcohol swelling their bellies.

And now my fear increased, for I knew these military men who were so sanguine when sober, would be capable of unimaginable bestial acts under the effects of alcohol.

To my surprise, the first one I saw was the young officer who had brought me here from the village. From a distance I smelled the beer and tobacco on his breath and recognized the self-confident smile of one who knows himself to be "a proud officer of the army."

He weaved slightly as he approached the pillar I was yoked to. "What happened, prof? Why have they tied you up like that?"

"The ones you left in charge of me beat me like savages," I said. The moderation he had shown earlier encouraged me to speak frankly with him and almost without fear.

"These stupid bastards always do the opposite of what they're ordered to," he said. "But don't worry, I'll have you set free right away." He called over a soldier and said firmly. "All right, I want this guy untied."

The soldier leaned his rifle against the stone barrier that divided the patio from the corridor and began to undo the thick knots that bound my waist to the pillar and pressed painfully against my throat.

As soon as he loosened the knots I rubbed my stiff fingers that were purple from the cold. After untying me, the soldier made an attempt to reassure me:

"Don't worry too much. They'll let you go tomorrow, because otherwise they would have taken you to the dungeon below with the other captives. They're much worse off."

"I hope to God you're right." I said.

The soldier called to the lieutenant, who had gone inside to write some messages, "Should I remove the ropes from his neck?"

"Yes, take them all off and then put him in the salon so he can find a place to sleep."

"Let's go inside," the soldier said, and I followed him like a starving and filthy beggar, eager to curl up in some out-of-the-way corner and wrap himself in trash or anything else he can find that will keep the cold from freezing his bowels. I understood then why beggars love their treasure trove of old and ragged things and why they sleep with one eye open to protect them at night, and why they guard them so jealously during the day. Whatever beggars have, beggars love. Those tattered bags full of fruit waste and rotting leftovers are precisely what I craved that night.

"Stay here," the soldier said, pointing to the cold tile floor. I sat down beside a large tin container that had been placed below a steady drip of rainwater through a poorly laid tile in the roof. The leaking raindrops did not splatter on the floor, but fell in the exact center of the tin, producing a dull monotonous sound.

The place the soldier picked out for me to lie down faced the main portal, which was kept open so that a moist, frigid draft lashed my face.

I did not bemoan my fate. At least I was still alive and had some hope of being rescued. I waited anxiously for morning and news of my wife, who would surely have made efforts to have me set free and would by now have approached influential persons in town to intercede for me.

In the midst of my whirling thoughts and hopes I momentarily shut my eyelids, not because I was sleepy, but because my eyes smarted from the cigarettes the soldiers smoked as they lay on their green bunks.

The coarse idiom of these brutes was unmoderated by the lateness of the hour. "Who the fuck took my blanket?" one of them yelled.

"Your whore of a mother," another replied.

"Shut up, motherfuckers, turds, and let me sleep," grumbled a third from a corner.

Seated on the cold floor, I reclined my back against the wall as the cold winds outside continued to blow.

Matters of the Heart

for Thomas McGrath & James Cooney

Old Tom, your rasping low voice
is so soft it's hard to imagine machine gun
bullets among the strikers in New Orleans
or the hard clubs on soft round heads
by the docks in New York City;
Jim, shuffling along with your walking stick
like an angry shepherd, kind as a good Samaritan,
first American printer of Miller and Nin:

"The deepest part of a man is his sense
of essential truth, essential honour, essential
justice: they hated him because he was free,
because he wasn't cowed as they were . . ."

"Wild talk, and easy enough now to laugh.
That's not the point and never was the point:
What was real was the generosity, expectant hope.
The open and true desire to create the good."

You rascals. What am I supposed to do?
Storm the White House? Picket Chase Manhattan?
What? I've tried it all, believe me; nothing
works. Everyone's asleep, or much too busy.

The point is: things are different now.
In the age of the MX missile and the Trident
nuclear submarine and the 20-megaton bomb
multiplied by a couple of thousand or so.
what are the odds I'll ever see
the same age you are now?

Did it seem so bleak in 1940
in that awful twilight when half the world
plunged headlong into darkness
out of the decade of comradeship and hope
while the other half stood poised to follow?

Four more decades have passed since then,
and you're still at it. The Pole Star's gone;
even the dreams we steered by only ten years ago
are gone. Where do you get your strength?

I'm tired of being swatted like a bothersome fly:
pariah, voice in the wilderness. My friends
look at me with pity in their eyes.
I want to own a house, raise a family,
draw a steady paycheck. What, after all, can I do
to change the course of a whole mad world?
I'm only a man; I want to forget for a while
and be happy . . .
     and yet your lives,
your words, your breath, your beating
old tired fighters' unbowed hearts
boom through the stillness of excuses
like a stuck clock forever tolling:

"Don't give in. Go on. Keep on.
Resist. Keep on. Go on."

Responsibility

The Congress shall have power to lay and collect taxes . . . to . . . provide for the common
defense and general welfare of the United States.
—*Art. I, Sec. 8, Para. 1, U.S. Constitution*

The sun taps on the kitchen table;
coffee boils. As birds awaken
trees beyond the window, I think of you
upstairs: your naked body curled
around a pillow, your gentle face
an easy dream of last night's love.
It's Friday; summer.

Somewhere
in another country to the south,
government troops are stalking
through a nightmare; a naked body
in the dusty street behind them
sprawls in rubbish, and a woman
in a house with the door kicked in
pounds fists on empty walls. There,
the news is always bad, the soldiers
always armed, the people
always waiting for the sound
of boots splintering wood.

What if you and I were wrenched from sleep
by soldiers, and they dragged me out
and shot me? Just like that; just
the way it happens every day:
the life we share,
all the years ahead we savor
like the rich taste of good imported coffee,
vanished
in a single bloody hole between the eyes.

Would you fix the door and go on living?
Or would the soldiers rape and shoot you, too?
Idle thoughts. Things like that don't happen
in America. The sun climbs;
the coffee's gone; time to leave for work.
Friday, payday, security:
money in my pocket for the weekend;
money for my government;
money for the soldiers of El Salvador,
two hundred bullets to the box.

From *Mother Tongue*

He stayed awake, talked to me; I didn't feel the doubts women sometimes feel when men fall asleep after making love, doubts delicate yet dangerous as asbestos fibers. Sometimes we held one another and listened to the shortwave radio which we had brought down from its place on the kitchen window sill. I remember a BBC commentator saying something about South Africa, and how his descriptions shattered like crystal wine glasses at the sound of a woman crying out in grief. But the sounds diminished as our bed bobbed away on the tide of sleep. Holding on to Jose Luis, my head pinned to his chest, I held on to the night, refused to let it slip through my hands. There were times I felt sad after making love. Intercourse often disappointed me. I could feel like a linear fitting of parts, a far cry from the creative pleasures of foreplay when we painted on the caves of one another's flesh. Perhaps it would have been different had I wanted a baby. Maybe then the act, with its audacious committing of present to future, would have touched the flaming core of my being. But I'm deceiving myself again. Lying. For a long time after Jose Luis left me I continued to believe a man could touch my essence, make me whole. All that time I could have been writing, touching the fires of my being and returning to the world, purified and strong.

You see, I was one of those women who is at her best when she wants something very badly. The mating dance, the yearning and flirting, surrenders and manipulations: I was good at that, so good at the pursuit that when I actually got what I wanted, such as a lover, terror appeared. Terror that wore the silly mask of disappointment.

Book II

I wish there were a way I could tell her. Say to Maria, you're inventing Jose Luis. And your invention may be very different from who I really am. She sees my scars and thinks I was brave for having survived. She doesn't understand that you don't always need to be brave to survive the most brutal injuries. Unfortunately (or fortunately?), wounds will often start healing even if you don't want them to, even if you would rather die quietly in the corner of a cell. The body's will to live sometimes is greater than that of mind or spirit.

I wish I could say to her, nothing I have done has required courage. When you're being shot at, it doesn't take courage to duck. Animals do as much. Me and my compañeros were being shot at so we dived for cover. And when we were not dodging bullets, we were asking questions about who made and sold the bullets, who bought them, and why they always end up in the hearts of poor people. We tried to figure these things out, to use our minds, our reason. Me and my seminary classmates are people of the book, Bible readers. Our cry has been, not by the gun but by the Word made flesh in collective action. How naive it sounds now. Like a dream of poets and mystics writing in blank notebooks in far away North America.

If there is courage to be found, maybe it is in the hearts of those who have headed for the mountains with guns of their own. The rebels feed the people, teach them to read and write. But they also teach them to defend what they have gained. That is the courage of choosing not to be a martyr. I thought I had made that choice, too, by coming here. And by day, when I am speaking to the other dishwashers about their situation, or helping volunteers translate human rights alerts, I know I am doing the right thing. Using words to educate people who have the power to influence the U.S. government. But at night, when I can't sleep, the torture starts up. I think of friends sleeping under ceiba trees or on dirt floors in cement block cells. I am tormented, wondering if I did the right thing. Or if I should be in my country, fighting. With words. Or with guns.

Sometimes the torment is so great that I turn to Maria for sleeping pills or sex or both. Sex to escape or at least to get me breathing again, to stop the cold shaking inside. And the next morning I have to live with my guilt at having used her. It wouldn't be bad if she just loved sex. But she loves me.

Or perhaps what she really loves is the idea of me. A refugee, a dissident, spokesman for a cause she knows little about, ignorance she seems to have made her peace with. She is trying to separate me in her own mind from my history. She thinks by loving the "real" me, the me before the war, she can make my memories of the war end. It is so American. The belief that people can be remade from scratch in the promised land, leaving the old self behind. I really think she believes if she loves me enough the scars inside me will disappear.

And dammit, I love her too. I love her for believing that I can be whole, for loving me even if I exist largely as a figment of her imagination. My Maria with a heart as big as this house.

She makes a big deal out of the fact that I read the Bible. She says she has "fallen away" from the spiritual life. I hate it when she talks about me as if I were half god. She won't give me the gift of flaws. And this is what worries me the most, that she wants me to save her. She talks about how beautiful our love is, how wonderful it would be if we got a little house in the valley and brought my friends and relatives up from Salvador. Any woman who talks that way a month into a relationship wants to be saved — from what, I don't know.

If I knew, I could at least offer advice. But Maria doesn't want advice. She wants a whole new self. It's too great a burden for me. It's all I can do to keep my own mind in one piece far from the knowledge that I might never return home. How do I say these things to her? Do I just let things continue until they fall apart? The warmth of her flesh is all I have to make me forget. But alcohol does the same thing. Am I using her? Or is she using me each time she looks at me and loves what is not there?

—JL Romero

Until now, I haven't had the nerve to translate one line from Jose Luis's journal. I should have just buried it. I might have saved myself the pain of having to open it up to identify the remains. Before he went away he asked me to keep his notebook because he feared the authorities could use it against him if they found it on him and pieced together his true identity. Now, all these years later, my life has come to a halt because of words written long ago by a man whose name I didn't even know. One new testament is all it takes to warp time, to call into question the neatly bound volume of trivia and revelations you thought was your history. He was right to leave his notebook with me. It has not betrayed his identity. But it is betraying mine, handing it over to be tried before a court in which I am the jury and judge.

I said earlier that I have forgiven myself; it is not true. I look back and see a woman who was naive and sad, who looked to a refugee to save her from fear: the kind that destroys, cell by cell, because it rampages undetected, unnamed. No, I haven't forgiven myself for being disappeared from myself anymore than I have forgiven him. You see, there is more to the story than I have let on, more than I ever intended to let on. All these years I have told myself that he returned to El Salvador, that the authorities found him and killed him; this was what happened to most Salvadorans who got deported. But the truth is, I don't know what happened to him.

And all these years I have avoided calling Jose Luis by his true name, desaparecido, disappeared one. My altar should have a photograph of him: the date of his birth and a question mark for the date of his death should be inscribed below his face. But I'm a coward, I couldn't bring myself to draw a question mark much less live with it day in and day out. But God was wiser. He carved that question mark into my heart and kept watch over it until I could wake up and cry out. Jose Luis disappeared. He defied the ordinary scheme of things in which one is either dead or alive and I cannot forgive him for this. And I cannot forgive myself for loving him now, twenty years too late, in ways I could not love him when I looked to him to swim out in the dark waters of my life and save me.

I have not laid hands on this story for six days, have not gotten near the paper. It has taken me this long to move beyond the resentment I feel at having told you the part of the story I had intended to keep to myself. Resentment, because in telling you—whoever you are—I opened the wound: I told myself the part of the story I had hoped to keep from myself, the disappeared part. But the unspoken words were turning into hooks, they were caught in my throat. Once a story is begun the whole thing must be told or it kills. If the teller does not let it out the tale will seize her, she will live it over and over without end, all the while believing she is doing something new. The Great Circle will come to represent not life but stagnation, repetition; she will die on a Catherine wheel of her own making.

Things began to happen: there were times he didn't call, times he didn't say I love you, nonevents that hurt in little ways, like paper cuts, but that added up. It could be these nonevents had happened all along, the normal ups and downs of relationships. But at a certain point, I began to perceive that he was pulling away from me and thinking about other things. And the fear ate at my heart like battery acid. But it's very likely that I only imagined him pulling away, imagined the whole thing. You see, the fear I am best at is always based upon a myth. It could be that the whole time Jose Luis was growing closer to me. He used to clip flowers from Soledad's garden and give them to me, stems wrapped in foil, one of hundreds of small ways he showed he cared. But all these acts took place against a backdrop of flight: the assumption that to survive, one sometimes must flee all that is loved. This is what terrified me. His body was branded with the equation, love equals flight.

Sometimes we made love in my Old Town house, the mud house the sun baked and cracked. The thick sheets of plastic I taped over my windows for winter insulation were down and the lace tablecloth I had pinned to a curtain rod could not thwart the gaze of tourists who occasionally mistook my house for a shop. So before we made love I took a length of golden cloth that was seared with red Farsi characters and tacked it to the wood frame above the window. I don't know what the characters meant. A man who sold lamp parts at the flea market had it among his wares; he couldn't say where it came from but he swore it was the color of luck. The forked letters were beautiful: The sunlight that strained through them dyed my bedroom a golden yellow; I felt I was moving through flames. In the heat and light we made love like the last two animals on earth. We struck at each other with our tongues like cobras. We twisted around one another and vowed never to let go. The fear that he would one day leave me jetted through my arteries. Fear was my yoga: it loosened my limbs and elongated my breath. It opened my third eye to the myriad possibilities of misshapen mattresses on nineteenth-century floorboards.

The silence of the golden room with its blue walls and white door frames was astonishing. At most, we whispered to one another. To try and keep the room cool we kept the door leading outside open. A sarong from Bali, the color of apricot skin and just as thin, hung over the screen; it was all that separated us from the din of tourists. Keeping quiet, we read the Braille of one another's bodies. Keeping quiet, he moved on top of me, found his way in. Afterward, he whispered, I love you. I love you, I said. I remember how those words moved up and down my thighs, how, over time, they evoked not happiness but a thrill. You see, after a certain point nothing resembling peace filled me in that room except perhaps, for the smoky gold light. No, it was all a thrill, exactly as one might feel after parachuting from a plane, joy dependent upon fear. Jose Luis's body un-clenched, he kissed my eyelids, my nose. He would have been happy, I'm sure, to rest. But I roused myself, roused him, and we had at it again. To this day I'm not sure what aroused me more — sex itself or sex the symbol, emblem of a bond all the more magnificent because it would be torn asunder. I prayed he would stay but assumed he would not, assumed he would leave me for his war or for another woman. My mother's cells had fought one another, a civil war that took her from me. When I was three, a woman lured my father from home. This story is not about them but it would be dishonest to disregard the role their ghosts played in my life, maybe still are playing: I had to make something beautiful out of abandon-ment. Long before Jose Luis left me I was using sex to weld our bodies together into a bronze statue so magnificent I knew even its shattered pieces each could stand alone.

I remember how the room used to spin after we made love. It was always the same; to staunch the strange feelings of panic I got up, got dressed, turned on the classical station, and then took down the cloth with the Farsi words. What might have been a pleasant ritual turned into a series of regimented acts. I took down that beautiful bolt of cloth and folded it like a flag. I guess it was a way to make the room stop spinning although I never would have admitted to myself that making love with Jose Luis was churning up something like chaos in me. Chaos that creates or destroys worlds, whichever comes first.

You see, real love is quiet as snow, without chaos, hard to write about. Perhaps that is why I haven't mentioned the man I have been seeing for a year: or maybe our love is just too new to have accrued meanings beyond pleasure. Our idea of a good time is bed and breakfast in northern New Mexico where he works for the state, weatherproofing houses of the low-income and elderly. When he visits here every other weekend our time together is joyful blessedly nondescript. He loves life in a way peculiar to those free of reverence for authority, who can see through its claims, its need to order and crush life. When he comes over he tells stories of how he defies the state bureaucracy, weatherproofing in ways beyond those detailed in the code book, using whatever materials are at hand. In their simplicity, his stories exorcise the inner authorities that say, quiet, don't tell, that keep women like me from speaking the truth about their lives.

The Extremely Funny Gun Salesman

When Rodrigo Huertas opened his eyes the morning of October 24, he understood in a flash that he had exhausted all of his choices save one: suicide. He stayed in bed a few more minutes and observed every detail of his wife's nude body: the still-firm breasts, the strong thighs, the silken torso he had caressed so many times with genuine pleasure. But Rodrigo Huertas had for more than two years been unable to smile, to enjoy life's pleasures; he could not even make love, for all his wife's beauty. He caressed the back and the buttocks that for so many years had aroused him, found yet again that he felt nothing, and decided suddenly, if a bit sadly, that the time had come: he must commit suicide that very day. But first he would kill her. He could not possibly leave her alive: a beautiful and sexy widow, with a fortune to squander on other men; the very idea drove him crazy. He would put an end to it once and for all: life was worth nothing.

That morning, after she had gone to work, he put his papers in order and made a holographic will leaving everything to his mother. At noon he lunched on lobster at his favorite restaurant and then went into the San Judas Gun Shop. In a whisper, even though the place was deserted, he told the handgun salesman that he wanted to buy the best and most expensive gun of them all. The salesman pointed to a nickel-plated Magnum 357 lying by itself, on black velvet, on the second shelf under the glass countertop.

"A deadlier pistol is impossible to find, sir. In the whole world, on the entire planet, there is no better gun. Just let me get it out of the cabinet and I will let you feel it. Or if you like I'll whistle and it'll come on its own. Of course, of course, sir, just a joke. Don't take offense, eh? I like jokes. Here, take its weight, feel the balance. So, are you going hunting? Need protection from criminals? Perhaps you're going to shoot your wife? Caught her with another man, did you? Of course I'm joking, sir, of course I am. It doesn't really matter to us. As a matter of fact, you don't even look like a married man. You are? But so young! What was it, an arranged marriage? You were married off when you were a boy? Ha, ha. Come on, don't be so serious. I just like to lighten up my life. Ha, ha. Here, feel it, caress it. So young — I can't believe it! Now does it feel? We have every kind of bullet, you know, even silver ones, to kill the Werewolf and Dracula. We bought them from the Lone Ranger when he retired. Ha, ha. It's very easy to clean. It comes apart in a matter of seconds. How does it feel? Oh, but don't forget its looks. I always say a weapon is the last resort, don't you think? Look how fierce it appears. Because the tiger is not as fierce as its stripes. Get it? The stripes are fiercer because they're riding the tiger. Ha, ha. That's a joke my kid told me last night. Ha, ha. The boy is extremely funny, just like his dad. Ha, ha. But around here we say looks don't lie. The gun looks fierce, and it is. It's intimidating all by itself, you know. You're face to face with a bandit and you say to him 'Don't move or I'll blow your brains to hell' and I guarantee you he'll piss himself. Because with one of the little ones, with a 22 or whatever, they look at you and break out laughing. But when they see this little animal I swear they'll fall to the ground and cry, and beg, and pray, and even recite poetry. Ha, ha. Pay no attention to me, eh? It's good to smile once in a while. This monster earns respect with her looks alone. Clothes make the gun, see? Ha, ha. And there's no better weapon for committing suicide. Look, it's very easy. In fact, the instruction manual explains how to blow one's own brains out. Ha, ha. That's a joke; I'm just kidding. You don't need instructions for that. Nothing to it. Place the barrel here at your temple, like so, and squeeze the trigger . . ."

The flash blinded Rodrigo Huertas. The gun salesman's brains splattered the ceiling and the walls and spilled all over the counter before the body, an enormous hole above its right ear, fell to the floor. When the smoke cleared and Rodrigo Huertas understood what had happened, he could not control the urge to laugh. He roared with laughter. He laughed as he had not laughed in more than two years. He laughed until he almost lost his breath, until he was doubled over, until his stomach ached and he tasted salty tears in his mouth. He laughed the rest of the afternoon at home, as he waited with a fierce desire to see his wife, as he listened to music and danced in the living room for the first time in more than two years. He opened the windows and let the sun in. And he was still laughing that night when he made love; and so contagious was his laughter that his wife laughed too, and they both laughed, and they made love laughing, and they could not sleep that night because every time Rodrigo Huertas remembered the extremely funny gun salesman he was overcome with an uncontrollable urge to laugh and to cry and to reach out for the pleasures of love.

Translated from the Spanish by Ted Kuster

Miami Beach Farmer

He awakens an hour before true dawn,
as he has on nearly every morning of his life.
Even though there are no cattle to feed,
and no ice to break on the pond so they can drink,
the atavistic instincts of 87 years
still define the man.

He lies alone for another half-hour or so,
carefully flexing his gravelly joints,
and talking quietly to the palpable presence
of the gentle woman who bore him one child, a son,
killed somewhere in Vietnam, just three months after high school
        graduation;
and who, herself, slipped away in this very same bed back in '85.

He gets up, creaks into the tiny bathroom —
reminded of the outhouses of his youth —
and voids his thin bowels immediately.
He washes his dry skin with a threadbare washcloth,
vigorously brushes his own strong teeth,
and dons a freshly starched pair of faded bib overalls and a long-sleeved
        Western shirt.

He closes the room door gently,
and makes his way down the darkened hallway
to the lobby.
The nighttime guard is asleep — as usual —
So he lets himself out the front door,
and crosses the deserted wide boulevard in front.

He buys weak and overly hot coffee in a styrofoam cup
from an angry Haitian who speaks no English
at a Japanese-owned 7–11 store down on the corner.
Then, it's through the garbage-strewn alley
for two blocks,
before arriving at his destination.

He sits down slowly on his favorite cracked concrete bench
overlooking a wide expanse of littered dirty sand.
With cobalt eyes beneath a wild shock of hair the color of January snow,
he watches the familiar sun rise
over endless waves of ripe Kansas wheat,
and waits patiently to die.

One Night in January

On a dark bitter evening in January, I found myself standing with a small group of students, faculty, and townspeople on the mall in front of the university bookstore. I was cradling a small white candle inside a paper cup, trying to prevent an icy wind from blowing out the tiny fragile flame. The two dozen or so folks huddled around me were subdued, silent, nearly stunned. No one was speechifying. No one was chanting. No one was even carrying placards.

Most of those in the little crowd were too young — thankfully — to know how to effectively plan or execute a peace demonstration. So it was mostly by word of mouth and common concern that we had gathered together that night; because once again, the United States was stumbling into a big war. And once again, some of us ordinary citizens felt angry, helpless, and disheartened.

The shock effect of America's newest military adventure was especially jarring for me, as I'd just returned the day before from a month-long trip through Vietnam, my sixth such visit to southeast Asia since serving there with the 25th Infantry Division in 1967–68. It was as a direct result of my army experience that I became a writer and teacher, and I've been actively involved in Indochina scholarship and reconciliation work for over two decades, including such projects as Vietnam Veterans Against the War, 1st Casualty Press (publishers of *Winning Hearts & Minds* and *Free Fire Zone*); The William Joiner Center for the Study of War and Social Consequence, the U.S.–Indochina Reconciliation Project, The Indochina Arts Project, and others. For the past ten years I've been a member of the English faculty at Southwest Missouri State University, where in addition to introducing and teaching Vietnam literature, I've also helped establish the Southeast Asia–Ozark Project. SEAOP's mission is the promotion of educational, cultural, and humanitarian dialogue and exchange between the United States and Laos, Cambodia, and Vietnam. For example, in 1991, I took a college film crew to Hue, where we shot a video documentary, *The Bicycle Doctors: Life in a Vietnamese Hospital.*

On every trip to Indochina, I've continued to search out indigenous written works, music, and films which I use to enhance my teaching curriculum and personal research — materials which will facilitate additional student insight into the Vietnam War, and the people, both Western and

Asian, who fought or were affected by it. I have devoted my entire adult life to the pursuit of peace and understanding, convinced that my efforts as both a witness and a teacher could make some contribution to the manner in which the new generation would think and act about war.

But while the restless ghosts of nearly 60,000 American soldiers and more than three million Indochinese still haunt shopping malls and rice paddies . . . there I was, standing with a few shivering souls in the freezing night air of Missouri, holding my small candle and wondering if my life's work had all been for naught. Since it was a spontaneous gathering, there was no rally leader, and no preplanned agenda. We stood quietly, each of us lost in our own sadness. Finally, a young coed, wanting to make some type of statement of unity and peace, but uncertain about what might be considered proper in the face of the overwhelming war hysteria sweeping the country, began to softly sing "America the Beautiful." Most of the rest of the group joined in, their thin ragged voices mostly lost in the winter wind.

It was by then rather late in the evening, and the campus was virtually deserted. However, even before the song was finished, our presence began to attract attention. At first, the few late-night passersby just glared at us, some shaking their heads as if to ward off a bad dream. One student spat defiantly in our direction. Suddenly, a bunch of girls appeared in the windows of a nearby dorm and started chanting shrilly, "Death to Hussein" and "Love It or Leave It."

Quickly, the commotion began to spread, and before long, an openly hostile crowd of young men and women — including some of my own students — started to congregate on the sidewalk across the street from our location. Some of them had yellow head or arm bands. Others were waving or were wrapped in large American flags. Many were wearing "Nuke Saddam" or "I'd Go 10,000 Miles to 'Smoke' a Camel" type T-shirts. Several were carrying signs: "War is sexy," "Kill the Ragheads," and "Screw Peace!"

At first, they were content to mutter at us, or give us the finger. But as their numbers increased, they became bolder, and their taunts became more vocal and nasty: "Pinkos!"; "Wimps!"; "Chickens!"

From my position near the rear of the rapidly dwindling peace group (which was fleeing in the face of the growing and unexpected hostility), I watched with profound sadness and incredulity. I almost couldn't believe what I was seeing and hearing. I couldn't shake the feeling that it was all just a surreal dream; some kind of '60s apparition gone mad. But I knew better.

I wanted to leave too. Needed to flee. But I wouldn't allow myself to abandon my little patch of frosty grass. Couldn't bring myself to snuff out my feeble candle. Refused to abruptly surrender my oh-so-hard-won outpost of idealism.

My mind and heart were wrenched back to the jungles of Cu Chi, and to the pale-faced young lieutenant — who was killed on his very first patrol in Vietnam, a mission I'd sent him on . . .

While fifty feet away, a college student, his face contorted with hate, yelled, "Traitors! Traitors!"

I was recalling the terrible grief and guilt I felt when writing to the lieutenant's parents about his death . . .

While just across the street, a young girl draped in an American flag screamed, "Communists! Communists!"

I was remembering the angry accusations of the lieutenant's fiancée, when I encountered her later in New York City . . .

While nearby, underage fraternity brothers swigging cans of beer, bellowed, "Faggots! Faggots!"

I was mourning the names of the 58,175 American soldiers on the Vietnam Veterans Memorial, and the 24 of them that I'd known fairly well . . .

While just a dozen yards away, a growing rabble of unruly students chanted in unison, "Cowards! Cowards!"

Even though they didn't necessarily represent the total tenor of campus opinion, at that moment, I hated those kids. Hated them nearly as much as I hated the government that had contrived a nice big war for them; and then given them the xenophobic mandate to hate Arabs (as well as fellow Americans) so openly and unquestioningly and proudly.

And just as criminal, my own nation was forcing me — once again — into the absolutely untenable position of either loving the warriors and publicly embracing their war or abandoning my soldier-students and colleagues, in the face of near-total social and academic ostracism.

Part of me wanted to wade into that mob of righteous smart alecks and try to knock some sense into them. Another part of me wanted to reach out to them with truth and history and reason. But even from across the street; even in the near-dark, I could see that either of those two approaches was hopeless. The burning brightness of their eyes and the earnest innocence of their faces told me that they were already way beyond the reach of any teacher. Despite our best intentions, we had somehow failed them; and now, although barely old enough to vote, their ignorance was permanently unassailable.

They'd never heard of Norman Morrison or Allison Krause or Thich Quang Duc or James T. Davis. Their war heroes were Oliver North and Sylvester Stallone and Chuck Norris and now, Norman Schwarzkopf. Those kids wanted blood, and they wanted it now! No Viet Cong or North

Vietnamese soldiers I ever faced were so unreasoningly fanatic, nor frightened me so deeply.

For a long time, I stood rooted to my small patch of lawn in the coldness of that January night, clutching my candle and feeling a resurgence of the rage I thought I'd conquered years and years ago.

Finally, I slipped into the shadows, and left the campus quietly. For blocks, I could still hear the mindless incantations of the still-growing prowar throng, as they echoed through the crisp night air.

And sometime during the long walk home, my candle went out.

The next morning, after a restive, sleepless night, I got up early, took a cold shower, drank two cups of extra strong coffee, and returned to campus to resume classes. Clearly, there was a lot more teaching to be done . . .

From *The Angel of History*

Surely all art is the result of one's having been in danger, of having gone
    through an experience all the way to the end.

As the last helicopter lifted away from the deck of the Manitowac and the
    ship turned

Bonsoir, madame. Je m'appelle Ellie.

A colander of starlight, the sky in that part of the world.

A wedding dress hanging in a toolshed outside Warsaw.

Bonsoir. Est-ce que je vous dérange?

On the contrary, I'm happy to practice speaking.

*Then you aren't French. How fortunate for me. I couldn't have shared this room
with a French woman.*

While the white phosphorous bombs plumed into the air like ostrich
    feathers of light and I cursed you for
        remaining there without me, for tricking me into this departure.

Parlez-vous français? Est-ce que vous le parlez bien?

So beautiful, ma'am, from here, the sailor said, if you don't stop to think.

And it went on like that all night, questions in French, and it went on,
   radiant white
      feathers along the coast of Lebanon, until Ellie Slept.

How can one confuse that much destruction with one woman's painful
   life?

Est-ce que je vous dérange? she asked. *Et pourquoi des questions?*

Because in French there is no auxiliary verb corresponding to our English
   did

   As in
Did you wait for him to come back? and Did he return from the war alive?

   Or

Did you decide in Beirut to go on without him?

As if someone not alive were watching:
Bonsoir. Est-ce que je vous dérange?

Night terrors. A city with all its windows blank.
A memory through which one hasn't lived.

You see, I told Madame about my life.
I told her everything.
And what did she say?

The Garden Shukkei-en

By way of a vanished bridge we cross this river
as a cloud of lifted snow would ascend a mountain.

She has always been afraid to come here.

It is the river she most
remembers, the living
and the dead both crying for help.

A world that allowed neither tears nor lamentation.

The matsu trees brush her hair as she passes
beneath them, as do the singing strands of barbed wire.

Where this lake is, there was a lake,
where these black pine grow, there grew black pine.

Where there is no teahouse I see a wooden teahouse
and the corpses of those who slept in it.

On the opposite bank of the Ota, a weeping willow
etches its memory of their faces into the water.

Where light touches the face, the character for heart is written.

She strokes a burnt trunk wrapped in straw:
I was weak and my skin hung from my fingertips like cloth

Do you think for a moment we were human beings to them?

She comes to the stone angel holding paper cranes.
Not an angel, but a woman where she once had been,

who walks through the garden Shukkei-en
calling the carp to the surface by clapping her hands.

Do Americans think of us?

So she began as we squatted over the toilets:
If you want, I'll tell you, but nothing I say will be enough.

We tried to dress our burns with vegetable oil.

Her hair is the white froth of rice rising up kettlesides, her mind also.
In the postwar years she thought deeply about how to live.

The common greeting dozo-yiroshku is please take care of me.
All hibakusha still alive were children then.

A cemetery seen from the air is a child's city.

I don't like this particular red flower because
it reminds me of a woman's brain crushed under a roof.

Perhaps my language is too precise, and therefore difficult to understand?

We have not, all these years, felt what you call happiness.
But at times, with good fortune, we experience something close.
As our life resembles life, and this garden the garden.
And in the silence surrounding what happened to us

it is the bell to awaken God that we've heard ringing.

Gisela Brüning

Why should I remember now? More than 20 years . . . The Paris
    Opéra! My first trip to Europe.

    In the next box: Gisela Brüning and her handsome
    blond son. Had she sensed how lonely I was —

    or just how uncomfortable, craning
    from the back of my box to see the stage?

    ". . . Maybe you would like to join us?"

They helped me over the partition (an usherette
    outside, on guard against people
    sneaking in where they didn't belong).

Her English was good; her son's
    better . . . He'd have been 16 — small for his age,
    with a tense, serious look on his pale,
    baby face; I was 24 . . .
                "From Hamburg, we are.
    My husband stays at home."

    (They resisted my attempt at German: I was
    their opportunity to practice English.)

Even from the Brünings' front-row seats, the opera was
    hard to see. *Roméo et Juliette* —
                      singers I'd
    never heard of. The soprano, "mature" for
    Juliet, wore a hip-length blond wig.
    (At least she could sing the famous Waltz.)

Our discussions animated the intermissions. Past midnight,
    lingering near the Metro, we eventually
    decided to meet next day. Gisela
    wanted Holger to see Chartres —

so we went to Chartres.

* * *

They embarrassed me, and I was embarrassed
    for them, these cultivated travelers turned
    tourist stereotype —
                    shouting to each other from
    opposite ends of the vaulted nave: f-stops and
    light-meters; which film; what scene to shoot.

(One photo they'd send — a chapel with
    burning candles — came out rather well.)

"It is good to remember such scenes," Gisela said.

* * *

We corresponded. Each air-letter had a motherly
    postscript: concerts they'd heard;
    museums she'd taken Holger to.

And the same invitation: Wouldn't I
    please visit? There was a bed for me. Plenty
    to eat. Operas. Museums. Hamburg was a
    great city: so very many fine things to do —

please do not refuse.

* * *

The following summer, I planned a trip to Greece — and a week
    with the Brünings. (They'd have loved to come
    with me: Gisela wanted Holger to see Greece.)

Would I mind? Holger had written they were
      vegetarians. And sure enough:
                      sunflower seeds and
raisins for breakfast; sunflower-seed-and-
raisin sandwiches for lunch. Bowls of
seeds and raisins on the table all day long.

      In the War, Gisela and her husband were forced to eat
      stray cats (if they were lucky to find any) —

      she could never eat meat again.

Herr Brüning was much older than his attractive,
      high-strung wife:
                    reticent, accommodating,
avuncular (more Dutch than German?); happy to be
so thoughtfully taken care of; "courtly."

      And proud of his only son's accomplishments: first oboe
      in his high school band (though too
      shy to practice at home).

Gisela took us to the museum. She loved
      the German expressionists — recognized
      where all this luxury of color

      could lead, but loved the danger
      too, the brinksmanship.

Holger followed where she led, debating light-meters
      and floor-plans (how to get "There" from "Here").

      Gisela hardly minded contradiction from such a clever
      boy who knew his own mind (even if she was never
      completely convinced he was correct) —

      they argued like sparrows.

We went to the opera. One night,
    Rigoletto: arias in Italian, choruses in German;

    once, Benjamin Britten's *Ein Sommernachtstraum* —
    a midsummer night's dream of a production (all lights
    and shadows); its sublime quartet

    of awakening lovers . . .

*   *   *

She took us to the red-light district. Young men, she said,
    should know about such things (and it was
    Hamburg's most famous attraction).

Olive-drab military barriers guarded each end of one
    narrow street:
                rows of narrow houses
    with wide, open windows; buxom women leaning down
    and out in gaudy peasant blouses (low-cut
    elastic bodices digging into fleshy chests);

    crowds of men cruising, stopping to inspect, to
    "negotiate."

We nudged and giggled, but Gisela was serious. She
    approved of this system. Men, she said,
    need to be relieved of their tensions.
                      And at least
    these women were forced to stay clean.

Holger's outspoken, enlightened mother made him blush.

They took me to meet Holger's English teacher (his favorite).
    Distinguished, dapper, his suit meticulously
    pressed — he pressed my hand, pressed
    me to return . . .
            But Gisela had every minute planned:

so many interesting things for a visitor to do.

* * *

One excursion took us to Lübeck: Bach's church; Thomas Mann's
    house;
        bathing cabinets, bikinis, and naked
    children frolicking in the gray Baltic.

Was this the field trip I have the photo from? Holger in
    lederhosen, I in my brown English raincoat;
    a deserted grassy ridge.
               We're perched on a bench,
    sitting on our crossed legs, eating — like tramps
    out of Beckett. (Gisela must have taken this picture;
    I'd forgotten she was there.)

* * *

Once, the Brünings had company: three or four
    stylishly dressed women — old friends.

    There would never have been a war, they were
    still complaining, *if it wasn't for the Jews* . . .

Gisela never commented on this visit.

* * *

Once before I left she asked what was my
    favorite food: she would make, she
    insisted, anything I liked.
               I was dying for

a steak.

Was it thirty years since Gisela had prepared a steak?
　　　　She must have cooked it over an hour (like
　　　　cat?).
　　　　　　　　I ate every leathery bite, while
　　　　the Brünings munched their healthy legumes.

*　*　*

Gisela packed me a lunch for the train: bread and
　　　　sweet-butter, raisins, fresh eggs.

　　　　We shook hands warmly (she had a vigorous
　　　　handshake: a tight squeeze, then two brisk pumps).

　　　　When I later cracked open an egg, it was
　　　　still soft (*Gisela!*), the entire compartment
　　　　laughing themselves to tears at my eggy mess.

*　*　*

Holger's letters began to arrive at
　　　　ever-widening intervals. He'd formed his
　　　　own wind ensemble (photo included); was studying
　　　　harder than ever at school.

　　　　The last one had bad news.

Gisela had bought a car, and taught him to drive.
　　　　They were touring; there was an accident (he
　　　　was driving) —

　　　　his mother had been killed.

*　*　*

I can't remember the house.

I see a big, old-fashioned kitchen: on the table, bowls of
　　　　raisins and sunflower seeds. In a cramped bedroom, Holger
　　　　sleeping soundly in the next bed,
　　　　　　　　　　　　just out of reach . . .

In one dream, I'm locked in an opera box — everyone
        singing a different language. Or I'm all
        alone:
                window-shopping in the red-light district . . .

Gisela trying to placate her reddish frizz; brushing
        the cornsilk strands out of Holger's eyes (his narrow,
        ironic smile).
                        Herr Brüning at the breakfast table:
        his pipe in his left hand — his contented,
        knowing look.

There's no car. Every day we walk to the station, on our way
        to a museum — Gisela preparing us for the morning's
        treasures:
                her arms are exclamation points; her
        voice shrills with excitement . . .

But the street is blank. The house is a blank.

Why can't I picture what it *looked* like? Why should this
        particular gap in my

        memory disturb me so?

Malebolge

The Bachelor Officer's Quarters. A Sunday morning,
   my eyes drifting vaguely
over the gypsum ceiling tiles, and over cinder blocks
   as desolate as craters.
Outside the sugar cane hisses, palm fronds clack,
   and a rainstorm darkens
a quadrant of sunlight. Next door, the junior supply
   officer has begun to stir
under his cadre of taped-up Playmates smiling down,
   an air-brushed, backlit
canopy for the boy pasha. In my room, hands behind
   my head, I am deciding
to quit the Marine Corps as a conscientious objector.

Nei-San is how it might be spelled phonetically.
   Sister or *Miss*
in Japanese, but we use it for the Okinawan maids.
   My roommate has
what is called a "ranch" and spends his weekends
   with our *Nei-San*
in a house outside the gate. How easily we all take
   to the minor pleasures
of empire: *Nei-Sans* to Brasso our belt buckles, to wash
   and starch our uniforms,
to spit-polish our boots. Our presence helps, we are told,
   "the local economy."

In the morning when we leave for our work, the *Nei-Sans*
   are setting up, squatting
near the soapy showers, their hot-plates lit, tea water
   simmering, and Ryukyuan
radio music tuned in. A hard, flattening light pours in
   onto a faded tatami.
I want to linger behind and listen to their jokes about us,
   the young lieutenant-sans.

In Book VI of the *Iliad*, Adrestos falls to Menelaos.
  Wrapping his arms
around the wronged king's knees, Adrestos begs for his life,
  and Menelaos wavers
but as the gods would have it, Agamemnon discovers them
  and rebukes his brother
for softness bordering on the feminine. Then he spears
  Adrestos in the belly,
and as he withdraws the blade, sets his foot on the man's
  ribs for leverage,
saying not even children in the womb are to be spared.
  I dream I am under arms,
helmeted in bronze, with a raised horsehair plume.
  My enemy wrestles me
into submission, and I bite him full on the calf.
  His blood wells up
like a spring, tasting like smoke and quicksilver.
  I sip it and do not die.

The strangest moment in the *Inferno:* when Dante's arms
  are wrapped around
the shoulders of Virgil, who is himself climbing down
  the coarse-haired flank
of Satan, whose enormous body is locked in a lake of ice.
  Suddenly Virgil seems
to be climbing back up, and Dante is bewildered,
  terrified as a child,
and needs to be told they have just passed through
  the core of the fallen
world and they are now hand over hand on their way
  to the earth's other side.

In Tengan, in Camp Smedley T. Butler, named after
  a general who in disgust
at the "banana wars" turned in his medals and quit;
  on a thickly flowered,
half-jungle hillside overlooking the Brig and a sea
  of sugar cane the escapees
loved like life itself; in a white blockhouse, on a spartan
  single bed, in skivvies

and flip-flops, I ask myself again what *would* I
    be willing to trade,
what part of my body, how much of my life would I pay
    for one poem, one true
line about this war. Then a voice not quite my own,
    but close to my face

and as if behind a wire mesh wonders just how grand,
    how filled with epiphany
the poem would have to be if the cost was an arm or more
    belonging to another?

Ganesh, son of Shiva and Parvati, has a pot-bellied
    human torso and an
elephant's head. Beloved by all, he blesses beginnings
    businesses, marriages,
births. He is also the patron of writers, an inspirer
    of epic poems.
He might as a series of small tremors step through me
    when he rises out
of the cane fields into clouds swollen with rainwater
    from the east.
I wish I could seek his protection in the months it will
    take me to get out.
He would set my penance at twenty years of silence,
    my words curling up
like leaves and blowing away. But even if this were so,
    I would still claim
the quick, half-audible "no" I said out loud was mine.

Okinawa, 1970

We're Substance Now and Time

If I have spoken about something
beyond
the violations
of childhood,
if I have been something
more than
one of the *wretched*
unloading his insolent shadows,
it's likely because out of the sun's glare
of the '60s one among many
said a word one day.
He said it to no one.
He said it to everyone
and everything came together,
then everything was different.
In this way the man
I know best
gained sharpness and courage,
and I also
made a covenant with the new acts
of the men and women
of mirrors and light.

We're substance now and time,
because it's the transparent weight
of ourselves,
and not History by itself alone
that marks
a different direction of the air,
different roads.

Translated by James Hoggard

From *Scene from the Movie* Giant

FIGHT SCENE: FINAL FRAMES

. . . And now it must end. Sarge with too much muscle,
Too much brawn against Bick Benedict with his half-idea
To stay alive in the fight, but his shoulders, all down
To his arms, can no longer contend to come back, cannot
Intercept the wallop that up-vaults him over the counter,

As over a line in a house divided at heart. He steadies
Himself upward, all sense of being there gone, to meet
Sarge (*upward shooting-angle*), standing with fists
Cocked to strike and he does, once more and again. You
Can see and can hear Rock Hudson's daughter give out a

Long-suffering cry, "Daaaddyyy!," and for Sarge to "leave
Him Alooonnne!" But in a wrath like this there can be no
Pity upon the earth, as the blows come harder from Sarge
Like a fever in him. Then it happens: Sarge's one last,
Vital, round-arm punch, one just measure of power, turning

The concept of struggle around. The earth, finally, is
Cleared of goodness when Rock Hudson is driven to the
Rugged floor and does not rise, his wife, Elizabeth
Taylor (Leslie), kneeling to be with his half-life,
Illuminated body and heartbeat. Whose heartbeat? Whose

Strength must be summoned to make his graceful body
Arise? Who shall come forth and be followed? What
Name do I give thoughts that collapse through each
Other? When may I learn strongly to act, who am caught
In this light like a still photograph? Can two fighters

Bring out a third? To live, must I learn how to die?
Sarge stands alone now, with all the atoms of his power
Still wanting to beat the air, stands in glory like a
Law that stands for other laws. It remains with me:
That a victory is not over until you turn it into words;

That a victor of his kind must legitimize his fists
Always, so he rips from the wall a sign, like a writ
Revealed tossed down to the strained chest of Rock Hudson.
And what he said unto him, he said like a pulpit preacher
Who knows only the unfriendly parts of the Bible,

After all, Sarge is not a Christian name. The camera
Zooms in:

> WE RESERVE
> THE RIGHT
> TO REFUSE SERVICE
> TO ANYONE

In the dream-work of the scene, as it is in memory, or
In a pattern with a beginning and an end only to begin
Again, timing is everything. Dissolve and the music ends.

The Other Alamo

San Antonio, Texas, 1990

In the Crockett Hotel dining room,
a chalk-faced man in medaled uniform
growls a prayer
at the head of the veterans' table.
Throughout the map of this saint-hungry city,
hands strain for the touch of shrines,
genuflection before cannon and memorial plaque,
grasping the talisman of Bowie knife replica
at the souvenir shop, visitors
in white biblical quote T-shirts.

The stones in the walls are smaller
than the fists of Texas martyrs;
their cavernous mouths could drink the canal to mud.
The Daughters of the Republic
print brochures dancing with Mexican demons,
Santa Anna's leg still hopping
to conjunto accordions.
The lawyers who conquered farmland
by scratching on parchment in an oil lamp haze,
the cotton growers who kept the time
of Mexican peasant lives dangling from their watch chains,
the vigilantes hooded like blind angels
hunting with torches for men the color of night,
gathering at church, the capitol, or the porch
for a century all said this: Alamo.

In 1949, thee boys
in Air Force dress khaki
ignored the whites-only sign
at the diner by the bus station:
A soldier from Baltimore, who heard nigger sung here
more often than his name, but would not glance away;

another blond and solemn as his Tennessee
of whitewashed spires;
another from distant Puerto Rico, cap tipped at an angle
in a country where brown skin
could be boiled for the leather of a vigilante's wallet.

The waitress squinted a glare and refused their contamination,
the manager lost his crewcut politeness
and blustered about local customs,
the police, with surrounding faces,
jeered about tacos and senoritas
on the Mexican side of town.
"We're not leaving," they said,
and hunched at their stools
till the manager ordered the cook,
sweat-burnished black man unable to hide his grin,
to slide cheeseburgers on plates
across the counter.
"We're not hungry," they said,
and left a week's pay for the cook.
One was my father; his word for fury
is Texas.

This afternoon, the heat clouds the air like bothered gnats.
The lunch counter was wrecked for the dump years ago.
In the newspapers, a report of vandals
scarring the wooden doors
of the Alamo
in black streaks of fire.

Them

They sit in a circle, a semi-
circle, as if onstage, and you
are the audience, watching them beat
their drums in the dim light.

They dance in a circle, a shrinking
circle, their skins glisten, and you
are the victim tied to a stake, the center
they circle, shifting their thick spears.

Of course they do not speak
to you, but they know something you
don't know, a deeper dark you'd like
to know, you in your circle, shrunk

with fear, beating your tiny drum
drum drum (they slink, they crouch,
they huddle, they jump) and what
they know is you, is us: they bear

our weapons, they carry our fears,
another country but distance
is nothing, no one, the country
they are is difference, someone

or other, you or they — curtain
down, houselights on, we sit
in a circle, our hands our drums, we
are center, circumference, everyone.

Rain

In the rain, the bark of the plane trees shines
in the colors, the shapes of camouflage:
trees looking like men looking like trees.

When the sun shines, the trees shade
the grass a darker green, the thick veins
of giant leaves, a giant's hands —

Terrain with deep cracks, that old puzzle —

In California, it rained on the queen
and the president, it rained on the good
and the bad, it rained on me.

In the jungle, it rained, it has rained,
it rains on bodies fallen
like leaves, on bodies that walk —

In the rain, the shadows disappear.

In a larger rain, things are lost.

In the largest rains, borders emerge —

A puzzle coming apart, becoming the world.

The Border

Hasta luego and over you go and it's not
serapes, the big sombreros, not even coyotes,
rivers and hills, though that's more like it, towers
with guards, Stop! or we shoot and they do but you don't
need a border for that, a fence will do, a black
boy stuck to its wire like a leaf, a happy gun
in the thick pink hand that wags from the sleeve, even
a street, the other side, a door, a skin, give
me a hand, and she gives him a hand, she gives him both
her hands, the bones of her back are cracking, the string
has snapped, she's falling, she's pleated paper, paper
is spreading and there you are again, over
the edge, you open your hands and what have you got
but confetti and what can you do with confetti, our
side won, a celebration, shaken hands, it matters
now, whatever it is, but how close
you are, your street, the fence behind your house
is the zero border where minus begins, roots
turn branches, cellar is house, you close your busy
mouth to speak, an anti-lamp darkens
the day, and you love that street, its crazy traffic,
you climb that fence, you wave across, there's a rock
in your hand but it's not your fault, you like to travel,
the colorful people, but what if you fell, your house,
your children, the work that gets you up in the morning,
the language gone, the grammar, the rules, the family
talent, those searching eyes, but think of the absence
of eye, a higher tower, a little more wire —
Border? You crossed the border hours ago.

What Makes Us Think We Are Only Here

Gallery Talk, 1994

What is it that I'm going to do? I'm going to dredge up my life. As I traveled here today, I went back to my diary from 1978, when I was in Nicaragua, the first time that I was in a war situation. I looked at my diary and I found these words, "there is the stink of rotting flesh in the rubble, a column of vultures turns above the city. The barricades have been bull-dozed under, clusters of desperate people pick about in the ruins searching for bodies, salvaging bits of wood, cardboard, metal, anything with which to begin again: the archeology of yesterday, the old figures lined up in a doorway to buy milk, a liter, for a half-day's wages. The luminous vacuum that surrounds disaster will fade. Water and words will be wasted anew. The regular petty intrigues will resurface. Selfishness and mistrust will regain their degree. For those who were not there, who were too young will say, 'oh ever since the war' or 'he's not really all there' until they too become witnesses."

Further down the page I found the words of a Nicaraguan mother: "The three of us crouched in the corner of the house trembling and crying all at once, thinking that surely we would die here as the bullets and shrapnel were destroying our small wooden home. We decided to leave and find a safe place to hide. So we went through the back, through the kitchen, my husband carrying our young daughter in his arms. A plane flew very low and seemed to be coming directly at us and firing rockets all over, striking my daughter in the back and my husband as he carried her. From where I was, only a few paces behind them, I saw only the heart and the entrails of my child. She seemed to have been blown apart, completely destroyed. My husband stumbled some thirty steps with his arms torn away, blood pouring out of him till he fell dead. There was a great hole in his chest. Part of it was still smoking, a smoking rocket was lodged in one leg. The other was stripped of all flesh to the bone. I wanted to pick up my daughter but there were only pieces of her. I was desperate. I ran and found her arm and tried to put it back on her, tried to put back everything that had spilled out of her. But she was already dead. She was my only child and it was hard for me to have her. I dressed her myself for parties. Spoiled her. I don't know what I'm going to do."

I think she is asking us to perceive what they call in Spanish, *la toma de conciencia*, the *taking of consciousness*, which is that moment in our lives when we come to make a decision and our being is made decisive and present in that decision.

For me photography is not something alienating, but a way to reach out. I always think of photographs as artifacts of a relationship. But it's the person who is of interest to me. So when I chose the title for the show of "What Makes Us Think We're Only Here" it was like an accent on each one of those words that our identity is larger than the "I."

A student of mine from Ethiopia put it so clearly. He said, "What happens to the *we* that I am when I have to become the *I* that Americans want." He came from a "we" based culture, to the United States where he felt he had to be an "I" and he didn't know what to do. I thought, "that's right, that's the beginning, that's the first rupture." Once broken, how does one come back inside the "we" again?

So when I chose the only photograph from Nicaragua in the exhibit, I didn't pick a particularly dramatic picture from a single aspect; I chose the single consciousness of a boy on top of a white bus roof surrounded by thousands, and that mass consciousness of history and event, of 80,000 people in the square on the day of the victory. It was that relationship between the individuated consciousness and the historical consciousness that I felt was most of interest. That really is what the photograph is about for me.

So many times I have walked into a situation of massive human suffering and been shocked into silence, have walked into a place where people were as deeply wounded as amputees and found myself so shocked that I couldn't speak. So I am looking in the mirror of myself and I'm worried about my feelings because I'm so shocked at what's happened to these others until I go over and engage in conversation and they start joking and opening me up. Again from the diary:

During those years, I was picking coffee on the wet highlands of Venezuela on hills so steep your shoulders almost touched the hillside, staying up all night reciting Pablo Neruda in Syria; going to Catholic christenings, Jewish weddings, and Moslem funerals; looking into the faces of The Disappeared on the *Plaza de Mayo* in Argentina and seeing the tiny portraits of disappeared children; standing on the steps of a mosque in Beirut and staring at the hands of the old women holding tiny photographs of their sons disappeared in the war; feeling the rasp of stone from a hundred monuments commemorating valor and sacrifice in the service of one's country; standing over an acre of freshly turned earth mixed with common garbage where civilian bodies were buried. I have discovered that rockets made in China, Russia, France, landing, all have the same effect and all their bullets are fatal hornets.

When first going back through these photos, I chose a few pictures from early years. Then I thought that what I want to do was make a series of peace monuments. I began traveling around Washington, D.C., where I live. There are 114 war monuments in Washington, D.C. There are no peace monuments. I began looking at the 114 war monuments and thinking about the pieces of them and then I found out there were archives that have the names of all of the people who have been killed in the different wars, and there are people who keep track of such things. The archive for World War II weighs 800 pounds and takes up more than 54,000 pages. I began to think about those lives and those names and then I began to think about Korea and Vietnam and Desert Storm and those other names.

People sometimes ask how often do I photograph every day? I worked at the mathematics. I photograph about two and half minutes a year. Writers are very fortunate, they're always concerned that they don't get to do enough writing. My wife is a writer and I know she spends at least several hours a night, if not more, writing. I only get to photograph two and half minutes a year. And what is that about? The average exposure is a sixtieth of a second. If I take two rolls of thirty-odd exposures each, that's one second. And if there are sixty seconds in a minute, then I take 150 rolls a year. That means the aperture's only open two and half minutes a year. And what is that aperture? Is that aperture my eye, my heart, my memory? What is that aperture through which we can see? So it's not just the mechanism of the twisting dials, the difficult little numbers. It's that opening, that relationship, that is the critical thing, and that which lasts.

In San Salvador (I)

Come   look   they said
here are the photograph albums
these are our children

We are called The Mothers of the Disappeared
we are also the mothers of those who were seen once more
and then photographed   sometimes parts of them
could not be found

a breast   an eye   an arm is missing
sometimes a whole stomach
that is why we are called The Mothers
of the Disappeared   although we have these large
heavy photograph albums full of beautiful
torn faces

GOING BACK

Going Back

As time passed and I gained a greater understanding of what Vietnam had done to me, I came to feel a desire, no, a need to return to the place that held the most painful and most important memories of my life. In May 1982, I was chosen to be part of a delegation of Vietnam Veterans of America to go back to Vietnam. There were nine of us, mostly Vietnam veterans, and our task was very different from the one we'd had so many years earlier. Then, we went as warriors. This time, we came in peace.

We were to continue the work that had been started six months earlier by Bobby Muller and three other members of the VVA board of directors. They had gone to Vietnam at Christmas 1981 to try to open a dialogue with the Vietnamese concerning the Americans who continue to be missing in action (MIA) from the war, the continuing questions about Agent Orange, and the problem of American-Vietnamese (Amerasian) children remaining in Vietnam after the war.

The Vietnamese had agreed to work with VVA to move toward a resolution of these issues, and our delegation's task was to continue this work. The trip would be very much a working one, but it would give me the opportunity to see again some of the country that was so much a part of me.

The leaders of our delegation were Tom Bird, a Vietnam combat vet who had founded and was director of the Veterans Ensemble Theater Company in New York, and Greg Kane, a Marine Corps veteran of Okinawa during the war, who was a member of VVA's board of directors. Tommy had been in the first delegation, so he would direct this one. There were also Bob Holcomb, Scott Higgins, Dave Aldstadt, Gary Beikirch, and me, all of us Vietnam veterans. In addition, there were Leslie Platt, VVA's special counsel on Agent Orange, and Joseph Papp, a well-known director, who had produced some of the earliest theater works about Vietnam.

We flew together from New York, taking the eastern route instead of the Pacific route I'd flown in 1969. We left on the evening of May 25, all of us taking a van from Joe Papp's Public Theater in lower Manhattan out to JFK Airport.

Greg played coach, handing out our tickets when we needed them, then collecting them again when we had boarded. He had a terrible fear that someone was going to lose one, and at times it felt like we were on a school field trip.

We finally took off around 10 P.M. Dawn came quickly as we sped to the east, and soon we were in Frankfurt.

On the next legs of the flight, I sat with Scotty, and between eating, sleeping, and watching movies (*On Golden Pond* and *Absence of Malice*), the time flew. I wrote in my journal a great deal, and while wandering through the darkened plane to stretch my legs, found Bob doing the same. We talked for a while about our need to remember everything of this trip, and Bob said he'd noticed everyone writing in journals. It seemed we all had that need.

As the second day and night wore on, I began to remember the confusion I'd had on my first flight to Vietnam thirteen years ago. As on that occasion, I couldn't figure out what time and day it was at any given point, and when Scotty tried to explain why, I just got more confused and decided to stop trying. By the time we landed in Bangkok, I was grateful just to find out the local time and date.

The next day, we returned to the airport for the final leg of our journey back to Vietnam. This time we would be taking Hang Khong Vietnam, the Vietnamese airline. As we checked in at the counter, I began getting nervous. I wandered off to buy a few small souvenirs and suddenly found myself feeling weird, talking to myself, giggling; I couldn't even remember Bob's name. Joe was walking with me and assured me that I was behaving normally for the situation, that is, off the wall. Strangely, that felt comforting.

Once on the plane, an ancient 1950s model that hadn't seen much refurbishment since it was built, I came face to face with the memory of the heat of Vietnam. It was as though they were trying to prepare us. It must have been 120° or 130° inside, and as I noticed the sweat beginning to pour from me, from all the usual places, then from the backs of my hands, and finally from under my fingernails, I knew. I was going back to Vietnam.

We were greeted on the ground in Hanoi by about a half-dozen Vietnamese men, well dressed in short-sleeved shirts and slacks. A few Vietnamese Army soldiers were scattered around the terminal, and it gave me a start to see the familiar gold star on the red background of their collars and hats. Tommy had been similarly startled when he had seen them on his previous trip, but he had warned us about this, and that eased things a bit.

The civilian men were to be our guides and translators. Most of them knew Tommy from his trip the previous December, so they had a very friendly reunion while the rest of us cleared the paperwork of customs. I was touched by another recollection as I filled in the declaration. The paper was thin slices of wood pulp, as was almost all the paper we were to see for the rest of the trip, including the toilet paper. It struck home how poor this country still was.

I was startled from my writing by the sound of MiG fighters flying overhead. I dropped my pen and ran outside to watch as they passed. It reminded me of the ever-present American jets during the war, and I wondered if this was a demonstration of pride or some sort of strange welcome. There were about six planes, and they made their screaming passes four or five times. Finally, I went back inside and finished my paperwork.

After collecting our luggage, we were directed to a line of black Russian-made limousines in front of the terminal, and we got into them for the long drive into Hanoi. Though I had never been in northern Vietnam before, the land seemed very familiar. As far as the eye could see there were rice paddies, just as I had remembered them. Men and women in black pajamas and conical hats were bending over, working in the fields. We talked very little during the drive, each of us peering intently into the descending dusk for glimpses of the familiar and the unknown. We drove through villages that looked much like those around Pleiku, and when we got to the Long Binh Bridge at Hanoi, I was struck again by the legacy the war had left here. It was the only one of five bridges over the Red River still standing after the many American B-52 strikes, and because of this, it took at least a half-hour to cross on its narrow lane, following unending lines of bicycles and pedestrians.

When we arrived at the Thang Loi Hotel, most of us were exhausted from the flight and long day. It would have been heaven just to go to sleep, but we were expected at the Government House to meet the Vietnamese Committees on MIA's and Agent Orange. I found my room down a long covered walkway and took a quick shower before racing back to the lobby to join the others.

The meeting was held in the main reception room in an old French colonial building. There were introductions all around. I had boned up on Vietnamese before the trip and I had my first chance here to practice the language. The men seemed very pleased, and I found out that they thought it was a difficult language for most people to learn. They greatly appreciated it when foreigners made the effort to try. I spoke in Vietnamese with almost everyone I met during the trip, and when I did, I invariably received a broad grin. The hours of study and practice had been well worth the effort. We spoke of many things, what we had done during the war, what I had remembered from my time here, the futility and destruction of war, what our lives were like now, our families, and our work. I found myself liking these people, Luu, Khanh, Quang, Ngo Minh. They were becoming individuals to me now, not mere extensions of a war.

We returned to the Thang Loi about 11 P.M., and I fell into my low narrow bed immediately, forgetting even to pull down the mosquito netting. In the morning, I cursed myself for that omission. I awoke at 4 A.M., scratching the bumps left by the hungry fellows, hoping none of them had been the females who carry malaria, and I realized the sun was already rising. I decided to join it. I brushed my teeth and exercised, then put on my running shoes and went out for a few miles' run. I'd expected to be alone on the roads, but I soon remembered how early the day begins in Vietnam. The dirt paths were filled with people on their way to work, to the fields, and to the market. For the first time, I realized that there was a middle-aged population here. I'd never seen anyone who wasn't very young or very old during the war, and here was the missing generation. Or perhaps it was that those who were young when I'd last been here had finally had the chance to arrive at middle age. After all, that's what I was now, so many years later.

The people stared at me as I ran in my shorts, running shoes, and a T-shirt with writing in English. I smiled at everyone and was rewarded by their smiles each time. I marveled. They were the same people who had been here before, but I didn't have to worry there was a knife or grenade to accompany the smile. We weren't at war, and I was safe. It was a revelation for me. I stopped a few times and spoke with people at village entrances and at kiosks selling fruit, cigarettes, and various and sundry machine parts. I greet all of them in Vietnamese. Chao, Ong. Chao, Ba. Chao, Bac. Bac manh gioi khong? Ten toi la Lynda.

They responded with smiles and warm greetings. They asked where I was from, and when I said I was an American, the response was always friendly. I had expected the reverse, anything but friendship, but I was mistaken. They seemed happy to see me. I thought that perhaps it had to do with my being an American woman, instead of a man, a soldier who might have been trying to destroy them during the war, but when Les and Dave went out later that day they got the same warm reception.

I didn't know what to make of it. I'd expected them to hate me, and I was finding friendship everywhere. I personified the perpetrators of their most recent war and still they seemed to like me.

I headed back to the hotel, showered, then went to the lobby to join the group to go to the first of the many meetings of the week, the MIA meeting. Tom, Greg, Scotty, Bob, Gary, Joe, and I were ushered off in the same collection of cars we'd arrived in last night. We honked and weaved our way through the bicycles and pedestrians in a scene reminiscent of driving in Italy. Our drivers seemed to use only two parts of the car, the accelerator and the horn. We passed Ho Chi Minh's mausoleum, and I remembered how scared I'd felt when he died. Now I wished only that I could see this leader who'd had such an impact on my life and on those of people I'd known during the war.

The meeting was long. The Vietnamese talked of how difficult it was to find remains of our soldiers. As they spoke of the triple canopy jungle, the heat, the humidity, the insects, the wild beasts, I remembered how those things had affected me in Pleiku, and I began to understand how difficult it was for them to get out and search for MIA's. The people of the villages would have to cooperate in the searches, and I thought of how they would feel about trying to find American remains when there were hundreds of thousands of their own people still missing from the war.

I had little time for thought, only transcription, until Ngo Minh said that they had news of some MIA's who had been found since the previous delegation's visit. Goose bumps stood out on my arms as I recorded the names of people they had found. I thought of the families who would be getting notice of their loved ones, and I shivered. Would they see an army green sedan roll up at their front doors like I'd imagined for Gene's family? Would they get a phone call from the state department? Or would they just see it in the newspapers? I wanted to call each of them and tell them. I wanted them to hear it from someone personally, as I'd wished to be able to talk with the families of so many of those who had died under my care during the war. During a break, I asked Tom and Greg if there wasn't some way we could speak with or get word to the families of the people we'd been told about before the news people got to them, but there was no phone communication between Vietnam and the United States, and we had no way of notifying them.

During the rest of the time in Hanoi, we were kept very busy on the MIA's, Agent Orange, the Amerasian children, and cultural exchange. I visited the History Museum, the Museum of Science and Technological Achievements, and the Hanoi Conservatory of Music. I saw art and history and music, and I began to get a sense of these people as I'd never understood them before. There had been no time during the war to go to history museums, and I had never known how many eons these people had faced war. America had been only the last in a long line of countries that had tried to conquer this nation throughout its existence of thousands of years.

I began to gain a feeling for the people and the country that had not been available to me before. War destroys so many things, and one of the first casualties is the ability to think of the enemy as human beings with a history and a future. If you do so, it will not be possible to destroy them and the land. You must depersonalize someone to kill him, and that is what the war had done to all of us. We were now finally having the opportunity to see each other as humans. It was an important step for me.

Before we left for Ho Chi Minh City (formerly Saigon), we were received by the foreign minister, Nguyen Co Thach, and by the deputy foreign minister, Ha Van Lau. Both meetings left us feeling very good about the chances for resolving the issues before us in a humanitarian manner. But more than that, I felt again a sense of friendship from these two men.

As I wondered once more about the friendly meetings we were having, Mr. Thach and, later that evening, Ha Van Lau expressed their belief that America's Vietnam veterans were as much victims as they were. They had no love for the U.S. government, but they understood that there was a difference between the warriors and the war. I was learning more all the time.

Monday morning we left Hanoi for Ho Chi Minh City, feeling as though we were leaving friends. Mr. Quang came along to continue interpreting for us, but there was a real sadness at leaving our other new acquaintances.

On the flight down-country we all peered constantly to catch glimpses of familiar locations. When we passed over the area that had been the DMZ, I half-expected to see some kind of great wall or marker. As we got closer to the landing at Tan Son Nhut Airport, I became very nervous. My muscles felt weak, my stomach was churning, and I was staring out the window of the plane trying to take it all in forever. Everything about the airport looked familiar, the terminal building, the camouflaged hangers, the sky, the fences and towers. I'd left Vietnam from this very airport and until this moment, I'd remembered almost nothing of it and my last day in Vietnam.

We landed smoothly and taxied up to the terminal, and I was glued to my seat. I just couldn't get up yet. I was intent on memorizing everything I saw. After everyone else had left, I rose and gathered my things, then walked down the steps of the plane to touch my Vietnam. Hanoi had been important but this was the stuff of my time here. I stood on the flight line for several minutes, looking in all directions. Yes, there were the guard towers, and over there a few military planes painted in camouflage colors. I saw so many things I recognized but what was more familiar were the feelings inside me. I was remembering everything of that last terrible day here. I walked toward the gate area, knowing exactly where I was going.

I pushed through the swinging door I'd gone out of almost twelve years ago. It was the same gate area, but something was missing. In my mind's eye, I saw a dozen or more benches here, with GI's sitting on them, the sadness of a lifetime in their eyes. Duffel bags were everywhere. Flak jackets and helmets were strewn on the floor. Flight announcements were constantly being made.

All those things were gone now. The room was open and bare. The benches were missing. The only announcements were in Vietnamese. I walked over to a place where there should have been a bench and bent over to touch the holes in the floor where the benches had been bolted down. What happened to them, I wondered? It was as real as if it had been yesterday.

I turned and walked back to the windows from which I'd stared out so long ago. The feelings of fear returned in a wave. I felt again the incredible sadness, the fear of all the Vietnamese around me, the longing for home, and the deeply rooted fear that I would never get out of here alive.

I was surprised to feel tears dropping on my folded arms. I began to realize that this was not twelve years ago; it was now, I had met and gotten to know Vietnamese this time, and they were people, just like me and my family and my friends. I didn't have to be afraid anymore. The tears came washing over me, this time, finally, in relief. It was over. The war was over for me.

As I stood there alone shaking and crying quietly, Colin Campbell, the *New York Times* reporter, came over and put his arm around my shoulders. "Are you all right, Lynda? Can I do anything?" he asked.

"It's OK, Colin," I answered. "It's good this time. I needed this to happen. I wanted to come back here to find something I had left, and I just found it. It was my youth, my innocence. I know now that I can never get them back, but I've touched them, and it's OK. I know where they went. I even think I know what they are. It's so sad." I buried my head in his shoulder and let the tears wash away the war.

It was Memorial Day. Waiting until near sunset in Vietnam, sunrise in America, we nine gathered in a garden. Quietly, without real plans, we formed a circle on the grass, sitting cross-legged in heat, moisture, and mosquitoes. Such were our memories of the surroundings of the war.

I'd chosen a branch of a Plumieria tree, with flowers of a heady perfume and a pure simple beauty. We placed it in the center of our circle and grew quiet. We held hands, and Gary began to speak, the soft gentle words of a minister. We were reminded by his prayers of our fallen friends — the

57,000 who lost their lives here, the many hundreds of thousands who gave, by their blood, to the war, the millions of our brothers and sisters who had fought here.

One could nearly touch, see, what we thought and felt. All gazed at the grass, the Plumieria, the blue of sky, but we saw the others' hearts in our own.

I reached for the branch of blossoms, and chose one for myself. Plucking it, I passed it to Dave who did the same, then it continued the circle around to Joe, who took the last one and returned it to me. I gently replaced the shorn branch in the center and Gary asked for our silent prayers.

The voice of that silence could be heard in the drop of humid air upon a leaf, the wisp of a breeze in our ears, the chirp of a gecko in a bush, the song of a bird in flight. I thought of my cousin Steve, of Gene, of Sharon Lane, of so many who had passed through my life here. We sent our prayers for our warriors to the heavens, our prayers for their peace and respite, and our prayers for the world. Ours were the prayers of those who know dearly the cost of war and who know deeply the meaning of peace and freedom. Our silence was unbroken, like our circle.

A shared look for us all, and we returned from our private reveries. Gary intoned his and our heartfelt hopes for the rest of our brothers and sisters, alive and not, Americans all, who answered a call and gave of themselves. And we prayed for peace for ourselves as well.

So ended the sun for us on Memorial Day 1982. Another Memorial Day for us, in Vietnam.

Fever Dream in Ha Noi

The gold red and green carp
surfaces in the lake where I struggle.
Angry and impatient with me
he shakes his head
big as a baby's head
towards the lake's center.
I'd been half-swimming,
half-treading water
to try to make the shore
where small lights
blinked around the perimeter
before tiny stands
where women squat
in that particular
Vietnamese way
selling their few packs of cigarettes,
their few bottles of warm beer.
Lovers linger too
among banyan trees tangled.
They nuzzle each other.
They coo and laugh
for these stolen minutes
away from the crowded
family houses. The lights
and the confessional lovers
all seem to call to me
when I wake in the lake
of the returned sword.
The carp shakes his head
towards the shrine
on the island
lit only with the light
of the Buddha's eyes.
I thought my life was calling
from the lamp-lit lover's shore.

I thought my death called too
from the dark water, deeper.
The carp shakes his head,
old hooks and fishing line
strung in the moon like a beard.
He swishes the fan of his tail
splashing green water across my face.
I'm on my back,
floating somehow towards the temple,
the face of the carp
changed, a human smile
on his lips, the Ha Noi moon
slashed across his back
so I see scales shine
and the blood gills pulse.
The lovers turn away from each other
to the lake's black edge,
and the old women
blow out their small lanterns
and turn too towards the lake
as if in prayer.
I'm being towed now,
the gold carp's hooks
snagged through the skin on my back.
With his eyes
He tells me not to fight.
He tells me of my perfect death
waiting at the shrine
like a spirit,

and then I wake,
burning with fever
in the guest house on Nguyen Du
by the lake where lovers walk
in the dark
evening's desire.
Two men and a boy
hold coal-hot doss sticks
to points on my wrists and feet
where my cold blood is still.

Another man taps needles into my back,
down my spine
until a cry or grunt
escapes my lips
and he nods
his happy affirmation
as my guts begin to stir,
a snake coming alive,
uncurling itself inside me,
my head swimming,
my skin hot, then cold,
then hot again,
musky waves of sickness
through which he tows me
with his needles
and I float.
I let go of everything.
I let go my family
the thousands of miles away.
I let go my days
and my hours
and my sad minutes.
I let go the love
of those in whose minds
I can't find myself.
I let go the songs,
each note a white bird
descending.
I let go the words.
Every word ever uttered.
I let go the world.
I spin off the world,
hooks in my back
pulling me upwards, upwards and away.

A Reed Boat

The boat's tarred and shellacked to a water-repellent finish, just sway-dancing with the current's ebb, light as a woman in love. It pushes off again, cutting through lotus blossoms, sediment, guilt, unforgivable darkness. Anything with half a root or heart could grow in this lagoon.

There's a pull against what's hidden from day, all that hurts. At dawn the gatherer's shadow backstrokes across water, choreographed for an instrument played for gods and monsters in the murky kingdom below. Blossoms lean into his fast hands, as if snapping themselves in half, giving in to some law.

Slow, rhetorical light cuts between night and day, like nude bathers embracing. The boat nudges deeper, with the ease of silverfish. I know by his fluid movements, there isn't the shadow of a bomber on the water anymore, gliding like a dream of death. Mystery grows out of the decay of dead things — each blossom a kiss from the unknown.

When I stand on the steps of Hanoi's West Lake Guest House, feeling that I am watched as I gaze at the boatman, it's hard to act like we're the only two left in the world. He balances on his boat of Ra, turning left and right, reaching through and beyond, as if the day is a woman he could pull into his arms.

The Hanoi Market

It smells of sea and earth, of things dying and newly born. Duck eggs, pig feet, mandarin oranges. Wooden bins and metal boxes of nails, screws, ratchets, balled copper wire, brass fittings, jet and helicopter gadgets, lug wrenches, bolts of silk, see-through paper, bamboo calligraphy pens, and curios hammered out of artillery shells.

Faces painted on coconuts. Polished to a knife-edge or sealed in layers of dust and grease, cogs and flywheels await secret missions. Aphrodisiacs for dream merchants. A silent storm moves through this place. Someone's worked sweat into the sweet loaves of bread lined up like coffins on a stone slab.

She tosses her blonde hair back and smiles down at everyone. Is it the squid and shrimp we ate for lunch, am I seeing things? An adjacent stall blooms with peacock feathers. The T-shirt wavers like a pennant as a sluggish fan slices the humidity into ribbons.

I remember her white dress billowing up in a blast of warm air from a steel grate in New York City, reminding me of Miss Firecracker flapping like a flag from an APC antenna. Did we kill each other for this?

I stop at a table of figurines. What was meant to tear off a leg or arm twenty years ago, now is a child's toy I can't stop touching.

Maybe Marilyn thought she'd erase herself from our minds, but she's here when the fan flutters the T-shirt silkscreened with her face. The artist used five shades of red to get her smile right.

A door left ajar by a wedge of sunlight. Below the T-shirt, at the end of two rows of wooden bins, a chicken is tied directly across from a caged snake. Bright skin — deadly bite. I move from the chicken to the snake, caught in their hypnotic plea.

Nui Ba Den: Black Virgin Mountain

For Crisp

1

In dreams you've returned before.
Last night, smoking
cigarette after cigarette,
pacing across the room,
ship lights blinking
up and down the Saigon River,
I saw you again
and all the others.

What mouth could speak
that last fear?

2

Highway 13.
The dust penetrates, ages us
inch by inch as it rises
along the road.
In tropic heat, whirlwinds —
taunting brown ghosts —
rise up from the ground,
at every bend
and are gone.

We drive straight into the landscape —
a flat panhandle,

unpeopled, and spare.
A sole shape beckons,
the Black Virgin Mountain:
Nui Ba Den,
the widow who waits her soldier's return.

3

Standing below the mountain,
I see you here again
after twenty years.
Red hair gleaming in the sun,
faded brown fatigues
stuffed with letters to Miriam
back in Georgia.

What green thoughts
rise in your mind,
what grace is found
in so much loss?

4

Jungle trails
still lead back
up the mountain,
past streams and caves
where children hide.

One last time
I kiss the red dirt
that holds you,
suck in again
your last breath,
return it to the wind
that blows down
Nui Ba Den, home
at last.

The Arts of Love and Hydrology
as Practiced in Hanoi

For Thuy

During the monsoon
in the North she digs
a hole outside
the stucco complex
where she shares
a nine-square-meter flat
with her father, mother,
and younger brother.
In the mornings at five,
she rises from her
hammock and begins
her chores before leaving
for the ministry.
Last, she dips the jars
of smoky glass down
into a fetid pool,
sets them by the hearth
then takes the route
she always has,
past the old school and canal.

It seems so distant now
that day she dove and dove
for him. She'd been
among the first pulled
back from the canal,
the bombs still falling.
They couldn't understand her
as she gestured
back to the water.
Then she left them, dove back in,
found him and drew him

up the bank where she pumped
the brackish waters
from her brother's chest.
Some of the children trampled,
she later learned, rushing from road
and school into the flooded ditch.

Still, evenings she returns
the same way; arriving home
again she checks to see
if the clay has settled
in the jars so she can cook.
Some nights the hues of crimson
in the rice will trouble
her as she lies in her
hammock dreaming late
of a lover laying
fresh-water pipe across
the broad green
fields of the delta.

River Music

One by one the lanterns
swim off down river.
A green one first, then red
and yellow. Each one calls
back a friend. Like dancers
they turn in circles.
One for my wife, one for my son,
one for our new child in spring.
Back and forth they swing
in twos and threes, seeking
ever newer combinations.
We drink rice liquor, toast
ten reasons men fall
in love on the river.
The old men smile into their instruments.
A woman sings, such beauty
even the moon might die
on her shoulder.

The Snail Gatherers of Co Loa Thanh

The legends of Co Loa Thanh, Old Snail City,
tell how spirits of Mount Tam Dao
tried to stall the citadel
by slipping down the hills each night
to undo the labor of the day.
One night a golden
tortoise crawled up river,
gave the king new weapons, bows
to slay the spirits of Tam Dao.
And so the city rose
carved from carcasses and shells.

Tonight, from old city walls strange shapes
rise on the night and wind
down old trails.
Some bear lights in hand;
others on their heads like miners.
From the balcony of the guest house
I hear their voices call.
How have they gotten past the guards,
breached the compound walls and lake?

At every tree, shadows pause.
Some move on hands and knees,
examining each blade of grass.
And why not? What gems
compare with these: the snails of Co Loa,
and their gatherers back again.

And we without our bows.

That Country

This is about the women of that country
sometimes they spoke in slogans
They said
    We patch the roads as we patch our sweetheart's trousers
    The heart will stop but not the transport
They said
    We have ensured production even near bomb craters
    Children let your voices sing higher than the explosions of the
        bombs
They said
    We have important tasks to teach the children
    that the people are the collective masters
    to bear hardship
    to instill love in the family
    to guide for good health of the children (they must
    wear clothing according to climate)
They said
    once men beat their wives
    now they may not
    once a poor family sold its daughter to a rich old man
    now the young may love one another
They said
    once we planted our rice any old way
    now we plant the young shoots in straight rows
    so the imperialist pilot can see how steady our
    hands are

In the evening we walked along the shores of the Lake of the Restored
    Sword

I said   is it true?   we are sisters?
They said,   Yes, we are of one family

The House on Lotus Pond

This blue sky is now ours.
Ours also these perfumed plains,
These streams heavy with brown silt,
This homeland — it is ours.
— *Nguyen Dinh Thi 1924–*

Traffic thickened as our airport van entered Chuong Duong Bridge one summer day in 1990. Below, the Red River, rich in iron oxide, swept by in a graceful curve, giving Ha-Noi its name, "Inside the River." But whereas the river moved at a stately pace, we had stopped. Two trucks — battered veterans of the American War — blocked the bridge, their hoods raised.

"Welcome to the Ho Chi Minh Trail!" Flower said. Her round face was soft and exuberant, like a peony in full bloom.

I relaxed, relishing the sound of Flower's laughter. We hadn't seen each other since my first trip to Ha-Noi during the war fifteen years before. Now, I'd returned for a four-month assignment to set up an office for the American Friends Service Committee, known in Viet-Nam as Quaker Service. I would be among Ha-Noi's first American residents; Flower was to be my Vietnamese partner.

"Remember the first time we crossed that old bridge?" Flower said, pointing upriver. "It's only used for bicycles and cyclos now."

I glanced at the lacy French artifact, which looked as frail as a child's Erector-set model. Dragon Bridge — once the sole road link between Ha-Noi and Peking — had been a prime U.S. bombing target during the war. Back then in 1975, stuck in traffic on Dragon Bridge, I watched lines of women carrying yoked baskets of earth, which they emptied into the craters.

But now in 1990, the riverbanks below Dragon Bridge were verdant with cabbages and greens; the bridge itself was a blur of bicycles. However, as had often happened during the war, motorized traffic entering Ha-Noi on the new companion bridge had stopped. Up ahead of us, a man inserted a steel shank into the crankcase of his truck and gave the rod a twirl. Soon, the truck lurched off, its engine spewing acrid smoke.

"Whew!" Flower said, waving the air.

I had made a dozen trips to Ha-Noi since the end of the war and had often asked after Flower; I knew she'd married and had a daughter. Still, despite my inquiries, we never met. But intimacy can grow across a void. Now, we were like old roommates reunited in giddy friendship. My one worry—whom I would work with—dissolved. And so I relaxed as our van made its way through downtown Ha-Noi to Rice Soup Street, where I settled into the room that would double as temporary office and living quarters.

In December 1990, Flower and I moved the Quaker Service office to Lotus Pond Street. In preparation for the family of four who would replace me, we hired the landlady's mother, Hien, as housekeeper and cook. In her mid-sixties, Hien had strong cheekbones and a high forehead accented by a widow's peak. Out of respect, I called her "Senior Aunt"; in comparable regard, she called me "Older Sister." Aunt Hien adopted me. Soon every morning I joined her friends for badminton in Lenin Park.

I left the house before dawn, pushing my bicycle out into the dark and shuttered street. As I locked the gate, a neighbor from several doors down tugged her noodle cart toward the corner. The cart's wheels knocked against the cobblestones in a cloppity rhythm.

"Good morning, Older Sister," I said, walking my bike alongside her cart. I savored the aroma of the chicken broth steeped in cinnamon, ginger, and coriander. Soon she would pour the broth over rice noodles, serving the neighborhood *pho*, a traditional Vietnamese breakfast.

"You're early today," she answered. At the corner, she removed a low table and four tiny stools from the back of her cart, transforming the sidewalk into her noodle stand.

Across the street, another stall added the aroma of fresh-baked bread. The vendor, an older woman with hair wrapped around her head in the tradition of northern Viet-Nam, pulled a tiny loaf from the warming oven she'd improvised from an old oil drum. "Sister!" she called to me. "Have some bread before you go to the park!"

"Thank you," I called over my shoulder. "Please, Auntie, save me a loaf as always."

"You'll need it," she answered, clicking her tongue. "The uncles will run the meat off your bones!"

I turned onto Nguyen Du Street, named for the famous poet who wrote Viet-Nam's epic poem, *The Tale of Kieu*. The street runs along one of Ha-

Noi's many lakes. Two men in a small rowboat, their voices subdued, hauled in a net filled with silvery fish. Nearby, an elderly gentleman practiced *tai chi* on the grassy bank, his long white beard floating like the mist.

But as I passed Thien Quang pagoda, the quiet turned to uproar. The buses from the provinces had arrived. Cyclo drivers swarmed, yelling at the women lowering sides of pork and huge baskets of vegetables from the bus roofs. The bottom of one basket broke, its cabbages bouncing like soccer balls. A boy snatched a rolling cabbage and tore off down the street.

"You're early today, Older Sister," a cyclo driver called.

I waved and pedaled through the gate of Lenin Park.

Hien was already playing, her knot of long black hair bobbing with each shot. I shed my wool cap, scarf, and sandals and, choosing a badminton racket, joined Hien and her friend, Noi. I missed shot after shot. I couldn't see the birdie against the gray, predawn sky. None of the others, all older than I, wore glasses, and so I'd left mine at home.

"How can you see that thing?" I called to Noi, finally hitting the birdie over our imaginary net.

"Pretend you're watching for airplanes." She returned my volley.

One by one, Hien's friends took me on. After demure Noi, came gracious Mai who, like Hien, wore the traditional round-necked Vietnamese blouse and black satin trousers. The women rested in turn, but I kept playing until I shed down to my own round-necked blouse.

"Are you tired yet?" Duc asked, stepping in front of me. Years before, rheumatism had crippled both Duc's arms. Then he took up badminton as therapy, first for his right arm, then for his left. Now, he played two rackets. Clapping their handles, he twirled between shots like a circus acrobat between feats.

Xuyen, unusual in her plumpness, joined me against Duc. Her touch was soft and her movements graceful.

"I used to have a Westerner's belly!" she announced, waddling in imitation of her former self.

"Beautiful," she said each time I returned the shuttlecock. The birdie floated between us like easy conversation.

The sky shifted to light gray and then to blue. Xuyen and I joined two men using a net. My partner, the only other person playing barefoot, wore his beret tilted at a rakish angle over his white hair. He served the shuttlecock as if firing a bullet.

"*Chet!* — Dead!" he shouted each time he whipped a return over the net. "*Chet!*" "*Chet!*"

"So many deaths," I said. laughing at his vigor.

"Like the B-52s," he answered. He sizzled the birdie at Xuyen, who lobbed it back to me. "I lost my wife and child during the Christmas bombing. Are you French?"

My concentration snapped; the birdie landed at my feet. It lay there, lifeless, like a corpse.

"Uncle, I'm American."

The corner of his mouth quivered. "My only son. He was two."

"So many deaths," I said: "So much pain."

He picked at a string of his racket as if playing the plaintive one-stringed zither. "Sometimes," he said, "old memories are sharper than yesterday's."

From the next court came the *plick, plick* of a birdie bandied. Nearby, a man with one leg snapped branches into burnable lengths and loaded them into a hand cart. A kiosk vendor turned on his radio, and the park filled with news of Baghdad and U.S. preparations for war.

"Uncle," I said, "can you forgive us?"

He twisted the sole of his bare foot against the asphalt. "It was a long time ago."

"Yes," I said. "But time is slow in its solace."

"But look at us now," he said, tapping his racket against the asphalt. "You and I on the same side, and we just lost a point! It's your serve, Sister."

I served, and Xuyen returned. My partner whipped Xuyen's return back to her; she responded with a graceful lob, which I sliced over the net. But her partner was equally quick. The birdie flew forward and back in an extended volley.

"What is she?" a bystander asked. Out of the corner of my eye, I could see that his jacket hung on him.

"Ask her," my partner answered. "She can talk."

"I'm American," I volunteered in Vietnamese. "What are you?"

"I'm Vietnamese," he answered in crystalline English. "I'll play you tomorrow!"

My partner and I played on until Uncle Khoai arrived on his bicycle. At seventy, Uncle Khoai's hair was as white as the feathers on a new birdie. He looked like a court jester in his blue sweat suit. His elfin expression fit his cap embroidered with "THIS MEN."

"*Di, di!*" Uncle Khoai ordered, using on me the same expression — "Move it!" — that American GI's had once hurled at Vietnamese. He sent me racing, side to side. "Where are you?" he called out, laughing as he flicked the birdie. "Now where are you?"

"You're stiff," he challenged. "Are you a tourist?"

"No, Uncle!" I said, diving for the birdie. "I'm not."

"Look!" said a bystander. "The American knows how to run."

"But not in sandals," added his companion.

I missed the shot.

"Bend like this," Uncle Khoai said. Exaggerating his own grace, he crossed one leg in front of the other and, sweeping his racket, dipped so low his knees rested on the pavement.

"We should book you into the Central Theater," I muttered. Sweat streamed down my arms and dripped from my elbows; my breath frosted into small clouds.

"Time for *pho*," Hien called.

Uncle Khoai caught the birdie I returned. As we walked to my pile of sweaters, he patted the pouch of acupuncture needles in the pocket of his sweat pants.

"Any ailments today?" he asked.

"Creaky knees," I said.

"You need to grease your joints. Eat more pork fat." Uncle Khoai laughed and mounted his bicycle. "See you tomorrow!" he called as he rode off.

It was 7 A.M. At daybreak, the park had been like the woods at home when the birds burst into sound. By now, with full sunlight, it was quiet. The runners completed their last loop around the lake. Two fencers stopped to talk to soccer players gathering around their bicycles. My bare-foot badminton partner unhooked his net. He waved as Aunt Hien and I passed on our way to the park gate.

The Christmas bombing that had shattered my badminton partner's life careened into every conversation I had in late 1990. The United States was revving up for the Gulf War. It may have generated ebullience among Americans, but Vietnamese faced a mine field of memories. I constantly blundered into explosions of pain.

One day just before Christmas, Aunt Hien and I sat down to lunch. Flower had gone off to a wedding. Aunt Hien filled two bowls with steaming white rice. I set the spring rolls and fish soup on the table. Sitting opposite me, Aunt Hien paired the chopsticks according to height and offered me a set.

"Please," she said, tucking a strand of hair into the knot at the nape of her neck as she invited me to eat. She dipped her chopsticks in the soup and placed a morsel of fish on my rice.

Always shy with strangers, I wondered what to talk about. I settled on a safe topic. "Tell me about your grandchildren," I said.

"I have a granddaughter in America."

The fish stuck like a bone in my throat. From the street outside came the laughter of children jumping rope. The rope struck the cobblestones, *slap, slap.*

"A year ago," Aunt Hien continued, "my daughter-in-law took my granddaughter to America through the Orderly Departure Program. My granddaughter was thirteen. I had raised her since she was two, but then her mother came and took her away to America."

Aunt Hien set a spring roll on my rice; she toyed with her own food. "When you return to the States, will you carry a package to my granddaughter?"

"Of course."

The noon siren began with a low moan, then rose to the wail that had once announced American bombers.

"I went to An Duong today," I said, changing the subject. An Duong had been the first site struck during Nixon's Christmas bombing. "They wanted an American to join their ceremony commemorating the people who were killed."

Once again Aunt Hien caught me by surprise. "That's when my husband died. During the last hour of the Christmas bombing."

What could I say?

Outside, the children skinned their jump rope, *Slap! Slap! Slap! "Mot! Hai! Ba! Bon!* —One! Two! Three! Four!"

"I'm sorry," I murmured. "We Americans have never taken responsibility for what we did."

Aunt Hien placed another spring roll on my rice. "Will they do it again?" she asked. "Bomb the Iraqis the way they did us?"

"I'm afraid so."

"But why?"

"Greed," I said. "Oil. Pride. We lost the American War in Viet-Nam."

"But suppose Americans had lived under bombs . . ." Aunt Hien looked at me. "Could you bomb so easily?"

"Probably not. Except for Pearl Harbor—and that was a military base—we can't remember war on our own land."

"We're so different," Aunt Hien said, touching her hair, which had strands of gray. "People my age, we've scarcely known peace."

When I left Ha-Noi in early 1991, Aunt Hien gave me a Vietnamese cook book to take to her granddaughter in America. For my father on his ninetieth birthday, she sent a youthful beret and lotus seed candy. My gift was a photograph of her family taken on the anniversary of her husband's death.

In the photograph, Aunt Hien stands in the rice paddy where the fateful bomb exploded. She bends in prayer over a white crypt. Smoke from the incense sticks pressed between her palms drifts over her grown sons and daughters, their spouses and children. One grandchild is missing: she is somewhere in Massachusetts, far from her grandfather's grave.

Over the years, I have heard many different stories of American bombing in both northern and southern Viet-Nam, but never so many as in late 1990 and early 1991, during those weeks leading up to the Gulf War. Somewhere in each conversation, there was silence. Always, out of the silence, came the same question.

"They won't bomb, will they?" Autumn, a friend I'd met in the early 1980s, asked at supper one evening at her house.

"Yes," I said. "They will."

"*Bom bi,*" her husband, Huy, muttered. "How can the Americans bomb again?!"

"*Hrmmmmmmmmmmmm,*" Autumn said, imitating a bomber. "Boom! And then the *bi* clatter." She held her thumb and forefinger an inch apart. "Once, I found a *bi* stuck in the straw of my manhole lid. I was that far from death."

"Americans don't know about bombing," I said. "After all, I've never seen a *bi.*"

"Oh!" Huy said. "I'll show you." He left the table and pulled a box from under the bed nearby, rummaging. "The baby bombs each burst into hundreds of these *bi,*" he said, handing me a tiny package.

"*Bi*" is the Vietnamese word for "marble," but what Huy set in my palm was no toy. Here was a dart the size of a straight pin but with flanges of steel.

"A baby bomb would kill you," Autumn said. "The *bi* wounded."

I nodded. I knew the tactic: don't kill; instead, maim. An enemy buries its dead and moves on. But the maimed immobilize the enemy's resources by tying up medical staff and family members.

I jabbed the dart against my fingertip, feeling its prick. "In the United States," I said, "we call this a 'fleshette.'"

"Will they use fleshettes on the Iraqis?" Huy asked.

"Yes," I said, "but this time, they'll use plastic."

"Plastic?" Autumn served me more rice and stir-fries. "Because it's cheaper?"

"No," I said. "X-rays."

"X-rays?" Autumn's brow furrowed. Then her eyes widened. "Oh! Because then the arrows won't show up!"

"Exactly," I said.

"I have two fleshettes." Huy set down his chopsticks. "If you want, you can take that one back to America."

And so I did.

At home in the States, I carry Huy's fleshette in my wallet as a reminder of how I, a taxpayer, bought and continue to pay for the American War.

Sometimes late at night I awaken from a recurring dream, where Americans and Vietnamese together pluck those fleshettes from earth and flesh, gathering them from the face of Viet-Nam and from the faces of Vietnamese. They lay the arrows side by side, end on end, until their flanges fuse into a span of steel strong enough to carry all the stories that separate us.

MOUNTAINS AND RIVERS
Works from Viet Nam

VU CAO

The Couple of the Mountains

From the diary of Nguyen Van Luc

Seven years ago you were seventeen,
I had just turned twenty.
Two villages, Xuan-Duc and Doai-Dong, two rice fields.
One day you would come to me,
And one day I would come to you.

On the path between mountains
That the villagers called Lover's Mountains
You teased me about how clever Heaven was
To create the husband and wife mountains
Side by side.

During the summer rice harvest
The enemy came.
Trees burned in the pagoda hamlet.
We had just proposed, but lost our chance to marry.
Since then we've been apart.

I joined the forces that went northeast.
Year after year I fought without thinking of myself.
When I met conscripted workers at the front
I would ask if they knew of Xuan-Duc, Doai-Dong.

I thought: our village could be occupied by the enemy.
The hundred thousand hatreds
And indignations would not disappear.
When fog surrounds the place of our enemy
I feel alone, apart from the world
And I long for you whom I left behind.

Comrades in my unit told each other
Our midland villages still waited for us.
And that you still crossed back and forth
On the river between the two mountains.

For days we were excited to go home,
Then the order for cease-fire finally came.
We took a short cut across the district's river
I stopped to visit my family and the two mountains.
I stood at the pier on the pond.

Then the news came like lightning
That under the pine trees
The enemy had killed only you.
Midnight, troops had surrounded Thua military post.
You lived loyally and died faithfully.

I look up at the two mountains:
Rows of pine trees, lush grass grown over our path,
The dusted sunlight suddenly dim with smoke.
The mountains stay together but I lost you.

People in Phu Ninh market
Said you were the youngest girl
In the village to become a guerrilla.
They wondered why you never married.

From the mountains to the river the road is blocked.
Xuan-Duc and Doai-Dong are thick with wild grass.
Bomb-cratered yards have become ponds, houses burn,
Destroyed in the dust and broken tile.

Our white-haired parents help each other return.
They love every root of every tree.
They build temporary huts from bamboo trees.
Gradually, day and night, they forget their grief.

On the way to the market I heard someone say
The next harvest would bring much rice.
The mountains remain side by side
And I remember our love.
As long as the enemy is here, I will fight.

The villagers wrote your name as a heroine
On the white steles in the center of the field:
Here the girl of Xuan-Duc died
For the happiness of the people of this land.

Reading your name I wanted you back.
I love you and call to you as a comrade.
One heart in a thousand hearts.

Red star on my hat
Always guiding my way,
I joined the troops.
You are the flower on top of the mountain.
In all seasons you send out your fragrance.

Translated by Thanh Nguyen and Bruce Weigl

Hope

To Tran Manh Giang,
a close friend met on the warring path.

Clouds shift above the stream.
Pink skies surround the mountains.
We have crossed many hills, many valleys
And rested our heads on the Truong Son mountains,
The rocks worn by our many steps.

We shiver with fits of malaria
That come and go
Yet we move into our future.
We walk a thousand miles
And still the promised life stays in our eyes.

The burning and killing will pass.
The enemy will be driven from our country.
Although our legs are weary,
Our voices hoarse,
We sing the songs of rebuilding.

All of our lives we struggle to be happy in our work,
To build a bridge to tomorrow.
Vietnam is a country of great seas
And long rivers.
We struggle on the road to move forward.
In this hardship, we need songs of hope.

23 February 1967

Translated by Thanh Nguyen and Bruce Weigl

Despair

Unbearable heat this afternoon.
The wind blows dry and hot.
The trees are withered,
Their branches dry, their leaves yellow.
I grieve for the roses that blossom only to die.

I blame the universe that revolves,
The wheel of life that turns so skillfully
And dazes me with longing.
If spring would come to stay,
The bees and flowers would never part.

Who could be so unfaithful
To keep the bees from their flowers?
Only those who believe money and power
Determine our fate.
Never think of me in this unjust way.

Finished on 29 July 1966

Translated by Thanh Nguyen and Bruce Weigl

My Thoughts

I want to write, in my little book,
Many pages of what I long for, what I feel.
A wandering life is no life at all.
I'm sick and I'm tired of this damned life.

Corrupt people look down on us here.
They teach us meaningless lessons
On how to shit, how to sleep.
They spy on who eats what and when.

They talk nonsense and wonder
Why those who eat so little shit so big.
If I had more teeth, I would eat a village of frogs.
I would eat a meal of rotten food
And see if they'd still want to watch.

"You're so rich, do something to me now," I'd say.
Until the victory, I'll try to believe in you.
Until my family can feast on fish, rice, and duck,
I will strike with my cane he who spies on me.

I have a life in this world.
Why stay quiet only to suffer loss?
Life in war is so short.

26 February 1967

Translated by Thanh Nguyen and Bruce Weigl

The Pole at the Village Pagoda

A lantern sways from the Banner Pole,
the East wind rattles its panes.
My love for you is deep aching, endless.
In the tipped dish, I grind ink for a poem:
a poem . . . three or four, saying
Wait for. Hope for. Remember Love.

Translated by John Balaban

The Colonial Troops Transport

The troop ship whistles once; I still waver.
Whistles twice, and I step down into the boat.
Three times, and the transport pushes north.
I grip the iron rail as tears stream forth,
and ask the helmsman for a rag for my tears.
Now the husband is North; the wife, South.

Translated by John Balaban

Ship of Redemption

The bell of Linh Mu Pagoda tolls,
awakening the drowsy soul,
probing, reminding one of debt,
washing one clean of worldly dust.
A boat crosses to the Western Lands.

Translated by John Balaban

Phoenixes and Sparrows

Phoenixes compete, so do sparrows.
They call before the shrine, behind the pagoda.
I can use men who are loyal, if not elegant.

Translated by John Balaban

Tavern by a Mountain Stream

Legs crossed, I look out on the valley,
its paths winding towards a deserted tavern
thatch roof tattered and decayed.
Bamboo poles, laid down on gnarled pylons
and lashed together at creaky joints,
bridge the emerald stream uncurling
long grasses in the wavering current.
Happy, I forget my old worries.
Someone's kite is angling high above.

Translated by John Balaban

The Lieu Quan School of Vietnamese Buddhism

Buddhism came to Viet Nam during the first century A.D. The religious practices were introduced to the Vietnamese by Buddhist monks who accompanied merchants coming from India by sea. By the second century, the Red River Delta region (North Viet Nam) had become an important center for the study of Buddhism, and it drew many scholars and monks from China. Throughout its history, Vietnamese Buddhism was to continue to receive influxes of Chinese monks and Zen masters. Particularly at times of civil war in China, many Chinese scholars, mandarins, merchants, and Buddhist monks took refuge in relatively peaceful Viet Nam.

Thien Buddhism (more familiar in the West as Zen Buddhism) was established as a distinctive school in Viet Nam in the sixth century by Vinitaruci, an Indian monk. Vo Ngon Thong, a Chinese master who studied under Bach Truong before coming to Viet Nam, set up another Thien school of note; however, a truly Vietnamese Thien school began only in the early thirteenth century with the Yeng Tu school, named after a mountain in North Viet Nam where its principal monastery was built. The practices of Vo Ngon Thong's tradition and those of other schools, including the teaching of the twelfth-century Chinese monk Lam Te, were combined in the Truc Lam school. At the beginning of the fifteenth century, troops of the Chinese Ming dynasty invaded Viet Nam and their twenty-year occupation had devastating consequences for Vietnamese culture. The invaders burned all Vietnamese books and art works to enforce their program of assimilation. Among the books that were destroyed were many containing essays and treatises by Vietnamese Thien teachers. Now only the titles remain.

In the mid-seventeenth century, a Chinese monk from Kuang Tung (Canton) came to Thua Thien, central Viet Nam. His dharma name was Minh Hoang-Tu Dung; he belonged to the thirty-fourth generation of the Lam Te school. Tu Dung had An Ton (now called Tu Dam) temple built in Hue and traveled through South Viet Nam to teach and give dharma instruction to hundreds of followers. One of his outstanding students was Lieu Quan, who established a school of Buddhism in Viet Nam that continues up to the present day. Most of the Buddhist temples now in South Viet Nam are led by monks of the Lieu Quan school.

Lieu Quan was born in 1670 in Phu Yen province in central Viet Nam.

His mother died when he was six years old. At the age of eleven, he became a novice under the tutelage of Te Vien, a Thien master. For eight years, until the death of Te Vien, Lieu Quan led the life of an ordinary novice: gardening, cooking, reciting the sutra, learning the precepts, and meditating. When he was twenty, Lieu Quan left his first monastery and went to Thuan Hoa, more than three hundred kilometers to the north, traveling most of the way on foot, through the mountains. He reached Hue and Thien Tho temple (now called Bao Quoc) and studied under the master Giac Phong. A year later, upon hearing that his father was gravely ill, he returned home and worked for four years as a woodcutter in order to care for his father. In principle, a Buddhist monk, once having entered into a temple, severed all family ties. However, Lieu Quan's reason for leaving the monastery was in keeping with Vietnamese tradition, which adopted the Confucian duties of a son toward his parents as part of his duties toward Buddha, the dharma, and the Sangha. In 1695, after the death of his father, Lieu Quan went back to Hue to receive the ten precepts of a Sa Di (Sramaner) from the master Thach Liem, a monk of the Tao Dong school. At that time Thach Liem conducted one of the largest ordination ceremonies in history; it lasted more than twenty days, and 1,400 monks received their precepts. The lord Nguyen and his family attended many of the functions; two of the lord's brothers also received the Bodhisattva's fifty-eight precepts for lay people.

In 1697, at the age of twenty-seven, Lieu Quan accepted the 250 precepts of a bhiksu. In search of the higher learning of the Buddha's teaching, he traveled from one monastery to another, studying with several masters. In 1702 he met Tu Dung at An Ton temple, in Hue.

Tradition tells us that at their first meeting, Tu Dung gave Lieu Quan the following Cong An, a subject for meditation to provoke his awakening: "All dharmas return to one, where will the one return to?" To work on this Cong An, Lieu Quan returned to his native province of Phu Yen, living mostly alone for five years. In 1708, he came back to see master Tu Dung. At this meeting, the master showed him a gatha in the form of a short poem:

> Go down to the abyss
> alone by yourself
> to die then to be reborn.
> Who could blame you after that?

Lieu Quan clapped his hands and laughed. Tu Dung shook his head, "Not ripe yet!" Lieu Quan responded, "The hammer is made of iron." Tu Dung shook his head again.

The following morning, Tu Dung was in his chamber when Lieu Quan passed his door. The master called out to him, "Our talk of yesterday has not ended yet! Let's continue; you go first." Lieu Quan said, "If I had known that the lamp is fire itself, I would know that the rice is already well cooked." The master was delighted! He praised the student's state of awakening.

This story is typical of a Thien encounter. What was transmitted between the two Zen monks was hidden beneath the surface of their words; it could not be expressed with language. Only in the context of their face-to-face meeting could the master discern the state of mind of his student, and only then could he judge whether his student had been enlightened. The rest of this story is a skeleton which demands deep concentration and meditation to flesh out.

At this meeting Lieu Quan was considered to have received the transmission of Tam An — the seal of the mind — from Tu Dung. He became the master of the thirty-fifth generation of the Lam Te school of Thien Buddhism. The lineage history tells us of another encounter between the two masters. In 1712, Lieu Quan and Tu Dung met at a large gathering of Buddhist monks in Quang Nam. Tu Dung asked, "Patriarch transmitted to patriarch, Buddha transmitted to Buddha, what was transmitted between them?" Lieu Quan answered with two verses:

> The Bamboo shoot sprang out of stone to grow ten feet high.
> The broom made of turtle's hair weighed three pounds!

Tu Dung replied:

> On the mountain ranges I rowed my boat.
> On the deep dark sea, I rode my horse.

Lieu Quan responded:

> I struck the buffalo's horn (as striking a musical instrument)
> all night long.
> From dawn to sunset I play the guitar with no strings.

After this meeting Tu Dung was completely satisfied with his student Lieu Quan, who was forty-two years old at that time. He had been teaching at several temples and monasteries, from Phu Yen, his native province, to Hue, which was then the capital of South Viet Nam. In 1708 he built one of the most important temples, Thien Tong, which means Dhyana school, or Zen sect. Thien Tong is a monastery on Thien Thai mountain. The temple is there to this day, in an isolated area outside the city of Hue. Until 1975, fifty monks lived permanently in the monastery.

Before Lieu Quan's time, Buddhism in southern Viet Nam was greatly influenced by teachers from China, such as Nguyen Thieu, Tu Dung, and Thach Liem. Lieu Quan set up a new tradition. He altered Buddhist practices to adapt them to the Vietnamese people. Besides Thien Tong, Lieu Quan and his students built several other temples. Among these, the best known are Vien Thong temple in the city of Hue, Hoi Tong temple in Co Lan, and Bao Tinh in Lieu Quan's native province of Phu Yen. From 1733 to 1735, Lieu Quan presided over four large ordination ceremonies. Two other large ordinations were organized in 1740 and 1742. In all, Lieu Quan had more than four thousand disciples.

On an autumn morning in 1742 (the twenty-first day of the eleventh month of the lunar calendar), Lieu Quan knew that he would soon die. He asked the novice who attended him to bring him a pen and paper. He wrote this gatha:

> During seventy or more years I have been in the world of forms and
> emptiness.
> I have lived the same way through forms or emptiness.
> This morning, all vows fulfilled, I am going back home.
> Do not tire yourselves asking about schools and patriarchs.

He then sat quietly, drinking tea. The monks in the temple gathered about him, some in tears. The master said: "Please, do not cry. Even the Buddhas had to enter Nirvana. My coming and going are clear. There is no reason for sorrow." People then regained their composure. The master and his disciples talked. Lieu Quan asked: "Has the Mui hour come yet?" (1:00 P.M. to 3:00 P.M.). They all answered: "Yes." The master said: "After I have gone, please keep in mind the impermanent nature of all things; remain diligent in the practice to realize the prajna in yourselves. Those are my words for you." Sitting in the lotus position, the master died.

The remains of Lieu Quan are now in a stupa at the Thien Tong temple he built. For the future generation of Lieu Quan's school, he left this gatha:

> That Te Dai dao
> Tanh hai thanh trung
> Tam nguyen quang Shuan

Duc bon tu phong
Gioi dinh Phuoc hue
The dung vien thong
Vinh sieu tri qua
Mat khe thanh cong
Truyen tri dieu ly
Dien xuong chanh tong
Hanh giai tuong ung
Dat ngo chan khong

A translation by Nhat Hanh follows:

The great way of reality is the pure ocean of the true nature.
The source of mind has penetrated everywhere.
From the roots of Virtue springs the tradition of compassion.
Vinaya, samadhl, and prajna.
The nature and function of all three are one.
The fruit of transcendent wisdom can be realized by being
wonderfully together.
Maintain and transmit the wonderful principles in order
to make known the true teaching.
For the realization of True Emptiness to be possible,
Wisdom and Action must go together.

Lieu Quan's lineage name is That Dieu (Real Wonder), the first word of which, *That* (also read Thuc in Vietnamese), is the first word of the gatha. All of his disciples belonging to the second generation of Lieu Quan's school were given lineage names beginning with *Te* (the second word of the gatha); disciples of the third generation were given lineage names beginning with *dai*, the third word of the gatha, and so on. The venerable Nhat Hanh, who belongs to the eighth generation, has the lineage name of Trung Quang, *Trung* being the eighth word. His disciples have lineage names beginning with *Tam*, the ninth generation of Lieu Quan's school and the forty-third generation of the Lam Te school.

For three centuries, the rhythm of life in the temple remained mostly unchanged. Following the Lam Te tradition, the monks labored to earn their living, tending gardens and rice fields. Monks and novices were awakened before 4:00 A.M. by a bell sounded by the Tri Tang monk, the temple's librarian. After a long strike of the bell, the Tri Tang recited four verses, which ended with recitation of the Buddha's name. Monks and novices from all corners of the temple followed, reciting the Buddha's name in unison. Then came the sitting meditation, each monk and novice on his own bed or sleeping mat. The Tri Tang walked silently around the temple to make sure that everyone was awake and sitting correctly. After their meditation, the monks and novices worked, doing housekeeping chores. Some of the monks remained in the main hall for the morning Cong Phu (literally, effort, or the recitation of the sutras). After breakfast at 6:00 A.M., there was more work and study. At the offering of the meal to Buddha, the Bodhisattvai, and the ancient patriarchs at noon, all monks and novices gathered again to have lunch in silence. Work and study resumed at 2:00 P.M. Cong Phu was set for 4:00 P.M., followed by a light supper at 5:30.

The evening activities began at 8:00 P.M. with Tinh Do or Pure Land practice, a practice that stresses human aspiration toward the most perfect human society, when all monks and novices gathered at the Buddha's hall for recitations of the Tinh Do sutras, the Buddha and the Bodhisattva names, for an hour. At 10:00 P.M., everyone returned to his own bed or sleeping mat, when a long strike at the bell signaled the beginning of the evening meditation period.

In all other temples of the Lieu Quan school, this practice has also been followed. The venerable Thich Vien Dieu, a monk in Montreal who had lived in the Thien Tong temple from his childhood, has said that life in the Thien Tong temple continued in this way until 1980, the time he left Viet Nam to come to Canada as a refugee. The venerable Thich Vien Dieu is now the monk-resident at the Thuyen Ton temple (which is the Vietnamese name for Thien Tong, his original monastery) in the city of St. Laurent.

In Viet Nam, Thien (Dhyana, Zen, or meditation) and Buddhism are interchangeable terms. Buddhist temples are called Cua Thien, literally Thien gate. Large temples are also monasteries, which are open to the public for three major events each year. Small temples in populous areas with fewer monks and novices also follow the rhythm of monastic life, but because of time spent in public service, the days are less strictly regulated. To compensate for the lack of rigorous monastic practices, monks from small temples gather at the larger temples, mostly the To Dinh (patriarch house), during the summer for a three-month period of An Cu (literally, calm living or retreat). Lay Buddhists are encouraged to attend twenty-four or forty-eight-hour retreats in the temples, Bat Quan Trai, during which time they live the daily life of a novice. The Lieu Quan school combines Thien (Zen practices) with Tinh Do (pure land practices) to satisfy the spiritual needs of the monks and the populace at the same time.

Nhat Hanh, whose translation of Lieu Quan's last gatha has been quoted above, is more widely known in the West than any other Vietnamese living master. In 1964 he set up a new order in the tradition of the Lieu Quan school, the Tiep Hien (Interbeing) order, which includes monks and laity. Tiep Hien members take vows to practice the fourteen precepts that reflect the spirit of the fifty-eight Bodhisattva precepts. In the Mahayana tradition, the Bodhisattva precepts represent a Buddhism that gets involved with the well being of society. A monk in the Lieu Quan school usually takes the vows of the Bodhisattva precepts even after being ordained by taking the 250 precepts of a bhiksu. A bhiksu pledges never to kill. By taking the vows of the Bodhisattva precepts, a bhiksu also engages in preventing killing in the world around him. Compassion is not merely a passive stance; it means taking an active role. This tradition of engagement is now carried into the Tiep Hien precepts that were designed to deal with the problems of today's world.

In 1967 Nhat Hanh was forced into exile because of his activities in the peace movement in Viet Nam. For the last twenty years, he has been teaching Thien practice to tens of thousands of Westerners. He has accepted hundreds of disciples into the Tiep Hien order. *Butsu Mon*, a Buddhist bulletin of San Francisco, considers him the most popular teacher of the new wave of Buddhism in North America. His books and teaching emphasize that Buddhism, as a spiritual movement of humankind, should be integrated with the spiritual tradition of the West. This integration of Buddhism into local beliefs and cultures has occurred in Tibet, China, Japan, Viet Nam, and Thailand. Nhat Hanh believes it must be achieved now in the West as well; otherwise Buddhism will not be true to itself. During a visit to Montreal a few years ago, Nhat Hanh met with Father Brodeur, the provincial at a Franciscan monastery.

"Jesus Christ told his disciples to eat bread as if eating His own flesh," Nhat Hanh said. "I see in His words the true spirit of Thien. A practitioner of Thien does everything in mindfulness, the same way we eat our daily bread as if the Lord is present."

Translated by Nguyen Ba Chung

Nonattachment

Let's gather every fragment of our memories
It's all that we have at the end of our life
Warring days and nights, showers of sun and rain
What's left of love?

Let's gather what remains of our memories
It's all that we have at the close of our life
Warring days and nights make us wonder
Should the bundle we gather be empty or full?

Parting

Sunlight falls through the clouds
On the day of her return, whose hair is long
The one who returns doesn't speak
About the passionate days

We met, but didn't say a word
I didn't know how to speak
Whatever words I might say
Could only hide the words unsaid

We said good-bye; we parted
I don't know when we'll meet again
We leave the lost days alone
In a whirlwind of dust and rain

White Circles Revisited

To Pham Tien Duat

Twenty-three years ago
you went in search of the sutra
and stopped at Hoa Xa,

A village of two thousand
whose only industry
was making mosquito nets
for the people's army,
white cloth spun and dipped in green,
the army's camouflage nets.

Half the village children
wore white arm bands.
There were so many,
white circles circled the roads;
white cloth blanketed the village;
whiteness blanketed the sky.

Eight hundred sons went south.
Eight hundred daughters remained
spinning white cloth
into white circles.
Few returned.
White circles circled the road.
White cloth blanketed the village.
Whiteness blanketed the eyes, the mind.

You remembered the days of childhood too,
and the white band on your forehead
that remained an unbearable emptiness:
a father's voice you had never heard.
A father's love you would never have.

Twenty-three years,
yet deep and untouched
that unbearable loss remains.
A war, yes, a war.
But who among us
can make those white bands disappear?

The Path

We have to learn as if for the first time
How to eat, how to speak, how to work
Lessons of history —
    Van Hanh, Quang Trung
    passions that draw blood
A century to rethink everything
    throw away the stinking, ruinous ideas
That have singed our grasses

Path of Meiji
    flowers of Israel
    rivers of Western thoughts
An opportunity
    for a Dien Hong campaign
Return to the source
    through one thousand paths

All pain, every wound of two centuries
    in the heart of the Vietnamese
Come to an end
To bear fruit.

Motion

Like an ancient town buried underground for thousands of years that is just now waking up, the snails creep across the garden under moonlight as dazzling as sunlight in summer. The tops of their shells flash like the diamond beads of a queen's crown on a festival evening. Their soft wet bodies glide, trembling with tenderness. Their antennas rise toward the sky to catch the waves of strange sounds. What secret language, happy or sad, is calling the snails?

The moonlight is quiet, the trees are quiet. The snails creep over sleeping grass and fallen leaves. Their bodies glide over sharp-cold bits of broken glass. I can't tell whether they cry or curse. What I hear is the sound of water, rising to flood the moonlit night.

The snails hid in banana plants, in thorn-bushes. Awake now, they silently slip away. Is my garden their native land, or the next garden, or still another garden? Are they running away from their native land, or finding their native land? It doesn't matter: I sing a song tonight because their departure is as marvelous as a dream, or a festival evening.

The last snail creeps over the old wall surrounding my garden. As the top of its shell disappears, the last diamond light of the queen's crown fades away. The snails leave glittering streams of light in their paths, and the streaming stars change position in the sky.

Behind the window of my house tonight, I whisper Good-bye to the snails.

Translated by the author and Martha Collins

The Inn of Snake Alcohol

The snakes are buried in alcohol.
Their spirits creep over the mouth of the jug,
They lie in the bottoms of cups.
Creep on, please creep on through white lips —
Listen: Drunk is shouting his vagabond song.

With the top of a hat, with a pair of shoes
With glazed eyes that search the horizon
With anger setting fires in the temple
A whole life stunned by nothingness —

Like a broken stone, like a bending reed
With the startling turns of a poem
With a frenzy of fears that lick like fire
With the laugh in the sleepwalker's crying —

Creep on, spirits of snakes, creep on!
Dazzling venom spurts from the jug.
There's a man who drinks nothing but memories
Whose veins are the paths of snakes.

The little inn buries the great night
The forest recalls the name of Autumn
Alcohol carries the spirits of snakes
And Drunk is making a song from his own venom.

Translated by the author and Martha Collins

Time

I sit holding my little daughter.
Both of us are sick —
We talk to each other in fits of coughing.

Dry branches crackle:
The sacred flame stirs and wakens.
Invisible footsteps circle the fire
Raising gusts of warm ashes.

Farther back, in a red autumn,
Gray snakes creep across a garden.
Farther back, crying with summer, I see
Another me walking, flying in the garden.

Farther back, still farther,
Time is a place where I sit by a fire,
One fever holding another,
Our coughs, now one, waiting to break in two.

Translated by the author and Martha Collins

On the Highway

Women carry bamboo shrimp pots, move in a single row
Close to the left side of the highway,
Wearing black. Only their hands,
Legs and eyes are not covered,
But they are all black too.
The pots are crescents picked up from the mud.
Creels at their hips are clean-shaven heads
Swaying with their marching steps.
Their shadows black puddles on the highway.

They move silent as defeated soldiers.
The pot handles bent down
Like rifle barrels without bullets.
Their torn clothes in the pots are
Flags of closed village festivals,
And the fish scales glitter like medals.
They don't wait to be welcomed.

Like summer clouds floating heavy and muggy
Before a coming storm, the women carry bamboo shrimp pots
And move in a single row along the left of the highway.
With the smell of crab and shellfish
Around them, where did they come from?
And where will they go?

Translated by the author and Yusef Komunyakaa

New Students, Old Teacher

for the American poets, on the occasion of their readings

We're the only people left in the world.
We lift our faces to pray, to utter our final words.
Three-eyed poems fly across the home of darkness.
We're prisoners, we're free;
We're recent corpses, we're living bodies
Who measure our breaths carefully:
We've hidden our lungs in smoky kitchens,
We've lost them in rotting jungle leaves.

We're the only people left in the world.
We bathe in muddy marshes of fear and pride
Where bubbles open their mouths to curse us.
We dry our waterless faces before a fire of howling blood
While one-winged bats speak many languages,
Flying about in eye-glasses, in search
Of the new breasts of our musty women.

Our noses chime, like terrified bells.
Our hearts dig deep holes; they sniff graves.
Our half-deaf ears fall like autumn leaves
And new ears sprout in the spaces between our fingers.

We're the only people left in the world.
A waterless river flows over our heads,
Where fish without fins or gills find their way to class
And an old teacher breaks cloud after cloud of smoke
With his winter coughs. He plucks
Off a ringless finger to write on the blackboard
And makes a comma that looks like a slanting eye.
Then he sits down and sews his pants,
Waiting for new students to come, their books filled with zeroes.

Translated by the author and Martha Collins

Those Days of Happiness

In April 1945 my family moved to Do Huu Vi, a street full of Hanoi government officials, to live with my aunt. The move would be good for all of us. Our rent would be lower, and we could rely on my aunt and our cousins during the chaotic days under both the French and the Japanese. My aunt would feel safer renting to her sister, and any extra income helped during this difficult time. I didn't feel any great joy at the move; this would be a house full of women who were sad and cold. My aunt was by nature strict and distant. Her two daughters were just as distant and loved to judge and make fun of others. They used to call me a dummy because I was always shy and a bit slow. My aunt had four children: a first-born son who had married and was a doctor, and three daughters. The second died suddenly at the age of twenty-five, unmarried, without even a sweetheart. Her funeral was still and white. The horses were draped in white, the carriage was painted white, the feather pompoms at the four corners of the carriage were white, and all the mourners were dressed in white. However, there was one man who kept a distance from the hearse, who wore a black suit. He held a package wrapped in newspaper in his two hands in front of his chest. After the internment, when everyone had left, he stepped in front of the grave, opened the newspaper package and put down a bundle of white flowers. Then he knelt.

The other two sisters were Linh who was twenty-five, and Nga who was twenty-two. Both had passed the sixth grade, with an upper elementary school certificate. They both stayed home, however; they had few friends and lived a solitary and cold existence. A woman, even an intelligent, knowledgeable one, could end up with a hard life. It wasn't easy to find a man she could fall in love with. "Who would dare to marry those two fiends? They'll both be spinsters," my aunt often lamented to my mother. All her life my aunt never dirtied her hands with housework. All she did was make obeisance at the temples and play cards. Despite her utter uselessness, her husband held her in high regard and her daughters never dared to cross her. When she went out, the house became as noisy as a marketplace; when she returned, everyone tiptoed about like ghosts, speaking in whispers. My mother said, "She's born happy, from birth to old age. We all have our fate."

2

That's how it was. When we moved in, things in my aunt's family had changed considerably. My uncle had died in early 1945. He was a chemical engineer who had graduated in the 1900s in France. He suffered dysentery during his last few months; his body wasted away and smelled. His son, the doctor from Haiphong, came home one evening when it was already dark. Carrying his medicine satchel upstairs, he sat down and talked with his father until midnight. Then he came down quietly, telling his sisters, "Let father sleep." Early next morning he told his mother, "Father passed away last night." My aunt stayed home every day, every week. There was no money left to play cards in any case. She closeted herself upstairs, withdrew into herself, and only came down at mealtime. My two cousins also changed their routines and behaviors. Speaking softly, they treated others with consideration and ease and they began to go out quite often, either for an afternoon or the whole day. Whenever they went, the two would spend hours picking out their clothes, arguing about the colors, and experimenting with putting on make-up so that it would appear they wore no make-up. Then they would look at each other, make this and that comment, recount this and that joke, and burst into innocent, carefree laughter. My aunt didn't say a word. She sensed something unusual but pretended she didn't notice.

The doctor, however, still kept his customary way. His lineage gave him stature; his medical degree gave him stature, his being the son-in-law of a governor-general gave him stature, fame, and wealth. The world's fortunes might change, but nothing could touch his exalted position. I just didn't like the way he called my mother "Madam," while referring to himself in the informal way as if she were a stranger, or the way my mother sheepishly addressed him as Mr., laughing and talking obsequiously. Once he stopped by the house on his way to Hanoi. He said to the two sisters, "Let me have dinner with you tonight." Immediately Linh said, "Why don't you go to the restaurant. There isn't much at home." He frowned unhappily. Linh continued the conversation with my mother without missing a beat, as if nothing had happened. Another time he said something to them while they all sat at the little table in the middle of the yard eating cake and drinking tea. The two sisters said something back, laughing. He shouted angrily, "Don't listen to those commies, the Japanese will chop our heads off. Their swords are sharp as hell." Linh shot back loudly: "Only a dumb animal would just sit there, waiting to be beheaded." He stood straight up, grabbed his satchel, and walked out, his face red with anger. Nga called after him, "How can a man be that weak!" During dinner my aunt asked: "Has your brother already left for Haiphong?" "They got into a tiff so he just left," my mother said. My aunt frowned, "After a father dies, there's the elder brother. If the elder brother cannot keep the peace, isn't it a cursed family?" Linh smiled wryly, nudging her sister lightly: "He's an educated man but he does not prize his dignity. All he wants is to be a servant to someone else, French or Japanese." My aunt dropped the pair of chopsticks on the table, her face purple with anger: "Idiots! If this house didn't eat French rice, could we have survived on rice water until now?"

3

In July my aunt had to sell off the bed with the carved legs, the tea cabinet, and a whole series of earthen pots, said to be antiques. Then came the damask silk tunic and the fur coat. Finally the Omic pedicab, the only means of transportation for the whole family, was also sold. The meals continued to be great — a tray of roasted meat, baked fish, mushroom soup, minced meat stuffed with snails and ginger leaves. Always a truly sumptuous feast. So thought my mother and I, but my aunt couldn't stand sitting in front of a meal with only two or three dishes. Even if she didn't eat, she had an inveterate desire to sit in front of a grand, fanciful meal, just to be able to look at it. After a few months of eating together, my mother asked to be allowed to have our meals separately. My aunt glowered at her, "If you want to eat separately, then don't live with us. You and I are sisters. Why bother having two kitchens? Won't people curse us for doing such a thing?"

My mother had to go along, but the three of us shared the meals with a great deal of discomfort. Yet at night things got quite merry. The whole family, except my aunt who would go upstairs after dinner, gathered closely together under the dim light listening to Linh, who always read in a whisper the paper of the Viet Minh general command. The paper was small, the size of a notebook, and poorly printed, but it was the only one that dared to call the French "colonialists," or the Japanese "fascists," the Tran Trong Kim government a servile, "figurehead government," and the king, "a figurehead king." In those days I didn't know anything, but was proud to be able to take part in such rebellious adult acts and to be able to live in such a secretive adult atmosphere. That made me stand tall among those of my age. Then Linh and Nga started entertaining male friends at home, something quite extraordinary. At first it was a young man who had looked like a college student. Sometimes he wore white shorts, sometimes a yellow suit, the look of a wealthy family in Hanoi. He usually came by in the afternoon, and they would talk together in low voices until dark. The young man did most of the talking; the two sisters sat still, listening respectfully, their faces bright, full of innocent and exquisite beauty. My mother would ask: "He is the friend of which one of you?" Linh blushed, saying not a word. Nga said: "He is a cadre." Then came another man, perhaps another cadre, and perhaps someone even more senior. They drank tea and ate sweet cakes around the small table in the inner yard. This man seemed the oldest, with a mustache and a pair of sun glasses. He neither spoke nor smiled very much, and retained a sense of mystery and secrecy just like the Ky Phat character in the Pham Cao Cung detective stories. It seemed that thereafter, more and more people came to talk to the two sisters. It was safe to carry out secret works in this house. The street was quiet, the house had only one owner, and although my family stayed there, we came and went without prying into anyone else's business.

––––––––

At the beginning of August, some tradeswomen who bought old bottles, copper scraps, and duck feathers, repeatedly banged on the door. It turned out that they weren't looking for anything to buy. From the bottom of their baskets they pulled out packages wrapped carefully in newspaper and gave them to the two sisters: the red and yellow cloth to make into flags. There were two sewing machines in the house. The two sisters and I labored to drag them into the room next to the kitchen. The two sisters sewed from morning until midnight. Then my mother came in to give them a hand. My aunt asked, "What do you two sew all day long?" My mother said, "A charitable association asked us to make some cheap clothes to give away." My aunt asked again, "Do they pay anything?" Nga replied, "It's charity work; how can we ask for pay?" My aunt didn't pursue it any further. The old maid now had to go to the market by herself, and then do the cooking by herself. The meals became much poorer: a plate of boiled vegetables, a bowl of vegetable broth laced with sapindus, plus a dish of meat or fish baked in salt. We ate that for the entire week, with no variety. My aunt suddenly became much more forgiving, and ate whatever was served without a word of anger or complaint except for some contemptuous looks, and an occasional sly smile, which made people uncomfortable.

Then the Revolution came. A Hanoi wrapped in red, young and free. Not a shot was fired, and not one person was killed, which made it an especially joyous event. Even the man who lost the most, the king, felt happy and proud to be a citizen of an independent Vietnam. Two days after the Revolution, the two sisters were called to work. I wondered what work they would do, and it turned out to be as food workers for a security agency of the Revolution stationed at the former French Security Office. The two women, thin and weak, who had never before had to engage in any heavy activity, or wait on anyone, now woke up at dawn, went to the market, and then cooked for more than twenty people. And yet they looked younger, prettier. What wonder was the power of hope, of love! It could bring the dead back to life.

Once in a happy conversation among the whole family around dinner my mother asked my aunt: "Did you know that they had joined the Viet Minh in those early days?" My aunt laughed disdainfully: "If I hadn't known, do you think I would have left them running around from morning till night?" No one understood what she meant. She continued: "I saw through the fellow with the fair skin and a ready smile right away. And the mustached fellow wearing sun glasses could have been caught, had things gone on like that a few more months. The way he looked, like a secret agent, raised a lot of suspicion. The upstairs room had a window looking down into the inner yard. The window was covered with a shade so no one could tell if someone kept watch behind it."

4

At the end of 1946 my family left Hanoi for Hung Yen, the city of my mother's family. Then came the nationwide Resistance. Throughout the eight years of fighting against the French, I had no news of my aunt's family. In 1955 when I returned to Hanoi, I went to visit her. She was then over seventy, living with her daughter-in-law, nephews, and nieces. Her only son, the doctor in the French army, was killed by a mine on Route 5 in early 1953. With his death the family's fortune declined. With too many children, my aunt and her daughter-in-law had to live from hand to mouth. There was not enough food. My aunt had to accept her hard lot. She didn't even have money to buy areca nuts. I offered her a few thousand piasters, from an author's fee I had just received. She took it with both hands, saying: "I'm deeply grateful. Please come by and see me once in a while." The two sisters had joined the Resistance, and I heard that they had married and had children, but they hadn't brought their families back to see my aunt. The following year my aunt died, but I was busy with an assignment and couldn't go back and so I missed the chance to meet the two sisters. In 1970, I had the opportunity to pass by Yen My district. The district's main street had reverted to its former noisy, happy self because the United States had stopped the bombing in 1968. I was walking about, looking over the sandals made out of old automobile tires, when someone called my name. I quickly turned around. A heavyset woman, with drooping eyes, baggy cheeks, and half-white hair cut short, stood in the door of the photography studio, staring at me intently. She was a complete stranger but I answered nevertheless, "Yes, I am K.H." She hurriedly stepped forward, seized my hand, and pulled me inside. "Get in here, boy; get in here, boy. You deserve a spanking!" I was in my military uniform, a major's insignia pinned to my collar, striking quite a tall and imposing figure. If she called me "boy," she had to be someone very close, but who could she be? She pushed me down into a chair, standing arms akimbo in front of me, smiling mischievously: "Dumb, dumb! Don't you recognize me?" Good heavens, it was sister Linh! Oh my sister Linh, how could you age so fast, get that shabby so fast. I was overcome with tears and could only utter, "Good Heavens!" I didn't dare say anything more. A bare-chested man with closely cropped hair walked out from the back in a threatening manner. Sister Linh said: "My husband!" I stood up to say hello. He nodded his head, and looking at my insignia, said curtly: "Such a young major?" "He's my cousin," Linh said, "son of my mother's younger sister." He sat down right in front of me, pulling at the water tobacco pipe that was filled with dregs and ashes. His voice sounded muffled. "So you two just met each other?" Such a dirty, tiny studio. I wondered if he was the photographer? But Linh said photography was her trade; he had worked as a nurse for the district hospital but quit because of asthma.

"What about . . . ?" I started to ask but didn't know the man's name. I remembered him from those early, secretive days. After the Revolution, he didn't come by the house anymore; he and his colleagues could now meet where they worked, and I hadn't seen any need to pry. What was his name? Linh smiled sadly: "You want to ask about Hanh? He was my first husband. After we had a daughter together, he passed away after catching an acute form of malaria in the northern highlands. In 1951, I married Tung here. We had two more children. I can never forget those days on Do Huu Vi Street; what a grand time, what joy, wasn't it, K.H.?"

I couldn't find much to say. I sat there thunderstruck, looking at the sister I had just found, my stomach churning at the changes time had wrought. Without much conviction she said, "It's almost noon, why don't you stay to have a meal with us?" I didn't have a chance to say no when her husband blurted: "Have your lunch in the district and then come back to visit us. With only the two of us, anything will do, but it's not really proper fare for a guest."

The following afternoon I went to say good-bye on my way back to Hanoi. Linh told me to be sure to pay Nga a visit if I ever had a chance to go by Tuyen Quang. I would know Nga's husband: the man with the mustache and sun glasses who looked like a character from a detective story. He had been the liaison agent of the group then. Having just joined, he liked to act mysterious. For his sake it was fortunate the Revolution came about when it did. I asked for Nga's address. Linh asked her husband and he went to look for it and then grumbled at her. They hadn't written to each other for such a long time; the address was lost.

I took my satchel and walked slowly to Yen My bus station. Filled with sadness, I didn't dare turn around and look back even once. Well, one shouldn't feel too sad about the barrenness of human life. That's how it is; how it always is. Everyone has a time when they live for hope, for love, for a dream, perhaps tinged with airy bubbles. Those beautiful dreams, those beautiful lives, those exquisite faces will always exist in time, like an infinite series that follow each other to eternity.

August 1992

Translated by Nguyen Ba Chung

The Alabaster Stork

When rain blackens the sky
>> in the east,
when rain blackens the sky
>> in the west,
when rain blackens the sky,
>> in the south, the north,
> I see a stork white as alabaster
> take wing and usher in the rain . . .

Rice in the paddy ripples
>> like a broad flag,
potato plants send up
>> their dark green leaves,
and the palm tree opens
>> its fronds to catch the drops.
Toads and frogs sing
>> all day and all night,
and fish dance merrily
>> flickering to that tune.
> But no one sees in the branches
> the stork shivering in the cold . . .

When rain blackens again
>> the sky in the east,
when rain blackens again
>> the sky in the west,
when rain blackens again
>> the sky in the south, the north,
> I see that stork white as alabaster
> take wing to proclaim the rain again.

English version by Fred Marchant and Nguyen Ba Chung

Quang Tri

Everywhere we dug there were white bones.
What could we do? Could we just leave them?
What kind of foundation would they make for our house?
My friends were perplexed. Were they our bones, or their bones?

No, I told them, there are no American bones here.
The Americans left years ago.
These skeletons, scattered all over our land,
Belong only to the Vietnamese.

Translated by Nguyen Ba Chung with Bruce Weigl

New Year Fireworks

The whole city seems to explode.
Fireworks thunder in the distance.
An old man with a stick and bag
sobs quietly by the train station.

The whole city seems to be on fire,
the sky suddenly streaked with flares.
A woman picks through the garbage,
shrivels up beneath a bridge.

The whole city seems awash in smoke.
The smells of fires fill the sky.
A streetwalker greets the New Year
alone beneath a tree.

The whole city seems to crack open.
Firecrackers cover the pavements.
A child lives alone in the dust,
curls up beneath a veranda listening.

Smoke rises, explosions rumble.
What battle has just passed through?
A man on a wooden crutch sits by the river,
dreaming of home . . .

Midnight, New Year's 1992

Translated by Nguyen Ba Chung and Kevin Bowen

Red Earth, Blue Water

Bombs ploughed into the red earth, berry red.
Scorching sunlight burned the noon air like kiln fire.

Bomb-raked funnels turned into rose water wells,
A noiseless stream of blue water gushing up.

That's our country, isn't it friend.
The maddening agony, the honey comes from within.

Translated by Nguyen Ba Chung

A Small Song of Peace

For M. Tka chop

I listen as you read from the pages of *Truth*
strange   yet,
Men everywhere are alike. They love their leisure, to tell their schoolboy
       tales.
In one place war rages on,
in another men congratulate each other on peace.

Down through the years the blood rolls on.
Tell me what century hasn't burned its millions in war?
Rifles firing, bombs exploding, a fine rain falling over the face of the
       earth.
One part of the earth engulfed in that rain and, in another, in ten
       thousand accents, men
sing songs of peace.

When I was a young man I walked through a land flooded in fire.
Now
I slap my thigh and laugh, drink beer above the high tower of Ottankino,
and the battlefield is a soiled and distant place.

Tonight, across the earth people turn up their wide faces.
All over the scarred continents, Africa . . . Asia . . . Nicaragua.
Lines of smoke and fire; hearts, like houses burning.
We have our calm and happy house; everywhere, someone enjoys calm.
In Palestine, where the earth is scarred and burned,
where soldiers' bones are strewn across the roads and men die in suicidal
       ambushes;
when the fighting stops, they are all only victims.

And the war criminals.
After all the murder and killing, they go on living, right out in the open.
They look so like normal people, the rich and cunning.

2

Every age has brought its madmen.
How many temples have they destroyed to bring about their changes?
How to guess how many of their own they've slaughtered,
the madness of war passed down through generations?

How many bloody battles can these old pine trees lay claim to?
How many mad years,
   how many mad months,
     how many mad days,
the fires still burning in the tender green shoots?
One mad second, the smallest kernel of time, all that is necessary,
just one moment, one missing second,
enough to burn the entire world, everything that's ever been born.
No men left.
   No subjects left.
     No human beings remaining.
The face of the earth barren, nothing likely to survive.

Are our voices calm, or are they dissembling?
Is this the thread of a prayer or is this only music?
How many years may the earth survive;
how many years temples live in the shadows of cities?

3

We slap our thighs and drink beer.
Half a kilometer away
towers send pictures end over end.
Over our old heads — space stations, information satellites.
Over our old heads — space shuttles and cosmonaut stations.
Over our old heads the stars reign.
We foolishly feel the distances narrowing.

The immaterial waves of electricity go searching, but they don't lie.
The basis of any intelligent literature is to seek the basis of others.
People of this world wish to meet people from outer space.
Things once thought unbelievable have come true.
How much time wasted to wish back;

not the time of armies, of policemen, of border guards, frontiers,
but of men and women living in unity, free of worry.

We want change,
but truth is crucial.

These nations face those as enemies.

One group annihilates another.
How do the people of the earth reach out to each other across these great
      distances?

How to plough down these incorporeal distances?
How to understand an electrical current?
How do the ions alternately collide and pass through each other?

4

Suddenly tossed in mid-air we pass between heaven and earth,
we skim by the soft white clouds, dusting them,
past the ravines of Mercury, its hills spotted with traces of steles.
You and I can remember our small conquests there.
But now do we know what they are doing?

We keep on entering the old frames — singing our boyhood songs.
Under the umbrella of your sharp tones and my hard voice,
the nerves in our brains rising,
together we sing these tunes of peace.

Our raucous voices
draw everyone to us.
The hope of man dissolving all these tensions.

All over the earth, the face of hope returns.
Only love poems now,
and news of love . . .

Moscow — Ho Chi Minh City, September 1985

Translated by Kevin Bowen

Contributors

John Balaban is a professor at the University of Miami and the director of its MFA program in writing. A conscientious objector, he served in Vietnam as a volunteer with the Committee for Responsibility to Save War Injured Children. A winner of the National Poetry Series, the Lamont Prize, and a nominee for the National Book Award, he has published nine books, including *After Our War, Ca Dao Vietnam, Coming Down Again, Remembering Heaven's Face, Blue Mountain,* and *Words for My Daughter.*

Lady Borton worked as an American Friends Service Committee volunteer in Quang Ngai Province during the Vietnam War. She returned to Asia in 1980 to assist Vietnamese boat people and has most recently worked as director of Quaker Field Services in Vietnam. She has been a columnist for the *Akron Beacon Journal* and a regular commentator for National Public Radio. Her essays have appeared in *Harper's* and the *New York Times.* She is the author of two books, *Sensing the Enemy* and *After Sorrow.*

Kevin Bowen is the director of the William Joiner Center for the Study of War and Social Consequences. He served in Vietnam in 1968–69 with the 1st Air Cavalry Division. *Playing Basketball with the Viet Cong*, his first collection of poems, was published by Curbstone Press in 1994.

Cao Tien Le was born in Nghe An Province. He served in the Army of the Viet Minh and was wounded at the final assault at Dien Bien Phu when he was sixteen. He has published eight collections of short stories and several novels. His most recent novel is *Experiencing Dien Bien* (1994). He lives in Ha Noi where he is editor-in-chief of Youth Publishing House.

Phil Caputo served in the Marine Corps in Vietnam. He is the author of two memoirs, *A Rumor of War* and *Means of Escape,* as well as three novels, *Indian Country, DelCorso's Gallery,* and *Horn of Africa.* He won the George Polk Award for his coverage of Palestinian guerrillas and a Pulitzer Prize in 1972 for his work as part of a team of investigative reporters at the *Chicago Tribune.*

Chu Lai was born in Hai Hung Province. He served in the Iron Triangle area as a sapper during the war with the United States. A novelist and playwright, he is the author of more than a dozen works of fiction. His most recent works include *The Ungrateful Circle, The Street of Soldiers,* and *Begging the Past.* He lives in Ha Noi where he is a senior editor at *Van Nghe Quan Doi.*

Martha Collins teaches creative writing at the University of Massachusetts, Boston. She is the author of three books of poetry, the most recent of which is *A History of a Small Life on a Windy Planet,* which won the Alice Fay DiCastagnola Award. Her other awards include a Pushcart Prize and fellowships from the National Endowment for the Arts, the Ingram Merrill Foundation, and the Bunting Institute.

Do Quy Toan Do is a veteran of the Army of the Republic of South Vietnam. He is a poet whose publications include *Dien Viet Nam* (1966), *Nang* (1968), and *Co va Tuyet* (1988). His works have appeared in many journals in the United States, Canada, and Vietnam. Currently he is a professor at the University of Quebec in Montreal.

W. D. Ehrhart served in the Marine Corps in Vietnam in 1967–68. He is the recipient of an Academy of American Poets Prize, a Mary Roberts Rinehart Foundation Grant, and the President's Medal from Veterans for Peace, Inc. His works include *To Those Who Have Gone Home Tired* and *Just for Laughs* (poetry), and *Passing Time, Going Back, Vietnam Perkasie*, and *Busted* (nonfiction). His most recent collection of poetry is *The Distance We Travel*. He was awarded a Pew Fellowship in 1993.

Gloria Emerson, a former foreign correspondent for the *New York Times*, covered the war in Vietnam from 1970 to 1972, and won a George Polk Award for her reporting. Her book on the war and its effects on the American people, *Winners and Losers*, won a National Book Award in 1978. She has written more than thirty magazine articles. She is also the author of *Some American Men* and, most recently, *Gaza: A Year in the Intifada*, an account of Palestinians under Israeli occupation.

Martín Espada is a poet and lawyer. He was awarded a fellowship from the National Endowment for the Arts in 1992. He has published five books of poetry: *The Immigrant Iceboy's Bolero, Trumpets from the Islands of Their Eviction, Rebellion Is the Circle of a Lover's Hands, City of Coughing and Dead Radiators*, and, most recently, *Imagine the Angels of Bread*. He is a recipient of the Paterson Poetry Prize and the PEN/Revson Poetry Prize and is currently an associate professor of English at the University of Massachusetts, Amherst.

George Evans has published three books of poetry in England: *Nightvision, Wrecking*, and *Eye Blade*. *Sudden Dreams* was his first collection published in the United States. A recipient of fellowships from the Lannan Foundation and the National Endowment for the Arts, he is the editor of *The Complete Correspondence of Charles Olson and Cid Corman* and of *Streetfare Journal*, a national program that displays poetry and art on posters in buses. He served in Vietnam as an Air Force medic.

Carolyn Forché lived and wrote in El Salvador during the late 1970s, observing the evolution of the political crisis there firsthand. Her books of poetry include *Gathering the Tribes* and *The Country Between Us*, which was the 1981 Lamont Poetry Selection of the Academy of American Poets. She is the editor of *Against Forgetting: Twentieth-Century Poetry of Witness*, which was published in 1993. Her most recent work, *The Angel of History*, a collection of poetry published by Harper Collins in 1994, won the Los Angeles Times Book Award.

Larry Heinemann is a novelist whose book *Paco's Story* earned him the 1987 National Book Award for fiction. His first novel, *Close Quarters*, appeared in 1977. *Cooler by the Lake*, a comic novel set in his native Chicago, was published in 1992. His shorter work has been featured in numerous periodicals, including *Atlantic, Harper's Magazine*, and *Playboy. Vietnam by Train* is a work in progress.

Ho Xuan Huong was born in Ha Noi in the late eighteenth-century. Twice married and widowed, she wrote poems that have been widely translated and are well known throughout Viet Nam for their beauty, wit, and word play.

Huu Thinh was born in 1942 in Vinh Phu Province. He is currently editor-in-chief of *Van Nghe*, the journal of arts and literature of the Writers' Association. He served in the Peoples Army of Vietnam from 1963 to 1990 as a soldier, correspondent, and editor, rising from the rank of private to lieutenant colonel in the tank corps. A veteran of Khe Sanh, the central highlands, and the Ho Chi Minh campaign, he is a poet whose collections include *Echo from the Trenches* (1966), *On the Way to the City* (1979), and *From the Trench to the City* (1985). He was awarded the national prize for poetry in 1980 and 1995. His most recent collections are *Winter Letter* (1995) and *Song of the Sea*.

Wayne Karlin is a novelist and the author of *Crossover, Lost Armies, The Extras*, and, most recently, *US* (1993). With Le Minh Khue and Tran Vu, he is editor of *The Other Side of Heaven: Post-War Fiction by Vietnamese and American Writers*. He is the recipient of three State of Maryland Individual Artist Awards in Fiction and a recent fellowship from the National Endowment for the Arts. A nominee for a Pushcart Prize, he received the Prairie Schooner Readers' Choice Award in 1992. He teaches at Charles County Community College in Maryland. His new book, *Rumors and Stones*, came out in the fall of 1996.

Yusef Komunyakaa is a professor of English and African American studies at Indiana University. Among his books of poetry are *I Apologize for the Eyes in My Head, Lost in the Bonewheel Factory, Dien Cai Dau*, and *Toys in a Field*. His most recent works are *Magic City* and *Neon Vernacular: New and Selected Poems*, which was awarded the Pulitzer Prize for poetry for 1994. He was the Holloway Poet at the University of California at Berkeley in 1991–92.

Le Luu was born in 1942 in Hai Hung Province. He worked as an army signal man and correspondent on the Ho Chi Minh Trail in the Troung Son Range. He is currently an editor at *Van Nghe Quan Doi*. A novelist, his main works include *Those Who Carry Guns, Near the Sun, Forest Clearing, Border Line, A Time Far Past*, and, most recently, *Chuyen Lang Cuoi* (1993). He was awarded the national prize for fiction for *A Time Far Past* in 1987.

Le Minh Khue was born in 1949 in Thanh Hoa Province. She joined the army at the age of fifteen and spent much of her youth on the Ho Chi Minh Trail. A short story writer and novelist, her works include: *Summer's Peak, Distant Stars, Conclusion, An Afternoon away from the City*, and *A Girl in a Green Gown*. She won the Writers' Association's award for short stories in 1987. She is an editor at the Writers' Association Publishing House. Her most recent collection is *Little Tragedies*.

Luis Lopéz-Nieves is a professor of literature at the University of the Sacred Heart in San Juan, Puerto Rico. His publications include *Seva* and *Escribir para Rafa*. He is the author of numerous short stories and poems, and has written scripts for television. He has served as literary correspondent for the television program "Hoy," and has been a recipient of a Ford Foundation Fellowship.

Fred Marchant served in the Marine Corps and was granted status as a conscientious objector during the war in Vietnam. He has received fellowships at MacDowell, Yaddo, and the Ucross Foundation. Poetry editor at the *Harvard Review*, he is currently chair of the humanities and modern languages department at Suffolk University in Boston.

Demetria Martínez is a poet, novelist, and journalist. *Turning*, a collection of her poetry, was published with the manuscripts of two other Chicana poets in *Three Times a Woman*. As a journalist, she worked for the *Albuquerque Journal*. Currently she is a columnist for the *National Catholic Reporter*. Her first novel, *Mother Tongue*, which was published in the fall of 1994 and will be reissued by Ballantine, won the Western States Book Award.

Robert Mason's newest book, *Chickenhawk: Back in the World: Life after Vietnam*, is a sequel to *Chickenhawk*. He has also written two science fiction novels, *Weapon* and *Solo*, a sequel. He lives in Florida with his wife, Patience H.C. Mason, who is the author of *Recovering from the War: A Woman's Guide to Helping Your Vietnam Vet, Your Family, and Yourself*.

Harry Mattison is a photographer who has covered wars in Central America and the Middle East. His photographs have appeared in major journals throughout the world and have been featured in exhibits nationally and internationally.

Marilyn McMahon served as a U.S. Navy nurse in Vietnam in 1969–70. Her observations of war and its consequences infuse her poetry, which she began writing a few years ago. She has published one book of poems, *Work in Progress*, and is at work on a second. Her poetry has also appeared in various anthologies. She is the subject of a book, *Another Silenced Trauma*, which appeared in 1987.

Victor Montejo's work focuses on his native Mayan culture and includes four books. *El Kanil: Man of Lightning* is a long poem based on a traditional Mayan tale. *The Bird Who Cleans the World* is a collection of Mayan folk tales. *Testimony: Death of a Guatemalan Village* recounts the destruction of a Mayan community, as does his latest, *A Very Brief Account of the Continuous Destruction of the Maya*.

Nguyen Ba Chung is a poet and translator whose work has appeared in the *Boston Review*, *Compost*, *Manoa*, *The Nation*, *New Asia Review* and other places. He is cotranslator of Le Luu's *A Time Far Past (Thoi xa vang)* and author of two collections of poetry in Vietnamese, *Tuoi nao thuong em (Time of Love)* and *Di toi khong ngung (Pressing Forward)*.

Nguyen Duy was born in Thanh Hoa Province in 1948. He served in the infantry in the war against the United States. A poet, his major works include *Cat Trang* (*White Sand*, 1973), *Duong Xa* (*Distant Road*), and *Anh Trang* (*Moonlight*, 1984). He was awarded the national prize for poetry in 1985 for *Anh Trang*. He is currently a co-director of Mekong Film Studios and southern editor of *Van Nghe*. His most recent work is *Sixes and Eights*.

Nguyen Khai was born in 1930 in Ha Nam Ninh Province. During the wars with the French and the United States, he was an army medic and a journalist. His short story collections and novels include: *Ground Nuts Harvest*, *The Conflict*, *They Live and Fight at Con Co*, *Lanes in the Clouds*, *Father and Son*, and *Year End Meeting*. He was awarded the national prize for fiction in 1982.

Nguyen Mong Giac is best known for his novels and short stories. Currently living in California, he has most recently published a three-volume saga of modern Vietnam, *Mua bien dong*. He edits the Vietnamese-language monthly review, *Van Hoc*.

Nguyen Quang Sang was born in An Giang Province in the Mekong Delta in 1932. During the French and American wars he served as a soldier, writer, and official of the Writers' Association of the National Liberation Front. His works include the novels *Diary of a Person Who Stays*, *Land of Fire*, *The Monsoon Season*, *The River of Childhood* and the short story collections *Native Country Man* and *The River That Sings*. He received the Writers' Association Award for Fiction in 1993.

Nguyen Quang Thieu was born in 1957 in Ha Tay Province. He is a poet, short story writer, translator, and editor at *Van Nghe*. He won the national prize for literature in 1993 for his collection of poems *The Insomnia of the Fire*. His other works include the collections *The House of Green Age* (1990) and *The White Haired Woman* (1993, short stories) and three novels. He has translated the works of many American writers into Vietnamese for various journals and publishing houses. Adaptations of his short stories into film have won awards at film festivals in Vietnam and Portugal.

Nguy Ngu was born in Hue and currently resides in Ho Chi Minh City. He served in the Army of the Republic of South Vietnam (ARVN) during the war and was imprisoned both during and after the war. He is a short story writer and screenwriter.

Tim O'Brien served in Vietnam in the Americal Division, 1968–69. He won the National Book Award in 1978 for *Going after Cacciato*. His other works include *If I Die in a Combat Zone*, *Northern Lights*, *The Nuclear Age*, *The Things They Carried*, and, most recently, *In the Lake in the Woods*.

Grace Paley is a short story writer, poet, and activist. She has won numerous awards including a Senior Fellowship of the Literature Program of the National Endowment for the Arts and the PEN/Faulkner Award. Her works include *Little Disturbances of Man*, *Enormous Changes at the Last Minute*, *Later the Same Day*, *New and Collected Poems*, and, most recently, *The Collected Stories*. She visited Vietnam in 1969 with a peace delegation and was involved in one of the first prisoner exchanges.

Pham Tien Duat served as a soldier and poet along the Ho Chi Minh Trail for ten years during the war. His work has received numerous awards including the national prize for poetry. He is currently editor at *Van Nghe*, the journal of arts and literature of the Writers' Association, and the host of a weekly television program on poetry in Vietnam. His collections include *The Moon Ringed with Fire* and *Poem of a Day's March*.

Leroy Quintana served in Vietnam as a member of a Long Range Reconnaissance unit in 1967–68. A poet and short story writer, he has written four collections of poetry, *Hijo del pueblo*, *Interrogations*, *The History of Home*, and *Sangre*, for which he won an American Book Award. He is editor of the recent anthology *Paper Dance: 55 Latino Poets*. He is an associate professor at San Diego Mesa College.

Oswald Rivera lives in New York City. He served with the Marines in Vietnam and was awarded the purple heart and other honors. His novel *Fire and Rain* is based on his Vietnam experience. He works as a staff analyst for the New York City Police Department.

Larry Rottmann served in Vietnam with the 25th Infantry in 1967–68. He was a contributing editor for *The Indochina Story* (1970), *The Winter Soldier Investigation* (1972), *Winning Hearts and Minds*, and *Free Fire Zone* (1973). He is the author of the novel *American Eagle: The Story of a Navajo Vietnam Veteran* (1977). His most recent collection is *Voices From the Ho Chi Minh Trail* (1993).

Lloyd Schwartz teaches creative writing at the University of Massachusetts, Boston, and is both classical music and poetry editor of the *Boston Phoenix*. He is the author of two books of poetry, *These People* and *Goodnight, Gracie*. His work has appeared in the *New Yorker*, the *Atlantic Monthly*, the *New Republic*, *The Pushcart Prize Anthology*, and *Best American Poetry*. Coeditor of *Elizabeth Bishop and Her Art*, he is the commentator on classical music for National Public Radio's *Fresh Air*. He won the Pulitzer Prize for his criticism in 1994.

Lamont Steptoe served in the 25th Infantry Division with the 38th and 46th scout dog platoons. He is an accomplished photographer and the publisher-founder of Whirlwind Press. His books include *Crimson River*, *America Morning/Mourning*, *Small Steps and Toes* (with Bob Small), and *Uncle's South China Sea Blue Nightmare*.

To Nhuan Vy is the director of the Arts and Literature Association of Hue. A former correspondent and student leader in Hue, he was wounded during the Tet offensive. He is the author of numerous short stories and novels, as well as an executive editor of *Song Huong*, Hue's journal of art and literature.

Tran Dang Khoa was born in 1958 in Hai Hung Province. He published his first collection of poems at the age of eight. He currently works as an editor at *Van Nghe Quan Doi, (The Army Journal of Arts and Literature)*.

Lynda Van Devanter served as a U.S. Army nurse in Pleiku Province during the Vietnam War. She has recounted those experiences in her book *Home before Morning*. Her writing has appeared in magazines and newspapers throughout the country, including the *Los Angeles Times* and the *New York Times*. With Joan Furey, she is editor of *Visions of War, Dreams of Peace: An Anthology of Women's Poetry from the Vietnam War*.

Van Le was born in Ninh Binh Province. He served in the war in the Iron Triangle and around Cu Chi with the Youth Brigades. He has published three collections of poetry and ten books of fiction. He has received awards for both his poetry and his fiction, most recently in 1994 for *If You Survive*. He is a film director for Giai Phong Studios. His most recent film, *A Time Difficult to Forget*, focuses on women who served in the Youth Brigades.

Tino Villanueva is a preceptor in Spanish at Boston University. He received a Ford Foundation graduate fellowship at Boston University where he earned his Ph.D. in the Department of Modern Foreign Languages and Literatures. The founder of Imagine Publishers and editor of *Imagine: International Chicano Poetry Journal*, he is the author of four collections of poetry: *Hay Otra Voz Poems, Shaking Off the Dark, Chronicle of My Worst Years*, and *Scene from the Movie "Giant,"* for which he won the American Book Award.

Bruce Weigl is a poet and professor of English at Pennsylvania State University. His books of poetry include *A Romance, The Monkey Wars, Song of Napalm, What Saves Us*, and *Sweet Lorrain*. *Poems from Captured Documents*, a work he translated with Thanh Nguyen and Vietnamese poet Nguyen Quang Thieu, was published by the University of Massachusetts Press in 1994. A recipient of a grant from the National Endowment for the Arts, he has also been awarded fellowships at Bread Loaf and Yaddo. He has been associated with the Writer's Workshop since its inception.

Daisy Zamora is a poet, painter, and psychologist. A combatant of the National Sandanista Liberation Front, she served as Vice Minister of Culture after the 1979 revolution. She currently lives in Nicaragua where she is active with groups concerned with women's issues. Her collections of poetry include *En Limpio Se Escriba La Vida, La Violenta Espuma, A Cada Quien La Vida*, as well as the anthology *The Nicaraguan Woman in Poetry*. Her works in English include *Riverbed of Memory*, published by City Lights in 1992, *Clean Slate: New and Selected Poems*, published by Curbstone Press in 1993, and *Life for Each*, published by Katabasis in 1995.

Credits and Permissions

Demetria Martínez, excerpt from *Mother Tongue*, a novel by Demetria Martínez. Copyright © 1994 by Demetria Martínez. Reprinted by permission of the author, Ballantine Publishers, a division of Random House, and Bilingual Press, Tempe, AZ.

Robert Mason, excerpt from *Chickenhawk: Back in the World* by Robert Mason. Copyright © 1993 by Robert C. Mason. Reprinted by permission of Viking Penguin, a division of Penguin Books USA Inc.

Harry Mattison, "What Makes Us Think We Are Only Here," a talk given at the William Joiner Center Writer's Workshop, University of Massachusetts at Boston, June 23, 1994. Reprinted by permission of the author.

Marilyn McMahon, "Knowing" and "Wounds of War" first appeared in *Connections* 3, no. 2, published by the William Joiner Center. Copyright © 1990 by Marilyn Mc-Mahon. Reprinted by permission of the author.

Victor Montejo, from *Testimony: Death of a Guatemalan Village* by Victor Montejo. Curbstone Press. Copyright © 1987 by Victor Montejo. Reprinted by permission of the author and Curbstone Press.

Nguyen Ba Chung, "Nonattachment," "Parting," "White Circles Revisited," and "The Path" by Nguyen Ba Chung, translated by the author. Reprinted by permission of the author.

Nguyen Duy, "Do Len," "Moonlight," "New Year Fireworks," "Red Earth, Blue Water," from *Sixes and Eights (Sau va tam)* by Nguyen Duy. Culture Publishing House, Hanoi, 1994. "A Small Song of Peace" from *Distant Road (Dung xa)* by Nguyen Duy. Ban Tre Publishing House, Ho Chi Minh City, 1989. Translations of these poems by Nguyen Ba Chung and Kevin Bowen first appeared in *Manoa* (Winter 1995). Copyright © 1995 Nguyen Ba Chung and Kevin Bowen. Reprinted by permission of the author and translators.

Nguyen Khai, "Those Days of Happiness," a short story originally appeared as "Da Tung Co Nhung Ngay Vui" in *Su Gia Chua Tham Va Ong Dai Ta Ve Huu* by Nguyen Khai. Writers Association Publishing House 1993. Translated by Nguyen Ba Chung. Reprinted by permission of the author and translator.

Nguyen Mong Giac, "The Slope of Life," from *The Horse with a Played-out Leg* (short stories) by Nguyen Mon Giac. Published by *Nguoi Viet*, 1984. Reprinted by permission of the author and translator, Le Tho Giao. Another version of this story in translation appeared in *The Other Side of Heaven: Postwar Fiction by Vietnamese and American Writers*, edited by Wayne Karlin, Le Minh Khue, and Truong Vu. Curbstone Press, 1995.

Nguyen Quang Sang, "The Ivory Comb," from *The Ivory Comb* by Nguyen Quang Sang. Giai Phong Publishing House, Republic of South Vietnam, 1968. Reprinted by permission of the author.

Nguyen Quang Thieu, "The Examples," "The Inn of Snake Alcohol," "Motion," "Time," "On the Highway," and "New Students, Old Teacher," from *The Women Carry River Water (Nhung Nguoi Dan Ba Ganh Nuoc Song)* by Nguyen Quang Thieu.

Culture Publishing House, Ha Noi 1994. Translations of "The Inn of Snake Alcohol," "Time," and "New Students, Old Teacher" by the author and Martha Collins. Translations of "The Examples" and "On the Highway" by the author and Yusef Komunyakaa. Reprinted by permission of the author and translators.

Nguy Ngu, "An Old Story" first appeared in *Van Nghe Quan Doi*, the Vietnamese Army Journal of Arts and Literature, January 1995. Translated by Nguyen Thi Kim Thu. Printed by permission of the author and translator.

Tim O'Brien, "How to Tell a True War Story" from *The Things They Carried* by Tim O'Brien. Houghton Mifflin Co./Seymour Lawrence. Copyright © 1990 by Tim O'Brien. Reprinted by permission of the author and Houghton Mifflin Co./Seymour Lawrence. All rights reserved.

Grace Paley, "Connections: Vermont Vietnam (I) and (II)," "In San Salvador (I)," and "That Country," from *New and Collected Poems* by Grace Paley. Published by Tilbury House. Copyright © 1992 by Grace Paley. Reprinted by permission of the author and publisher.

Pham Tien Duat, "White Circle," translated by Nguyen Quang Thieu and Kevin Bowen, and "In the Labor Market at Giang Ho," translated by Nguyen Ba Chung and Kevin Bowen first appeared in *Manoa* (Winter 1995). "Truong Son East, and Truong Son West" and "Drivers of Lorries without Windscreens," translated by Nguyen Khac Vien, first appeared in *An Anthology of Vietnamese Literature*, edited Nguyen Khac Vien, Red River Press, Ha Noi. Reprinted by permission of the author and translators.

Leroy Quintana, "Armed Forces Day, Albuquerque High School 1962," "The First Day, Headquarters, Co. 101st Airborne, Phan Rang Vietnam," and "First Encounter" from *Interrogations* by Leroy Quintana. Published by Viet Nam Generation, Inc. & Burning Cities Press. Copyright © 1990 by Leroy Quintana. Reprinted by permission of the author.

Oswald Rivera, excerpt from *Fire and Rain*, a novel by Oswald Rivera. Copyright © 1990 by Oswald Rivera. Published by Four Walls Eight Windows Press, New York. Reprinted by permission of the author and Four Walls Eight Windows Press.

Larry Rottmann, "Miami Beach Farmer" and "One Night in January," reprinted by permission of the author.

Lloyd Schwartz, "Gisela Brüning" from *Goodnight Gracie* by Lloyd Schwartz. Copyright © 1992 by Lloyd Schwartz. Published by University of Chicago Press, Chicago, IL. Reprinted by permission of the author.

Lamont Steptoe, "Return the Missing" and "Parts" published in *Chiron Review* 10, no. 1 (Spring 1991). Republished in *Mad Minute* by Lamont Steptoe. Whirlwind Press. Copyright © 1993 by Lamont Steptoe. "Survivors" published in *Mad Minute* by Lamont Steptoe. Whirlwind Press. Copyright © 1993 by Lamont Steptoe. Reprinted by permission of the publisher and the author.

To Nhuan Vy, "Over There Is the Horizon." Translated by Ngo Vinh Long. Reprinted by permission of the author and translator.